ALICE DANIELS

CAN'T LET YOU GO

AN IVY RIDGE NOVEL

ALICE DANIELS

This book is intended for mature audiences.

ISBN: 978-1-964971-06-3

Editing: Aria Harding

Cover Design by Jillian Liota, Blue Moon Creative Studio

CONTENTS

Sometimes it's okay to fall—they'll be there to catch you.

PLAYLIST

Another Love- Tom Odell
Bigger Than The Whole Sky- Taylor Swift
FOOLS- Troye Sivan
Glitch- Taylor Swift
Green Eyes- JOSEPH
Green Eyes- Judah & The Lion
the grudge- Olivia Rodrigo
Guilty as Sin?- Taylor Swift
How Did It End?- Taylor Swift
In The Light-The Lumineers
I Wish I Was- The Avett Brothers
Laughter Lines- Bastille
Never Grow Up (Taylor's Version)- Taylor Swift
Never Say Never- Cole Swindell, Lainey Wilson
She Lit A Fire- Lord Huron
Shouldn't Come Back- Demi Lovato
Woman-Mumford & Sons

To listen to whole playlist, scan the code!

Dear Reader,

Can't Let You Go contains subjects that may be triggering to some. This content includes on page scenes depicting a miscarriage, grief, on page discussions of a drug overdose (not FMC or MMC), and addiction. Mentions of death of a parent from cancer, divorce, cheating (not FMC or MMC), child custody agreements, and emotional manipulation/abuse from an ex-husband.

Fallon struggles with her confidence as a plus size woman after her divorce to a man who picked at her insecurities. There is also brief mention of a drug overdose of a teen in the context of a police investigation.

This book includes explicit language and graphic sexual scenes. Reader discretion is advised.

Take care of yourself. Your mental health matters more than a book.

AUTHOR'S NOTE

Dear Reader,

I strive to write characters that are authentic and Fallon's story is one of those. While I love a confident plus size FMC, sometimes, they aren't always that way. In this book, Fallon struggles with confidence and self-image due to the way she was treated and things that were said to her by her ex-husband. Throughout the book, she mentions that she is working on her confidence, but she is not always as confident as she could be. If you love books where the plus size FMC is always confident no matter what, this might not be the book for you. There are internal conflicts that she has with her body, but Jason helps her see how beautiful she is, and loves her body the way that it is, and helps her continue to grow confident in herself again.

Please note that a lawyer was consulted in regards to the child custody case, but this is fiction, so there were a few liberties taken.

I hope you enjoy Can't Let You Go.
xoxo, Alice

1

―――――

FALLON

"Ma'am, your insurance is coming up as 'inactive', do you have another card we can try?" I'm pulled out of my foggy thoughts by the nurse's sweet voice. I look up, taking in her pale blue scrubs and graying hair. Her badge reads *Pam*, but I'm sure I won't remember in ten minutes.

"What?" I ask, not totally understanding.

She repeats herself.

"No," I whisper. "That's the only insurance I have. What does it mean if it's inactive?"

"It could be that the policy is expired, or you didn't pay the premium. Something like that," she explains. The pity in her eyes makes me think she might know something I don't.

"My..." I swallow hard. "My husband, he's the one in charge of insurance. We get it through his work. I can't reach him though. He's on a business trip," I explain.

She nods, reaching out to take my hand, squeezing gently. "I'm sorry, sweetie. You shouldn't have to do this alone. I'll tell registration to run it again. Maybe they entered the number wrong."

I avert my gaze to my lap, where her wrinkled hand is clasped in mine. "Okay," I reply. She gives my hand one final squeeze, leaving me alone in the cold, brightly lit room.

Brad, my husband, should be here with me. Instead, he's away on one of his frequent business trips. I'm alone, dealing with something no woman should ever have to deal with. When I started spotting this morning, I called the nurse line right away, and they didn't seem worried at all, telling me to monitor it and to come in if it got worse.

We'd been trying to get pregnant for so long after Presley was born, wanting so badly to have a sibling for her to grow up with, but after four years and no luck, I figured it wouldn't happen. Then a few weeks ago, I felt crummy, and Brad suggested I take a test.

The shock I felt when it came up blazing positive was soul lifting. Brad seemed so happy when I came out of the bathroom, holding the stick with a giant smile on my face. Things seemed to be coming together.

After we found out I was pregnant again, he became the most attentive husband, like he was after we first got married. We've been married eight years, so yes, there have been rough times and fights, but that's normal in any marriage. Work has been so stressful for him as of late, and his attentiveness has faded over the years with his parents hounding him to move up in his company, to be the head honcho. They expected greatness from him which he wasn't delivering, so he had to step up his game, at the expense of his personal time, unfortunately.

I do what I can to be a good wife and support him through the hard times at work. I make sure the house is clean, and Presley is happy when he gets home from work every night. I take care of him, and I love him. He is my husband, the person I want with me through thick and thin.

I lay my head back on the stiff, crinkly hospital pillow. Why isn't the insurance active? I brought Presley in for her well-child check a few weeks ago, and everything was fine. I pull my phone out from under my leg, careful of the IV lines. I bring up his contact, pressing the call button. It rings, and rings, and rings. I have no idea if he will answer the phone. I haven't heard his real voice in just over a week since he called me after landing in Orlando. All I've received are scattered texts, letting me know he's busy with the conference and that he'll call when he can. Something's off, but I can't place it.

In the past, when he's gone to conferences, he's been responsive, making sure to call and text all the time. That's why I've never really minded when he leaves to attend them. He goes to one every few months, and usually one or two of his colleagues go with him. There was only one other instance a few months ago when he had to extend a trip, but even then, he apologized for weeks following.

I'm not surprised when his voicemail picks up. "You've reached Bradley Douglas, leave me a message, and I'll call you back when I can." His familiar voice momentarily eases the anxiety, but then it ramps up again. What kind of CPA conference is so busy he can't spend five minutes on the phone every night with his wife and daughter?

"It's me. Again," I say, my voice rising with irritation. "Please, call me, Brad. I'm worried and I need you." I press the button to end the call, closing my eyes again. A knock on the door pulls me out of my self wallowing, and the doctor walks in with a grim look on his face. He glances down at his clipboard containing what I assume are my lab results.

And then he speaks the words I never wanted to hear.

My heart breaks, the pain cracking and shattering me

into pieces. A nurse sits by my side with my head resting on her shoulder as they prep me for the procedure, holding my hand, keeping the shattered pieces of me together.

"Should we try to call your husband again?" she asks. "Or is there maybe someone else you want to call?"

I shake my head into the crook of her neck. "No, but I should call the person who is watching my daughter. Let her know what's going on."

When we were house hunting, Brad chose where we were going to live, not giving me a say, or listening to my desire to be closer than an hour from my mom. I fought him hard on it, knowing I would need my mom after I gave birth to Presley, and knowing his parents wouldn't support us the way my mom would. In the end, I gave in to his desires. He is the one who brings in most of the money, so he made it known that it was his choice. Situations like these are exactly why. When I determined I needed to go to the hospital, I dropped Presley off at her friend's house. I know the mom, Sarah, well enough but we aren't super close.

Now, I'm stuck at the hospital, with no way to get home as I'm sure they won't let me drive myself following the procedure. My mom is on a cruise, though I know if I called her she'd move hell and high water to get to us, but I won't put that kind of stress on her. I could call Sarah, but... I don't know. I told her I was having pain, but had brushed it off as kidney stones at the time. I'm not sure I want to say the truth out loud yet. Sarah and her husband are both nice. I trust them with Presley, so I know I could trust her with this. Though I would rather have someone I *know*.

My best friend, Megan, is a doctor in a small town, but she's over an hour away from here. No one even knows I'm pregnant.

Was pregnant.

I lean back, wiping at the tears under my eyes. With shaky hands, I look at the time, realizing it's about Presley's bedtime. I press the call button and Sarah picks up right away.

"Hey, how are you?" Sarah asks.

I sniffle. "I'm okay. I need to have a procedure, but I wanted to check in on Pres."

"She's doing good. I can tell she's worried about you, but she's hiding it well."

"Thank you, Sarah. Can I talk to her?"

"Of course," she says. I hear her call Presley's name and the sound of my daughter's rushing footsteps.

"Mommy?" her sweet, soft voice sends another bout of tears streaming down my cheeks.

"Hi, sweet girl," I murmur. "Are you having fun?" I clear my throat, trying to hide my emotion from her. It guts me knowing she lost a sibling when she didn't even know she was going to get one in the first place.

"Yes! We went to Pizza Hut for supper and got ice cream. We're watching a princess movie now, and Millie's dad is making us popcorn."

"Wow, that sounds so fun!"

"It is. Are you with Auntie Megan?"

I shake my head, even though she can't see. "Not tonight. Mommy's relaxing tonight."

"Oh. I miss you." I can hear the twinge of sadness in her voice, and my heart aches. She hasn't had a sleepover anywhere besides her Grandma's house, and it's probably a little early for it now, but I'm out of options.

"I know sweetie, but I'll pick you up right away in the morning. Sarah and Seth are going to take such good care of you." God, I wish I could be there right now to hold her.

In the background I hear her friend's voice. "Presley, the movie is starting!"

"Okay, I love you, Mommy. When is Daddy coming home?"

"Only a few more days, I think," I tell her, but at this point, I don't know. It's so unlike him to go radio silent. "I love you more, Pres."

There's a shuffling noise, and then Sarah is back on the phone. "Do you need a ride? Someone to sit with you?"

"Not right now. I'll be here for a few more hours at least."

"You shouldn't be alone, Fallon."

My heart clenches. She doesn't know what's happening, and yet, she's willing to come and be with me. Her kindness makes tears burn my eyes again. "I'm okay. I'll call you if I change my mind." I would love to have someone to sit with me, but I have the nurses. And the doctor is really nice. I can cry and not worry about judgment with them. I'd be more worried if Sarah was here, and not with my daughter.

"Okay. I can pick you up, too. It doesn't matter what time, call me. I'll keep my phone on."

"Will do," I tell her. Perhaps I underestimated our friendship, and can trust her, but we're saying goodbye before I can pluck up the courage to tell her.

My nurse rubs a soothing circle on my hand. Before I second guess it with worries about taking up too much of her time, or that she might be working or sleeping before a night shift, I call Megan.

She answers on the second ring. "Hey you. I was just thinking about you."

"Hey, Meg," I say, my voice immediately betraying me.

"Fallon? What's wrong?" I can hear her fiancé in the background, whispering questions.

"Can you come here?" I whisper. My nurse nods, patting me on the leg as she stands, giving me some privacy. "I'm at the hospital."

"Of course, I'll leave right now. Which hospital? What's going on?"

In the background I hear Isaac again. "I'll go grab a bag for you," he says, and his hurried footsteps carry through the phone.

"I'm—" I choke on the words. "I'm having a miscarriage. I need to have a procedure, and Brad's at a work conference." I don't tell her about the lack of communication, that can come out later.

"Oh, Fallon. I'll be there as soon as possible. When are they taking you back?" Her voice oozes sympathy, and I know I'm making the right choice.

"Soon," I say.

"If I'm not there before you go in, I'll be there when you wake up. Tell them I'm coming so they'll let me in your room, okay?"

I nod, though she can't see me.

"I've got you. Where's Pres?"

"Spending the night at a friend's house. This is her first sleepover. I'm such a bad mom, Meg," I cry. "She's only four. She's probably not ready for this."

"She's okay. Text me the number of who she's staying with, and let her know I'll text her so she has my information while you're in the procedure." Isaac is back, whispering something to Megan as she talks to me.

A car door opens and closes. "I'm leaving my house now. I'll be there soon. Do you want to stay on the phone?"

"No, I'm okay. I'm going to try and relax a bit."

"Okay."

We hang up, and I send Sarah's number to Megan. I

give Sarah a heads up that Meg is going to be calling her, to which she responds with a heart and some more kind words.

When Pam comes back in, I tell her Megan will be here and that I want her there when I wake up. She tells me they still can't find an active insurance for me and my heart sinks a little bit more.

I send one final text, this time to Brad. I don't want to tell him I've lost the baby over a text, but I tell him to call me and that it's an emergency. The message is marked as delivered and then read. I get a small glimmer of hope, needing the comfort only my husband can bring as the typing bubbles appear and disappear as fast they appeared.

Seconds later, the status changes, letting me know his phone is on do not disturb. My heart drops, a sinking sensation settling in my gut. I'm in pain, my baby is gone, I'm alone, and he won't even call me back? It's almost like I'm numb. The reality is too raw, too painful to even think about, so I shut down. I can't process the loss of my baby *and* the way my husband is treating me right now, so it's almost easier to avoid it all together.

MY SENSES ARE groggy as I wake. The world is hazy and my body is heavy. Something squeezes my palm, warmth settling on my skin. Everything comes back to me as my senses slowly return. My eyes flutter open, taking in the small, dimly lit hospital room. I flick my gaze to the left where Megan sits. She's perched in the cushioned chair, but half of her body is resting on the bed.

"Hey." My voice is scratchy as I wake up. My lower

abdomen is sore and crampy, an unwelcome reminder of the loss.

Megan sits up at the sound of my voice. "Hey," she says, her voice sad and empathetic.

"I'm sorry," I whisper, heavy sadness washing over my body. "I shouldn't have called you. It's so late."

"Stop that right now," she scolds. "You have nothing to be sorry about. I'm glad I can be here for you, but I wish it was under better circumstances."

I nod, squeezing her hand. Megan has always been there for me, ever since my second year of college. We were randomly assigned to each other as roommates, and the rest is history. It's been too long since I've seen her, probably a few months. She lives an hour away from me in a small town called Ivy Ridge and is soon starting her residency in family medicine. "How long have I been asleep?"

"Not long. They just brought you in. He said they woke you up as soon as the procedure was done, but you've been sleeping since. Sarah texted me. Pres is fine."

I nod, thankful for the update on my daughter. I vaguely recall the doctor waking me up and nurses moving me over to a new bed, but barely. "Do you know if Brad has called back?" I ask, though, I think I know the answer.

"I didn't see any missed calls," she says mournfully. "Is he on a plane home?"

I huff. "I don't know."

"Fallon..." Megan drawls. "Where is he? He should be here."

"He's at a work conference in Orlando. He won't answer my calls, and all my texts have been left on read, or I get one-word responses. I told him it was an emergency, but I didn't want to text him that I lost the baby. He read the message and still didn't call."

"I'm going to beat the shit out of him." Megan nearly vibrates with anger. She's never been a huge fan of Brad, even during college. She has always tolerated him, but I suppose her not liking him maybe should have been a sign.

"It's fine," I say, though I don't believe the words. "Maybe he had a work emergency."

"How is this fine, Fallon? I get that he's across the country. I get that he's at a work conference. But to read a message from your wife after she tells you it's an emergency and still not call?" She leans back in the chair. Her blonde hair is up in a haphazard bun, pieces falling out to frame her face. "That, I don't get."

"Me either. I couldn't even get a new insurance card from him. They ran my insurance card like four or five times, and it kept coming up as inactive," I explain, that sinking sensation settling deep in my gut as I say the words out loud. Could the fact that he's not answering have something to do with the insurance? Megan doesn't say anything, but I can tell based on the look on her face that she has a theory as well.

"Let's not worry about that now. I'm sure he has an updated card, and they can backdate it so it gets covered." She waves her hand in the air flippantly as there's a knock on the door.

I SNUGGLE INTO THE COUCH, wrapped up in a fuzzy cream colored blanket. Megan left about twenty minutes ago to pick up Presley after making sure I wasn't in any pain and had water at my side.

My head is spinning, trying to process all the events

from last night. Brad still has not called me back, nor sent even a text to check in. I lost my baby.. I dreamed of bringing my new baby home, greeting Presley at the door while my mom stood behind her, taking photos of Pres meeting her new sibling. Something that won't be happening now. I never imagined this outcome.

I'm not sure what this will mean for our marriage. It doesn't exactly bode well for him at the moment. I look down at my bare ring finger, the place where my wedding band and engagement ring usually sit. They put my rings in a little bag before they took me back for the procedure and I have yet to put them back on.

A key clicks in the front door, alerting me to Megan and Presley's arrival. I'm excited to see my baby girl, and hope maybe she can help ease some of my pain.

"Megan? Presley?" I call when there isn't the familiarity of Presley's energy through the house. Instead, I'm greeted with heavy footsteps.

Brad appears in my line of sight, dressed in his suit and tie, like he's heading to work. "Brad?" I ask, my voice breaking in relief. *He came.* He cares. All my previous negative thoughts of him fly out the window as I shift to a sitting position. He must have rushed home the second he saw my message that I was in the hospital, right?

"Fallon, what are you doing here?" Brad retorts, his voice almost... accusatory. I sit further forward on the couch, unwrapping myself from the blanket.

"Wh-what do you mean?" I inhale a shaky breath. "I tried calling you, tried texting you. You didn't come home to see me? To help me?"

"God, you're so lazy. You can't even be bothered to get off the couch and do anything. No wonder why you can't lose all the extra weight." Brad scoffs, his face wrinkled in disgust as he takes in my appearance. Where did this come from? What is he talking about? I mean, I know I have gained a lot of weight since having Pres, and he's mentioned dieting and working out a few times, but is now really the time to bring it up?

"Brad, I… I was in the hospital last night."

"I met someone else." He speaks over me, running one hand through his hair, the other he holds up in front of him, halting me from speaking more. My gaze falls to his left hand. He isn't wearing his wedding ring.

His words strike me. A painful ache spears through my heart, like a bullet being torn through the muscle with no exit wound.

"Oh," I respond lamely, because what does a person say to that? Has he even processed that I told him I was in the hospital? Something he should have known after reading the text messages I sent him?

"Her name is Trixie. We met on a business trip last year. We've decided we want to be together."

Only then do I notice the empty duffle bags at his feet.

It's like my brain can't process any words he's saying. I only recognize the empty bags at his feet. "Why are the bags empty? What are you doing? I—Brad, what is happening?"

He exhales, pinching the bridge of his nose in exasperation. "I can't believe I need to lay this out for you," he mumbles under his breath. "Fallon, I'm leaving you."

"But I need you, Presley needs you." I clutch at my stomach, the place where our baby was only hours ago, and is now empty. "I had a miscarriage, Brad."

Brad doesn't seem surprised or even hurt by this news. He simply nods. "It's better that way."

"It's *better* that way?" I shriek. "How is it better? I'm being ripped apart piece by piece. My body aches, hurts from the loss of my baby, my heart is cracked wide open, and now my husband is telling me he's leaving me for someone else. How is that *better*?"

"It's better, because now you only have to be a lackluster parent to one child. I never should have agreed to get you pregnant again. Not after seeing the way you are with Presley. She's too dependent on you. I can't stand how whiny she is; you made her that way. She's just like you."

"She's four!" I shout, my throat burning against the words. How could he say such cruel things of his own flesh and blood—his own daughter? "Of course she's going to whine and be dependent on her mother! I'm a stay-at-home mom, I spend every hour of every day with her. I love her more than anyone. How can you say these things, Brad?"

"Exactly," Brad says through gritted teeth. He's unbearably calm. "You loved her more than you ever loved me. Shouldn't you love your husband more? You should have chosen me!"

I don't speak, don't even know what to say. Am I really that horrible of a mother that I pushed away my own husband?

"You'll hear from my lawyers." With that, he grabs the bags at his feet, and heads down the hall to our bedroom. My bedroom.

I hear the opening and closing of drawers and closet doors but choose to shut my brain off. His footsteps come closer until he steps in front of me. He doesn't say anything as he leaves his wedding ring on the coffee table and throws his duffle over his shoulder.

Once he's gone, I break again. Tears stream down my cheeks in rivulets. He's right. I could have paid more attention to him and been a better wife. I could have done more, been there for him more. I could have lost weight, could have... I can't even list all of the things I could have done, because now, I lost my chance.

I rise from the couch and slowly walk through the house. My body aches with even the smallest of movements. Every step is a reminder of the loss of my baby, of the way my life just changed so drastically. My heart no longer feels as though it's being shredded from the inside out. Now, it's empty. Like a shell.

I make my way into the bedroom, to where there is still the faint scent of his cologne. I slowly get into the bed, which I've never slept comfortably in after Brad insisted we buy a memory foam mattress. Pulling the covers up over my head, I start to sob.

Megan and Presley arrive home shortly after, having stopped somewhere to pick up breakfast. I put on a brave face for my daughter and best friend, only breaking down later in my best friend's arms.

I pretend it's all a dream. Maybe it's a horrible nightmare, one I'll wake up from and roll over to find my husband still in bed with me, cradling me in his arms. He'll kiss me on the head, and splay his hand over my stomach, caressing where our baby grows inside me.

But he won't.

It's not a dream.

The divorce papers arrive a week later.

2

———

FALLON

THREE YEARS LATER

September

"**F**allon, do you have a copy of the schedule? I seem to have lost mine," Isaac says, running his hand through his hair.

I laugh softly. "Yes, but remember, you aren't supposed to be working. That's what I'm for. It's your best friend's wedding. You're off duty."

Isaac narrows his eyes, but it's not malicious, more like he knows I'm right. "Fine," he says.

I shoo him away, glancing down at the clipboard in my hands. Things are going according to schedule, and I'm grateful. I'm still new and getting the hang of things here at Meadow Grove Winery, and I'm anxious to make a good impression.

Isaac took over the winery as the general manager a few years ago after his parents retired, and hired me on as the event planner. After Brad left, it took a long time for me to work through the stress and exhaustion as I figured out how to be a single mom. But we made it through, and finally I can say things are good.

Brad didn't just leave me. He left Presley too.

We haven't seen him since the day he left, sending waived custody the day he sent the divorce papers. Moving to Ivy Ridge three years ago made all the difference. We stayed with my mom for just under two years until we got back on our feet and moved into a townhome about three months ago. I'm happy here, especially being so close to my Mom and best friend. Presley loves her new school and has made so many new friends.

My phone rings in my pocket, and I pull it out. My mom's name is on the screen which is a little weird. She's watching Presley overnight, something she will do on the weekends I work a wedding or another late night event.

"Mom? Everything okay?" I answer.

My mom's voice is weak and scratchy. "I hate to do this, but I need to drop Presley off. Maybe she can hang out in your office or something. I've got some sort of stomach bug."

"Oh no," I murmur, my eyes frantically searching the room as if that will bring me some sort of answer to this new predicament. "Are you sure you can drive?"

"I'm not sure, but I'll be careful. I'll text you when we leave."

I frown as we say our goodbyes.

The winery is about thirty minutes outside of town, and I don't want my mom to be sick and trying to drive. My other babysitter is out of town this weekend, and everyone I would trust with Pres is here. Megan must catch my worried gaze from across the room, flitting to my side.

"What's wrong?" she asks, rubbing a hand up my arm.

"My mom called. She's got a stomach bug and can't watch Presley anymore. I don't want her to drive, but I might not have a choice. I can't leave, and anyone I trust is here." I gesture at her and then to Isaac across the room now in a small circle of guys, drinking a glass of wine.

"Let me check with Josie," Megan says, gesturing to the bride. Megan is one of Josie's bridesmaids and sings her praises. I've met Josie a few times, and even though she's the nicest woman, I'd feel bad about imposing. "I can meet your mom halfway or go pick her up. I still have her booster seat in my car."

"No, I can't ask you to do that. What if they need you?" I bite my fingernails, glancing down at the clipboard. In all honesty, there really isn't much left on the schedule tonight. The rehearsal is finished, and now dinner is being prepped, so everyone is mingling.

"They don't. Unless you need me here for something, I'll go get her. I'll call your mom." Without giving me another chance to fight her on it—not that I have much of a reason to—Megan gets Josie's attention, waving her over. Josie smiles, rushing to our side.

"What's up?" she asks. Her red hair is curled loosely, hanging in waves around her round face.

"Fallon's mom is sick, and she's watching her daughter. Do you mind if I run into town to pick her up, and she hangs out here tonight, and probably tomorrow?" Megan asks.

Fuck, I didn't even think about tomorrow. I'll have to be here from dawn till almost midnight. Between set up, the ceremony, and the reception it was going to be a long day anyway, and now, I have to throw Presley into the mix.

"I'm so sorry," I interject.

Josie waves me off. "Nothing to be sorry about. The more the merrier. I'm sure Lennie, Jason's daughter, would love to have someone to play with. It's no problem at all."

"Are you sure?" A weight lifts off my chest at how relaxed Josie is. Some brides would lose their mind if something like this happened, and I, for one, am grateful it happened tonight when Josie is the bride.

"Don't even think twice about it," Josie says. She reaches out, clasping her hand on my arm. "We might not be close yet, but whether you like it or not, we're friends. Friends help each other, so yes. Megan, go get Presley, and we will be fine here for an hour."

I nod, a prick of tears stinging my eyes.

Megan pulls out her phone. "I'll call your mom."

She walks away, leaving me alone with Josie. I take a deep breath, and settle my eyes back down on the clipboard in my hand, looking at what I need to do next.

In the time I've worked and lived here, I've barely made time for anyone outside of Meg and my mom. Meg has been begging me to meet up with her and "the girls" more, but I haven't had it in me. I don't want to let anyone down, so it's easier to keep to myself. I've been prioritizing my little girl for years now, and setting all my own needs to the side. Maybe I should start getting together with them more. Especially after the kindness they've both shown me today.

PRESLEY HIDES behind my leg as we make our way back into the reception hall. There are tables scattered with decor and other odds and ends, the finishing touches for the reception decorations.

Megan leads me toward a table where a young girl sits with a few coloring pages in front of her. Her long dark hair is hanging down her back, with a large ribbon tied into a bow on top of her head. She's beautiful, with deep chocolate brown eyes. She's dressed in a white tulle dress with a deep maroon bow around her waist.

"Hey, Lennie," Megan says. "This is Fallon and her daughter, Presley. We were wondering if you two wanted to play together. You're pretty close in age, and both really like princesses. Is that okay?"

Lennie looks us over, glancing behind my legs where Presley is being uncharacteristically shy. When the two meet each other's eyes, they both light up in the most adorable smiles. Presley lets go of my leg, stepping out from behind me.

"I love to color. Do you?" Presley asks.

"Do you want to pick one?" Lennie asks, offering up her thick coloring book to my daughter. "I have lots of different ones you can choose from." She has a subtle lisp, but one that is more than likely due to her age and not a speech impediment.

"Do you have one with a cat?" Presley asks.

"Yes!"

A sigh of relief falls past my lips. Now, I have one less thing to worry about. Nikki, Lennie's grandma, and the Mother of the Groom, smiles at me from the small table she sits at with the girls.

"I'll take care of her," she tells me. Weirdly, I trust her instantly though I don't know her all that well. I'm usually hesitant with who I trust around Pres, but with Nikki, I don't have that hesitation. She has such a kind heart, and though I've only met her for the first time today, I can tell she would do anything to take care of my daughter.

"Thank you," I gush. "You have no idea how much I appreciate this. I can pay you." I reach into my back pocket for my phone where I have some cash in my case, but she stops me.

"Nonsense. I doubt they will need me for nothing more than to appreciate their drawings and help choose what color to use. I can bring her up to the room, and you can pick her up when you're ready." Nikki stands, stepping in to give me a quick hug. Thankfully, the hotel is connected to the winery, making it easy for weddings and events.

We exchange phone numbers, and I lean down, pressing a kiss to the top of Presley's head. She barely pays any attention to me, fully focused on the coloring page in front of her.

I straighten and glance around the room. A small circle of people have gathered, and I recognize Megan's friend, Marley, along with three men I don't recognize. One of whom is clearly standing protectively next to Marley, whether she realizes it or not. The other two men stand in a semi-circle, their hands in their pockets. I was busy running around during the rehearsal, so I didn't get to meet any of the other groomsmen or bridesmaids.

One has a full head of blonde hair, and when he smiles I can barely catch a glimpse of a gap in his front teeth, and a set of prominent dimples. The other is taller than the two other men, dressed in a crisp button up like the others, but the top three buttons are undone, revealing a white under-shirt and the subtlest hint of dark chest hair peeking out from the collar.

When my gaze lifts to his face, I'm slammed with a sudden hit of recognition.

Holy shit.

Cunningham. The groom has a brother named Jason. *Jason Cunningham.* I can't believe I didn't put it together until now, but the more I look at him, the more I realize my eyes aren't playing tricks on me. It *is* him. It's been at least thirteen years since I've seen him, and while he looks so eerily similar to the last time, I can see the hints of aging and time in his features.

A memory flares through me, and before I can stop myself, I turn my eyes from him, and head down the hall to my office to give myself a moment to breathe, remembering that time in my life.

"Oh, come on, you can't be serious," Jason says with a laugh.

"I am!" I say, shrinking into the uncomfortable chair when the librarian walks by, shushing us with a finger to her lips, and a not so quiet shushing noise. My cheeks flame, and I glance back at Jason, my smile growing as I try to hold in my snickering laugh.

Jason's eyes widen as he looks at the old woman walking away. "Did she shush you?"

I drop my jaw. "You're the one who started laughing! It's not my fault you don't believe me that Professor Adams quoted Michael Scott and called it a great business mantra!"

"How can I?" he questions. His brown eyes are peering into my soul, and for the fifth time in the last hour, I have to remind myself that I have a date tonight. A date that is not with Jason.

"I'm a very trustworthy person," I say.

"Guess you'll have to prove it to me," Jason quips.

"You're on." Heart fluttering, I try to steady myself. I need to get control of my crush. He's four years older, and a senior here at the university. Maybe that's why I'm going on a date tonight, to remind myself of that fact.

The first day of classes last fall, Jason snuck into class ten minutes late. For some reason, he flopped down in the chair next to mine, and acted like it was no big deal he was casu-

ally late to the first day of classes. He had an air about him, something that screamed, "I'm a seasoned student." All his notebooks and binders were used. Not the fresh, unwrinkled ones everyone else in class seemed to have.

At the end of the first mind-numbingly boring lecture, he leaned over, offering me a hand to shake. Since that moment, we had slowly become friends, all leading up to now. Halfway through spring semester, we meet every Wednesday afternoon in the library to study, work on homework together, or commiserate about Professor Adams. After studying, we usually end up talking for hours. We don't have as many classes together as we did last semester, but we still meet every week.

We're both business majors, and surprisingly have a lot in common. Both of us are here on scholarships. He got a full ride through baseball, and I got many academic ones. That's the only way either of us could afford to be here.

Jason wants to open his own business. He's not sure what yet, but he's got a lot of ideas. His Grandpa also runs his own woodworking business that his brother plans to take over, so he wants to be able to help him too.

He's told me all about his siblings and parents. As an only child, I always get a little jealous when he tells me about his brothers' latest antics, but then again, I have my mom, and I'm thankful I have her, that I have the relationship I do with her. I also am glad I didn't have to watch a sibling go through the pain of losing my dad.

"How's the dear old roomie?" Jason asks, pulling me from my straying thoughts.

I sigh in contempt. "It's... fine," I finally say.

"It sucks you have to live on campus your first year," he says, pulling off his baseball cap and running his hands *through his hair. Instead of putting it back on normally, he puts it on so the bill is backward.*

Who allowed men to do that? Don't they know what a backwards baseball cap does to women?

I clear my throat. "Yeah. Not like I know who I'd live with though." We're part way through the spring semester, I've made one friend, Jason. My roommate, Shiloh, is only interested in going to frat and sorority parties. Her long-term goal is to move into a sorority house, so she has no interest in forging a friendship with me.

"I wish Marley were here, I bet you'd be great friends with her." Jason leans back, resting his hands behind his head. He's been training nearly non-stop, and the baseball season doesn't start for a few more weeks. His arms are thick with muscle, pectorals taut and strong. I look away, remembering what he said.

"Who is Marley?" I ask. I try to keep the accusation from my tone, but I can tell I didn't do a good job of it when he smirks.

"Marley," he says with a small laugh, "is my brother's best friend. Though, she's practically my sister. And if either of them get their head out of their asses, maybe someday she will be my sister."

"Oh," I reply. "Cool?"

"Yeah," he laughs. "She's great though. I think you would get along well with her."

I nod, twirling my pencil in my finger. The sun is setting, but it's winter, so it gets dark early. I take a look at the clock across the room and groan.

I don't know why I agreed to this date tonight. I'd much rather hang with Jason, but maybe I shouldn't want to. I should let him enjoy his senior year of college without some freshman hanging on his arm, desperate for his attention. He should be out with his friends, partying, or whatever it is seniors do.

"I don't know what I'll do next year," I say, bringing the conversation back around. "Usually people end up rooming with friends their sophomore year, and since I don't have any of them, I'm screwed."

Jason grimaces. "Well, I'd offer up my place, but..." he trails off.

I laugh. "Yeah, sorry, but not sure I'd want to live in your shared house, even if you weren't graduating in the spring. Rooming with four guys? Sounds... yucky."

"Hey," Jason protests. "I will have you know that we are very clean boys. Men. We are clean men. We have a chore wheel, and we get beer for each task we complete."

"I... I'm not surprised whatsoever." I laugh. "A chore wheel with beer as a reward? Yeah, definitely sounds like the place to be," I say, sarcasm lacing my words.

"Is it weird I wish I wasn't graduating this year?"

"Why?" I blink at the rapid change in subject.

Jason shrugs, looking up at the ceiling. He doesn't respond.

I pause, wanting to give him a moment. When we near a full minute passing, and he hasn't said anything, I speak. "Jason. Why don't you want to graduate?"

"It sounds silly to say out loud."

"Nothing you say is silly."

"I'm not ready. I've had four years to fuck around, go to classes and work my ass off to earn this degree, but yet, I'm not ready. The thought of starting out in the real world is terrifying."

"I hate to sound like something from an infomercial, but... You can do anything you set your mind to. You're going

to be amazing, Jason. Anyone can see that. I'm pretty sure you're the only reason I'm passing Econ."

"Liar," he says, some of his easy humor returning. "You passed the last test with flying colors. I didn't even have to write the answers on my hand to flash you during the test."

"Jason!" I scold. "You have never done that."

"Nope, but I would if you asked."

I shouldn't swoon over him offering to help me cheat on a test, but I do. "I won't ask." I laugh.

He shrugs, that smile I love so much appearing on his face. "What are you doing tonight?"

I shrink. "Um. I—"

I'm interrupted by someone sitting in the chair beside me, scooting too close for comfort.

"Hey babe," the person says. I turn, and realize it's Brad. We met in the cafeteria a few days ago, and he didn't really give me much of an option but to take his number. At the use of the pet name, I instantly regret agreeing to a date.

"Uh," I clear my throat. "Hi, Brad." I glance between Jason and Brad, regretting my entire existence. Jason looks back and forth, brows furrowing. "Jason, this is Brad." I don't introduce him with a title, because how does one say, "Hey, 'guy I'm totally crushing on but never have a chance with', here's the frat boy I agreed to go out with so I can get my mind off you?"

Brad reaches across the table, taking Jason's hand in a rough shake. I internally wince at my idiocy.

"I was just picking Fallon up for our date," Brad announces, and I look over at him with wide eyes. I definitely never told him to pick me up at the library. We agreed on my dorm at seven, and it's barely even six.

Is this some sort of pissing contest he is trying to win?

I'm incredulous as I glare at him, begging him to take a hint and leave.

He doesn't get it.

"Ready, babe?" he asks, standing and offering me his hand. I can do one of two things in this moment. I can go with him, or I can stay with Jason, and let my crush fester.

Do I do the sane thing, and stay with the man who's been nothing but nice to me? Or do I make the stupidest choice ever and put my hand in the palm of the boy who is wearing a salmon colored polo and khaki shorts in the dead of winter?

Obviously, I do the stupid thing.

The look on Jason's face as I say goodbye haunts me for weeks. He starts to avoid me, skipping our weekly meetups, only helping if I ask, and barely talking to me during and after class. Eventually, he goes silent altogether.

I swallow the lump in my throat as I push down the memories of that kind young man who helped pull me out of my shell. I was randomly assigned a roommate the next fall, and somehow got lucky and it was Megan. We became best friends, which was also in my favor because Jason and I never got back to what we used to be after that night. After he graduated, I never saw him again. Until tonight.

What am I going to say? Of course I'm going to have to interact with him. There's no way we won't. He's the brother of the groom and in the wedding party. Do I bite the bullet and get it over with? Or do I wait for a natural interaction that's sure to be awkward as hell?

I take a deep breath as I make my way back to the reception hall. I spot him walking over to the bar. It's now or never. I might as well do it. He gets another bottle of beer and thanks the bartender with a chin tip. I stride over to him before I can psych myself out of it. I smooth my shirt and silently curse myself for feeling self conscious. I'm not the same girl I was all those years ago, he probably won't even recognize me.

I clear my throat as I approach him. He turns, and it's almost like a punch to the gut. He's as handsome as he was then. His deep brown eyes are glazed as he takes me in, his gaze roaming up and down my body. "Um, hi, Jason?" I state, clearing my throat again when my voice cracks. "I'm sure you don't remember me, but, my name is—"

"Fallon," Jason breathes my name, recognition arising on his face.

3

JASON

My brother, Thomas, claps me on the back as I take a long pull of my beer. I'm absolutely exhausted. Work was nuts this afternoon, and then I had to rush to the winery to make it to the rehearsal dinner on time. Luckily, my mom was able to stop by my house and grab my daughter, Lennie's, dresses for this weekend, otherwise, I would have been in deep trouble with my future sister-in-law, Josie. Not really, Josie's amazing, but still. It would have been an inconvenience, so I'm eternally grateful to my mom for remembering to grab it.

"How's it feel knowing our youngest brother is going to be the first to get married?" Thomas asks, glancing over at the man in question, Andrew. He's staring at his wife-to-be with what can only be described as googly eyes. Their love story was a bit fast, but anyone that looks at them knows they're in love, and meant to be together.

I shrug. "Good for him." It's the truth. He deserves happiness, and he found that with Josie. I don't have any intention to fall in love again, not after the way things ended with my ex, my daughter's mother. Drugs can change a person, turn them into someone you don't recognize.

Now, I know that my entire focus is, and should be, my daughter. Making sure she's happy, healthy, and all the things a four, almost five-year-old should be. I glance over at my daughter to check on her quickly. She's sitting at a table, next to my mom, coloring. Guilt swarms in my stomach. My parents are amazing. They do anything they can to help me so I'm still able to run and help operate my brewery, Blue Ox Brewing. My mom watches Lennie every day, and picks her up from school during the school year. Most days, I can get away with picking Lennie up from my parents place at about five-thirty or six. However, nights where there is an event or a band, I'm stuck there till after closing. Perks of owning a brewery, instead of a bar, is our establishment closes around ten-thirty, rather than two a.m.

A second glance at the table has me eyeing another little girl with dirty blonde hair with hair down just past her shoulders that has appeared. She's not a family member, and I don't recognize her. She might be a few years older than Lennie, but it appears they are getting along well. Lennie points at something on her coloring page, and the little girl smiles.

"Who's the little girl with Lenners?" Thomas asks, drawing my attention back to him.

"I'm not sure," I respond, trying to place her in a memory or something. Nothing comes to me, and I turn my focus back to my brother. "How do you feel about our youngest brother getting married?"

Thomas stuffs his hand into his pants pockets and shuffles his feet. "Jealous." He stammers for a second. "Not that he's marrying Josie. No, that girl is like my sister. Just that he's getting married. I want someone to share my life with. You know?"

I don't. But I give him a slight nod anyway. "You'll find someone." I squeeze his shoulder.

"When I least expect it, right?" he chuckles, the sound almost rueful.

"Don't get down on yourself. It may happen before you know it." I gesture over to the bar. "I'm going to get another beer. Do you want one?"

He shakes his head. "Nah. I'm going to go sit with Dad and Gramps." He gestures to their table.

"I'll meet you there." I head to the bar and order myself a beer, thanking the young bartender with a chin dip and some extra cash in his jar as I turn, taking another drink. A person enters my line of sight.

Her hair is in loose honey-blonde waves which fall past her shoulders. Her green eyes are bright as she takes me in. She's dressed in a pair of black pants that hug her like a second skin. She's wearing a deep maroon blouse that ties at the waist, accentuating the swell of her hips. Her top shows a hint of cleavage, giving me a glimpse of her large, pillowing breasts. I might be more buzzed than I thought, because all I want to do is take a nap on them. I focus on her face, and I notice her lips are moving.

I fight the urge to shake my head to evade the haze she threw me into. "Um, hi, Jason?" her soft voice cracks, and it's like I'm thrown backward in time at the sound of it. "You might not remember me, but my name is—"

I interrupt her. "Fallon," I say on a heavy breath. Memories of classes together, library study sessions, and a Christmas party that almost changed things swirl in my brain. Wow. It's been ages since the last time I saw her— since my senior year of college—and to be honest, the memory isn't one I'm fond of. The earlier attraction I had to her hits me square in the chest, but I shake it off as the attraction is replaced by a familiar ache of loss and betrayal as I realize who this woman is. "It's been a long time. What are you doing here?" I ask.

Fallon clears her throat. "I work here. I'm the event and wedding coordinator."

"Wow," I mutter. "Small world."

"You could say that."

"It's, uh—it's nice to see you again. You look good." And she does. The extra curves she never had back in college fit her so well.

"Thanks, but I look like a mess. You look the same as I remember," she says with an awkward smile and a subtle shake of her head, her cheeks flaming.

"Do you live in Ivy Ridge?" I ask. Has she lived here for long, and I've somehow missed her? It's a small town, but I really don't go to many places outside of work, and my families' houses.

She nods. "Only recently. My daughter and I were staying with my mom a few towns over until I got the job here earlier this summer. We moved into a townhome in Ivy Ridge this month."

"You have a daughter?" I ask, my curiosity rising.

"I do." Fallon turns, pointing at the table where my own daughter sits. "Her name is Presley. She's six. Turning seven in May next year."

I gulp as I watch the two young girls interact. I nod toward them. "That's my daughter, Lennie. She's four, turning five in the spring."

"That's your daughter?" Fallon asks, her tone full of disbelief. I nod, and Fallon smiles. "She looks like you. And she's so sweet. You should be proud."

I let myself smile a little. "I am. She's the sweetest girl. Though, she looks a lot more like her mom, than me."

Fallon's smile grows. "Is she here? Her mom?"

I shake my head, my heart clenching. Talia *should* be here. Whether we're together or not, she should be here to see the important moments in her daughter's life. "Just me. It's a long story."

Fallon nods, her smile falling. "I get that. It's just me, too. I'm all Presley has. Lennie is lucky to have you, Jason."

I blink hard as I glance toward my daughter again. It would be so easy to confide in Fallon, someone who I once considered my best friend. She understands, she knows how hard it is to be a single parent. But I can't do it. I don't open myself up to anyone, so why would I with her?

"It was good to see you, Fallon." Without waiting for a response, I spin on my heel and head toward the table where my brother sits.

Fallon Vosk was someone I trusted, someone who I thought could be more than a friend. That ship sailed a long time ago, and I'm not about to try and jump aboard.

4

JASON

The wedding goes without a hitch, and now that it's done, my daughter won't stop asking about when she can spend more time with Fallon's daughter. Presley was around all weekend, so the girls spent a lot of time together. I'm thankful she made a friend to hang out with this weekend, since it's not like she has any cousins her age, but I'm not sure I want to spend more time with Fallon than I have to.

Maybe I'm still holding on to some lingering resentment from thirteen years ago, but she hurt me, more than I'd care to admit.

I roll Lennie and my suitcases into the lobby with her trailing at my side. It was easier to stay at the winery's hotel last night instead of making the short drive home, especially since I'd been drinking. We finished up the post wedding brunch about an hour ago, and now it's time to head home.

A voice calls my name from the opposite end of the lobby, and I turn my head toward it. It's Isaac, the owner of the winery and venue, and Andrew's best friend. He looks more than a little hungover this morning, but honestly, everyone does.

As Andrew's best friend, I've known Isaac forever. I'm older than the pair, so while we were in a different age group, I still hung out with them. Isaac was a talented baseball player, so he was on my team my senior year of high school.

Isaac makes his way to me, holding up his hand. "I wanted to run something by you before you left today. Do you have a minute to stop by my office?"

I look down at Lennie. She's probably exhausted, but I don't think a few more minutes will hurt. "Sure. Is Lennie okay to come with?"

"Absolutely. We can grab her a coloring page from the front desk on the way there."

I tell Lennie that we're going to Isaac's office quickly, and we follow him, only stopping momentarily to get her a coloring sheet and crayons from behind the front desk. Once in his office, I lean my suitcases against the wall, and sit across from him.

Isaac rubs at his temples. "I'm too hungover to even think about work right now, but I knew I needed to get the ball rolling on this."

"What is *this*?" I ask, my curiosity growing. Isaac sits up a little straighter, putting on the face of the business man I can easily admire.

"I have a proposition for you," he says. "We would have to look further into the logistics of it all, but do you have any interest in contracting with Meadow Grove Winery? We'd serve your beer, as well as our wine, exclusively at our events. Much like we are contracted with Josie for florals, we want to keep things local, really put some shine on our local businesses."

My mind whirs with the possibilities. It would mean more work, sure, and I'd probably have to hire someone on for events, or making the beer, but... it could work.

"Shit," I say, leaning back into my chair, and running my hand over my face and glancing over at Lennie to see if she caught my swear word. I've been trying to watch my mouth lately, but sometimes, I forget. "I mean, yeah, there's a lot of logistics to it, but... I'm definitely interested."

A wide grin pops up on Isaac's face. "Fuck yeah." He grimaces, also looking at my daughter, but she's lost in her own little world. He holds out a hand, and I give him mine, shaking it firmly.

"I'll get a meeting set up next week with you and we can go from there." Isaac drops my hand and rises from his chair.

5

FALLON

Of course, I'm running late on a day I absolutely should not be. Jason recently signed a contract to serve Blue Ox Brewing beer at weddings and events we have here at Meadow Grove. Today, I have a meeting with Isaac, Jason, and a few of Jason's employees to discuss the work flow for events.

I am a little nervous about seeing him again. He ended our conversation so abruptly at the rehearsal dinner, it felt like he wanted nothing to do with me any further . It stung a bit. I should have put on my big girl panties and apologized for the way I left things in college, but things had changed between us. It's my fault they did, but still. I was young and immature.

The day of his graduation, I had planned on talking to him again. I was going to find him, and congratulate him, but also apologize for ditching him, for ruining our friendship. That is, until I saw him being fawned over and kissed by a girl, someone with dark brown hair, and stunning features. I knew I couldn't compare to her, so I let it go. It's not like I expected him to ask me out or anything, but I wanted my friend back.

I texted Isaac a few minutes ago to let him know I was running late. He's a very laid back boss, and is always understanding when I'm a few minutes behind, or when Presley has to come hang out in the evenings with me for an event set up. I'm embarrassed though.

The meeting with Jason this morning is basically a meet and greet to go over the details of our agreement and get a taste for how his business works.

I pull my vehicle in the small parking lot in the back of the building, grabbing my purse and thermos of coffee in a rush. I don't run inside, because I don't need to be all sweaty and out of breath when I get into the conference room, but I'm definitely glad I had the foresight to wear a pair of flats today rather than heels.

The large reception area is empty this early in the morning. I love the quiet weekdays around here, always remembering them during an event when there's so many people you can barely make it through the crowd.

I stride through the room, my feet thwacking the ground in my rush. I fling open the door to the hall that leads to the offices, only to crash into a large body. My trusty binder goes flying, paper falling out as it tumbles to the ground. My thermos falls from my hand, landing on the floor in a loud *clang.*

"Oh no," I cry, bending down to grab it before it spills open. Thankfully, the seal is pretty good, but you never know. "I am so sorry. I can't believe I did that," I say without looking up. I've probably traumatized a vendor or someone else who works for the venue.

Great, exactly what I need.

Nothing like the event planner arriving to work in shambles to make you want to partner with the business.

"It's fine," a low, grumbling, *familiar* voice says. "Are you okay? I wasn't looking."

I tilt my head up, my sight meeting those beautiful chocolate brown eyes. Jason looks down at me, brows furrowed in an unknown expression—concern, or maybe irritation—as he tries to collect my papers and binder.

"I'm okay. I'm so sorry," I repeat, as my mind stutters like a broken record. "Are *you* okay? I crashed into you hard."

"You really didn't. I'm fine."

I nod, realizing I'm still bent at the waist. Jason rises, offering me his free hand, with the other clasping my strewn papers. My palm lands in his, and he helps me stand. I'm staring at him, probably slack-jawed. God, this is awkward.

I can't stop the embarrassment that flares inside me as a few of Brad's parting words flare inside my brain. *No wonder why you can't lose all the extra weight.* I've gained a hundred pounds, probably more, since he saw me last. It's taken me a long time, but I've been trying to be more confident in my new body after Brad wore me down time after time toward the last few years of our marriage. The worst part was I hadn't even realized he was doing it.

The comments weren't constant, in fact, they were strategically spaced out, or subtle-enough digs that I didn't process them as insults back then. I thought *I* was the problem. He was right, I didn't *need* the sweet treat after a trip to the park with Presley, or a second serving of spaghetti, because that was a lot of carbs.

After being freed from him, it took a lot of work and a lot of therapy, but finally I realized I wasn't the problem.

My mind refocuses on Jason in front of me. He hasn't

changed much. I didn't really take in his appearance the last time I saw him, but the signs of aging are there, but he looks like the same young man I remember so fondly.

We're still standing in the doorway, Jason still holding my papers, when the conference room door opens. "Hey, Fallon," Isaac's voice carries. "How are you this morning?"

I offer him a slight wave. "Good. Sorry I'm running late. Presley and I overslept a bit."

He waves me off. "You know I don't mind. We were going to grab some coffee. You can go get settled, and we will meet in ten minutes. Need some coffee?"

I shake my head, lifting my thermos. "I've got it covered. Thanks, though."

Isaac nods. "Jason, you coming?"

I glance back towards the man in question. He's staring at me like he's lost, but shakes it off. "Yep, be right behind you."

Isaac heads off, and Jason attempts to organize my papers into a pile for me. "Thanks, and... sorry again?"

He shakes his head, but the slight grimace on his face makes me uncomfortable. Gone is the man who offered a smile at the drop of a hat, doing anything to make you smile. "No need. It's good to see you, Fallon." His voice goes low and gruff, and it sounds like he's more irritated than anything. He passes off the papers, and our arms brush. He rushes off like he's trying to get away from me as fast as possible. I try to hold it back, but a shiver races through my body, leaving goosebumps in its path at the simple touch.

I feel like I'm nineteen all over again.

Ten minutes later, I've got my papers reorganized, and my coffee is mostly gone. My brain is finally functioning, and Jason and Isaac come back into the conference room.

One of the other managers, Laila, and one of Jason's employees enter, and I stand as they do.

I may be a bit of a hot mess, but I'm a professional, and good at my job. Before I had Presley, I was an executive assistant for a CEO in the heart of downtown Minneapolis. I worked my ass off, and I loved it. I'm not as sprightly as I was back then, being a single mom will do that to you, but I love getting to work again. Brad wanted me to be home for Presley and our potential future children, and at the time, I didn't have a problem with it. I loved being a stay at home mom, but I also love working.

Jason enters the room, Isaac close at his heels. Isaac chuckles under his breath. "You all know we are very laid back. You don't have to stand."

I laugh, the awkwardness settling in my gut. I won't have much to do in terms of setting up Jason's contract, but I'll be his go to when it comes to events, so it's important I'm here to guide him through how we run things, and what to expect.

Both Jason and Isaac sit down, and Isaac starts the meeting. He gives us a rundown of what to expect with this contract, and then Jason chimes in with what his process will be. I'm listening closely, taking notes so I'm sure of what to expect.

Throughout the meeting, I can't stop gazing up at Jason. His brown eyes are focused, brows furrowed as he concentrates and takes notes. He looks different, but I can still see the young man I once knew. Perhaps I'm romanticizing the short amount of time we were friends, and the infatuations I had for him, but I don't think so. He's changed, as to be expected when time passes. He seems almost jaded. He's not the happy man I used to know.

There's a constant furrow in his brow, and something

put it there. After the wedding, I peppered Megan and Josie with questions about him on a coffee date, all while doing my best not to share too much, only telling them that we knew each other in college.

They really only told me a fact I already knew. He's a single dad, and is a pretty closed off person. I got that vibe from him the night of the rehearsal dinner. He seemed happy to see me at the start of the conversation, but as the moments passed, it was like watching his memory of us slowly creep back in, and he shut down. As soon as I mentioned his daughter, he shut down completely.

The story of Lennie's mom seems to be a sore subject. I gently prodded for details, but neither Josie, nor Megan would give me any, which is fine. It's not their story to tell.

Jason's successful. He became the talented businessman he talked about being, despite some of his hesitancy toward graduation. In a way, I'm proud of him, proud of what he became.

Jason lifts his eyes from his paperwork, catching me staring at him. I inhale sharply, turning my eyes away. I keep my focus on the pile of paper and notes in front of me for the rest of the meeting.

"Fallon, do you have anything you need to add?" Isaac asks.

I shake my head, glancing down at the papers in front of me again. "Nope, I don't think so. Just..." I clear my throat, for some reason anxious about this next part. "I need to exchange contact information with Jason and the team members working out here so we can be in touch if need be."

I push a piece of hair out of my face, looking at Jason briefly. He's nodding to himself, finishing up a note. We finish the meeting, and Jason's employee, Laila, and I exchange information. She leaves the room, followed by one of our other employees who helps me out when I need. Isaac exits as well, heading off to another meeting.

I have a venue tour in an hour with a bride and groom, so I need to head out and type up my notes before they get here.

I clear my throat softly. Jason is still sitting at the large round table, clearing up his papers. He lifts his head. "Sorry, got lost in my notes for a second," he says, standing up.

Jason hovers over me. In my flats, I'm not as tall as I would be in my normal attire of heels. Even in heels, Jason would still be taller than me. If I remember right, he was probably six-foot-one or two, from his baseball stats, much taller than my five-foot-six. He steps over to me, pulling his phone from his pocket.

He passes his phone over, and I type my number in. Only, instead of going to add myself as a new contact card, my name pops up. A surprised gasp falls from my lips, but I'm quick to disguise it as clearing my throat. I didn't expect that, and it makes my heart flip flop into my stomach.

He still has my phone number saved. I don't know what to feel. Somehow, I haven't had to change my number ever, so it makes sense he would still have my number, especially if he hasn't changed his. It's listed under my maiden name, Fallon Vosk, and I wonder if I should update it. I never changed my name back after the divorce. I change it quickly, not telling him that that's what I'm doing.

When I hand him back his phone, I open my contacts, and search his name. My slight intuition was right, and I still have his number saved.

I swallow thickly. "I guess I still have your number saved. Do you want to check and see if it's the same?"

I offer him my phone, and he takes it into his large palm.

"I haven't changed my number, so I'm sure it's still the same." He glances at the contact card briefly, nodding. "Yep, the same."

"Cool," I say, taking my phone back, and offering him an awkward thumbs up. *Good god, Fallon. You're thirty-two years old. There's no reason to get all flustered over a man you knew when you were nineteen.*

Jason turns, heading toward the conference room door, holding it open for me. "So, what have you been up to all these years?" I ask, trying to fill the awkward silence. I get the idea he doesn't want to talk to me any more than he has to, but selfishly, I want to know him again. I still need to apologize, and I hope he lets me.

He looks down, an almost confused look on his face. "Well, the last five have been spent wrangling my daughter. She's like a little tornado."

"I know the feeling," I reply. I got that impression during the wedding weekend, so I can totally understand that. "Presley is a little ball of chaos. I love her with more than I am, though."

Jason nods, leading us down the hall. My office is in the opposite direction, and yet I don't correct him, or leave the conversation early to go separate ways.

"You recently moved here, right? What brought you to the area?" Jason asks, and I'm a bit surprised he's leading the conversation.

"Well, my mom is a few towns over, and Megan, Isaac's wife, is my best friend. She was my roommate my sophomore year of college, and the rest is history. After..." I trail off. "After my husband, *ex*-husband left, I wanted a fresh start. My daughter and I moved in with my mom, and after I got the job here, we found a little place in town. It's been an adjustment, but I'm really happy here."

Jason nods. "I'm glad you're happy here."

"Have you been back here since graduation?" I ask, curious about his whereabouts.

"Yeah. I moved home right away. My grandma passed not long after I moved home, and I decided I wanted to stay close to my family."

"Sorry to hear about your grandma," I reply. I can't believe I never put it together that he lived here. I mean I'm sure he mentioned it in the time we were friends, I just didn't connect the dots.

He shrugs. "Part of life."

We walk in comfortable silence for a bit longer, only stopping when we reach the main event center. "Can I ask you something?" I ask.

Jason's brows lift. "Of course."

"Do you think our girls could get together for a playdate someday?" I take a deep breath, trying to calm my nerves. "Presley has been hounding me, pretty much non-stop since Josie and Andrew's wedding."

"Lennie would love that," he says.

"I think they're close enough in age that they could become really close friends," I explain.

"I agree," Jason replies. For some reason in my brain, he was going to say no, so his easy acceptance is throwing me off. "I'm sure we can get something organized."

"Great," I say. "I—uh, I need to get back to my office, I have a tour soon. But it was good to see you again, Jason."

"You too, Fallon. I'll let you know about a playdate."

I offer him an awkward finger gun, turning and hiding my blazing red face before he can see my humiliation.

6

JASON

"Daddy, what time are they going to be here?" Lennie asks for what might be the hundredth time. We arrived at the indoor playground early, so they should be arriving any minute.

"I'm not sure, Lenners. Why don't you go play, I'm sure they'll be here soon." I gesture to the swings. "I can push you on the swing, if you'd like?"

Lennie shakes her head adamantly. "Not yet. I want to show Presley how I can jump off the swing when I get really high."

Her words send a spiral of panic through me, cause *what*? "What do you mean, jump off?"

"When I pump my legs really hard and get high enough, I jump off and land on my feet. Uncle Andrew showed me how to do it when he took me here last," she explains.

"Of course he did," I mutter, making a mental note to text my little brother to stop teaching my daughter dangerous things. Do I remember doing things like that when I was a kid? Yes, absolutely, but that doesn't mean I want my daughter doing them. I broke both my arms as a kid, and I'll do anything to keep Lennie from doing that.

I'm about to explain to Lennie why we shouldn't jump from the swings from heights, when she screeches, "They're here!" She runs across the room to greet Presley. Fallon walks in right behind her, unzipping her jacket and smiling when she sees Lennie bounding toward them.

Presley shouts Lennie's name, and pulls her into a hug. It's adorable how much their friendship has grown in a few short months since meeting at the wedding, and I'm glad Lennie has found a friend in her. Fallon takes off her winter jacket, revealing a black floral wrap dress. She has on a pair of black tights underneath, showing off her gorgeous legs and hints of her thick thighs. Her blonde hair is up in a messy bun, like she threw it up as soon as she got in the car after work. It's beautiful, showing off the gentle slope of her neck. She has such a natural beauty, that I forget to breathe for a moment.

Presley takes off her jacket and hands it over to Fallon, and then the girls are off running, heading right to the swings. "Hey Jason," Fallon greets when she's closer.

"Hey," I reply. I can't keep my eyes on her though, because if I do, I won't be able to stop ogling her. It reminds me of college. Her mind is as brilliant as her beauty, and I could never take my eyes off her, even if I tried.

"How was your day?" she asks, looking up at me briefly before turning back to the girls.

"Fine." One word answers. That's what I can do right now. I need to keep a firm boundary for my sanity, and if I'm honest with myself, I might still have some unresolved frustration with her over the way things ended between us all those years ago. I'm an asshole. I know this, and my mom would smack me upside the head if she knew the way I was acting.

Fallon shuffles, kicking at the padded floor with her wedged boot. We stand in awkward silence for a long few minutes, until I decide to go sit on one of the benches. She follows, sitting on the opposite end from me. Her back is ramrod straight as she sits as far as she can from me.

"I know this is probably the last thing you want to talk about," Fallon starts, and I look over at her. "But I wanted to apologize for the way I left things back—"

I interrupt her. "We don't need to talk about it."

"I-I'm sorry. Can I at least say that?"

I shift my eyes back to where my daughter is pumping her legs on the swings, Presley right beside her, mimicking the motions. They both swing higher and higher as I watch. Great, Lennie is totally going to jump the way Andrew taught her. My heart pounds with nervous energy as I grumble out, "It's fine, the past is the past."

From the corner of my eye, I can see Fallon look down at her hands in her lap. She twists her fingers in the hem of her dress, and I know I've made this way more uncomfortable than necessary.

"Um—okay then," Fallon states. Without another word, she stands from the bench, plastering a smile on her face and walking over to the swings. With each step, her hips sway, the curve of her ass on display as her body moves with grace, making my body react in ways I know it shouldn't. My pulse quickens, and there's a tightness in my jeans I choose to ignore. She pushes both of them, alternating between kids, and I watch how easily the girls shriek in happiness, all from the simplicity of a swing.

Fallon smiles easily now, laughing with the two young girls, even cheering them on as they test how far they can jump off the swings. I shouldn't let her do this, but it makes her so happy, and she really isn't jumping from that high. Fallon seems to be okay with it, so maybe it's fine. My heart pulses rapidly in my chest out of fear each time they jump, but when they stick each landing, the anxiety lessens.

Even though I was a jerk for no reason other than not wanting to dwell on the past, Fallon practically radiates sunshine. I've heard the tiniest hints of her past, and for her to stand as tall as she does, it's impressive. Everyone loves her and her daughter, and knowing her all those years ago, I know exactly why everyone does. She's amazing. Sweet, kind, beautiful, joyful, everything I'm not.

I have no qualms with Presley and Lennie being friends, but I know I can't open myself up to Fallon again. I can't deal with that hurt again.

7

———

JASON

"**L**aila, what do you need from me?" I turn my gaze to my bartender and manager.

"Not a thing," she says with a shrug, glancing out at the crowd of people. The cocktail hour of our first wedding at Meadow Grove Winery has gone without a hitch, and I'm grateful. It gives me hope that I made the right decision in partnering with the winery. Not that Isaac ever does anything lightly, but still. I put my trust in him, and it's paying off.

In the last few months or so since that first meeting with Isaac and Fallon, things have moved quickly. Work has been busy, and adding the contract with the winery has made things even busier, but that didn't stop me from making time for my daughter and my family. There have also been plenty of playdates with Fallon and Presley, and thankfully, Fallon hasn't tried to apologize again. However, that didn't stop me from thinking about her, thinking of memories and analyzing every conversation we've ever had.

Speaking of Fallon, she practically skips by the bar, clipboard in hand. Her blonde hair is twisted up in a curled ponytail, and she's wearing a black fitted blouse tucked into a pair of burgundy high waisted pants. I can't help but imagine what it would be like to peel off those clothes and see what's underneath.

Somehow, she's nearly running in a pair of heels, and I have no idea how she's doing it. Like every other time I've seen her lately, my body reacts the same way it used to back in college. It's like an involuntary reaction at this point. My pulse starts to thump heavily, and my thoughts narrow to only her, dreaming of what it would be like to have her in my arms, in my embrace.

"Slow down, Fallon!" Laila calls with a laugh, but Fallon doesn't say anything, only smiles toward her and continues on her way. It reminds me of a younger version of herself, always on the move, always heading off to her next class.

My phone buzzes in my pocket, and I check it quickly to make sure it's not from my mom. It is from her, but it's a photo of Lennie. They went to a craft festival today, so Lennie is having a fun day out.

A guest arrives at the bar, so I take their order, and Laila serves them. I won't have to be at every wedding we serve at, but for this first one, I knew it was important for me to be here, not only to make sure things go smoothly, but to represent my company.

One of the other girls that offered to work today arrives in time for her shift. "Nora," I greet with a head tilt. I'm not a talkative man, and my employees know that, but they also know I do whatever I can to be a good employer. I pay them well, and do my best to keep them happy.

I'm not totally naive, I know I do things some of my

employees dislike, but that's normal when you're the boss, you're not going to make everyone happy all the time.

And what can I say, I'm a grumpy guy. I've been told I'm intimidating as fuck until you get to know me.

Laila is giving Nora the rundown on how we're doing things, which is slightly different than our normal operations, when I see a flash of red hair run through the waves of people.

"*What the fuck?*" I murmur under my breath at the sight of my sister-in-law Josie, nearly sprinting through the room. "Josie," I call, catching her attention.

She breathes out a heavy sigh when she sees me, rushing over to the bar. "Oh thank god, I totally forgot you were here today. Marley was the photographer for the wedding today, and now she's having contractions, and I was sent to get her water, but I'm not going to lie, I'm freaking out a little."

Marley and Beau finally got together during Josie and Andrew's wedding, and now, Marley's about eight months pregnant with twins, a boy and a girl. Watching them finally give into the feelings we knew were there all along over the last few months has been amazing. Another one of my brothers is settling down and starting a family, and I'm happy for him.

"She's having contractions?" I repeat.

Josie nods frantically.

"Shit," I murmur. "Laila, Nora, can you handle this for a bit? I have to check on my sister-in-law." *Technically*, she's not my sister-in-law, but she will be someday.

"Go," Laila waves me away.

I rush around the bar to Josie's side, and she leads me down the hall. "Megan's here somewhere, right?"

"Yeah, I think she's in the office, I'll run and grab her. You grab the water. Where is Marley?"

"Front lobby," Josie replies, already turning toward the kitchen.

I run down the hall to Isaac's office, finding Megan sitting at his desk, with him standing behind her. He's pointing to something on the screen, but I don't care.

"Meg, we need you," I tell her. "I guess Marley's having contractions?" I say with a questioning tone, because I truly don't know what the fuck is going on.

"Shit," she stands immediately, and Isaac follows as we briskly walk down the hall. Marley's like my little sister, and I'd do anything to protect her and those babies, regardless of the fact that they are my niece and nephew.

We meet Josie in the entry to the lobby, and she tells Megan what's happening, and how she thinks Marley is having Braxton-Hicks contractions. We all collectively sigh in relief when we see Marley sitting on the couch, feet up on the table. She looks relaxed, and not at all stressed the way Josie is.

Josie cools it though, and is calm and collected as she strides up to Marley. Marley has her phone up to her ear, and she's listening intently to whoever is on the other line.

She finishes her conversation with what I'm gathering is a nurse, and Josie immediately asks, "Well?"

"They want me to come in. Just for evaluation though. She doesn't think I'm in active labor, but since things are a bit more risky with twins, she wants to be sure," Marley replies, setting her phone down.

Megan nods. "After Josie told me what was happening, I figured that would be the case."

She tilts her head back on the couch, taking a few shaky

breaths. I sit down on the edge of the coffee table, resting my hand on her shin.

"Marley," I say, my voice low. "Do you need anything? Hungry? Thirsty?"

"I'm okay, really. I'm tired, but otherwise, I think I'm okay."

"You sure?" I ask. "I can always get Thomas to give you a police escort. You know he'd do it." I raise my brow in a silent question, knowing full well Thomas would be here in a heartbeat.

She laughs softly. "No, I promise I'm okay. If things get worse, I'll let you know."

I still nod, and squeeze her leg. "I'm sticking around until Beau gets here."

She starts to cry, and I panic internally, worrying I did something wrong. "Why are you even here?" she asks.

"It's the first wedding we are serving Blue Ox at. I was over at the bar when I caught Josie running like a madwoman through the reception area."

Josie peeks her head in, smacking my bicep and giving her own two cents. "Hey now, I was on a mission. As soon as I told you what was happening, you were running faster than I was."

"I'm not denying it." I shrug as I look at Marley. I'll admit it, I was freaking out a bit. I care strongly for my family, and I'll do anything for them.

Something catches my attention, and I turn my head in time to see Fallon rushing toward us. Her face is flushed, and I fight the urge to stand up and see what happened. Is she hurt?

"Josie!" she calls across the lobby. "We need you, one of the drunken cousins knocked over the flower arch."

Josie sighs heavily and stands. Fallon is already long gone, and Josie says her goodbyes to Marley, making her promise to keep her updated. Isaac follows, leaving only Megan and I behind.

I move so I'm sitting next to Marley on the couch now. I'm reminded about the times when Talia had Braxton-Hicks contractions toward the end of her pregnancy. Something compels me to bring it up. It's not something I would normally do, but I do it anyway.

"When Talia was pregnant with Lennie, she got those early 'practice contractions' all the time. She had a super low pain tolerance, so we were going into the hospital every other day, it seemed."

Marley turns to face me a little more. Her eyes spark with remembrance. "Oh yeah. I remember that now. How did she do during her actual labor?"

I can't keep myself from rolling my eyes. The memories flash behind my eyes as I think about the long and painful days. I lean forward, resting my elbows on my knees. "Lots of screaming. Lots of begging for drugs and *lots* of curse words."

There was one particular contraction where Talia actually threatened the doctors if they didn't give her more medication. I spent a lot of time apologizing to the doctors and nurses, but they wouldn't hear it. I remember all the people who helped deliver Lennie though, so I try to give them free beer whenever they come into the brewery, as sort of a thank you.

"That's usually the norm, though," Megan tries to say.

I shake my head, wincing before I explain. "Not like this. The doctors struggled with how to tell her no, that she was maxed out on her meds, and there was nothing else they could do. I knew she'd had a problem with drugs in the past, but never realized it was that bad. She swore she was clean and ready to be done with that life. I should have seen it coming. Shortly after Lennie was born, she fell off the deep end."

A subtle shiver rocks through me with the memories.

Marley reaches out her hand, squeezing the top of my arm in consolation. "It's not your fault. You couldn't have known, Jason."

I shrug, knowing she's right, but there will always be the guilt that settles deep in my chest when I think of Talia. Could I have done more? If I'd done one thing differently would she have stayed clean? Would we be a family right now? Would Lennie have a mom, and more siblings? I brush it off, saying, "Lennie is safe, and that's all that matters, right?"

There's a beat of silence, and then Marley is squeezing the absolute shit out of my arm. I almost yank it away, before I realize she's probably having another contraction.

I let her grip my arm as hard as she needs. Megan kneels in front of her, coaching her through her breathing. I don't say anything but stay here as a strong pillar for her. I can be her strength until Beau gets here.

As if I summoned him, loud footsteps echo through the lobby, and my younger brother appears, looking stressed as hell. His long hair is disheveled, eyes wide as he scans the room in search of his love. I catch his attention, waving him over. He's over to her in two beats, dropping down beside her and taking her palm in his.

He holds her close, while she still has one hand clenched around my arm. Beau whispers reassurances in her ear, words none of us can hear, something that's only for them.

It warms my heart knowing they've finally made their

way to each other. I may be a man who knows I'm destined to be alone, I don't know that I could ever open myself up to someone again after Talia, after she broke my trust one too many times, but I can admit how happy it makes me to know my brothers are finding their person.

Once the contraction passes, Marley lets go of my arm. Her eyes widen and she profusely apologizes as she takes in the red marks on my skin. I laugh. "Nothing to be sorry about, Mar. If you guys need anything, let me know." I stand, rubbing at my arm dramatically to give her shit. She swats at my leg and I laugh. Beau rises, giving me a tight hug.

"Thanks for being with her," he murmurs. I nod into the embrace. I pull away first, giving them and Megan a wave before heading back to the reception area.

I spot Josie and Fallon trying to get the flower arch set back up. Fallon is standing back a bit, while Josie is on a stool, rearranging the flowers. I glance over to the bar, and note that Laila and Nora seem to have things well under control, so they should be alright for a few minutes.

"Jason," Josie calls, pulling my attention back to her. "You're tall."

"Um, yes?" I respond, frowning and stepping up to the arch.

"Can you lift this piece so I can pin it down?"

I nod in agreement, and she shows me which vine to grab, and where to place it. She pins it delicately, but while also making sure it's stable. She leans back, taking a glance at a new angle. "Perfect," she mutters to herself. "Kenzy usually helps me, but she's gone already, and I didn't trust Fallon to be on a stool in her heels."

I glance back toward Fallon, and give an agreeing nod. She's still in her tall heels, and I'm grateful I was here when

I was. Wouldn't want her to fall and hurt herself. I offer Josie a hand, and she steps down off her little stool, shoving her clippers and wire into a little utility belt I didn't notice before.

"Thanks," Josie says. "I'll probably head out here shortly, so if I don't see you, I'll see you at brunch tomorrow?"

"Yep." Every Sunday since I was a kid, my mom hosts Sunday Brunch. Our family, and our neighbors, Marley's parents, will come over and have brunch with us. We've always been close with Marley's family, and even spend most holidays together. As our families have slowly started to grow, so have brunches. Josie is now in attendance every Sunday with Andrew, and every so often, her parents will make the trek down too.

Soon, Marley and Beau's twins will join in when they're born, and I'm sure Thomas will find a girl soon, and she'll become part of the family.

It makes me happy that my family is starting to grow, and even happier that Lennie will have some cousins to play with soon. Even though she'll be five years older than them, I know she will still love to have them around. She's been the only kid for so long.

Josie and I say goodbye, and she runs off to Fallon, giving her a quick and brief hug. I stand by the arch still, watching the wedding take place. Everyone is still mingling, slowly finding their seats as the cocktail hour winds down. Once we get through dinner, I'll make my way to my parents' house and pick up Lennie. I promised her we'd have a *Barbie* movie night tonight, and while I'm not looking forward to the movies, I'm always excited to spend time with my daughter.

A tap on my shoulder startles me. Fallon is standing

right by me, taller in her heels, so her chin is at the same height as my shoulder. "Don't you love weddings?" she asks, a lovestruck look in her eyes.

I can't help the grumble that builds in my chest, narrowing my eyes as I look at her. "Not exactly."

"Why?" she questions, her voice light and genuinely curious.

"Too many people, everyone is drunk and annoying." What I don't say is that it can be hard to see people getting the happy endings I thought I might have gotten with someone.

"That's fair. For me, It's the huge display of love. I love that everyone is there to celebrate two people, and it's such a combination of worlds. I mean, they have people here from all walks of their lives. Work friends, family, school, an obscure cousin you haven't seen in ten years, but no matter what, everyone is here to support them."

I really look at her as she takes in the crowded room around us. She really is beautiful, and so optimistic. I've learned the bare minimum about what she's been up to in the last ten-plus years, only that she was married, and now she's not. Maybe someday I'll get to know her better, but for now, I think I should keep my distance, keep her as a friend, or someone from my past.

"Even after..." I trail off, stopping myself before I say anything more. "Never mind."

"You can say it," Fallon says, glancing up at me with those deep green eyes. "Even after my divorce?"

I grimace. This is the most she's talked to me in months outside of the short conversations we have while our girls have their playdates. I do my best to keep my distance. She's too easy to talk to. It would be so easy to fall back into the old cycle, confiding in her for everything and then having my heart ripped out and shredded in the end. I'm a dick, because she tries to start conversations, but I shut down. I don't engage.

She shrugs, dropping my gaze and glancing around the room again. "Even after my divorce, yeah. I still love weddings. My wedding day was a shit show if I'm being honest. I should have taken everything that went wrong as a sign maybe. The wedding planner quit the day before the wedding, my florist was in a car accident on the way to the venue, and my veil ripped. I took it in stride though. I find that doing what I do now, it helps me come full circle. I had a shitty wedding day, and well, to be honest, a shitty marriage," she says with a scoff. "But that doesn't mean I lost hope on love. I want these couples to have the best day, and if I can help them, then I will."

"I get that," I reply. Talia and I never married, so I never had that feeling of overwhelming love from all sides, but... hearing her describe it, I get it, and why she does what she does. I force myself to keep the conversation going. "Will you ever get married again?"

She shrugs. "If it's the right person. My marriage to Brad changed me. I'm still figuring out who I am outside of that marriage. I'm not going to force it though. I'm happy, me and Pres. We are doing our best to make a good life for ourselves, and honestly, the thought of going through what I did again..." Fallon shudders. "Right now, I'm happy."

"You deserve to be happy," I tell her honestly. The drop of the name of her ex-husband has me reeling. Did she really marry the guy she left with that day in the library? The one that barely let her get two words out? If it's the same guy, I'm glad she got out of the marriage, even if it hurt her. She's better off without him.

"Are you happy?" she asks me.

I think to myself for a long moment. I'm happy to be a dad, happy I have my daughter, but am I really, truly, *happy*? Before I can answer, someone calls Fallon's name. She stands straighter, looking around to find the person. "I gotta go," she says, waving to me, before running off to fend off another drunk cousin, fix a ripped veil, or who knows.

8

FALLON

I mentally slap myself as I run away from Jason. God, word vomit much? I was spewing how much I love love, like a freaking Valentine's Day Hallmark movie. Meanwhile, he's standing there next to me, the epitome of uninterest, probably thinking how absurd I am. We have barely talked since. Most of the time during playdates, he's focused on watching Lennie, or gives me one word answers. Our conversations are short and to the point nowadays. I want to break down the walls he's put up, but I doubt I'll be able to.

To be honest, I have no idea how I still believe in love after what Brad did to me and Presley, but I do. I saw what true love was when I was a kid, watching my mom and dad, and now, I see it in my best friend, and her husband, as well as my other friends.

Do I think I'll find love for myself again? Probably not. I have too much baggage after Brad, but like I told Jason, I have Presley, and that's enough. I have so much love for her that it's all I need. I wish her sibling could be here for Presley, someone to have at her side, besides me. Having a sibling is different from a mom, but the cards didn't fall that way. A pang of grief hits me square in the chest, but I shake that off.

I bring my focus back to the task at hand. The mother of the groom called me over, complaining that the bride and groom are taking too long for portraits. I've tried explaining to her that they aren't running behind, they still have at least twenty-five minutes before they're due back, but she's not having it.

"I don't understand why they are taking so long," she continues. I do my best to keep a straight face and not roll my eyes. "I could have sworn I saw the photographer a few minutes ago, so wouldn't they be with her?"

In all reality, I know they're not taking photos anymore. They specifically slotted themselves thirty minutes of alone time between their portrait session and when they are due for the grand entrance. Marissa, the photographer, and I are the only ones who know they technically aren't doing their portraits right now. I have no idea where they are, or what they are doing, just that they're alone. Honestly, I think it's smart. It's good to get some time to themselves, whether it be for a quickie, or time to recoup from the craziness of their wedding day.

"Mrs. Swenson, I promise, they're on time. They're finishing up here in about—" I check the time on my phone, "—fifteen minutes, and then it's time for the grand entrance."

She huffs again, clearly not pleased with my answer. I have an inkling she is one of those moms that has a hard time letting her baby boy go. Though, from what I've seen of the bride, she's not putting up with it, and neither is the groom. The mom won't take a hint.

She spins away from me, and I watch her to make sure she doesn't follow as I head in the direction I saw Marissa sneak off to with a plate of cheese and crackers. Thankfully, she's pulled in the opposite direction by another guest, so I let out a sigh of relief and make my way back to the bar area. Jason has rejoined his staff, and Isaac is doing his final rounds of the night before he heads out.

I head over to where he is leaning against the bar, talking with Jason. My phone buzzes on my way over, and I pull it out of the pocket of my slacks. A fresh wave of guilt floods my body when I read the message.

MOM

> If you can spare a minute, Presley needs a goodnight call tonight. She's having a rough day.

I knew that was going to happen. Sometimes, she is fine to go to bed without hearing from me, and other times, she needs a call from me to be able to sleep. I do my best to call regardless when I know I won't be home at bedtime, but sometimes, things come up.

ME

> I should be able to make it work. Did something happen?

MOM

> She saw a photo of your dad on the mantel, and asked if he left the way her dad did.

Fuck.

I've told her about my dad, her grandpa, and how he passed away and is in heaven, but sometimes that's a lot for a seven-year-old to grasp.

MOM

I told her no, that he'd passed away, and
that's why he's not with us anymore.

ME

Shit, Mom. I'm so sorry.

I know how hard it is for my mom to talk about my dad.
She grieves the loss of him so much.

MOM

It's not your fault.

It didn't end well. She's so stuck on why
her dad isn't here if he's not dead. She
keeps asking if he didn't love her.

ME

I'm so sorry, Mom. You shouldn't have had
to deal with that.

MOM

It's alright, honey. Just… try to call tonight
if you can.

ME

I'll make sure of it. Give me an hour?

MOM

Of course.

"Fallon, as always, wonderful job," Isaac says, pulling
my attention back to the world in front of me.

"Thank you," I reply, putting my phone face down atop
my clipboard. "It's been a successful day so far."

"Have a drink," he says. "Having Blue Ox here is a hit."

It's been a hot day, and a cool drink sounds wonderful.
"That sounds great," I say.

I glance up to find Jason's eyes on mine. There's something different in his eyes, something I haven't seen from him. Almost... interest?

"What can I get you?" he asks.

"Umm, what's your favorite?"

He glances behind him, looking at the taps. "Depends on what you like. Do you want a beer? Or a cider?"

I make it appear like I'm pondering, though really, I'm not a beer girl. I *hate* beer.

"Cider," I reply.

Jason smirks, like he knew that's what I was going to say. He probably did. "Or, I have a hard lemonade you can try."

I shake my head, ignoring the tug of a memory on the edge of my mind of a Christmas party in a run down college house. "Not a hard lemonade fan anymore."

"Noted," he says, giving me a knowing look, like he's remembering the same thing I am. "Do you trust me?"

I nod, almost breathless at his words. I never thought I would trust a man again, but for some reason with this, I trust him. He turns, heading back to the taps. He grabs a glass, and fills it with a rich golden colored cider. He sets it on the bar in front of me, gesturing for me to take a sip. I lift the glass to my lips, letting the flavor settle on my tongue before I swallow the softly bubbling liquid.

The flavor hits me all at once, and I fight back the groan of pleasure at the taste. "What is that?" I ask. It's sweet, tart, and so damn good.

"Strawberry Rhubarb," he replies.

"Holy moly, that's good." I take another long sip, loving the flavor. It's subtle, but so freaking good that I can't get enough.

"It's a favorite at the brewery," he tells me.

"I can see why."

My phone buzzes again with another text from my

mom, and I try to subtly look at it while also keeping my attention on the people in front of me. I glance down at the message, seeing a photo of Presley. She's cuddled up on the couch in a blanket I recognize as one from my childhood with her favorite teddy bear in her arms. The message from my mom reads, *cuddled with her favorite. She's missing her mom a little extra tonight.*

"Everything okay?" Isaac asks.

"Huh?" I ask, distracted. "Oh, yeah. Everything's fine. Presley is missing me tonight."

He nods. When I look up again, Jason is looking down at me, a look of almost... irritation on his face? I don't know why he'd be irritated, but it rubs me the wrong way. I take a sip of my cider, and check the time. It's about time for the grand entrance, so I really should be on my way to go and find the bridal party.

"I'll see you guys in a bit, I'm off to get everyone organized." I wave, taking my drink with me as I go.

"HI, SWEETIE," I say to my daughter. Her cheeks are flushed pink, and tears glisten down her skin.

"Hi," she says, her voice thick with emotion.

"Are you feeling better?"

"Not really."

I sigh. "I'm sorry I can't be there tonight. Want to tell me what made you sad today?" I'm all about making sure she knows that she can tell me any thoughts or emotions she's experiencing. I should probably take my own advice and talk to someone, but Presley is my focus right now.

"If my daddy didn't die like grandpa then why isn't my

daddy here? Doesn't he love me? Did I do something wrong? Is that why he left?" Presley asks, her tears falling steadily.

God, I wish I could hug her, hold her right now. I need her to know how loved she is. How much I love her.

"Of course not, Presley. You did nothing wrong. I do know that your daddy loved you, and I don't know why he left the way he did. It hurts, and I'm so sorry."

My throat thickens, and I try to swallow down some of the emotion clogging it. "But I will *never* leave you. Ever. I need you to know that."

She turns her face away from the camera. I understand why she doesn't believe me when the proof is right there that people *do* leave, but I don't know how to get her to understand.

"Lennie has a daddy, but not a mommy. All my other friends at school have both. Why don't we have both?" Her voice wobbles.

Looking up at the ceiling to try and stifle my own tears, and stop my lip from trembling, I reply, "I don't know why Lennie doesn't have a mom, but she has a daddy who loves her so much, like I love you. I love you, Presley. So, so much. I will do anything I can to make sure you are happy. I know this is so hard for you, but I'm here."

Presley sniffles. "I love you too," she murmurs. She has so many big emotions. "Can you come lay with me when you get here?"

"Of course," I tell her, hoping she's forgiven me at least a little bit.

"Do you have to go?" Presley asks.

"Not for another minute. The bride and groom are dancing, so I have time." That makes her face light up. Presley is like me. She loves weddings.

"What does her dress look like?" she asks, eyes bright now.

I go into great detail describing the gorgeous dress the bride is wearing. I'm in my office, the door is wide open, so I'm not really paying attention when a figure appears in the doorway. I figure it's probably Isaac or Megan, so I'm surprised when they don't step over and say hi to Presley. Presley loves her Aunt Megan and Uncle Issac. I glance up after I'm finished telling her about the flowers, confused when it's Jason standing there.

He's not exactly glaring at me, but the look on his face isn't exactly inviting. When he sees that I notice him, he steps in further.

"Who are you looking at, Mom?" Presley asks.

I stammer, clearing my throat. "Um, it's Jason, Lennie's dad."

"Oh!" she exclaims, her excitement rising again. She asks him a question, even though she can't see him. "Mr. Jason, can I play with Lennie again next week?"

Jason rounds my desk, coming up behind me. He leans down so he can look at my screen. "Hi, Presley, yes, you can. Your mom and I will get something organized."

I try to ignore the way he smells—so clean and fresh—but I can't. He's in my space, his body heat mingling with mine, and I can't stop the way my heart starts to pound.

Presley continues to talk to Jason, all while I try to ignore the thumping heat flowing through my veins at our proximity.

Jason listens as Presley talks animatedly. Presley says my name, and I'm brought back to the present.

"What honey?" I ask.

"Grandma says it's time for dinner."

"Oh," I pause. "She's right. I'll come in when I get there,

okay?" She nods, her earlier happy mood when talking to Jason dimming. She waves to him as he's still behind me, and he waves back, standing to his full height and backing up. "I love you so much, Presley."

"I love you too, Mom." I blow her a kiss through the screen, and she blows one back, and then we're hanging up. For a second, I forget Jason is still in the room. He clears his throat.

I sit up straighter in my desk chair, spinning it to face him. "Sorry about that. What's up?" Heat flushes on my chest.

He furrows his brows. "Isaac wanted me to come grab you for something." Jason doesn't elaborate, and takes a step back toward the open door.

"Oh, um, thanks," I say. I stand from my chair, wiping my sweaty palms on the fronts of my pants, ignoring the slight ache in my feet after a long day. He stands in the doorway stiffly, like he's unsure whether he should wait for me or not. "Thanks for talking to Presley." I break the awkward silence.

Jason shrugs. "No problem. She's a good kid."

"She's been having a hard time lately." I blurt before I can second guess myself.

Jason raises a brow.

"With the divorce. She remembers her dad, but she doesn't understand why he left. She thinks it's something she did to make him leave. It breaks my heart every time, and I hate it. She didn't do anything to make him leave. If anything, it was me." I shake off the thought, not willing to dive deeper into that conversation with him right now. I don't know him well enough. "One day he went to a work conference, and the next, boom, signed divorce papers."

Obviously, there's a lot more to that story, but that's not

the point right now. "I can't give her a two parent home when I'm barely hanging on by a thread myself. Being a single parent is hard. I can't be the type of person someone deserves in a relationship, so it's going to be just us. I know what I said earlier, but the truth is, I can't handle anything else. I hate that he put me in this position, that she doesn't have any answers. She deserves to have a dad that loves her, and I can't give that to her. " When the words are out, I realize how callous my words are. I don't know the situation between Jason and Lennie's mom.

A flare of *something* burns in Jason's gaze, and my chest clenches. "I'm sorry. Forget I said anything," I stammer.

"I get it," Jason murmurs. "Lennie doesn't ask about her mom often, but when she does, it fucking sucks. It's so hard. I mean, how do you tell a five-year-old about drugs?"

I don't know what to say. This is the most information he's freely given me, and I realize how difficult this must have been for him.

"Forget I said anything," Jason snaps, running a hand through his hair.

With a nod, it settles in that we at least have something in common. We don't know what to tell our kids. And that sucks. As parents, it feels like we should have all the answers for our kids, but that doesn't always happen.

"We should get going," Jason says, pulling me from my thoughts.

I agree with him, and walk to the door. He steps out, and I pull the door closed behind me. "Where's Isaac?"

"At the bar still." I nod, following him down the hall to the main reception area where the bar is. We don't speak for a moment, and I know I've overstepped between our conversations earlier today. "Marley's fine," he says, surprising me.

"Oh, good," I reply. I was meaning to ask Megan if she'd heard anything, but I kept forgetting.

"It was some practice contractions, she's home now."

"Good." I shove my hands in my pockets, twisting my finger around a loose string. Why is this so awkward suddenly? I can't handle this. We make it to the reception area, and I spy Isaac sitting at the bar. He waves us over, and I sigh in relief, thankful to be free of this awkward interaction.

9

———

JASON

I should have left twenty minutes ago, but I can't stop my gaze from finding Fallon every so often, from checking in on her. The interaction between us was something I didn't expect, and it settled like a stone in my gut. Even though she acts like everything is fine and dandy, it's not. She's going through a lot of what I'm going through. We're both doing everything we can to be the best parents for our daughters, and it has to be enough, though sometimes it's not.

The nights Lennie cries and asks about her mom are some of the worst nights of my life. It breaks my heart over and over, knowing she yearns for a mother, but will never have one. I have to be enough for her, and I don't know that I ever will be. Drugs took my daughter's mother from her. I would love to be able to tell my daughter her mother was able to put her past behind her, but unfortunately, I can't.

I have to hope I'm enough for her.

"Go home, boss," Nora says, pulling my attention from where Fallon is currently being pulled aside by the mother of the groom, again.

72

I nod, not really acknowledging her words, though.

"Jason," Laila says with a laugh. I finally pull my gaze from Fallon. "Seriously. We've got this. This is no busier than a Saturday night at the brewery, and we've got everything we need. If we need you, we'll give you a call. Go have your *Barbie* movie night."

I groan, though really, I look forward to these nights with my daughter, spending one on one time with her, something that doesn't happen nearly as often as it should with my work schedule. Her movie tastes are not typically my first choice.

"Alright, fine," I grumble. "But you promise to call me, right?"

Nora holds her hand to her brow in a salute. "Promise."

I wave at Isaac from the opposite end of the room. Dinner is finishing up, and Lennie's going to have a late bedtime tonight, but it's fine. She's getting older now, so it's not as big of a deal for her to stay up a little late now and then.

Isaac strides over, a smile on his face. "Heading out?" he asks.

"Yep."

"Well, I'd say tonight was a success. People loved it, and especially loved having the extra option of beer as well as wine."

I agree with him, giving a few very minor suggestions on things we can do in the future to improve things even more. We say our goodbyes, and I'm heading out the door before I get sidetracked again. I spare one final look back to Fallon, who is totally sucked into a conversation with someone.

She's so gorgeous, even though I can tell she's starting to feel the effects of the day. She's not standing quite as tall and confident. She lost the heels she was strutting around in earlier, now wearing a pair of black flats.

She must sense my stare, because she turns, catching me as I reach the door. She offers me a genuine smile and a wave, and I only nod in return. My face is probably nothing more than a scowl right now, but I don't have it in me to smile at her. I'm not in the right headspace to start something with someone.

Being in her space earlier, our faces nearly touching when I was talking to Presley on the phone, taking in her sweet scent was enough to nearly bring me to my knees. It made me dream of what it would be like to hold her in my arms, and all at once, a fantasy conjured in my mind of holding her in the early morning before our girls woke up. But that can't happen. I can't give anyone but Lennie my focus right now. Anything else wouldn't be fair to her, and of all people, Fallon would understand.

Thirty minutes later, I'm pulling onto the street of my childhood home. The sun is still shining, and as I round the final corner, I see the familiar peaks of the roof.

Lennie is in the driveway, her long, dark hair braided over her shoulders and loose strands covering her face. She's got a bright pink chalk stick in her palm, and she's drawing something. Her bike is toppled on its side in the grass next to the driveway. My parents, as well as my Gramps, are sitting in their lawn chairs, watching her work. Marley's parents, Gabriel and Jane, are also sitting in the driveway with them. They live next door, and are another set of grandparents to my daughter. I'm so grateful for all the people I have in my corner.

When she hears my car, Lennie stands, a giant smile taking over her face. I park on the street, getting out of my vehicle and heading over to Lennie. As soon as my feet hit the grass, Lennie is running over to me, arms wide open as she flings herself into me.

"Daddy!" she calls.

"Hey, peanut," I greet her, lifting her up into my arms, spinning her in a circle. "What are you drawing?"

She talks so fast I can barely catch what she's saying. I shift her to my hip as she points down to the driveway, covered in lines and shapes. "I'm making a town. See, that's the grocery store and the library, and the road to get to the grocery store. There's our house," she points to an odd shape, and then to another. "And there's Grandma and Grandpa's." She continues to point. "Then, I drew Uncle Andrew and Auntie Josie's house on Grandma Jane and Grampa Gabriel's driveway, and Auntie Marley and Uncle Beau's house too. I even drew the babies in their house."

"Wow," I say, when she finishes her explanation. "Looks like you've been busy."

She nods. "You're standing on Uncle Thomas's house." She points under my feet, where I'm standing on a drawing of a dog, I'm assuming to be Arson. I step off when she gives me a knowing look. She smiles. "Then, I ride my bike on the road I drew, and I get to visit everyone."

"That's so cool," I tell her.

Gramps chuckles. "Did ya catch all that?"

"Think so." I smirk at my grandfather.

"She's been running around like a little maniac all day. Made my back hurt watching her bend over like that," he says with a grimace, rubbing at his back like the thought of himself trying to do it is too much. His cane sits in his hands, and he uses it to point to us. "I don't know how she still has so much energy. I had to take two naps today, and she's still running without one."

Lennie wrinkles her nose at her great-grandpa. "You're old, Gramps. That's why."

Gramps jumps in mock aghast, clutching his chest. "You little stinker."

My daughter laughs wildly. "He snores really loud, Daddy."

"Yes, he does," I agree. "He always has."

"You snore too," she says matter of factly.

"Yes, I know." I groan, rolling my eyes.

Gramps cackles. "Maybe you're getting old too, son."

I laugh and agree. "Well, should we go? I think we have a few movies waiting for us."

Lennie drops from my hold to her feet. "Yes!" She runs off, giving all of her grandparents hugs and kisses. She puts her bike and chalk in the garage, and runs back to me in moments. It's nice now that she's older and we don't have to worry about diapers, or formula. My parents also have a few sets of pajamas and clothes at their house.

We say our final goodbyes, and then I'm getting Lennie buckled into her seat and heading toward home. When I pull into the driveway of our home, I let out a deep sigh. It's been a long day, but it's good to be home with my girl. Even if I have to watch animated *Barbie* movies.

"Daddy, can we have sprinkle popcorn?" Lennie's voice pulls me out of my head. A few months ago, I threw some multi-colored sprinkles on her popcorn for a little extra fun. She loved it, and requests it all the time now.

"You bet," I reply, unbuckling and climbing out of the vehicle. I help Lennie get out, and she runs up the front lawn to the front door. I amble behind her, unlocking the door and flipping on the front entry light. Our house isn't anything special, a two-bedroom two-bath with a small room that could be considered an office or an extra bedroom if there was a legal window in it, but it's used as Lennie's play area for now.

Lennie runs through the house toward the living room. "I'm ready!" she calls.

I kick off my shoes, hanging up my work backpack on the hook. "First, you need to put on your pajamas and help me make the popcorn," I call back.

Her footsteps tumble down the hall, and I hear the tell-tale sounds of her door opening and closing. I head toward my own room, changing out of my dress shirt and into a pair of sweats and a Blue Ox tee. Lennie rushes into my room, a whirlwind of pink and purple.

She has on her favorite princess themed night gown, and her hair is pulled out of the neat braids my mom had put it in. "Daddy, can you fix my hair?"

"I can try," I tell her. "Why did you take your braids out?"

She huffs. "It got stuck on my shirt when I was taking it off, and then I decided to take the other one out so it would match."

I hold in my groan. I suck at doing her hair, and I don't have it in me to ask her to cut it. She always talks about how much she loves her long hair, and for a kid her age, her hair is crazy long. It reminds me so much of her mom's with how thick and dark it is.

"Go get your brush and ponytails while I start the popcorn, okay kiddo?"

She nods, rushing back to her room. I swear, this kid does everything at a run. Gramps was right, it's exhausting.

I head into the kitchen, grabbing the microwave popcorn bowl from the cabinet. I get everything I need, throwing the kernels into the bowl, and popping it in the microwave.

"Got it!" Lennie calls as she runs past me in the kitchen.

The kernels start to pop as I grab the sprinkles from the spice cabinet. They don't add any flavor to the popcorn, but it makes things extra fun for Lennie. I also decide to make us both Shirley Temples, complete with maraschino cherries and crazy straws. Lennie's is in her bright pink Disney cup, while mine is in a normal glass. The microwave beeps, and I let it sit for a moment to finish popping before pulling the bowl out.

I separate Lennie's into a smaller bowl, and throw a few shakes of sprinkles on it before setting it on a small tray to carry it all into the living room. Lennie is curled up on the couch under an array of blankets with the company of her stuffed animals from her room.

She shimmies with giddy excitement when she sees me coming, reaching for her bowl before I even set it down on the coffee table.

"Ah, ah," I tsk. "We have to fix your hair, first."

She sighs, dropping her arm. "Okay." Lennie scoots off the couch and onto the floor, crossing her legs and wrapping her arm around her stuffed bear.

After arranging the bowls on the table so they don't fall, I grab her hairbrush and ponytail holders. "What movie are we watching tonight?" I ask.

"Hmm." She considers for a long moment. "The swan one."

"*Barbie Swan Lake?*" I ask, though I know the answer. To be honest, that one might be my favorite of them, it's at least tolerable compared to the newer movies.

"Yes!" she exclaims. I grab the remote and queue up the movie from a streaming service, and once the opening credits start, I get to work on her hair. The women in my life have been trying to teach me how to do her hair, and I can do a basic braid, but the strands never end up even, causing it to look blocky and weird. I have a love-hate relationship with doing her hair. I love the uninterrupted time I get with her. When we aren't watching a movie, I'll usually ask her about her day, or we will talk about school, her friends, or anything that comes to mind. It helps me stop and enjoy the time instead of always rushing to the next activity or work day.

Once her hair is done in two chunky braids that fall down her back, I sink into the couch cushions. "You're done kiddo, now, I need some snuggles."

Lennie snickers, reaching up to grab her popcorn bowl and climbing back onto the couch. I grab the bowl from her so it doesn't spill everywhere while she settles, handing it back to her once she's tucked into my side with her blankets covering her lap. I pass her the covered Shirley Temple, and she takes a long drink of it. Once she's done with her snack, she snuggles herself into my side more, and starts playing with my shirt.

At the end, when the Prince and Odette get married, Lennie tilts her head up, looking at me with her chocolate brown eyes. "Daddy, when you get married, can I be in the wedding?"

My gut twists at her words as I reminisce on the earlier conversation with Fallon. Her words struck more than I'd care to admit. We've had more conversations like this as she's gotten older, and every time, it gets harder. "I don't know if I'll ever get married," I tell her. "But if I do, of course you can be in the wedding."

"Can I wear a pretty dress, like I did for Auntie Josie and Uncle Andrew's?"

"Absolutely."

"Why don't you know if you'll get married? Everyone wants to get married."

Whenever she brings up weddings, I fear the day she asks why I didn't marry her mom. Truth be told, I would have. I would have done anything to get her to stay.

"I'm not sure, honey. Right now, I'm focused on taking care of you, and making sure you're happy and healthy."

"I am happy and healthy," she counters. She narrows her eyes, sitting up a little. "I want you to be happy."

I sigh, pulling her into my chest for a hug. "Lennie, I am happy. You make me happy, and that's all I need. I don't need to be married to be happy, not when I have you."

When she pulls away, she twirls the end of her braid around her finger. At five, I'm not sure she realizes there is more to a wedding than a fun party with pretty dresses. Maybe I'm wrong, but I don't know if she is thinking about the fact that me getting married would mean she would have a step-mom. Not that that is a bad thing, but what happens if things don't work out? Before or after the marriage? Not only would I be breaking my heart, I would be breaking hers too. To have someone be a mother figure in her life, only to rip it away from her.

No, I can't do that to her. I can't put her through heartbreak, not now, preferably not ever. I never want her to experience the pain I've felt in losing her mom, in losing someone she loves.

She deserves more.

"I think you and Presley's mom should get married," Lennie shocks me by saying. I inwardly cringe, and run a hand down my face. I go to speak, but Lennie continues. "Then I would have a mom and a sister."

Oh, dear.

"Lennie," I start. "I'm not going to marry Fallon."

"Why not?" she asks innocently.

"Because... we aren't in love. We don't really know each other, peanut. We can't get married."

"So, get to know each other. I want to play with Presley more."

"You can play with Presley anytime you want. Fallon and I don't have to be married for that."

Lennie's brows furrow as she quips, "You're grumpy. Your face is doing that thing where your forehead wrinkles, Daddy."

"I'm always grumpy," I reply, crossing my eyes and sticking out my tongue at her.

She squeaks with laughter. "I think you're grumpy because you love Presley's mom."

I chuckle humorlessly. "And I think you're late for bedtime." I haul her into my arms, laughing right along with her as she squeals, kicking and screaming. I want her to be happy. Right now, I can keep her happy by being alone, despite what she thinks.

I plop a laughing Lennie down into her twin sized bed, sitting down on the edge of the bed. "I promise you, I am happy, Lennie. You don't need to worry about me."

She nods, sombering. "I love you, Daddy."

"I love you too, Lenners." I tuck her into bed with all her stuffed animals and blankets, pressing a gentle kiss to her forehead before flicking the light off and saying one final goodnight before closing the door.

Somehow, Lennie has always been a great sleeper. She's never wanted anything to do with sleeping in the same bed as me, unless she's sick. She much prefers to sleep alone in her bed.

Even as an infant, she would rarely fall asleep in my arms, preferring to fall asleep after I laid her in her crib or bassinet. If anything, I was the clingy one when she was that small. I had to always be by her side, make sure she was breathing, and safe.

Back when Talia was still around, she would tease me, telling me we had to enjoy it while we could, because who knew what she would be like when she got older. God, I wish I knew if Talia was okay or not. It's been years since we heard from her. I check in with her parents often. They live in California, and we FaceTime with Lennie and them. They come to visit every so often, but it's hard for them. They're older, and not as mobile. I can't fault them for it. They do what they can, and I want my daughter to know as much family as possible. They only hear from Talia every once in a while when she ends up at a shelter, or finds someone with a phone. I don't love her like that anymore, but as the mother of my child, I care for her enough to know if she's alive or dead.

Addiction is... well, addiction, and she might not have had a choice in the end, but it hurts all the same.

10

———

FALLON

June

"So, any guys have you interested lately?" Megan asks.

I scoff into my coffee cup. "You act as if I have time to date, and even if I did, why would a guy want to be with someone like me?" I glance up at my best friend as I gesture to myself. "All I have time for is swiping right or left on dating apps, and even that is nauseating."

Megan doesn't say anything, only glares at me.

"What?" I ask, though I can anticipate what she is going to say.

"You know what."

I do. Megan has been there since the day Brad left, has witnessed what that did to my self-esteem, has heard all of the negative words I've aimed at myself, and has watched as I tried to build myself back up. I'm not confident all the time, but I'm getting there. I tend to call myself out now before she can, because I am trying to cut the negative thoughts out at the source.

"Honestly, the thought of dating right now is daunting. I'm not the same person anymore," I say.

"All the more reason to put yourself out there. Find out who you are now. You're a kickass, hot as fuck, single mom. Show them that."

I glance down at my thighs. "I... it sounds silly, but I'm scared. I've only ever been with Brad, and he tore me down every chance he could without me even realizing it. Thinking about being... intimate with someone makes me nauseous. That, and dating in itself? Exhausting. I don't trust people anymore, Meg. It's impossible to."

"So take it slow," Megan says with a shrug.

"Dating apps are a cesspool of disgusting men, Megs."

"How bad can it really be?" she asks.

I scoff. "Oh honey." I pull up my Tinder, and show her a crude message I received this morning.

She visibly cringes. "Jesus, people really open up with that?"

"Yep."

"That's... horrid."

I sigh. "Which is exactly why I don't open the app. Honestly, I should delete it. Besides, I need to be focused on Presley."

Meg reaches across the table, clasping her hand in mine. "Presley is fine, Fallon. She's happy. She's adjusted. She has friends, and she loves her school and her teacher. It's not selfish to focus on your own happiness."

"Why does it feel like that, then? The guilt eats me alive anytime I'm not with her or I'm working." I take a deep breath, glancing around the coffee shop around me.

She squeezes my hand, and I turn my eyes back to her. "I can't say I understand it, but I will say this. You have a village now. Use us. We are here for you and that crazy little girl of yours. Try not to feel guilty about being an amazing mom who also has a life outside of her daughter."

I nod, my eyes welling up with unshed tears. The last few weeks have been so stressful. School ends in a few days, and each day has been a whirlwind of activities, projects, and field trips.

Presley will be spending every day with my mom this summer. Thankfully she's able to drive here every day so I don't have to go thirty minutes past work to drop her off. It's a lifesaver, but I'm still indebted to her.

The door to the coffee shop opens, and in strides Jason Cunningham. The man I can't seem to get out of my thoughts and dreams lately. It doesn't help that he's so sweet to my daughter during playdates, even though he still doesn't say more than five words to me outside of that wedding last month when I vented to him in my office. He walks up to the counter and orders without seeing us. Of course, Megan sees me watching him before I have the smart sense to look away.

"Oh, I see," she states, a sly grin crossing her face.

"No," I reply, holding up a finger. She cannot do this. No one needs to know about the little tiny feelings I still harbor for him. I need to keep that shit locked down.

She mimes zipping her lips shut, and I relax in my chair. Of course, I should have known not to trust her, because not a second later, she's calling, "Hey, Jason!"

My eyes widen to a comically large size as she waves him over. I don't even look up, because I am so mortified. How is it that after I take one look at the man, she knows I have some sort of school girl crush on him? That's really all it is. A crush. It's the same one I had back in college, and it's the same one I have now. Totally harmless, but yet, it's there.

We've had quite a few meetings together for work, as well as one more event since the first one a few weeks ago, and each time, I catch him watching me, only for him to look away. It's probably nothing. I mean to be honest, I'm sure I'm overthinking each look he gives me. But I can't help the small part of me wishes his looks meant something.

Jason stops when he's standing at our table, and I turn to look at him. "Ladies," he greets, taking a sip of the coffee in his hand.

"Hi," I reply.

"I heard you are officially an uncle as of yesterday," Megan says.

A small smile appears on his face, and *crap*, it's adorable.

It's so exciting that Marley finally had the babies. She sent a message in the group chat yesterday announcing their birth. It was an adorable photo of the two babies in Beau's arms, with a text stating, *happy and healthy*. She was so miserable the last few weeks, complaining in our group chat about how uncomfortable she was, and then FaceTiming us, crying, because she felt bad about complaining.

"Yep," he responds. "Lennie and I went to the hospital this morning, and she's already obsessed with her cousins." He pulls his phone from his pocket, unlocking it and showing us a picture. It's a photo of Lennie with the two infants in her arms, a wide, happy grin on her face.

"She looks so proud," I say, my own smile growing, though inside, I'm being ripped to shreds. I would have loved to have just one photo of Presley holding her sibling.

"She is." He swipes to another photo of him holding one of the babies in each arm. Beau stands beside him, an arm around his brother. Beau's eyes are tired, but filled with so much joy.

"They're so small."

"Hard to believe there was ever a time Lennie was that small," he says. "I'm sure you know the feeling."

I nod, suddenly lost for words. I do remember when Presley was that little, though what I remember most is being so overwhelmed. Brad's family was constantly hovering, his mom and dad giving me constant critique, down to the way I would hold Presley while breastfeeding. I haven't heard from them since the day Brad left, and while I grieve the relationship Presley might have had with them, I don't miss my ex-mother-in-law.

I'm happy for Marley that her pregnancy is finally over. I'll have to send her a message soon to see if she needs me to come over someday and watch the babies so she can nap, or I can even clean, too. Those first few weeks after delivery are rough, and they have twins, so they have double the amount of bottles, dirty diapers, *everything*.

"I do," I finally respond. "I've only really known them together, but it seems like everyone is happy they're finally together. Do you think they'll get engaged soon?"

Jason shrugs. "Who knows. If it were up to Beau, he'd have married her the day they found out she was pregnant, but he doesn't want to rush her. Right now, they're happy. Knowing them, they might take another fifteen years to get their shit together."

"Nope," Megan says, popping the p. "I'm sure it will happen by the end of summer, mark my words, Cunningham."

He raises a brow. "You think?"

She nods. "Oh yeah. They're done waiting."

He thoughtfully nods. "I guess we'll have to wait and see." He glances around the room. "Well, I should get going,

Lennie has a school event in thirty minutes I need to be at. It was nice to see you, Megan, Fallon."

My name on his lips makes me want to shiver, but I hold it in. "Bye," I respond.

"See ya later, Jason," Megan replies.

I turn back to my coffee, wrapping my hands around the warm mug. I'm about to lift it to my lips when Megan startles me.

"So, no one has caught your interest. huh?" she mocks. "I beg to differ young lady."

"*Young* lady?" I scoff. "And no... yes?" I groan. "It's a long story. We actually... We knew each other a long time ago."

Her eyes widen. "Why is this the first I'm hearing about this?"

I pinch my nose. "Because, there really isn't anything to tell. When I was a freshman in college, he was a senior. We had a few classes together, and for a while, he was my only friend. I sort of had a huge crush on him, but nothing could ever happen. He was older, graduating soon, and... I'm me."

Megan narrows her eyes. "I can't believe I never knew. I mean, it makes sense. He graduated the spring before I transferred there."

"Yeah," I reply. "We hung out all the time, but then I started dating Brad, and I know I hurt his feelings, not intentionally, but still. So we lost touch. After he graduated, I didn't see him again until the night of Josie and Andrew's wedding. To say I was shocked would be an understatement."

"That's so crazy. What a small world," she muses. "I say you go for it. Shoot your shot."

"What am I shooting my shot on? I told you I need to focus on Presley."

"And I told you no one is going to fault you for trying to find happiness, Fallon."

"I'm a mess, Meg. I can't do that to him, or anyone."

"You act as if he's not in the same exact boat you are. He's a single parent who also has to rely on his family and friends. If anything, he'll understand you more than anyone else can."

"I don't know," I say. "It seems like anytime we're together, he avoids all conversation. Or he ends any that I try to start. He won't even let me apologize for the way I left things between us way back when. I'm very different from back in college. I'm pretty sure he dislikes me."

She waves a hand. "I promise he doesn't. It took me years to get used to his weird attitude, especially when it got so much worse after Talia left, but I promise, there's a big softy under that hard turtle shell exterior."

I sigh. Again, my curiosity is piqued at the mention of Talia. At this point, I've gathered that she is his ex, and Lennie's mom, but that's it. I really don't know anything about his life. I can't stop thinking again about Jason, even when I know I shouldn't. He's my co-worker, probably considered my superior, and I shouldn't be thinking or even considering my feelings. Not that there are any. Nope. No feelings, no crushes here. Right? Push them all down and away. It's fine.

I take another long sip of my coffee, hoping my reactions don't give me away, though who am I kidding? Megan sees everything.

11
———

JASON

MOM

That inkling you had this morning about
Lennie getting sick? Yeah, you were
spot on.

ME

Crap. What's going on?

MOM

She's got a fever, a cough, runny nose, the
works.

She fell asleep on the couch, and she
hasn't done that in ages.

ME

Yeah, naps are no longer in her vocabulary
if she can help it.

I can be there in an hour to pick her up.

MOM

No, it's fine. Finish your evening, I've
got her.

ME

No, I want to be there for her. I'll come get her.

Guilt sinks low in my gut. I peer up from my phone to my computer screen where I'm working on some inventory tracking, and call out to Nora. It's early evening on a Friday, not even five, so things are still slow before we have a band playing tonight.

"Yeah, boss?" Nora calls back as she strides into my office.

"Think you guys can handle the band tonight? Lennie's coming down with something. I want to check on her, make sure I don't need to bring her into urgent care."

"Of course. Laila will be here in thirty, and Max is punching in. We've got this."

"You sure?" I ask, already closing out the screens on my laptop.

"Positive. I know you like to be here for events, and it's appreciated, but I'm making the call on this. Go. I'll call you if we need something."

"Thank you." I got lucky with my staff, and they are some of the best, most trustworthy people.

"Tell Lenners to get better," she says, and I'm waving goodbye and walking out the door, sending a text to my mom.

LENNIE IS CURRENTLY PASSED out in the backseat, with green snot sliding out of her nose. It's disgusting. I feel horrible.

I picked her up about thirty minutes ago from my parents, and after we went through a McDonald's drive-thru to get her a sprite, I decided to stop by the pharmacy and stock up on medications. I'm not sure what we have at home since it's been a while that she's been sick.

Only now, the problem is that she's passed out in the backseat, and I don't want to wake her when she's feeling this crummy. I don't have much of a choice though. I've been sitting in the car for five minutes, trying to pluck up the courage to wake her, or at least carry her into the store with me.

With a resigned sigh, I turn the car off, and get out, opening her door. She doesn't even stir, and that's how I know she really doesn't feel good. I unbuckle her, and pull her into my arms. She lets out a little groan, but doesn't wake, burrowing herself into my neck. She's sort of awake now, but still she's dead weight in my arms. She wraps her arms around my neck, and her legs around my waist. "We have to get you some medicine, peanut," I tell her. "We can get you some popsicles for your throat, too."

She nods, and I head into the store. I grab one of the carts, figuring this way I at least won't have to carry everything in my one hand. I keep Lennie in my arms, since at least this way she's semi-comfortable, and can keep sleeping.

I head down the aisles toward the over the counter medication and put my aim straight toward the kids' stuff. Why are there so many different types of medications? Daytime versus nighttime. Name brand versus off brand. It's a lot to take in. I throw in a few different types of cough syrup into the cart, and I continue to stare at another array of boxes, getting irritated at the many versions of aceta-minophen. I can't seem to remember which one I usually get, when there's a soft tap on my shoulder, the one opposite of where Lennie is resting.

I turn, confused as to who could be tapping me in a pharmacy, and see Fallon standing beside me. "Hey," she murmurs softly. "Lennie not feeling well?"

I shake my head, glancing down at her. She's dressed in her business casual wear, a fitted pink blouse with a black cardigan and black high waisted pants. She's wearing flats today, but her hair is twisted in a neat braid on one side of her head. She's so gorgeous that I forget to respond for a moment.

"Nope. I hope it's a cold, but it's hitting fast and hard. I dropped her off at my parents' this morning, and she was starting to feel crummy, but nothing out of the ordinary."

"Poor girl," Fallon says. She glances at the section of medication, pulling one off the shelf. "Not sure if you are wanting advice, but this is usually my go to. It's kind of an all-in-one."

I nod, taking the box from her and looking it over. I've been lucky, Lennie has always been a pretty healthy kid, so it usually freaks me out when she gets sick. I throw the box into the cart, nodding at Fallon in thanks. She nods back, giving me an awkward wave.

"Uh, I guess I'll see you later," she says. Reaching over, she rubs a soothing hand down Lennie's spine. "Feel better, sweetie."

Lennie barely rouses at her touch. "She never sleeps outside of bedtime," I explain, my mind whirring with nerves. I don't know why I'm blurting everything out to her right now, but I feel like I can. "I didn't want to leave her in the car."

"You're a good dad, she'll be fine."

"Thanks," I reply. She waves again, and walks in the opposite direction toward the grocery aisle.

I grab a few more items, cough drop suckers, tissues, Vaporub, and two boxes of popsicles before checking out. Lennie sleeps the whole time on my shoulder, coughing occasionally. I can also detect a steady stream of drool and snot soaking my shirt. *Pleasant.*

She doesn't rouse the entire trip home, and I slowly get more and more nervous. I bring her inside first, settling her in on the couch, purposefully leaving her uncovered as I can tell she's got a fever.

I unload the few bags of things in the kitchen, and head down the hall to the bathroom closet, digging around for the thermometer. Light footsteps pull me out of my intense focus on the messy closet.

"Daddy, I don't feel very good," Lennie says. Her eyes are dull, not the usually bright chocolate color. She's pale and a little green around the edges. Shit, is she going to—

Lennie projectile vomits all over the—thankfully laminate—floor. I give myself half a second to gag and cringe before I'm rushing over, picking her up and bringing her into the bathroom. She gags again, this time thankfully making it into the toilet. She's crying as she continues to puke. My heart twists as I watch my little girl, unable to do anything right now but help hold her hair and rub her back as she pukes.

Once she's done, I help her wash up, and fix her hair into a ponytail. I carry her out into the living room again, carefully avoiding the pile of vomit. I lay her back down on the couch. "Stay here, peanut. I'm going to clean up and grab your medicine and the thermometer, okay?"

Lennie nods, sinking into the pillow and taking a deep breath. I hand her the remote, and she starts to search for something to watch as I press a kiss to her burning hot forehead. Crap. I really need to find that thermometer and get some medicine in her.

I rush down the hall and quickly work to clean up the vomit and scrub down the toilet and everything else with a disinfectant. I thankfully find the thermometer quickly after that. I grab the meds, a bowl, and a popsicle from the kitchen before heading back to Lennie in the living room. She's in the same spot I left her, curled into a tight little ball.

"Alright sweetie. Let's take your temp." I sit down on my knees in front of the couch, and she dutifully opens up her mouth without hesitation. I slide it under her tongue, and she closes her lips around it as we wait for the beep.

The shrill beep comes a moment later, beeping again and again to indicate a high temp. I pull it out from her mouth, and wearily glance down at the numbers.

One hundred and two point five.

I sigh, and turn, uncapping the bottle of medicine and pouring the syrupy liquid into the small cup. "Alright, I know you hate taking medicine, but I promise this will help you feel better, and I have a red popsicle with your name on it after you take it."

She nods, not putting up any fight with taking the meds. I help her sit up, and pass her the small cup. She swallows it down without a single complaint. My gut twists, because she's never done that before, and now I'm overthinking even more and worried she feels worse than she's letting on.

I hand her the popsicle, and she wraps herself in a blanket, scooting into the couch. I sit next to her, pulling her into my side. She eats her popsicle in silence, watching the Disney movie she picked.

An hour later, her popsicle is long gone, and she's asleep in my arms. I keep checking her forehead, but it doesn't really seem like her temp has gone down. Shouldn't the medicine have kicked in by now? Isn't a fever dangerous if it stays high too long? Should I give her more medicine? The bottle said you can only give it once every four hours.

I pull out my phone, debating on texting my mom for advice, until I remember she said that since I was picking up Lennie, she and my dad were going to go see a movie. I don't want to bother her, though she's kind of my only option.

That is, until I remember running into Fallon at the store earlier. She's a mom. Presley is a few years older than Lennie. Presley has more than likely been sick at some point, and she did offer up a suggestion on medicine, so she has to know more than me.

I pull up her contact, and see all of the messages we've previously sent each other, all related to work, meetings, and playdates. All of my messages are short, one word answers, and it makes me feel like such a jerk to be asking for help now when I've offered her nothing, not even a friendship.

As I'm about to start typing a message, those bouncing bubbles appear on the screen. Is she texting me? How did she know? My palms grow sweaty as I grip my phone, waiting for a message to come through.

12

FALLON

"Can I paint after dinner, Mom?" Presley asks as she takes a bite of her spaghetti. She has sauce all over her lips as she tries to slurp up a noodle.

"Sure, honey," I say, finishing my last bite. "As soon as we clean up dinner, I'll get your paint stuff."

She nods in agreement, and starts to try and eat faster. I chuckle. "Take it slow, Pres. You don't have to rush."

My words seem to appease her, and she slows her bites. I head back into the kitchen to pack up the leftovers and load all the dirty dishes into the dishwasher.

Minutes later, Pres walks in with her empty plate and fork. She puts them in the dishwasher, and we head down the hall to grab her painting stuff from the closet. I help her get set up, then I sit down at the table and watch her. My mind strays to earlier when I saw Jason and Lennie at the drugstore. The poor girl wasn't even awake and she looked miserable.

Jason looked a little frazzled too. He's been on his own with her for a long time, so he has to be used to her getting sick, but he seemed so worried. I get it though. Anytime Presley gets sick, I'm usually a mess of anxiety.

I wonder if I should text him to make sure Lennie is okay. That's totally normal, right? I can text him quick. Offer him a helping hand. Lord knows when Presley is sick I lose track of everything. The house ends up a mess, and I forget to shower for three days.

Decision made, I grab my phone off the table, and pull up his contact card. My heart flutters in my chest as I type out the message, and hit send before I can second guess it.

ME

> Hey. How is Lennie doing? Do you need anything?

The bubbles appear on his end immediately. I didn't expect him to reply so quickly.

JASON

> I don't know. Her temp is pretty high, and it hasn't come down at all with the first dose of meds. Should I bring her in? I'm kinda panicking

ME

> What was it?

JASON

> 102.5

> And she puked all over

ME

> Poor girl. What time did you give her the medicine? What did you give her?

My heart clenches. I've been there, and it's not easy having a sick kiddo.

JASON

An hour ago, and it was that stuff you put in my cart

ME

Have you checked her temp since giving her the medicine?

JASON

Yeah. I did and it's at 101.9, so down, but not much

ME

Give it another hour, then alternate with some ibuprofen. I saw that in your cart too. The med I gave you has acetaminophen in it. You can alternate the two of them every two hours.

JASON

Really? It's not going to hurt her?

ME

Nope, she'll be fine.

His worry is sweet, and I'm happy I'm able to help him in this situation. It's nice to have someone to lean on in times like this.

JASON

Okay, I'll set an alarm.

ME

In the meantime, you could give her a lukewarm/cool bath to help her cool down. Make sure she's drinking fluids.

JASON

I'm not sure why I'm panicking so much this time. She's been sick before. She's going to be sick again.

ME

Don't worry, I get this way too. Keep an eye on her tonight, and if the fever doesn't drop, take her into urgent care tomorrow. Or, if your gut tells you to. Worst that can happen is they say it's a cold and send you home.

JASON

That's a good point. Thanks. I feel better already.

ME

Of course. I'm happy to help, I'm sorry she's not feeling well.

JASON

Me too. She doesn't get sick often.

ME

It's funny how it always happens shortly after school ends too. You'd think they'd get so sick at the end of the school year when they're still around all of their classmates, but it's like as soon as school is done, boom, they get super sick. It's usually what happens to Presley, but so far *knocks on wood* she's been good this year.

Don't get me started on bringing them in to the doctor. It always seems like when you think you have to bring them in, so sure they have an ear infection or something, they're perfectly fine, and it's a cold. But then, the time you decide to wait it out, it ends up being an ear infection when you do decide to bring them in eventually.

JASON

Huh. I've never put two and two together. I know she's going to be bummed when I tell her we can't go visit the new babies tomorrow.

And right? Tell me about it. I can't count how many doctor bills I have for visits that we didn't end up needing to go in for.

ME

Yeah, that's going to be tough. But I'm sure she will understand when you explain that she doesn't want to get the new babies sick.

I look up from my phone, and see Presley painting a flower on her paper. "Wow, that's really pretty, honey," I tell her.

"Thanks," she responds, still completely engrossed in her art.

Jason doesn't respond again for a few hours, and I try not to overthink it. Is Lennie okay? Did he bring her to the doctor?

Once Presley is done painting, it's time to wind down for the night, so she takes a quick bath and snuggles in her pajamas. She picks out one of her *Junie B. Jones* books, and starts to read. She's such a fast reader. She can usually finish one of the books in a night. She doesn't have me read to her anymore, which is fine, but we still sit together each night. We do our usual routine after she reads, and she falls asleep as easily as always.

I pour myself a glass of wine and sit down on the couch. I pull out my phone, wondering if Jason has replied, or sent an update. The conversation was at a natural end, but I can't help but want to make sure both he and Lennie are okay.

With my phone empty of notifications, I settle in, putting on a movie I haven't seen in a long time. I'm finishing the glass of wine when my phone rings. Jason's name is on the screen, and I panic, thinking something is wrong with Lennie.

"Jason?" I answer.

"Hey," he says, his voice low and tired.

"Is everything okay?"

I can hear his heavy sigh. "Yeah. She's fine. The fever went down to ninety-nine, and she's asleep now. Her cough is ramping up, though. I might take her in in the morning, depending on how tonight goes."

My heart twists when I hear Lennie let out a cough in the background. Poor girl. I nod to myself before speaking. "Good. I'm glad she's doing okay."

"Me too," he replies, his voice turning gruff. "I wanted to apologize."

I pause before responding. What could he have to apologize for? "Apologize?" I ask.

"Yeah." He briefly pauses. "I shouldn't have bothered you earlier with my frantic messages."

"Jase—" I blurt the shortened version of his name before I can second guess it. I used to call him that all the time in college, and now, things are different. We're different. "Jason. You have nothing to apologize for. I get it. Sick kids are stressful."

I can practically hear him shaking his head. "I shouldn't have texted you though. I could have called my mom or something. I took your attention away from your own daughter."

I stop him before he can say anything more. "Jason, please. Don't apologize. That's what friends are for. And trust me, I get not wanting to call your mom. Plus, I texted you first, remember?"

He lets out a heavy, soul-weary sigh. "I don't want to be a burden to anyone."

"Being a single parent is hard work on a good day. Just because you're a single parent doesn't mean you have to do it alone." I repeat the words my mom tells me all the time.

The line is silent. "Do you feel guilty?" Jason asks after a long moment. "Like when your mom watches Presley, or you have to work and miss dropping her off at a birthday party or something? Do you ever feel guilty?"

I pause. Because yeah, I do. Every day. My mind automatically replays the conversation I had with Megan about this.

"Shit—" he mutters. "I overstepped."

"No," I interrupt him. "I was trying to come up with the words. I feel guilty all the time. It's exhausting. Every bedtime I miss, or when she has a bad night because she misses her dad, and doesn't understand why he's not there anymore, I have so much guilt I swear it's going to eat me alive."

"God, you have no idea how good it is to know I'm not the only one."

"Not by a long shot," I reply with a laugh.

"None of my siblings or friends understand. I can't talk to my parents about it, because they'd tell me they don't mind watching Lennie, that they love her so much and are happy to help."

"That's how my mom is too. Megan tries to help and understand, but she has such a busy schedule, that I feel bad venting about how tired I am, when she's literally saving lives."

The conversation hits a lull, and for a moment, I'm

reminded of our college days again. He's talking so freely, something he hasn't done with me since we've reunited.

"We should probably set the girls up on another play-date," he says, surprising me. I've been the one to reach out every time to set up a playdate. Never once in any of the time we've been going on playdates, has he initiated one.

"Yeah," I agree. "Presley has been wanting to go to the splash pad now that it's open. Maybe we could take them there?"

"Lennie would love that. She's a waterbug."

"So's Pres."

"My mom was thinking about taking Lennie to the Children's Museum in a few weeks. Would you want her to take Presley too? Maybe your mom could tag along. I'm sure our moms would get along no problem."

"That sounds perfect. I bet they'd love it."

"Do you remember the night of the Christmas party?" Jason asks, abruptly changing the subject.

"The Christmas party?" I ask, my mind drawing a blank. I haven't attended a Christmas event since living here, so I don't know what he's talking about, unless... "Wait, the one you had at your house in college?"

"Yeah."

The memories begin to flash through my mind one by one, as if playing on a movie screen.

"How could I forget?" I state. What I don't say is how I remember every moment of that night. Every unexpected touch, every flirty comment and the way he held me close, held me in a way he never had before.

"It was freezing that night," I chuckle awkwardly. "I thought I had to wear a dress and be fancy, then I show up to what was pretty much a frat house, and everyone was already drunk and you were wearing a Christmas sweater you *swore* you weren't going to wear!"

"Hey, I lost a bet, remember? I didn't have a choice," Jason retorts.

Those words are so similar to the ones he whispered against my ear that night as he held me close for the first time. The memory still sends a shiver down my spine.

"Sure," I say, sarcasm thick in my tone. "You were '*coerced*', right?"

"I was!" In the background, there's the sound of a door softly closing as he whispers. Jason sighs. "Remember how you grabbed a hard lemonade, even though you hated it? It was better than the beer though. It always tasted so watered down."

I laugh softly. "Yeah, that gross hard lemonade was much preferred to the beer."

"I had to take you on a tour of that shitty house to get you alone," he confesses. The memory practically replays in my mind. "In the few minutes you'd been there, I could already see five or more guys leering at you. They all wanted a piece of you, but you were my friend. Selfishly, I wanted to keep you to myself. We wouldn't have had a moment alone had I not brought you up to my room."

"Is that why?" I ask. I've always wondered why he was in such a rush to get upstairs when the party was on the main level. "It definitely confused me."

"In what way?" His voice is as confused as I was.

"You showed me your room."

"Can you blame me for wanting private time with you?"

My stomach swoops and I shake my head, even though he can't see. "No. If I'm being honest, at the time, I had this idea that things had been changing between us," I say, my voice shaking.

Jason hesitates, not speaking for a long moment, then, his voice cracks as he speaks. "Maybe they were." There's a long pause. "Can I tell you something, Fallon?"

Something about the way he asks his question sends my heart racing. "Of course."

He swallows audibly. "That night... I wanted to kiss you."

"You did?" I ask stupidly, even though I remember it so clearly. The way we sat side by side on his twin sized bed, his hand resting on my thigh as he leaned in, his dark eyes flicking between my eyes and my lips, and when he finally said my name, his voice breathless and whispered, I knew it was going to happen. I *wanted* it to happen.

Jason softly chuckles. "Yeah. I did, but then we were interrupted. Fuck, I was pissed at that guy. He ruined it, and I've been cursing him ever since."

I laugh in response, though my mind is whirling. He's been more open in the last five minutes with me than he has in the last nine months since we reconnected. What changed that he's suddenly talking to me? I don't say anything for a long moment, and neither does he. I think we are both reminiscing on that time in our lives.

"Why'd you leave?" Jason asks, his voice soft.

I grimace to myself. The moment after the almost kiss is painful to think about. "You were drunk," I whisper. "I figured it was the alcohol in your system, and you were acting on a whim."

"I wasn't," he admits. "Sure, I'd had a few drinks and was buzzed, but I knew exactly what I was doing. I wanted nothing more than to kiss you that night. To finally have your lips on mine. I was so scared to change our friendship and the way things were, but fuck, Fallon. I wanted you as more than a friend. I dreamt of it, dreamt of having you in my arms all the time."

His words hit me like a ton of bricks. "I'm sorry," I say, my voice breaking as tears well in my eyes.

"You don't have to be sorry," Jason says. "It's not like I ever told you."

"I am sorry. I wanted it too, wanted you to kiss me. And then I panicked, and soon went on that date with Brad. I convinced myself I imagined that night. That I was being a naive teenage girl, and that you'd never really be interested in me."

"I was. But the past is in the past, and we can't change it, right?" Jason says, trying to placate me.

"I guess that's true. You've changed a lot since then," I say, almost regretting the words. He was such an easy going person then, nothing fazed him. Now, though, he's focused on his daughter, and while I can't fault him for that, it seems like anything besides his family and his daughter makes him cranky.

He sighs. "Yeah. So have you. In good ways, though. You're an amazing mom. You're beautiful, and an incredible role model for both your daughter and mine."

His words surprise me. I wasn't expecting him to bring up the Christmas party, the night I thought things were going to change between us. "Why did you ask about that?"

I can practically hear him pondering his words through the phone. "It's one of my favorite memories of you."

I try to think of something else to say, but Jason speaks first.

"I should let you go," his words are abrupt, a fast change to the way he'd been speaking to me only moments ago.

I nod, knowing he's right. "Let me know how Lennie is. I'm always here for you, Jase."

"Thanks, Fallon," he replies. "Goodnight."
"Night," I say, and the call ends with a beep.

13

___

JASON

"Jason, what are you doing next weekend?" Isaac asks as we finish up our meeting. I try to join a meeting once a month since we started the contract with Meadow Grove. Fallon already left after giving a cheerful update about the feedback she's received from her most recent brides and how much they're loving Blue Ox.

It's exciting, and the brewery has been busier as a result. Laila has taken it upon herself to revamp our social media pages too, and that, coupled with the extra publicity from having the beer at weddings, has been an awesome upgrade.

I glance up at Isaac, who has his phone in his palm, the calendar app open.

"Um," I reply, pulling up my own calendar. "Right now, nothing. But you never know."

"I'd pay for it, but would you be interested in going to a conference in the Twin Cities with me?" He taps out something on his phone, showing me the screen. "It's an event and vendor weekend, and I thought it could be good for you to go, maybe get your name out there too."

He passes me his phone, and I look through the event and the schedule. In all honesty, I don't know how I feel about going. A few of the speakers look interesting, and I know I'd probably have a good time, but the thought of leaving Lennie on top of the overall effort it would take to leave for a weekend deters me from giving an answer right away. I would rather stay home and soak up some extra time with my daughter, but he's right. It could be good for business.

"I'd have to get back to you, it depends on if I can find someone for Lenners," I reply, passing him back his phone.

"No problem," he replies. "I've asked Fallon and a few of the girls to come too, so it would be a group of us. Let me know, and I can get your room booked."

"Great," I reply, but I'm trying not to react. I've been avoiding Fallon since our late evening chat a few weeks ago when Lennie was sick. I panicked, and I still don't know why I called her. I didn't need to dump all my feelings and emotionally vomit on her. But I did. Internally, I grimace. I can't let myself fall into something with her, not again. I was destroyed after she left the first time, and I was destroyed each time Talia left. People leave. I can't let myself get attached, and I definitely can't let Lennie get attached. It's not good for either of us.

I admit, it was nice to chat and it felt familiar, comfortable, but, still. I didn't need to do that to her, no matter how many times she said it was okay. And going as far as bringing up the Christmas party? I can't believe I did that. That night was something I tried to forget, but never could. It was the closest we'd ever gotten to something more. Something that will never happen between us. Hearing her say I've changed though? That settled deep in me. I wish I was still the person I was in college, but life happened.

"I'll let you know," I tell Isaac, standing up from the chair. I have to get back to the brewery today and get some work done there, so I head out of the conference room and down the hall.

"Jason!" I hear Fallon's cheery voice call. She's in a great mood today, if her voice and excitement during the meeting are any tell. I halt my steps, turning to face her. As always, she looks adorable in her business attire. Today she's wearing a navy blue blazer that brings out the hint of blue in her green eyes I'm so drawn to every time I look at her. "Hey," she greets. "How's it going?"

"Fine," I reply curtly . I can't let myself give her more, because I can't trust myself with her. I need to try and distance myself again after the talk of the Christmas party.

She raises a blonde brow. "Fine? Presley was raving about their trip to the museum the other day."

"Lennie was too," I say. "She had a lot of fun."

"They'll have to do it again."

"Sure," I state.

"Are you going to the conference next weekend?"

I shrug. "Not sure. I just found out about it. It depends on if my mom can watch Lennie. If I even want to ask her to."

Fallon nods in agreement. "I think it will be fun. If you can find someone for her, you should come."

"I'll try," I snap, already irritated that I have to ask my family for more help. *If I can get over my stupid guilt,* I think to myself. "I need to get going." I jerk a thumb over my shoulder in the direction of the parking lot.

"Right," she responds, her posture deflating. Great, now

I feel like even more of an asshole than I already am. "I'll see you later?"

I agree, and say goodbye, and then I'm heading out the door to my car. I can sense her eyes on me as I walk away, and know I hurt her feelings after opening up to her the way I did during that phone call, but I don't have the mental capacity to deal with that right now. I climb in my car and notice a bunch of messages in the group chat with my brothers.

BEAU

sends photo of Arlo and Ariel

Look at how freaking cute my kids are.

THOMAS

So cute.

Though, they still kinda look like wrinkly old men.

BEAU

sends photo of Arlo with his middle finger up

ANDREW

Dude, did you make your infant flick us off?

Maybe I need to have a kid so I can make them flick you off.

BEAU

You guys are ridiculous.

But yeah, you guys totally should have a kid. It's amazing. Jase gets it.

ME

I get it.

Yeah, it's amazing, but Beau also has an amazing partner to share it with. I'm doing this alone.

BEAU

See? He gets it.

ANDREW

Maybe I should ask Josie if she's ready to have a baby.

THOMAS

Anyone want to go for a drink tonight? I'm bored.

ME

Can't. If I'm going to ask Mom and Dad to watch Lennie next weekend for a conference Isaac invited me to, I don't want to make them watch her tonight too.

ANDREW

Wait.

I'm a genius.

Someone please tell me I'm a genius.

THOMAS

No one knows why you're a genius, dumbass. You haven't said anything besides "Wait."

ANDREW

What if Josie and I watch Lennie next weekend? That way we can figure out if we're ready for kids. I mean, I know Lennie's five, but maybe we can start there, and then I can borrow one of Beau's kids next.

BEAU

You're not allowed to "borrow" my kids, Andrew.

ANDREW

I didn't say kidS. I said KID. Single. Uno.

BEAU

Good lord.

ME

Wait, really? You and Josie would be open to watching her the whole weekend?

A heavy weight lifts off my chest. This would save me from the familiar guilt of asking my mom and dad for help yet again, and Lennie would get some one-on-one time with Andrew and Josie. I won't tell anyone, but I'm pretty sure Andrew is her favorite uncle. Or maybe Tommy. He's definitely a close second. I let myself get a hint of excitement over the prospect of going away for the weekend, but shut it down, because I don't want to get too overzealous when nothing is set in stone.

My phone buzzes in my palm with more texts.

THOMAS

Still guessing that's a no on the beer tonight.

ME

Shit, yeah. I forgot I told Lennie we could have a bonfire tonight. You can come over if you want.

THOMAS

Yeah. I might. I'm lonely, and I think Arson is bored of me.

ME

Bring him. Lennie will wear him out.

ANDREW

Great, what time should Josie and I come over?

ME

Oh, everyone's coming over now?

ANDREW

I'll bring chips.

BEAU

I'll ask Mar, but I think we're out. The babies are in a weird sleep cycle right now. Marley's barely sleeping.

ME

No worries. Let us know if you need anything.

BEAU

Will do. Gabriel and Jane are hanging out for a few hours today, so we're good now. I should be napping, actually.

THOMAS

Get some sleep, lil' bro.

I swipe out of the current group chat, and open up the one that is already buzzing with even more texts. Andrew's already making plans for the weekend.

ANDREW

I checked with Josie, she's totally down to take Lenners for the weekend.

ME

That would be amazing.

JOSIE

I can't wait to spend the weekend with Lennie! It's an Auntie and Lennie weekend!

ANDREW

Petals, I'm going to be there too?

JOSIE

I know, but still.

ME

I really appreciate this, you guys.

I let out a heavy sigh of appreciation for those two. Could I really go? In all reality, the choice is up to Lennie. If she wants me to stay home with her, I will, but if she's okay spending the weekend with Josie and Andrew, then I don't see why I couldn't go. I'm still wary of leaving for the weekend, but I have to admit to myself that it will be good for a change of pace and some time on my own.

14

FALLON

"You're sure it's okay?" I ask my mom for probably the thousandth time.

"Go," she simply replies. "Presley and I are fine. I am happy to help, and you know I love that I get to spend time with her."

I give my mom a look, searching her face for any hint of insincerity. I don't find any. I rush into her arms, giving her a tight hug. "Thank you. I will never be able to thank you enough for all your help." The familiar guilt is still there, but I'm grateful for the opportunity to spend the weekend away. In all reality, I don't think I've ever had an actual full weekend away from her.

Brad never wanted to be alone with her a whole weekend, so most of the time, I would end up going home a day early, or get a panicked call from him and have to leave altogether.

"Of course," my mom murmurs into my hair, squeezing me tight. We pull apart, and I head down the hall to find Presley. She's playing with some of her dolls on the floor of the room my mom has set up for her..

"Alright, sweetie." She peeks up at me. "I'll be back on Sunday afternoon, okay? We'll have lunch with Grandma, and then we'll head home and watch some movies."

"Okay, Mom," Presley says with a soft smile. It hurts a little knowing she is so unbothered by my leaving, but I don't show it.

"Give me a hug," I tell her, opening my arms. She crawls into my lap, and I give her a tight squeeze. "I love you so much."

"I love you too, Mommy."

"Have so much fun this weekend, okay?"

"We will. Grandma said we could make cupcakes and decorate them however I want."

"Woah. That will be so much fun," I say. "Save one for me, okay?"

"Okay."

I give her one final squeeze and then I stand, heading out her bedroom door, and thanking my mom again. I climb into my car and check my phone one last time before I set up the GPS. It's a small number of us coming, so we're all in a group message. A few of us were planning to carpool, but I said I'd drive separately so I would have a bit more time with Pres. I read the few messages I've missed from Isaac, and Cassidy, the assistant general manager and immediately start to panic.

ISAAC

Bad news. I have some sort of stomach flu or something, so I'm not going to make it this weekend. I've canceled my room, but you all still have separate rooms on the company card.

CASSIDY

I think I'm coming down with it too, and so is Laila.

ISAAC

Crap.

So that leaves Fallon and Jason. Are you guys okay?

ME

I'm fine, but if we need to cancel everything, I would understand.

JASON

Fine here, but also would understand.

ISAAC

No, you two go. Would it be too much to ask if you take peoples' info and call me with anything that seems awesome?

JASON

Not at all, happy to help.

ME

Agreed.

My heart flutters in my chest. If it's only Jason and me all weekend, that means there won't be a buffer between us. Things are still so awkward, even more so now after Lennie was sick. I've been trying so hard to be extra friendly, to get him to show me that side of him I used to know so well, but he's a tough shell to crack.

Another message comes in as I still sit in my mom's driveway.

ISAAC

You two are the best. I've got your rooms taken care of, let me know if you need anything. I'll send over the PDF of the schedule and event maps.

JASON

Perfect.

I shift my car into gear and start the drive to the hotel. I have no idea what this weekend will look like, but I do know that I'll apparently be spending a lot of time with Jason.

I'VE JUST PARKED my car in the hotel parking ramp when my phone starts ringing. I take a deep breath when I see that it's Jason. I slide my finger across the screen, and answer the call.

"Are you here yet?" he says, voice low and irritated.

"Well hello to you too, Mr. Grumpy," I reply.

He sighs, changing his tone. "Hi, Fallon. Are you at the hotel yet?"

"Yeah. I'm parked in the parking ramp. Are you here?"

"I'm in the lobby. Meet me here, okay?"

"Sure," I reply, and then he hangs up without another word, ending the call.

I scoff, and turn off my car. I grab my weekend bag and small rolling suitcase from the backseat, and head to the elevator that will take me down to the lobby. When I reach the automatic doors, I immediately spot Jason sitting on one of the plush leather couches. He looks stressed. He's leaning forward, elbows on his knees, and running a hand up and down his face. I reach him and sit down beside him, sinking into the deep couch. "Hey, what's going on?" I ask.

"They fucked up the reservation," he replies. "When Isaac called to cancel a few of the rooms, they misunderstood and canceled all the rooms."

"Oh no," I breathe. "Now what?"

"They were able to find a room, and it's an upgraded suite, but it's only a king size bed, with a pull out couch."

"Well that's not the end of the world," I say, trying to make light of the situation. Do I really want to share a room with him? Is it bad that I'm not upset about the prospect? Probably. But I can't get this man out of my head. Much like I couldn't all those years ago. "I'll sleep on the pull out."

Jason glares at me. "No way. Those things are so uncomfortable. We shouldn't have to share a room. I tried everything, but they're clean out. Apparently they had a waitlist with how booked the hotel was for the event, and the rooms Isaac canceled got booked up immediately."

I'm a little insulted at the vehemence he has toward not sharing a room with me. Am I that repulsive? I suppose Brad thought so, so why wouldn't Jason?

I think back to all our earlier interactions since reconnecting, and shrink a little further into the shell Brad shoved me in. I let my irritation with him show in my words. "So what then? We don't really have many options, and I'm thinking with the popularity of the conference, the hotels in the nearby area are going to be booked up too."

"They are, I checked."

"Got it," I say, a little more snippy than intended. I take a deep breath. "Is it really that bad to share a room with me?" I mean, clearly there's something wrong with me if both he and Brad are repulsed by me, but am I really so bad he can't survive a few days in a hotel room with me? The other night, he was telling me how badly he wanted to kiss me back in college.

But that was then. This is now.

"Fuck," Jason curses, reaching out and resting his hand over mine. The heat of his touch sends a jolt through my body, reminding me *yet again* of that freaking Christmas party with his closeness. "That wasn't what I meant. I just... I don't want to make you uncomfortable. It's one thing to be expecting a room to yourself, and another to share a room with a guy you don't know very well."

I... I don't really know what to say to that. I want to believe him, I do, but I don't think I would be uncomfortable sharing a room with him. I can sleep on the couch, and make myself scarce. It will be fine. I try to play it cool. "Honestly, are we really going to be in the room all that much, besides sleeping?"

Jason nods, his posture relaxing. "I suppose that's true. It doesn't make the fact that there's only one bed better, though."

"I can take the couch." Jason gives me a side-eyed glare. "Oh, don't give me that look," I scold, giving him my best "mom" look. I shake off the earlier irritation I had, and focus on the now instead.

"I'm taking the couch," he rebutes, and I glare at him in return. We will see about that. The man is tall. He'll barely fit on the couch, and I guarantee the couch itself will be better than the pullout. Ignoring him, I stand and grab my bag from the floor. "Come on, let's get settled in the room, and then get to the first event."

Jason stands and leads us toward the elevator. He punches the button for the tenth floor, and when the doors open on the floor, I follow him. I have no idea which room is ours, but he stops outside of ten-thirteen, and swipes the card in front of the reader, pushing the door open when it flashes green and unlocks.

He holds the door open for me, his own bag slung over his shoulder. When I step into the room, a burst of cold air hits me, sending a shiver down my spine. It's a beautiful hotel room, much nicer than the standard room I usually would stay in. To my immediate right is the large bathroom. The light automatically flashes on with my movement, revealing a walk in shower with glass doors and a rainfall shower head. There's also a giant soaking tub, and a standard toilet.

I glance around the rest of the room. The walls are painted a warm gray color, and the large king size bed is in the middle of the room, made with crisp white sheets and a perfectly tucked comforter.

On the opposite wall is the couch, which, compared to the rest of the room, looks a little sad. It's gray with small throw pillows and crooked cushions. Jason glances at it and does what he can to hide his reaction, but I see it. His face falls, a small grimace flashing on his face.

"Jason, really, I'll take the couch." I try to argue with him yet again.

"Nope," he says, flopping down onto the cushion, ignoring the squeal of the springs. He sets his bag next to him, and gingerly leans against the back of the couch.

I sigh, and set my bag at the foot of the large bed. I sit down on the edge of the bed, my body sinking into it. Yeah, this bed is nice. Guilt starts to eat at me, but Jason sees it, and points his finger at me. "Don't even think about it." I start to speak, but he cuts me off. "Knock it off, Fallon."

The words stun me silent. Normally, I'd react negatively towards those words. It's something Brad used to say to me all the time. I wouldn't even be doing anything bad, or saying anything, but he used it as a way to exert control over me. But... weirdly, coming out of Jason's mouth, it sounded hot. A tingling heat builds low in my belly, and I can't stop the shiver that breaks out on my skin, such a contrast to the cold hotel room.

I can't help but notice the difference in the way Jason said it too, the real reason it made my body heat. It was less of a scolding tone, and much more... caring in a way. He wasn't saying it to make me feel childish or silly, it was him doing what he could to stop the guilt from seeping through my veins, the guilt he could surely see written all over my face. The infliction in his voice didn't want to make me curl up and die, it made me want to lay myself out for him to preen over, something I never anticipated myself wanting to do.

The heat pooling low in my belly spreads throughout my body, flushing my chest and my cheeks in an embarrassing show. I stand, turning away from him to hide my reaction, and face toward the large windows that take up a majority of the far wall. Minneapolis stands before us, a sea of tall buildings the only thing I can see.

The view of downtown reminds me of the days when I worked here, the way I loved the constant hustle and bustle of the city, and the high energy of my job. Brad always thought I could be doing more, be something more important than "just an assistant" to one of the most influential CEOs in the city. He had so many mixed messages toward me. One day, I'd be so incredible, the next, I could be better. It only got worse as time went on, and even more so when I became a full time stay-at-home mom, by his insistence. He wanted to be the breadwinner, the one to provide for his family.

At first, I thought it was sweet. Now, I know it was

another way for him to control me, control who saw me. I needed to be the perfect little housewife for him.

Jason pulls me out of my reverie, saying, "Should we head to the event center soon? The first vendor set starts at four."

"Yes," I reply. "I should change though."

"You look really nice," Jason immediately replies, and I glance down at my black leggings and sunshine yellow blouse. I cringe internally, trying to shove down the thought that he's just saying that. He doesn't really feel that way.

I smile, trying to hide my emotions. "Thanks, but I should put on something a little more professional, especially if I'm the only one here to represent Meadow Grove. I'm glad I remembered to bring our business cards."

"Yeah, that's smart."

"Did you bring any of yours?" I ask as I rifle through my suitcase for my slacks and a new top.

"Yeah." He nods, shoving his hands into the front pockets of his pants. Once I have the items I want, I turn, and head toward the bathroom. I change quickly, and check my makeup in the mirror, as well as giving myself a fresh spritz of my favorite perfume. I wonder if he'll like my perfume, or perhaps he'll think it's too much? Will he compliment it? Do I *want* him to like it?

Wearing perfume is yet another thing I started trying to reclaim after Brad. I loved wearing perfume, even if it was a cheap one from Bath and Body Works. He hated the scents I wore, even when I changed it up a few different times. Said they were too "perfumey", and gave him a headache.

I slide my feet into ballet flats, figuring I should choose comfort today over attire. I do a lot of walking during events at work, but today, I don't think I have it in me to wear heels. Maybe tomorrow.

I exit the bathroom in my new outfit, a pair of black slacks with a black top I've tucked into the pants, and a mauve blazer. It's not a fabulous outfit by any means, but it's something. Who knows, maybe Jason will like this one better than the other outfit. "Ready?" I ask, catching Jason's eye as I close the door behind me.

Jason nods, his suddenly heated eyes glancing up and down my body. I try to ignore the way he looks at me, but it's hard. He changed while I was in the bathroom too, into a pair of khaki pants and a button up dress shirt. He looks *hot*. What is it about a button up shirt with the sleeves rolled halfway up a man's arms that does it for me?

"You look nice," I state, almost stumbling over the words.

He Adam's apple bobs as he swallows thickly. "You look beautiful," he says in reply.

I want to contest him, tell him that this outfit is nothing to write home about, but I don't. I take the compliment, thanking him. I sigh a breath of relief.

He holds open the door for me, and when it closes behind us, he reaches into his pocket, pulling out the extra room key. "Here. I'm sure we won't be together all weekend, and I don't want you locked out."

"Oh, thanks, I forgot about that," I admit, and put the key into the pocket of my pants. I have my small purse with me that I have over my shoulder, but if I need to come up before Jason I don't want to have to dig the key out of the bottom of my purse.

As we walk down the hall toward the elevator, Jason speaks softly. "Did you put on perfume?"

My heart stops. I knew the perfume was too much. "Um, yes. Is it too much? It's too much, isn't it. I can run back and wash it off quick, I'm sorry," I stammer over my words, spinning on my heel to walk back to the room.

Jason's hand reaches out, grasping my forearm. "No, don't." He pulls me close to him, inhaling deeply. "I like it. It's sweet. It smells like the one you wore back in college."

My lips fumble, trying to speak, not just make noises. I clear my throat, "Um, it's the same one. I don't wear it often, so it's the same bottle."

"Hm," Jason ponders, trying to come up with his next words. "You should wear it more often."

With that, he continues his jaunt down the hall, as if he didn't stop my world from turning in those few seconds, bringing my self-confidence up a few more notches and erasing all earlier thoughts of repulsion.

15

JASON

It's only been a few hours, but I'm already exhausted. I'm not great at marketing myself, but Fallon seems to be incredible at it. She's boasting both my business as well as the winery, and is killing it. She's exchanged information with so many people I've lost count. Spending this time with her, one-on-one has been enlightening.

We're heading back up to the hotel room, and Fallon seems as beat as I am. She's walking slowly, her posture not as straight as before, like there's a weight pressing down on her shoulders. I'm definitely not looking forward to sleeping on that terrible couch, but what else am I supposed to do? It's not like I'm going to make Fallon sleep on it, and we definitely can't share a bed.

I can't let myself get that close to her. All the infatuation I had for her back in college is starting to rush in anyway, and if I'm laying in a bed next to her, smelling that delectable perfume... I know if I let myself cross that boundary with Fallon, I wouldn't be able to hold back. I can't let myself go there with her. I can't do the relationship thing, and I get the sense that's where things would go if I let myself give in.

It's almost like Fallon reads my mind when I let us into the room. She starts to speak, and stops herself, before gaining the confidence to continue. "You're sure you don't want to have me sleep on the couch? Or we could..." She clears her throat. "We could share the bed."

I'm shaking my head before she even finishes her sentence. "It's fine, really."

She reluctantly nods, and turns back to her suitcase. "I'm going to get changed."

Five minutes later, I have what resembles a bed set up on the couch, knowing the actual couch is probably better than the thin mattress on the pull out. Fallon steps out of the bathroom, face washed and free of makeup, hair up in a messy loose bun on top of her head. It's crooked and pieces are falling out of it, but it's pretty cute. The sleep shorts she has on are barely covering the curve of her ass, and I do my best not to stare. My dick throbs. She has a loose shirt on top, and I can see the outline of her peaked nipples. Fuck. I withhold a groan, and shift so she can't see my hardening cock in my pants. I need to take a cold shower.

"Bathroom is all yours," she says, dropping her clothes into her open suitcase on the floor. I quickly grab my things from my bag, and head into the bathroom.

I take a deep breath, and stare at myself in the mirror. I beg myself not to give in, not to break, or even bend. I need to be there for Lennie, be the best dad I can for her, and as much as I want to believe it wouldn't be, a woman, any woman, is a distraction right now. Between work, the still new contract with Meadow Grove, and the winery, I'm stretched thin. I'm already not there enough for my daughter. If I can't give enough of myself to her, how can I offer someone a part of me that doesn't even exist?

My dick is hard as a rock, and I do my best to ignore it, but it's no use. Hopefully a shower will help. I start the shower, not bothering to let it heat up before I strip down and climb in. The cold water is like a shock to my system, making me gasp and shiver. My dick is still rock hard, clearly not deterred by the freezing water. I wash my body quickly, avoiding all contact with my cock, trying not to give into it.

After washing my hair, thinking of anything but the gorgeous woman in the next room, I'm still hard. There's really only one surefire way to get rid of it now, and as much as I don't want to give in, I also don't want to walk out of this bathroom with a clear as day erection.

I sigh, wrapping my palm around my shaft, and squeezing tightly. I swallow the groan that is threatening its way up my throat as I begin to stroke myself in quick, hard pulls.

My mind strays as I suddenly picture Fallon on her knees in front of me, hair wet and stuck to her face, her breasts heavy and hanging bare with water cascading down them. Her nipples are pointed and look eager for my touch. She looks up at me, those green eyes round and innocent.

My balls tighten and I try to stave off my climax, to give myself another minute to enjoy the fantasy, to live out this perfect moment that can never become a reality. I squeeze tight, almost to the point of pain, and in my mind, I'm touching Fallon, playing with those pert nipples and round breasts.

Her mouth falls open as I touch her, breathy gasps and moans slipping from her lips as I kneel before her, sliding my fingers between her slick folds, tasting her pleasure.

I come with a groan, white spurts hitting the wall of the shower as I come harder than I have in months, possibly years. I don't focus much on my pleasure anymore, using it more as a simple release than anything. I watch as the water washes away all signs of my orgasm, of my slip in self-control.

My dick is no longer hard, so I do one final rinse, and shut off the water. I dry myself off and change into my pajamas. Thankfully, I decided to bring a pair of pajama pants, instead of planning on sleeping in my usual boxers and no shirt.

My phone buzzes on the countertop.

JOSIE

sends a photo of Lennie snuggled into the couch with a bowl of popcorn and a huge grin on her face.

We're having so much fun!

ME

You guys are going to be great parents someday. Thanks for watching her.

JOSIE

Thanks, Jason.

ME

Let me know if you need anything.

JOSIE

Will do. Have fun this weekend! I heard through the grapevine it's just you and Fallon now.

I don't know why, but I want to confide in my sister-in-law. She's an easy person to talk to, and I know she'll be honest with me. I can't say I've ever confided in her before, but I hope she knows both Fallon and I well enough to help me in this scenario.

ME

I need advice. You can't tell anyone.

JOSIE

Wait!

I'm not good at secrets. At least not from Andrew.

ME

Crap. Nevermind.

JOSIE

You can't not tell me now!

ME

Fine, but at least try not to tell anyone.

JOSIE

🤐

ME

There was an error with the reservation, and Fallon and I are sharing a room. With one bed.

JOSIE

Oh my god.

ME

Yeah.

JOSIE

Are you sharing the bed?

ME

I'm sleeping on the couch. My back is not going to be pleased with me in the morning.

JOSIE

Is this... Are you trying to tell me
something?

Crap. Crap. Crap. I said too much, now she's going to
get all excited and think something is going to happen
between us.

JOSIE

Do you have a crush on Fallon?

Oh my god. You totally do.

You two would be perfect together. I can
see it now.

You should totally go for it.

ME

Josie. You're WAY ahead of yourself there. I
don't have a "crush" on her. We have
some... unresolved history.

JOSIE

HISTORY?? Why don't I know this???
Wtf?? Do any of your brothers know?

ME

I think history is a big word for it. We went
to college together when I was a senior
and she was a freshman, and I had feelings
for her then, but she met her ex-husband,
and I took it hard and kinda blocked
her out.

In all honesty, I think that's where some of
my issues with trust started. I thought we
had something, but she shattered it in the
blink of an eye.

The realization settles low in my gut. I mean, I know I

have trust issues, clearly. But I guess I never put it together. Maybe that was the start of them.

ME

I didn't see her after that, not until your wedding.

JOSIE

So are you telling me something might happen? Do you want it to?

ME

No, nothing can happen. I have to focus on being a dad.

JOSIE

That's not what I asked. I asked if you wanted something to happen.

ME

It can't happen, Josie. Regardless of whether I want it to or not.

JOSIE

You're depressing. I think you can be happy in a relationship and be a good dad, all at the same time. You don't have to sacrifice one for the other, Jason.

ME

I can't, Jos.

JOSIE

Fine, but... have fun this weekend. There's nothing out there that says you can't have fun and let go.

ME

Thanks. Don't tell Andrew.

JOSIE

I'll do my best, but he always knows when I'm keeping a secret.

ME

Thanks again for watching Lennie.

JOSIE

Anytime, seriously.

I step out of the bathroom and into the chilly room, noting that Fallon is already in bed, the covers pulled up and over her shoulders. She's lying on her side, and is scrolling on her phone.

"Should I get the lights?" I ask, and she nods, so I flick off the main light, leaving the room only glowing by the small lamp at Fallon's head.

"I still think this is stupid," she mumbles. "There's no reason we can't share the bed."

"Fallon, really, it's fine. I promise." I sink down onto the unforgiving spring couch, and pull the blanket up over my shoulder. I shimmy a bit as I try to get comfortable, and grimace as my back cracks, and the springs jolt.

"You're sure?" she asks, clearly seeing the look on my face.

"Positive."

She shakes her head, and flicks the light off, bathing the room in darkness.

16

FALLON

What a stubborn man. He could barely walk this morning when he rolled off the couch, and I could hear him moving and grunting all night, and yet, he still refused to share the damn bed.

It's so frustrating.

I'm finishing curling the last piece of my hair before we head down for breakfast and the first few hours of the day. Jason is already dressed and ready to go, but he opted to wait for me, instead of heading down by himself. I'm not exactly sure why. It's not like he ever wants to spend time with me, but I guess I don't mind. All of our conversations have been clipped and short while here, but I guess that's Jason's new normal. He doesn't share as willingly as he used to.

I give myself a final once-over in the mirror, and head out of the bathroom. Today, I'm dressed in one of my favorite black pleated skirts that is about mid-calf length with a bow around my waist. For a top, I'm wearing a baby blue blouse and another blazer over it. My hair is curled loosely around my face, and I went with a light makeup look. I'm definitely wearing flats again today. It's not worth it wearing heels if it's not a work event.

When I exit the bathroom, I spot Jason with his arms up above his head as he attempts to stretch out his body. His arm muscles are taut as he tries to massage and stretch out the tightness there. I skate my eyes up and down his body as he's distracted, taking in the softness of his stomach, and chest. He's not the same muscular man I knew in college, but honestly, I like the softness of him now.

I quirk my brow at him, narrowing my eyes. He does the same, like he's daring me to say something. I decide to poke the bear. "All I'm going to say is you can't complain. I gave you options so you didn't have to sleep on the couch. Now, you're a grumpy bear."

"I'm not a grumpy bear," he grumbles under his breath.

"Sure," I say with a small laugh. "Are you ready to go?"

He nods, doing one final stretch over his head, and grabbing his wallet and phone from the side table.

We head down to where breakfast is being served and find a table. We go our separate ways to get food, and end up back at the table eating a few minutes later. I check my phone while we eat, sending a message off to my mom to check in on Presley. She replies, letting me know everything is going fine as per usual. I send off a text to Megan, updating her on the circumstances of the weekend.

ME

So. Jason and I are sharing a room.

MEGAN

What?? Why? Isaac said he left two rooms for you guys.

ME

Long story, there was a mix up with the hotel.

MEGAN

Wow.

ME

It gets better.

It's a king suite, so there's only one bed.

MEGAN

OH MY GOD. Are you sharing a bed??
Please tell me you are.

ME

Nope. He's too stubborn. He slept on the couch last night, even though I offered to, and offered to share the bed. And now he's all grumbly and wincing in pain every five seconds.

MEGAN

When is Jason not grumbly, though?

I mean really, he's quite a grumbly guy.

ME

Trust me, I know. He's grumpier than normal though.

MEGAN

I can think of a way to make him less grumpy.

ME

Nope. Not going there.

MEGAN

You're no fun. You're living out the perfect romance novel dream, only one bed, and yet, you aren't even going to try??

ME

It's not going to happen, Megan.

MEGAN

We'll see. Have fun, I love you!

ME

Love you too.

As expected, breakfast is awkward. On those rare occasions I've been able to get more than a few words from Jason, I think I'm starting to crack his shell, but then he turns back into a one word responder again. Then he goes and waits to eat breakfast with me, but doesn't say a word the entire time. I don't know what to think of it. I wish things were the way they used to be, where conversation flowed between us with no awkward pauses or breaks. I want to get to know him again, not just try and reconcile this version of him with the old Jason, because clearly they are very different men.

17

FALLON

Jason and I make our way back to the hotel room after the last event of the evening. We did a lot more networking today, and left with twice as many cards and brochures than we came with. I met some really awesome event planners, and got so many ideas on how to make things run better at Meadow Grove. A giddy sense of excitement rolls through me as I think about all the things I have planned now.

Jason did his own exploring today, and didn't say much to me about what he found, only that he was glad he came.

As Jason unlocks the door to the hotel room, he asks curiously, "Are you planning on going down to the cocktail hour and dinner?"

"Yeah, I was planning on it," I say. "One of the people I met today wanted to chat a bit more, so I was going to spend some time with her."

He nods. "Sounds great."

"What about you?" I ask.

"I'll go down and eat, but not sure what the rest of the night looks like for me."

Twenty minutes later, we head down to the hotel bar, and I spot the woman I planned to meet up with, Penny, right away. I wave at her, and then turn to Jason. "Do you want to join us?"

He shakes his head. "Nah, I'm going to call Lennie, and grab a bite. I'll see you back in the room."

I nod, totally understanding that he wants to talk to his daughter. I called Presley earlier when we were in the room, and she was so excited to tell me all about the cupcakes she and my mom made today. I'm not surprised he didn't want to eat with us, if I'm honest.

I sit down by Penny and she starts talking immediately. "Who were you with? Is that your boyfriend?"

"Oh, Jason?" I ask, turning to look back at him. He's still looking at me as he sits down a few tables away. When he sees me looking, he darts his gaze away immediately. "No, he's not my boyfriend. He's a... friend? I think? It's a long story. His brewery is contracted with the winery I'm the event planner for."

"That's cool," Penny says, but something tells me she wants to dive deeper into the subject. My suspicions are correct when she continues, "He's totally interested in you. He hasn't stopped looking over here."

I wave her off. "He's not interested in me."

Penny raises her brow, like she doesn't believe me.

The waitress arrives at the right time, setting down full glasses of ice water, and asking for our drink orders. I take a quick glance at the menu, and order a Mojito. Not something I might usually get, but it sounds refreshing after a long day.

A full plate of nachos and two drinks later, I'm buzzed. Penny is super sweet, and I'm learning so much from her. I brought my notebook in case I wanted to take notes, and I'm glad I did. I've filled two pages of information. She's been an event planner for over ten years now and has so much experience.

"Want another drink?" Penny asks as the waitress comes back to check on us.

"I think I'm good," I respond. I don't want to get drunk, and I certainly don't want to lower my inhibitions more around Jason. I fear if I do, I'll say something stupid. Brad never let me have more than two drinks, because I would lose my filter, and embarrass him.

Penny orders herself another drink, and we continue our conversation. Her eyes dart behind me for a second, and she offers someone a soft smile, before turning her attention back to me. I'm aware of someone's presence, so I glance behind me.

A tall man stands right behind me, and when he sees me looking, he moves so he's standing in front of me. He's nice enough looking, with dirty blonde hair, and blue eyes, but to be honest, he looks too much like Brad, the rich, preppy kind, that I'm immediately turned away from it.

"Hey," he greets, his voice almost nasally. "Can I buy you a drink?"

"Um," I murmur, glancing back and forth between Penny and him. I don't know Penny well enough to know what the look on her face means. It's a mix of surprise and shock, something I don't know how to interpret.

I look down at the drink currently in my palm, still half full. "I'm good. Thank you for the offer, though. That's really kind."

He scoffs. "You've almost emptied your drink. Can't I get you another? I'd love to chat."

I try to hold back my shock. "I'm actually in a meeting, so it's really not a good time."

The man glances behind him at Penny, who awkwardly holds her hand up in a wave.

"When you're done then." He doesn't phrase it as a question, and that in itself pisses me off. This man reminds me of Brad in more ways than one, especially with his refusal to take no for an answer.

"Really, I'm not interested," I say, hoping this way he finally takes the hint.

"Come on, sweet cheeks," he murmurs, bending down so he's at eye level. I can smell the liquor on his breath, and that, along with the pet name, is disgusting. "You know you want to. Ditch your friend. I can show you the time of your life. I'm sure good dick is hard for you to come by, and all you need to do is get a drink with me."

God, I really hate men sometimes. Anger begins to fuel through my body, and as I'm about to rip him a new one, a low, grumbly voice sounds from behind me.

18
______

JASON

I've been watching this asshole all night. Watching as he ogles Fallon and adjusts himself under the bar repeatedly. It's fucking disgusting. When he goes from watching her to striding over to her table with what appears to be the swagger of an overconfident frat boy, I stand, making my way closer to the table.

I'm pretty sure she can hold her own, but that doesn't mean I want this guy anywhere near her. Some guys can't take no for an answer, and I want to give her some backup.

I catch her refusing his offer for a drink, and when he continues to try again, I'm ready to pop him in the jaw. He tries one last time, this time not giving her a choice, telling her when she's done with her meeting he'll buy her a drink, and I'm done.

"Really, I'm not interested," she says, and I watch as he bends down so he's at eye level. Fallon visibly grimaces, and her friend notices me approaching.

"Come on, sweet cheeks. You know you want to. Ditch your friend. I can show you the time of your life. I'm sure good dick is hard for you to come by, and all you need to do is get a drink with me," he slurs, giving me even more of a sign that her telling him no isn't going to be enough. He needs an outside force to get him away.

"What part of no don't you understand?" I say, my voice low in my irritation. The man's eyes widen as he looks up, taking me in as I stand behind Fallon. "You alright, sunshine?" I ask, bending down to press a kiss to Fallon's temple.

She stiffens, and I realize my actions might be over the top, but I'm feeling protective, and okay, maybe a *little* possessive of her right now. Even I'm surprised by my own actions. Was it another man showing interest in her, someone I have been feeling so back and forth with that set me off?

I don't have time to process it right now though, and I focus my attention back to the situation. Fallon nods, her eyes wide as she takes me in. I step up so I'm chest to chest with this asshole.

"I think it's time for you to leave my girl alone, don't you think?" Those two words, *my girl*, slip out before I can think better of it, but I'd be lying if I said it didn't make me apprehensive.

The man glances between Fallon and me, eyes wide. "Hey bro," he says, holding up his arms in surrender. "I didn't know she had a man. I was offering her a drink."

"Still doesn't make it okay that you don't understand what the word no means."

He steps away from me, but I follow, keeping myself close to him. "Leave them alone, and maybe do a little research into consent."

The man frantically nods, turning on his heel and stumbling back to the bar. He throws a few twenties on the counter next to his drink, and leaves in a rush. With him gone, I turn my focus back to Fallon. "You okay?" I ask.

Fallon glances up to me, and her eyes are dazed, from the alcohol, or the situation, I'm not sure. "Thanks. I was about ready to punch him in the jaw. Saved my hand from some bruising."

I offer a small laugh, all while internally relieved that the situation has been diffused. "As much as I would have liked to see that, I'm glad you didn't have to punch him," I admit. This entire weekend has given me whiplash. I don't want anything to do with women, relationships or drama, and yet, here I am protecting Fallon, calling her mine, and giving her a nickname.

"Me too," she says. She looks back to her friend. "Penny, this is Jason, he owns Blue Ox Brewery. Jason, this is Penny."

I lean over, shaking Penny's hand. "Sorry to interrupt your evening. I'll leave you to it." I point over at my table. "I'll be over there if you need me, but I'll probably head back to the room soon."

"Could you..." Fallon hesitates. "Could you wait? After that, I'm not really sure I want to walk up to the room alone. I don't think we will be much longer."

"No problem." I'm thankful she asked, because I wasn't really wanting to leave her alone anyway.

"Thanks," she murmurs.

"Take your time," I say, and wave goodbye to her and Penny, telling her it was nice to meet her. As I walk away, I hear a small gasp and shriek from Penny.

I sit down at my table and watch as Penny talks to Fallon animatedly, and keeps glancing over at me. It's hilarious, because I know they're talking about me. I keep thinking through the last ten minutes, trying to justify my actions to myself that I was doing what any man should do, protect the woman who is saying no to someone that won't listen, but yet, I can't. My mind is spiraling, telling me that really, there's something more between us, something I've been fighting and telling myself is nothing.

Not long later, they're paying their bill and hugging goodbye. Fallon walks over to my table, and sits in the seat across from me. She looks as beautiful as ever, with her hair in loose waves and the light makeup on her face. She has such a natural beauty. It's one of the things that attracted me to her all those years ago. Some girls looked like they were ready to walk down a runway with how much makeup they'd slathered on their face for an eight a.m. economics class, but not Fallon. There were days it looked like she rolled out of bed minutes before she had to be in the lecture hall. It was adorable, and while her job requires her to be dressed more professionally now, it's nice to see she hasn't changed all that much.

"Ready?" I ask, my insides quaking with nerves that everything is suddenly changing, I'm losing my grip on my self control.

She nods. When I stand, she does too, and I can't help but place my hand at the small of her back as we exit the restaurant. She's warm and leans into me as we make our way to the elevator.

"Thanks again for earlier. I didn't know what else to do to get him to take a hint. He was kind of an asshole."

"No thanks necessary," I reply. "Honestly, I'm glad I didn't punch him. It was a close one."

"Can I ask you something?" she says, her cheeks pinkening as I press the button to call the elevator.

The elevator dings its arrival. "Of course," I respond.

"Why'd you call me sunshine?"

"To be honest, it slipped out," I admit, running my hand over my face, trying to hide the emotions roiling inside me. "I knew I needed a way to get him to leave without being too aggressive, and staking a claim on you... that was the only thing I could think of in the moment. The name felt fitting."

She nods thoughtfully, not speaking any more on the subject as we exit the elevator and I let us into our room. I inwardly cringe at the thought of sleeping on that couch another night, but I'm not going to say anything. I don't want to do anything to make her uncomfortable. I already can't believe I called her a pet name and pretended to be her boyfriend. I could have approached the guy and made it clear she wasn't interested, but no, I had to stake a claim.

The worst thing is... she didn't deny it. She didn't push me off. She leaned in closer, let me get another whiff of the perfume that keeps infiltrating my senses every second. Both when the guy was still there, and then again now when we were making our way back to the hotel room.

I'm going to shower quickly," Fallon says, gathering her things from her bag.

"No problem," I reply, sitting down on the god-awful couch.

She heads into the bathroom a minute later, and after I change into my own pajamas, I decide to call Josie, and see if Lennie wants to chat since they were out and about earlier and couldn't chat then.

I pull her contact up, and start a FaceTime call. I hear giggles first, and there's a lot of blurriness on the screen, and then Lennie's face fills my phone. "Hey, peanut," I say, a smile crossing my face.

She looks so happy, her hair is in some sort of weird

twist on her head, and she's in her princess nightgown. "Hi, Daddy!"

"Are you having fun with Uncle Andrew and Auntie Josie?"

"So much fun. Today, we went and visited Gramps, and then Uncle Andrew took me to his shop and told me he would make me my very own jewelry box!" she babbles.

"Wow, that's so nice of him," I say, eyeing my younger brother in the background. He's already made her a toy box, and so many other things, there really isn't a need for more, but he loves to gift his family with things he makes.

"How's your trip?" Lennie asks, eyeing behind me. "Is the hotel pretty?"

"It's really nice," I say, standing up from the couch. "Let me show you." I flip the screen, and show her the room. I take her over to the windows and show her the view of the city in front of us. We chat for a while longer, longer than I thought, because the bathroom door opens, and Fallon strides out in her pajamas, her long hair damp on her shoulders. I try to flip the camera, but I'm not fast enough.

"Daddy, was that Presley's mom?" Lennie asks, her eyes bright and curious.

I inwardly curse, and glance over at Fallon with wide eyes. I'm not quite sure what to do. Fallon smiles softly, and walks over to us. She steps in right beside me, so close her head nearly rests on my arm. I can smell her sweet floral shampoo. It smells so good, and it brings me right back to my fantasy from last night's shower.

"Hi Lennie," she greets my daughter with a wave, directing my attention back to them. "How are you?"

"Hi Fallon!" Lennie says with so much excitement, you'd think I'd told her we were going to Disney World. "Is Presley with you?"

Fallon shakes her head. "Nope, it's only me. I'm at the same event that your dad is."

"Huh," Lennie says with a grin. I wait for the inevitable question about why we are in the same room, but it doesn't come. However, I can see Josie in the background, her face blazing red, trying to gesture at Andrew. I'm assuming she's trying to get him to shut up. Well, so much for keeping a secret. Though, it's kind of my own fault. I took the risk, knowing Fallon could walk out of the bathroom at any time.

Fallon talks with Lennie for a few more minutes, her body so close to mine I can grasp at her warmth. When Lennie yawns, I decide it's time to call it.

"Alright, Lenners, I think it's time for you to get to bed."

She shakes her head. "No, I'm fine. I want to keep talking to you, Daddy."

"We can talk tomorrow when I pick you up, okay?"

Lennie hesitates, then agrees.

"Have fun with Josie and Andrew, Lennie. I love you, and I'll see you tomorrow."

"I love you, Daddy." Lennie passes the phone back to Josie, and Fallon waves, then steps away.

Josie widens her eyes, giving me a look. I do the same, hoping to convey a glare that says, "don't bring it up." Thankfully, she doesn't say anything, but Andrew is standing behind her, glancing between the two of us, and he starts to mouth words.

I scoff as he continues to mime words to me I definitely can't understand. "Alright, well I'll see you guys tomorrow," I say, cutting off his silent rant. "Thanks again. Is she behaving?"

"She's perfect," Josie responds. "I think we might need to babysit the twins though, because if anything, she's giving me more baby fever, and I don't think we are there, yet."

I nod. "Yeah, a five-year-old is a lot different than a baby."

Andrew waves us both off. "Nah, we're ready. Lennie is a piece of cake, and I think a baby will be too."

Oh wow, he's in for a wake up call.

Josie rolls her eyes at her husband. "Have fun. We'll see you tomorrow."

"Thanks." We say goodbye, and disconnect the call, leaving Fallon and I alone. She's organizing a few things in her bag, and I toss my phone down on the couch. "I'm going to use the bathroom."

She nods, giving me a smile of acknowledgement. I head into the bathroom, letting the door close behind me as I try to prepare myself for another night of discomfort and pain on the couch.

19

FALLON

The bathroom door closes with a soft *click*, and I immediately jump into action. I got the idea for my brilliant plan when we were walking up to the hotel room, and now it's time to put it into action. I knew I needed to get into the bathroom first, that way, when Jason was using the bathroom, I could stand my ground.

I grab my pillow from the bed, and throw it onto the couch. I move his phone and charger over to the bed on the opposite side of where I was sleeping. If my plan fails, I'll be spending the night on the couch. Which will be fine, but not ideal for either of us.

Pulling back the sheets on Jason's makeshift bed, I lay down, adjusting the pillow behind my head, and scroll on my phone. I have to hold my ground. I can do this.

A few minutes later, Jason steps out of the bathroom, running a towel over his damp hair. He's shirtless, wearing only his pajama pants. The hem of his boxers is visible as his pants ride low, and I have to swallow down the extra saliva pooling in my mouth. *You can't drool over the man, Fallon.*

I need to shut down this attraction to him, for my own sake. I really don't think it's reciprocated, and I don't want to deal with that rejection.

Jason doesn't see me at first, but glances over at the bed, and sees it empty. His brows furrow, and then he looks over to the couch where I'm laying.

"What are you doing?" he questions, his voice gruff.

"Going to bed," I say with a shrug. "I figured it was only fair that I sleep on the couch tonight, since you did last night."

He shakes his head in what appears to be irritation. "No. Get up."

"No." *Hold your ground, Fallon.*

Jason tilts his head back, staring at the ceiling in exasperation. "Fallon, seriously. Get up."

"No," I simply reply.

He takes a deep breath, muttering something under his breath that sounds like, "worse than a toddler."

I hold in my giggle at his frustration, because this isn't going to work if I laugh. The ideal plan would be for both of us to end up in the bed, but if I have to sleep here, then so be it.

"Fallon." He gives me his best stern look, one I'm assuming works easily on Lennie.

"Jason."

"Come on. You're going to get hurt sleeping on the couch."

"Worse than you got hurt?" I refute. "You only started walking normally an hour ago."

He groans. "How can I get you to sleep in the bed?"

I hold in my smile. I've got him now. "I'll sleep in the bed if you do. It's stupid that you're insisting on sleeping on this couch when there is a perfectly good bed right there.

We're adults. We can share a king size bed, no problem. We can even put up the extra pillows between us to make a barrier, if you're that worried about it."

There's a long pause, and I stare at him the entire time. I can see the moment his resolve fully cracks.

"Fine," he mutters.

I try my best not to smile with glee as I stand up from the horrible couch, taking my pillow and phone charger and stride over to the bed. "Good. Glad we came to this agreement."

I climb into the bed after plugging in my phone, and roll onto my side. The overhead light flicks off, leaving us in the dim glow of the lamp. The bed dips as Jason opens the sheets and climbs in on the opposite side of me.

I turn off the lamp, leaving us in complete darkness. I turn so I'm facing Jason, and though I can barely see in the dark, I can tell he's facing me too.

"Goodnight, Jase," I say, my heart thrumming rapidly in my chest. He shifts, and it's almost like he's scooting closer to me.

My hand is resting in the empty space between us, and I swear I'm more aware of the heat of his body. "Goodnight, Fallon," he replies, his voice quiet, and almost... tense.

I'm not sure what prompts me to, but I speak. "It's been years since I've shared a bed with someone. Well, besides Presley, but even then, it's rare."

I'm met with a long beat of silence, then, "Me too. Lennie doesn't sleep in my bed unless she's sick."

"It's kind of nice," I admit. My face heats, and I'm grateful he can't see it.

"Yeah, it is."

My lips are moving before I have the forethought to keep them shut. "It sounds stupid, but it's one of the reasons

I miss Brad. Well, I'll take that back. I don't miss him. I miss the connection, the familiarity and comfort of something as simple as sharing a bed with someone."

"I miss it too," Jason responds. His voice is deep, and it sends a shiver down my spine. "But I don't want to talk about your ex while I'm laying in bed next to you, Fallon."

There's that tingling sensation again.

I find myself scooting a little closer to Jason. I crave his warmth. I know he doesn't want me, doesn't want anything more, and to be honest, I don't either. And yet, I can't help this draw I have to him, can't help the recent pining and emotions he's been bringing up in me. The same thing I felt all those years ago, and I messed it up, and lost him. I did that. Not him.

"This is nice," I say, my voice breathy.

"Yeah," Jason replies, his voice gravelly. It's like a magnet is pulling us together, because I move even closer to him. We meet in the middle of the large bed, and though we aren't touching, we may as well be with how close we are.

The second guessing starts back up. Do I move away? Am I pushing this too far? Pushing him?

I'm about to back away when Jason's large palm lands on my hip, pulling me that last short distance into him. I suck in a breath at the contact, and let my body sink further into the mattress, into his touch. My own palm moves on its own accord until it's flat against his bare chest. His skin is so warm and smooth that I can't breathe.

Our hips are pressed together, bodies as close as they can be to each other. Jason's free hand comes up, pushing away my still damp hair from my face to cup my cheek.

"I shouldn't do this," he says. He didn't say *we* shouldn't do this. He said *I* shouldn't do this. Does that mean he doesn't want to do this with me? Am I the problem? I panic and start to pull away, knowing I pushed too hard.

Instead of him letting me move away though, his hand grips my hip tighter, pulling me back to him. He's rock hard, pressing through the thin barrier of his boxers and pajama pants. Holy crap. Maybe he does want this. He just feels like he shouldn't.

Jason moves his face closer to mine, so close I can sense his shallow breaths on my lips. Is this happening?

"Fuck it," he breathes, and then his lips are on mine. I barely have time to react to the fact that he's kissing me, before I'm tangling myself in him.

My mouth opens, letting him in, my hand moving from his chest to tangle in his short hair, holding him to me. My leg lifts, hooking on his hip, pulling his body into my core. I react more than I think at this moment. He tastes so good, minty and fresh. Our lips twist and move together, and then the realization hits me. I'm kissing Jason. Jason is kissing me.

Holy shit.

I don't let my brain take over though, I give into his indescribable caress.

"Fallon," Jason breathes into my mouth, and I will never get enough of hearing my name fall from his lips. I pull him even closer, trying my hardest to keep any sort of contact with him. The contact is short lived, because Jason breaks us apart. My lips tingle from the loss, and my leg is still wrapped around his body, my hand still twined in his hair.

"What are we doing?" Jason asks.

I don't answer right away. "Seeking comfort from another person?" I finally reply.

"I..." Jason pauses. "I can't give you more than this, more than tonight, Fallon."

"I can't either," I reply. "I'm busy enough as it is. I can't offer you a relationship, or someone you can rely on. Presley is my entire world. She's my focus."

"So, we agree. Just tonight?"

"Just tonight," I say. We both know this is a one time thing. Even though there's a niggling in my heart telling me I want more, I shove it away.

Lips crash back down onto mine, and I let go of those thoughts, and lose myself in him again. My hand moves down his face, the roughness of his five o'clock shadow bristling on my skin. Jason's lips are expertly tangled in mine, and I've never been kissed like this. So slow, yet so passionate and full of lust. It makes me wonder what it would have been like to kiss him that night at the Christmas party. Would it have been soft like this? Or would it have been fast, hurried and eager?

My leg is still wrapped around his body, holding him so close to me. Wetness pools at my core, my clit throbbing, aching to be touched. Jason's hand on my hip moves, sliding around the hem of my sleep shorts. He slides up under my shirt, up the soft skin of my stomach.

I'm thankful we're swathed in darkness, or I admit, there would be a lot more self consciousness. I have a lot of resentment toward my body. I know I've done incredible things with it. I carried and birthed my beautiful daughter, but after my marriage to Brad, he didn't exactly help me instill confidence in myself. All the remarks about the weight I'd gained since Presley was born, and the stretch marks and cellulite that didn't go away sit fresh in my mind. I try not to let it get to me, but it does. But I can't think of that now. I'm finally getting what a younger me dreamt of.

Jason's hand is further up my top now, his large palm cupping my breasts. They're heavy in his hand, and he tweaks my nipples, pulling and making them even more sensitive. Jolts of unbridled pleasure make their way through my body, landing between my thighs where I'm starting to ache for his touch.

"Jase, please," I moan, needing more of him. "I need you to touch me."

He chuckles against my lips. "I'm touching you, sunshine."

I let out an annoyed groan. "You know what I mean."

My hand moves down his chest, to the waistline of his pants, and I slide my fingers underneath. His boxer briefs are still between me and his skin, but this will do for now.

Jason jumps under my touch, a shiver rolling through his body. "See," I croon, "You need my touch, too."

His forehead drops to rest against mine. I let my hand move down more, until the head of his cock peeks through the top of his briefs. He's so hard, so ready for this, and I lightly trail my fingertip over the crown. Jason shudders, letting out a low groan.

"Mmm, does that feel good?" I tease.

"Stop talking," Jason grunts, his lips attacking mine again as I do what I can to wrap my fingers around his shaft, giving him a gentle squeeze. He bites my lower lip between his teeth gently, almost like he's punishing me.

I squeeze harder, slowly moving my hand down his length. Jason's hand moves down my body, and he slides his hand into my sleep shorts, soaking up my warmth.

His fingers slide between my soaked folds, and he groans. "You're so wet. Is that all for me, sunshine?"

"All for you." I practically melt from his dirty words.

"Good," he replies, his fingers circling my clit. The zing of pleasure is almost instant, and I need to touch more of him, need to have his skin on mine.

I take my hand from his boxers, moving upward until I

can slide under the hem. I push them down as much as I can, and his hard cock slips out from the fabric. I immediately take it into my palm, slowly moving up and down the shaft. I use the pad of my thumb to swipe at the bead of precum, using it to aid my movements.

His fingers circle my clit in a torturous pace, and I rise closer to the edge of pleasure. I drop my head back, letting out a ridiculous moan. His touch is so good that I can't even process any thoughts besides him, of him finally touching me, having his hands on me.

I moan his name, and he bends down, kissing my cheeks and jawline, before kissing my neck, sucking and teasing me. It's probably going to leave a mark, but I don't care. It's incredible, and I would give anything to feel this way forever.

God, I want to taste him, to have him in my mouth, but I don't dare move. Don't dare stop his touch on me.

I continue to stroke him, trying to make sure he's experiencing what I am at this moment, because I need to know I'm not alone in this. An idea pops into my brain, and I let go of him for a moment, reaching to grab at his wrist. "Wait," I say. He stops, and I reach for the hem of my pants and underwear, shimmying them down and off my legs with his help. He does the same with his boxers and pajama pants, leaving him completely naked, and me with only my tee shirt on.

I take my fingers and swipe them through my core, gathering the wetness there, and using it to coat his cock as a lube. Jason groans loudly, and then he's kissing me again, his mouth rough and hard against mine as I stroke him. His fingers find their way back to my clit, circling it a few times before moving further down, to my entrance.

I gasp as he presses one long digit inside me, slowly

moving in and out. He adds a second finger, and then his thumb is back on my clit, pressing on it and circling as he pumps in and out of me.

"Oh god," I cry as my orgasm starts to build within. My nipples are practically pebbles as I press my body into him, trying to get as close as humanly possible. My leg ended up against his hip again, and I have no idea how we are making this work, with how tangled our arms and legs are, but I don't care, I only care that we're doing this, that I'm feeling him *finally*.

His cock twitches in my palm, and I keep moving, using my own wetness to aid in the movement. He's so thick in my palm, and I can't even see him. I yearn to see him, to know what his cock looks like, but for now, and maybe always, this will have to be enough. To know what he feels like in my palm, to know what his giant hands are like on my skin and inside my pussy.

"I'm close," I cry, moving my hand faster and harder on his cock. My body heats and explodes under his touch, the white hot pleasure barreling through my body as I clench around his fingers, and come hard. Jason continues to move, and his hips jerk in my hand and he loudly groans as the warm jets of his cum paint my skin. He curses under his breath, the sound sending a tingle up my body.

"Oh my," I breathe, no other words able to come to my mind. I'm completely and utterly satiated. I'm relaxed, my body unable to move. My hand is still wrapped around Jason's softening cock, and his fingers are still deep inside me. "That was..."

"So good," he finishes for me.

"Incredible," I agree. I reluctantly let go of him, and slide my leg off his hips. He slides his fingers out of me, leaving me empty again. Jason leans his forehead against mine again as we catch our breath. He leans back, but kisses my forehead before rolling out of the bed. I wince at the sting of loss, but logically, I know he's going to clean up.

The light in the bathroom turns on, and I hear the sound of running water. I roll onto my back, still trying to catch my breath and process what happened. It's one night, and I can't let myself think this can be something more. It won't be, and I need to accept that. This was a simple release for both of us. Expelling the pent up energy we've had for all these years.

Jason reenters the room, his face flushed pink. He's still naked, but I don't get a good glimpse at him, the light from the bathroom isn't quite enough. He has a washcloth in his hands, and instead of handing it to me, I'm surprised when he pulls the sheets back, and cleans between my legs himself. He even takes my hand, and cleans me up there.

When he's done, he stands, heading back into the bathroom, and rinsing out the washcloth. Even though he cleaned me up, I should still use the bathroom, so I stand, and head that way.

His body collides with mine in the doorway, and my face heats. "Sorry," I gasp, and turn, sliding between him and the door. "I need to use the restroom."

"You're fine, sunshine."

Every time he calls me that, my heart squeezes. It's such a sweet name, and it's... *right*. Brad never had a nickname for me, and I always wished I could have a cute nickname from my partner.

I take care of myself in the bathroom, and when I look at myself in the mirror, I flush a deeper shade of red. My still damp hair is tangled, and almost looks like a rat's nest on my head. My cheeks are bright red and scratched from the roughness of his stubble. Despite how chaotic I look, and the red marks on my neck from his kisses, I look content, and more relaxed than I have in ages. If that says something about me, I guess I'm not sure, but I feel amazing.

I turn the light off and close the door behind me, making my way into the room again. Jason has turned the light on for me so I can see, and he's in the bed, leaning up against the headboard. I'm not sure if he put any clothes on, but I decide I'm not going to put my shorts and panties back on. I climb into the bed next to him, and shuffle so I'm laying on my side by him.

He turns off the lamp, and scoots down, laying on his side and pulling me into him. He's wearing his boxers, but I'm fine with it. It's so good to have him hold me. His arm is wrapped around my waist, hand splayed across my stomach.

After pressing a kiss to my cheek, then the top of my head, he whispers, "Goodnight, Fallon. Thank you."

I repeat the sentiment and close my eyes, sinking into his embrace. I almost don't want to fall asleep, don't want to miss a moment of this. If one night is all we have, then I don't want to take any moment of it for granted.

20

JASON

I wake before Fallon. Our bodies are so entwined that it takes me minutes to disentangle without waking her. When finally I do manage my escape, I go down to get some breakfast, and decide to bring up some cinnamon rolls and bacon for her.

As I make my way to the elevator, I reminisce on last night. The sounds she made had me savoring the moment in a way I didn't expect to ever experience. I'm so thankful it happened, even if it could only be one night.

The elevator dings as I arrive on our floor and make my way to the door. I've got the plate of food for her in one hand, and a to-go coffee cup in the other. When I reach our door, I can hear music playing loudly on a phone speaker. I maneuver the cup into the crook of my other arm, and pull the room key from my back pocket, waving it in front of the scanner until it turns green.

I push open the door, and the pop song playing grows louder as it echoes off the bathroom walls. Fallon stands in front of the mirror, running a brush through her long honey blonde hair. She's humming the words under her breath, swaying her body to the beat. It's adorable. She turns when she sees me, a smile playing on her lips. Her cheeks turn pink, and I wonder if she's remembering what our night entailed.

"Hey," I say, offering her a wave.

She waves. "Oooh, they have cinnamon rolls downstairs? I'll have to grab one."

I gesture to the plate with a tip of my head. "I brought these for you."

"You did?" She steps out of the bathroom into the hall. "Thank you, that was really sweet."

I shrug. "No problem." I hold out the plate to her, and she gratefully takes it. Without thinking, I lean down, swiftly kissing her cheek. Instantly, I stiffen and pull away, knowing I already broke the rule of "only one night". My cheeks heat as I look away, and then, remembering I also brought her coffee, I grab that from where it's sitting in my elbow and hand it to her.

"Coffee, too?" she says, her voice growing an octave higher.

"Yep. You have it in your hand every time I see you at the winery, so I figured it was a safe bet."

"You figured right." She takes a deep inhale of the coffee, savoring the smell.

I glance around the room, seeing that she's pulled the sheets up on the bed, and has already collected her things. My stuff is ready too, shoved into my duffel bag on the floor. "Looks like you're ready to go. What time are you heading out?"

She shrugs. "Probably soon. There aren't any events today, and honestly, I'm ready to get home to my girl."

I shove my hands into the pockets of my jeans, staring down at the floor. "Yeah, I know how that is. Though, I'm a little scared that Josie and Andrew won't give me my kid back."

"I bet they're having fun."

"I think so," I say, running a hand through my short hair.

Fallon takes the coffee and plate from me, sitting down at the desk before taking a long sip of the coffee. She shivers as the warmth hits her tongue.

"For hotel coffee, this is surprisingly good," she admits. She takes another sip, and then dives into the cinnamon roll. The moan that slides from her lips sends a jolt of electricity through my body.

She made the same noises last night when I was making her come. My mind whirls as I consider the consequences of it. Sure, it was amazing, and in the moment it was perfect, but maybe we shouldn't have crossed that line. I shouldn't have given in last night and shared the bed with her, but I did. I made things twice as complicated than they were before.

What if she was only saying those things about not wanting anything more last night? Was she only saying them to appease me? Am I going to break her heart in the process of this? I meant what I said last night. It could only be one night, and it shouldn't have even happened.

I sit down on the end of the bed, pulling my phone out to scroll. I could leave right now, my stuff is packed and ready, but something is holding me back. *She* is holding me back. I don't want to leave without her. I want to take advantage of this one-on-one time with her.

I admit it. I spent pretty much the entire weekend at her side, and yet, I want more. *Need* more time with her. Even though I shouldn't. I know I shouldn't.

I aimlessly scroll, but I'm not really paying attention to what I'm looking at. My focus is on her. She's on her phone too, scrolling as she eats, and something about it makes me relax. Like there is no pressure to fill every silence with conversation.

After she's finished eating her breakfast, she pushes her chair back to stand. She heads into the bathroom, collecting the last of her things and shoving them into her suitcase. "Well, I suppose it's about time to go," she says.

I stand from the edge of the bed. "Let me help you with your stuff," I offer, reaching to grab her small duffle.

She shakes her head with a smile. "You have your own stuff to grab, Jason."

I turn my head to look at my bag on the floor. "Right." I bend down, grabbing my own bag and hauling it over my shoulder. "I can still take your bag though. I have another arm."

Fallon raises her brows, but I hold out my free arm, making grabby hands for her bag. She scoffs under her breath, and says, "Alright." She hands over the bag, and extends the handle on her rolling suitcase.

I glance over the room one last time, making sure we both have our phone chargers and anything else we might have forgotten. When I'm satisfied, I head toward the door. Opening it, I step to the side, allowing her to go out first. She smiles softly, looking down at her feet as her cheeks flush.

She walks through the open door, and I step through behind her, letting it fall shut after me. We make our way through the halls and into the elevator.

"Where did you park?" I ask.

"The parking ramp below the hotel. P2."

I press the button marked P2, and the elevator starts to move down.

Fallon starts to speak, filling the silence. "I had a great time this weekend."

I look over to her. She's glancing up at me, her green eyes sparkling. I could lose myself in those eyes. I rip my gaze away from her before I do. I need to pull away. I can't let myself get close to her again. The last time I did, I had my first encounter with heartbreak. It's not just my heart I can be careless with anymore. I have Lennie to think about.

Last night was a lapse in judgement. I can't do it again. I clear my throat, staring up at the ceiling. "Yeah, it was nice."

The elevator dings our arrival, and when the doors open, I hold my arm out in front to prevent it from closing on her. She walks through, pulling her suitcase behind her. When we are clear of the doorway, she stops, stepping off to the side of the sidewalk. "I guess this is goodbye." She holds her arm out for her bag but I shake my head.

"Where's your car? I'll walk you there." I can't be more for her, but I can give myself a few more minutes to pretend.

She points a few rows down, and I gesture for her to lead the way. We walk in silence, the only sound is the rolling of her suitcase on the pavement. When we reach her car, I wait for her to unlock it, and then open the trunk for her. I set her duffle in, and then reach forward, grabbing her rolling suitcase before she can.

She huffs, but doesn't say anything. I can't help it. I need to do this, need to be the one to help her. What if I wasn't here and her suitcase rolled away before she could put it in the trunk?

That's ridiculous. I know I'm being over the top. I know that I really can't bear the thought of letting her go yet, but I don't want to acknowledge it.

"Thanks," she murmurs, shifting back awkwardly on

her heels. I shove my free hand into my pocket, because if I don't, I'm afraid of what I might do.

"Wh—"

"I—"

We both speak at the same time, and I stop, holding my hand out and snapping my mouth shut for her to continue.

"What happened last night..." she speaks slowly. "I wanted to thank you. I know it was only a one time thing, but I had fun. Like we said, it was comforting to have another person by my side all night. One that doesn't kick me in the ribs when she lays sideways in the bed."

I chuckle, my mood lightening. "It was nice. I'm sorry it can't be more."

She shrugs. "We are both on the same page, Jase. There's nothing to apologize for. It's nice to have your friendship again. I've missed you. More than I realized."

"Me too," I respond with a nod. Guilt hits me for thinking that maybe she wasn't on the same page as me, but I realize now that we're both adults. For lack of better words, we used each other for a mutual release, mutual comfort, and that's all it was.

"Friends?" Fallon offers.

"Friends," I confirm with a nod. She gives me one of her gorgeous smiles, making my heart skip a beat. I lean forward, unable to stop myself. I open up my arms, wrapping her into my embrace. She smells so good, a soft floral, with a hint of warmth. I soak up every second I can of this, knowing it's the only time it will happen. "I guess I'll see you later," I say, pulling back from the hug.

With one final squeeze, Fallon does the same. "Thanks again." She surprises me by standing up on her tiptoes, and pressing a kiss to my cheek.

Her lips are soft, and it reminds me of last night. Of the

way her lips felt on my neck, my jaw, my mouth. She pulls away all too soon, and I take a step back, letting the sensation of her lips on my skin linger.

I awkwardly raise my hand in a wave, and turn away, walking backwards in the direction of my car. "Bye, sunshine," I say. The nickname slips out again, and I watch as Fallon's cheeks blaze, a smile coming across her face as she shakes her head.

"Bye, Jase."

I watch her get into her car, and then cross the parking garage to my own. As I get into my car, I send a message off to Josie and Andrew, letting them know I'm on my way home.

As I watch her car leave the parking garage from my rearview mirror, I can't help but wonder if I'm making a mistake by putting the barrier up between us, by shutting down my budding affection for the second time.

21

FALLON

ME

SOS.

MEGAN

Fucking finally. I've been sitting on pins and needles all weekend waiting for more information from you.

ME

Megan, I don't know what the fuck I'm doing

MEGAN

Breathe. I'll come over tonight, and once Pres goes to bed, we can talk.

ME

Okay. You can't tell Isaac anything.

MEGAN

I know. I'll see you in a few hours.

ME

You're the best, Megs.

MEGAN

"Mom, can we go to the zoo?" Presley asks me over dinner.

"Sure, honey. We might have to go sometime next week, unless you want to ask Grandma if she can take you." This upcoming week is busy with lots of meetings at work, and there's a wedding on Saturday I can't miss.

She shakes her head and her dirty blonde hair falls into her eyes. "No, I want to go with you. Can we bring Lennie? And maybe my friend Natalie?"

I mindlessly play with my rice, pushing it around until it turns into a little pile in the center. "Yeah, of course. I'll text Natalie's mom."

"And Lennie's dad?" she prompts.

I swallow the lump in my throat at the mention of him and nod. "Yeah. Him too."

"Yay!" she cheers. While I know last night was a one-time thing, I need to keep telling my stupid heart that. All day today, I've flipped back and forth between wanting to take that step and see if the risk is worth the reward, and shoving my heart back down into my stomach, forcing it to behave. We both agreed. One night. One amazing, *incredible*, pleasure-and-comfort-filled night. I need to get my head back on straight and stop daydreaming about the way his fingers felt inside me, or the way his lips felt as they tangled with mine.

There's a knock on the front door that pulls me out of

my daydreams. Megan announces her arrival, making her way through the house to where we sit at the dinner table.

"Hello!" she says in a cheery voice. She's in a pair of cozy sweats and sweatshirt, her hair pulled into a high bun, perfect for tonight's activities. She has a plastic container in her right hand filled with those frosted sugar cookies people either love or hate. I'm personally a fan of the cookies, and so is Presley.

Presley shrieks in delight when she sees Megan. "Auntie Megan! Are you here for a sleepover?"

"No sleepover," Megan responds. "But we can watch a movie and snuggle before you go to bed. I brought a treat for us."

Presley giggles in delight, and I let out a sigh of relief. Being in my best friend's presence helps to slow my racing thoughts.

She sits down beside me, pulling me into a tight side hug. Once Presley and I finish dinner, the three of us move over to the couch and we let Presley pick a movie.

Presley snuggles in between me and Megan. A pile of blankets cover us, along with a group of her stuffed animals. We watch the movie and eat our cookies. I ignore the guilty notion of taking my best friend away from a night at home with her husband, knowing that if she didn't want to come over, she wouldn't have.

When it's finally time for Presley to go to bed, she does so easily and without complaint. I tuck her in and kiss her goodnight, and leave her room, shutting the door behind me.

I let out a heavy sigh and head into my living room, flopping down on the couch next to Meg. She pulls me into her arms, tucking a blanket around me. "Time to spill the beans," she says.

I sigh, and tell her every detail from the weekend,

updating her on the events that happened after my last messages to her. She gasps when I tell her how he commented on my perfume and helped protect me from that man. She shrieks with delight when I tell her how Jason and I *helped* each other last night in bed.

"So now, I'm a mess. My brain is telling me all the reasons that we both agreed on are right, and we can't go any further, but my heart is being dramatic, telling me to chase after him and show him we could be good together, despite all the reasons holding both of us back."

Megan sighs heavily. "You know what I think. I think you're both being ridiculous. You clearly are both stuck in some delusion that your responsibility to your children or the way your past played out is more important than your own happiness. You're allowed to have fun and do things for yourselves, too."

"But we can't!" I argue. "We have our kids to think about."

"Yeah, your kids, who are practically best friends." She scoots up on the couch, leaning forward to flick my nose. "You aren't going to get any sympathy from me, Fallon. It's been three years now since Brad left. You've grieved your marriage, and the life you had. You've created a wonderful new life for you and your daughter, and no one will tell you that you can't give into your feelings and pursue something with someone. Nevermind the fact that this man is one of the best men I've ever met in my life."

I swallow harshly. "That doesn't change the fact that he isn't interested in something more. I shouldn't have given in to my desire for him last night."

Megan reaches over, taking my hand and squeezing it. "I'm not able to speak for him, but if I had to guess, I would say he's experiencing a lot of what you are right now. I mean, you two have a history. You knew each other before the worst times in your lives, and now you are building your futures. He could be more interested than you think, and is simply holding himself back. You never know, Fallon."

I lean into Megan, glad she's here and talking this through with me. "I won't force it either way. If it happens, then I guess it happens. My apprehensions about it aren't going to go away though."

"I'd never expect them to. Like you've said, it's not only you that you have to think of, and I'm proud of you, and Jason, for recognizing that."

"Thanks," I say, though I'm not quite sure I mean it. I'm still a mess. This conversation is not helping as much as I would have liked it to.

22

FALLON

Sometimes when I'm overwhelmed, I like to go for a walk during my afternoon break for a little change in scenery on the days I'm stuck in my office. Lately, I've been going down into the wine cellar. It's quiet, cold, and usually a nice break in the day.

I've been wandering down here for about fifteen minutes, taking in the names of some of the new barrels of wine lining the walls, and admiring how much work goes into making wine.

Josie and I have a meeting with a potential client in about thirty minutes, so I should really head back to my office soon. I needed a breather after a rough client this morning. I have an inkling she's going to be a bit of a bridezilla, and I'm already not looking forward to her wedding. Never mind the fact that it was a rough morning for Presley.

I'm about to head back up the stairs when I hear the creaking of the door opening and footsteps coming down the stairs. I'm expecting to see one of the vineyard workers, or maybe even a lost guest, but to my surprise, it's Jason who comes around the corner.

His eyes are curious as he takes me in, glancing up and down my body with an unexpected hunger. "Hey," he greets, voice low and thick. "What are you doing down here?"

"Taking a break before a meeting. I needed a minute."

"Is everything okay?" Jason asks, stepping toward me.

I shrug. "Rough client this morning. She's going to be a tough one, I can already tell, and then throw in Presley having a rough morning, and it made for a perfect storm."

"What happened, if you don't mind my asking?" Jason questions.

"I don't mind. Every once in a while she struggles with the pain she has over her dad not being around."

Jason nods. "I'm sure that's tough on a young kid. Does she remember him?"

I shake my head. "Not really. At least I don't think so. I think she more so remembers the idea of him, and that's what hurts. It's always hard to leave her when she has these times. Usually something triggers it, but I can't think of what it might have been today. Last winter, they had a daddy-daughter dance at school, and it absolutely gutted her she couldn't go. The following few days were really rough. She was really clingy to me, and I couldn't even blame her."

"They really don't have an alternative for kids that don't have a male figure in their lives?" Jason asks through gritted teeth.

I shake my head. "Isaac offered to go with her, but at that point, she wanted nothing to do with it anymore."

My chest hurts from the pain of leaving her today, so I

change the subject. "What are you doing here? There isn't a wedding or anything today."

"Isaac asked me to stop by and I wanted to have a meeting with my bartenders here." He shrugs, shoving his hands in his pockets and rocking back on his heels. He looks sexy in his worn jeans and tee. His hair is tousled today, growing longer on the sides. "And when I didn't see you in your office, I saw Josie and she told me you like to go for walks sometimes."

My mind goes blank as I try to process why he went in search of me. "You went to my office?"

He glances up, his chocolate brown eyes locking on mine. "Yeah."

"Why?" I ask.

He doesn't answer, looking down at his feet again.

"Jase," I state his name. "Tell me."

"I wanted to make sure you were still okay with how we left things the other day."

"I'm fine," I mutter, a little irritated. "Why didn't you text me that?" I shake my head. "Never mind, I should get going. I have a meeting of my own." I start to walk toward the stairway, but as I'm passing Jason, he stops me with a hand on my wrist.

"Jason?" I breathe his name, internally hoping he might say something, anything, to keep me down here with him, while at the same time wanting *out*. "Can I get by, please?" I finally ask when he doesn't make a move to let by.

"No," he mutters. I don't fully see what's happening, because my gaze is still at my feet, but Jason steps toward me until we are standing toe-to-toe. "You need a hug."

And then his arms are around me. My arms go limp at my sides. I wasn't expecting a hug from him. Annoyance trickles through my veins. He's like a freaking sour candy. Sour, then sweet. The hot and cold I've experienced with him until this point has been fucking with my head, but the strength of his arms around me is so good that I let myself give in once more.

Jason holds me tightly, and the internal wall crumbles. The walls holding back my emotions of the pain Presley experiences over the lack of answers about her dad crumble to dust. I'm overwhelmed by the pain I have that I can't make it all better. I'd give anything to make her pain go away. Longing for the man holding me, even though I know I shouldn't. Silent tears stream down my face. I let myself be held by this man. His large hand cups the back of my head, stroking my hair gently. I don't care that he's probably making it frizzy, or messing with the loose side braid I have it in. I only care about the way I react to him.

I sense a loss of control around him, and yet, he grounds me, all at once. His other hand is around my shoulders, pulling me into his chest. My own arms lift from my sides, wrapping around his soft torso, and pulling myself even tighter against him.

It's one of those moments where you don't realize what you need until you have it. Apparently, I really needed a hug.

He holds me until the silent, soul shaking tears stop. In all reality, I don't even think the tears were from today. I think it was a combination of the last few years of my life.

When I drop my arms from him, he slowly steps back. "Better?" he asks.

I nod, because while I do feel immensely better, now, the embarrassment starts to creep in. "Sorry," I say, taking a few rapid steps back, my heels clicking on the stone floor.

"Don't be. We all have to let out a little emotion sometimes," he replies, shoving his hands back into his pockets and rocking on his heels.

"Do you?" I ask before I can think twice. "Let your emotions out, I mean."

Jason seems indifferent to the question. He doesn't answer right away, then shrugs. "Haven't found a way to let it out yet."

"You should," I say, as if I've found a healthy way to let out my emotions that doesn't include hugging the man I definitely shouldn't have tingly feelings for. Jason looks up at me. Our eyes lock, his brown eyes burning with something so intense, I can't seem to name it. He takes a step toward me, and I step back, giving him more room. Only he follows. He reaches out, grasping my wrist in his warm, rough hand. He pulls me back into him, making me stumble.

"The last time I felt relaxed, like I got my emotions out was at the hotel," he says so low that I have to strain to hear him. "I haven't felt that good in years, and I haven't felt it since that weekend."

I gasp at his admission. "We..." I swallow thickly. "Jason," I say, his name coming out soft and strained, not at all confident.

Neither of us are looking at each other, avoiding gazes like we'll be scorched if we catch the other's eye. I'm hit with a wave of heat, a tension that crackles between us, and I can't take it. I glance up, and so does Jason.

Our eyes meet, and something snaps. I'm lunging back into his arms, this time, my arms flying up and around his neck. His hands cup my face, and our lips crash together in an anguished kiss.

I press my body as close as possible to him. My heart pounds rampantly in my chest, like it's trying to burst out of my skin to get even close to him. The last time we kissed doesn't even compare to this one. Jason is pouring his emotions into this, and maybe I am too, but I can't get enough.

My hips move, pushing up against his hard groin. Jason grunts against my lips. "Fuck, sunshine."

I bite down on his bottom lip at the nickname, prompting him to groan, low and long. His chest rumbles, tickling my skin. Jason moves his hands that are cupping my face, one down to slowly wrap around my neck, the other to rest on my hip. He breaks the kiss for only a moment, moving down to kiss along my jaw.

I gasp when his hand around my throat tightens in the slightest. I can still breathe, but it's like he wants me to know he's there. The hand on my hip tightens, gripping the love handle I secretly hate and wish I could change, but he's gripping me like he can't get enough of me. It makes me start to love it, knowing he loves it.

He groans, shifting his hips so his hardening cock presses against me. "Jase," I breathe, my head falling back. I'm floating, falling into nothing.

Hearing his name, he pulls back completely, dropping his hand from my throat. I think he's going to put a stop to this, and I nearly whimper. My panties are growing wetter by the second, my tummy swooping with each second that passes. Instead of calling it off, he pushes me back against a wall of barrels.

I let out a small shriek, and Jason silences me with his mouth, his tongue pressing between my lips. He stops his kiss for only a moment, and I'm confused when he bends down, his head level with my chest. Both hands on my hips, he traces down, bending until his hands are at the backs of my thighs.

He pulls me up and into his arms, my legs flying up and latching around his waist. "Jason!" I shriek, and he kisses me again.

"Quiet, sunshine," he growls.

"Put me down," I whisper angrily. He can't hold me like this.

"No," he simply replies. I pant against his mouth, so focused on clutching to his shirt in case he drops me. Brad would never have even tried to lift me during sex, let alone hold me while he kisses me like I'm the only person in the world.

His cock presses against my slick panties, and he thrusts, giving me the smallest amount of friction. "I need more," I whimper against his mouth.

Jason shifts, pushing me back against one of the sturdy barrels that are firmly held on shelves against the wall. My ass, covered by my panties and pink wrap dress, now rests on the very edge of one of the large wooden barrels.

With one hand, Jason hooks my right thigh higher, and pushes the other off his hip, opening me to him. My heeled foot is tall enough that the ball of my foot steadies me on the ground. Jason's brown eyes are dilated, the black of his pupil nearly as wide as the iris. I nod when I see his searching gaze, and his fingers reach for the hem of my soft cotton thong, pulling it off my pussy and to the side.

His fingers trail up through my core, sending a shiver through my body. This was so unexpected. I came down here to take a breath, and now Jason's fingers are sliding through my soaked pussy.

One tentative finger presses inside me, and I drop my head back against the barrel with a dull *thud*. Jason plunges in and out of me, his thumb finding my clit and circling it at a leisurely pace. I try to shift and get more, more pressure, more *everything*, but he doesn't let me. "Don't move," he murmurs, bending in to kiss me. "I've got you, sunshine. I'll get you where you need to be."

I trust his words implicitly. He adds a second finger, and the added pressure is wonderful. His fingers are long and thick, and add in his thumb on my clit, and I'm close to a life altering orgasm in mere minutes. Wetness coats Jason's fingers and hands, and while I hurtle toward a release, I also can't wait to experience the fullness of his length inside me. I didn't get that last time, only had him in my hand. I need it this time. He does too.

His mouth teases mine open, and fuck, he's such a good kisser. He tastes so good, always the hint of a flavor, though I can't quite grasp what it is. It's fruity, but also has the tang of something else.

With one more flick to my clit and thrust of his fingers, I'm sliding into my orgasm, my pussy clenching around him in a steady rhythm. I hold my breath so I don't scream and bite down on Jason's lip again. He kisses me through it, tangling our lips together until my orgasm is through. I take in a heavy breath once I'm convinced I won't scream out in ecstasy any more.

As soon as his fingers slide out of me, I'm using one hand to reach into his pants, the other still wrapped around him for balance. Jason reaches down too, unzipping his pants and helping me get his cock out. Wetness beads on the slit, his crown red and desperate for touch, friction, release.

I wrap my fingers around him, pumping a few times to give him some sort of relief. Gently, I pull him by his cock so he's closer to me, closer to my drenched pussy that needs him.

He hesitates for a moment, and I fear we've gone too far.

"Are you ready for this?" he asks, his voice eager and yearning, pulling me from my fear.

"So ready," I murmur, trailing my hand up his neck to thread in his hair and kiss him roughly. He lines his erection up, and presses gently in.

That's the last of the gentleness, though. Once he's inside me, he thrusts hard, jolting my body with the motion. He fills me up so deeply that I'm fuller than I ever have before. I use my leg still around his hip to pull him tighter, and my hands around his shoulders hold me steady.

One of his hands is still wrapped under my thigh, the other sliding up my torso to cup my breasts. He squeezes as he pounds in and out of me. I breathe heavily, the movements of his body inside me almost euphoric.

"Oh, god," I mewl. Jason tugs at the bow around my waist, pulling the wrap dress apart to get a glimpse at my chest. I'm in a simple black bra, but that doesn't stop him from looking at my breasts like they're the greatest things he's ever seen. He yanks one cup down, freeing my boob and tweaking the hard nipple between his fingers. I gasp, throwing my head back again. I'm going to have a headache after hitting my head on this freaking barrel so many times. *Worth it.*

After turning my nipple to a pointed peak, he frees my other breast, repeating the motions until my nipples tingle with every tease.

I'm about to lose my mind with pleasure. I don't think I'll come again, but having him inside me is so fucking good. Jason must know I'm close to screeching, because he moves his hand from my breast, up to wrap his fingers around my neck again. He squeezes so gently, a warning. I do my best to stifle my cries.

His eyes stare down at mine in question, checking to

make sure he hasn't crossed a boundary. "Don't stop," I breathe in an answered whisper. "More."

Jason's fingers tighten ever so slightly, still not enough to cut off any air supply, but it helps to hold in my moans of pleasure. His thrusts become harder, less rhythmic as he gets closer to his orgasm.

"Fuck, you feel so good, sunshine," he groans, kissing me again. "You want me to come? You want to see what you do to me?"

"Yes," I say, trying to contain my cries. He tenses his fingers around my throat in a warning. I nod, and he moves with me.

"That's my girl," he praises, and a gush of wetness pours out of me. He thrusts a few more times, and I know he's about to come.

The sound of a creaking door pulls us out of our crazed moment. A voice calls down the long stairway, echoing into the cellar. "Fallon? Are you down there?"

Josie. Of course she would come looking for me.

I squeak and start to panic. Jason's eyes widen, and when I hear the first step of Josie's feet on the stone stairs, I wrap my fingers around Jason's wrist, yanking his fingers from my throat and covering his own mouth with his hand.

"I'm fine!" I call, begging silently that she doesn't come to investigate. Jason adjusts us, and that's when his cock jerks inside me. Hot spurts of warmth fill me, and slowly drip out of my pussy as Jason shudders around me. His brows furrow in pleasure, and I drop my head back onto the barrel yet again. "Did you just cum?" I whisper.

Jason nods with a grimace, and slides his still hard cock out of me, his release dripping as he does. I internally groan, knowing this is going to be a hassle to clean. I'm going to have to book it to the bathroom.

I hoist my tits back into my bra, and work on righting my dress. I scramble off the barrel, both feet now firmly on the floor. Jason tucks his cock back into his pants, his eyes searching the room, hopefully looking for a towel or something to clean us up with.

"Are you sure? It's been a while," Josie calls.

"Fine! I needed a minute to breathe. I'll be right up," I yell.

"Okay. Things are okay up here," she reassures. "So if you need another minute... let me know?" she says as a question.

"I will, thanks, Josie!"

Her next question causes me to internally combust. "Have you seen Jason anywhere? Laila is here and has a question for him."

I freeze in my tracks, a chill running through my body. "Um, nope!" I try to keep my voice level, but it cracks. *Fuck.*

Josie's perceptive enough that she'll figure it out. If she didn't already assume he was down here, she knows for sure he is now. Especially after that FaceTime at the hotel, she has to think something is up between us now.

I glance behind me, my cheeks flaming red, to find Jason shoving himself into his pants. He shimmies to adjust himself, and I fling my gaze anywhere but at his still hard dick.

Did we really just fuck in the wine cellar? Oh, fuck me.

23

JASON

Josie's not going to let this go. I can already tell. She knew I was down here. I literally asked her if she'd seen Fallon, and she was more than happy to direct me to her. She's such a little shit. She and Andrew really are the perfect match, because this is exactly the type of shit he would do.

I look up at the ceiling for a moment, praying my dick softens sooner rather than later. It's currently throbbing against the zipper of my jeans, still reeling after the best orgasm I've had since... well since the hotel with Fallon. I glance around again to look for a towel, and find one against the far wall. I head over to grab it, and make my way back to Fallon.

She's standing where I left her, trying to right herself in her dress. "Stop," I murmur. Somehow, she's got everything even more twisted than it was before. I use the towel to clean between her thick thighs, swiping the fabric delicately, hoping to get as much of my cum from her as I can so she isn't too much of a mess.

Once that's done, I drop the towel to the ground for

now and reach out, untying the bow she haphazardly placed at her waist, and open the dress. With it completely open, I get a glimpse at her full figure, something I haven't seen completely before. When we were in the hotel, she was covered from the waist up, and earlier, I only uncovered her breasts and her pussy.

She's beautiful. Her stomach is soft and dimpled, and a few stretch marks linger from her pregnancy. My fingers itch to reach out and trace the marks, but I don't. I've wanted to see what was beneath her clothes for so long, that this feels like a dream, making my head hazy. Her hips have the perfect amount to grab onto, something I was all too happy to do mere minutes ago. I adjust her dress to cover her again and tie the bow, making sure her cleavage isn't showing too much. Then, I reach up and fix her braid, making sure her hair isn't too much of a mess.

Once there isn't a single hair out of place, I slide my hands down her body, over her breasts and stomach to rest on those hips again. "There. That's better." Fallon winces, and I pause, realizing what I've said. "Not that I want you covered up, sunshine. Fuck, I wish I could unwrap you again, but that's only for me. No one else gets to see what's mine."

"Yours?" she hesitantly asks. I shouldn't have said that, because in reality, she can't be. But my stupid brain got ahead of me. I don't say anything, and Fallon nods. "Right," she murmurs. "Thanks, Jason."

I can see the look of disappointment on her face. I don't trust my voice, so I nod, shifting my asshole demeanor back into place.

Fallon steps back, and leaves the wine cellar, her heels clicking against the tile stairs, the sound echoing with each step until it ceases all together.

When I know she's gone, I kick at one of the walls, my irritation with myself growing. I shouldn't have even come down here in the first place. Clearly, I can't be trusted when it comes to Fallon Douglas. I can't be alone with her and not lose myself in her, in that easy smile I'd do anything to be on the receiving end of.

Now that I've been inside of her though, I fear I'm not going to be able to hold back. Her warmth around me, her slick heat clenching around my cock with each thrust? Fuck, it's enough to make me nearly finish in my pants, something that clearly wasn't able to happen before.

I give myself time to wallow in my irritation with myself, because I let her walk away. While cleaning myself up, I realize something huge. I didn't use a condom. Fuck, do I even have condoms? If I do, they'll surely be expired. I need to talk to Fallon, apologize for my carelessness. I take a deep breath before heading back up the stairs to rejoin the real world.

When I make it up the stairs, Josie is standing at the bar, talking with Laila and Nora. She spots me, and a devilish grin appears on her face. That little shit.

"Hey, big brother," she says with a smile when I approach.

"Josie," I greet.

"Did you find Fallon?" she asks, her face a mask of total innocence.

"Nope," I lie, avoiding all eye contact and glancing around the room. I find myself unintentionally looking for her, and snap my eyes back to the bar, to anything but the beautiful girl with the honey blonde hair and green eyes that suck me in without even trying.

"Hmm. I could have sworn I saw you follow her into the wine cellar, but maybe I was wrong."

"You were wrong," I say through gritted teeth.

"You know it's not a bad thing if you and Fallon... explore whatever is between you, right?" Josie states, already striding away from me.

I try not to let my thoughts stray, knowing I can't get into this right now. "What's up?" I ask Nora and Laila as I step behind the bar.

Laila raises her pierced eyebrow at me. "I have no idea. You told me to come here for a meeting. Is there a meeting?"

From the corner of my eye I spot Fallon talking to a client. She has a sweet smile on her face. She nods along to something she says, and I rip my gaze from her. I need to stop searching for her in every room.

"Hey, boss?" Nora's voice thankfully distracts me.

I turn to her and respond, "Yeah?"

"Not to be... rude, but, what are we doing here?"

I raise my brow. "What do you mean?"

She shrugs. "Well, we could have met at the brewery if you wanted to have a meeting. We have a really good system now for the events, and we don't have to meet here for meetings." Her eyes widen as something else occurs to her. "Unless of course you want to, then that's fine. You know what? Forget I said anything." Nora's cheeks heat in embarrassment.

"Nora, you're fine," I tell her. "I guess I have been wanting to make sure this transition is going well."

Laila, ever the instigator, feigns a coughing spell. "*Fallon,*" she says through her fake cough.

Nora's brows raise. "Ohhh, I see."

"Stop it," I say through gritted teeth, pointing a finger at my best employees. "She has nothing to do with it."

"Sure," Laila says in a teasing lilt. "Whatever you say. I see the way you watch her."

I groan. "I don't watch her."

Nora smiles. "I cannot believe I didn't put two and two together. It makes so much sense now."

"And their girls love each other. When Lennie was in the brewery the other day, she was telling me all about how they're going to go to the zoo soon! It's adorable."

"Stop," I mutter. "You two are lucky I need you, or I'd be firing your asses."

"You would never," Laila says. She's worked for me for years now, and has become absolutely invaluable to me. She's my right-hand-gal, and I owe her a lot of the success we've had.

"You're right, but still. Nothing is going on between us," I lie. The lie is bitter on my tongue, and they see right through me.

The girls are looking behind me at someone, and somehow, I know it's her. Sure enough, when I turn, Fallon is striding up to the bar, client in tow.

"Hey guys," she greets. "This is Kay. She's wondering if she can do a taste test since you're here."

"Of course." I offer her my hand, and give her a professional shake. "What are you thinking?" I explain what we have to offer, and am pleased when she picks one of our top brews.

We get her squared away, and I decide maybe it's best for me to go. But first, I need to talk to Fallon. I shouldn't, but I'd rather talk to her in person about the condom situation, and our upcoming plans with the girls.

Fallon is in the zone, barely even seeing me as I reach out to grab her arm. "Hey," I say when she is pulled to a stop by me.

"Oh, hey," she says, her cheeks pinkening as she looks

up at me, clearly remembering our activities not even an hour ago. "What's up?"

I clear my throat and lower my voice while leaning in closer to her ear. "I didn't wear a condom. I needed you to know that... I'm clean. I—it's been a long time."

When I lean back, her cheeks are bright red. If anyone were to look over at us, surely they would suspect something is happening between us. Fallon nods. "I have an IUD. It's okay. And... I'm clean too. I got checked after the divorce. And I haven't been with anyone else."

I let out a relieved sigh. Guilt swarms me, knowing I even put her in that position of concern. I should have been paying more attention, should have had the forethought to think of her before sticking my dick inside of her, but when it comes to Fallon, I lose all rational thought.

I clear my throat and change the subject. "Are we taking the girls to the zoo next week?"

"Yes!" Instantly, she's pulling her phone out, looking at her calendar. "Is that okay?"

"Definitely," I say. "Lennie has been bugging me to come with her, so I figure now is the best time."

"Agreed," she says. "Would Wednesday work?"

With a glance at my own calendar, I nod my agreement. "It's a date," I confirm, and immediately regret my choice of words. "Not a date, it's a..." I trail off, trying to hide my idiocy.

"I know what you mean, Jase," Fallon says, though she's actively avoiding my eyes.

"I, uh," I clear my throat. "I'll text you later for timing and such. Sound good?"

"Peachy," Fallon squeaks, and shoves her phone into a pocket of her dress. Huh, that's neat. Didn't know her dress had pockets.

"About earlier—" I try to bring it up again, but she holds up a hand.

"It's fine, Jase. We don't have to talk about it. If anything, maybe we... shouldn't talk about it." Her green eyes are looking at anything but me.

"Okay," I say, and then without another word, I wave goodbye and head out the door. I need to get out of here before I do something I shouldn't.

24

———

FALLON

"Mom, where is my sparkly scrunchie?" Presley calls from the bathroom.

"In the drawer with all your hair things," I call back to her. I'm staring into my closet, trying to find something to wear to the zoo today. It's nearly one hundred degrees, plus humidity and it's only going to get hotter as the day goes on.

I thought about rescheduling, but something about spending the day with Jason and his daughter, only the four of us, with no interruptions, seemed too good to pass up. Presley's friend, Natalie, was supposed to come, but her family went out of town this week. I have on a pair of comfy jean shorts and am debating on a tank top to wear. It shouldn't be this hard of a decision, he's seen me naked, but yet, I can't help but overthink it.

I throw my hair up into a ponytail, knowing I'll need it up and off my neck today.

"Mommy!" Presley calls, and I pick the first tank top I see, a powder blue one and slide on my comfortable shoes, knowing I need practical over cute shoes today for footwear.

"Coming," I call.

When I reach the bathroom, Pres is running a brush through her dirty blonde hair. "Can you braid my hair?" she asks.

"Sure, honey. What do you think about a French braid into a ponytail so it's off your neck? I don't want you to get too hot today," I offer, hoping it's a fair compromise.

"Yes!" she heartily agrees. "But only if we use my purple sparkly ponytail. I want to match my purple tank top." She points to the purple top she's wearing with Disney Princesses on it.

"You got it, sweetie."

Ten minutes later, her hair is braided and ready to go. I brush my teeth and swipe a few coats of mascara onto my lashes. My phone buzzes in my back pocket with a text from Jason, telling me he's here. I shoo Presley out the door and grab the bag I packed with our water bottles, snacks, and extra sunscreen before locking the front door behind myself.

Jason's SUV is parked in the driveway of my townhome, and he must have seen Presley's booster seat sitting in front of the garage door, because he's helping her get buckled.

The sun is beating down on my skin already, and I'm grateful I thought to put a layer of sunscreen on us already. I push my sunglasses off my head and down over my eyes to block out some of the harsh sun.

"Hey," I greet Jason when I reach the passenger side back door. He's buckled Presley in, and she and Lennie are already happily chattering. "Thanks for buckling her in," I say.

"No problem," he replies. "Ready?"

"Yep." I climb into Jason's passenger seat, and Jason closes the door behind me. It's stupid really, but the simple action is enough to give me butterflies. It's not something Brad ever did for me.

When Jason climbs into the air conditioned vehicle, I notice he wipes a drop of sweat off his brow. "Are you sure we shouldn't go to the beach, or reschedule?"

He glances over at me. "It's really up to you. I've got enough water to hydrate ten people, but if you don't want to go, we don't have to."

I shake my head. "No, it's fine. If anything, we can go to the inside exhibits if we get too hot."

"Exactly. It will be alright," he says. The girls in the backseat are totally oblivious to our conversation, only talking about which animals they're excited to see.

Jason reverses out of my driveway, and we start the drive in silence. I don't exactly know what to talk to him about, seeing as every conversation with us leads to something deeper and I'm not sure I'm ready for that so early in the day.

"Miss Fallon," Lennie says, pulling my attention to her. "Are you married?"

I swallow thickly. "Um, no, Lennie, I'm not. Why?" I ask.

"I think you should marry my daddy."

I nearly choke on the spit in my mouth, and cough.

Jason sighs. "Lennie, we talked about this."

I shift in my seat to look back at her. "That's really sweet that you want me to marry your daddy." I can't say anything else, because I'm being interrupted by both girls.

"Then we could be sisters," Presley chimes.

"And you could be my mom!" Lennie yells.

I don't know what to say. I look to Jason for help, but he apparently doesn't know what to say either. I guess the girls have been plotting against us for a while. Well, I guess I get to be the one to break their hearts. "I know you two would love for us to get married, but we are only friends. Friends don't really get married. People who are in love get married, like your Uncle Andrew and Auntie Josie," I say to Lennie, hoping an example will help.

"Or my Uncle Beau and Auntie Marley? Are they in love?" she asks.

"Yes they are," I agree, thankful she's getting it. "And maybe soon they'll get married." If the text I received from Beau earlier this week is any hint, I'm thinking it will happen sooner rather than later.

"Auntie Megan and Uncle Isaac got married too, Mom," Presley pipes in.

"Yes, they did, because they're in love." I need to veer this conversation away before we get into the territory of why I'm not still married. "What animals do you guys want to see first?" I ask, and thankfully, that helps to change the conversation.

In their own world again, I shift so I'm facing forward in the seat. Jason glances over at me.

"Good job," he says, and I raise my brows.

"You weren't much help," I tease.

He shrugs, an apologetic look crossing his face. "Sorry. I was trying to come up with something, but you beat me."

"Right." I give him a gentle shove on the shoulder. "Well if it happens again, it's all you, buddy."

We pull into the parking lot of the zoo, and for it being so hot, it's still quite busy. We find a parking spot and get the girls out, grabbing our bags and a few extra water bottles to throw in the bags.

I slather sunscreen on Presley, and Jason does the same to Lennie, and ten minutes later, we are walking into the zoo entrance.

Once we've paid, the girls are already pointing out the

exhibits they want to see. The decision is made to see the monkeys first, so we head in that direction.

Jason and I walk side by side in silence, and as the minutes pass on, the awkward tension grows. In college, I never felt the need to fill the silence with him, but for some reason, I do now. Though, before I can think of something to ask him, Jason speaks.

"Can I ask you something? You don't have to answer, I guess I'm curious."

"What's up?"

"I've heard bits and pieces, but I wanted to see if you'd be willing to tell me the story of why you moved here?" He sounds so tentative, so worried, that I immediately want to open up and tell him everything, something that is no easy feat for me.

"I can. It's really not all that great of a story to be honest. Long story short, Presley and I needed a fresh start."

"That must be the super condensed version."

"It is."

"Tell me the rest of it."

"You really don't want to hear that whole sob story."

His eyes grow serious as he looks at me. His tone gives no hint of argument when he says, "I really do."

"Alright, well you might want to buckle in, cause you're in for a bumpy ride."

"I'm ready," he offers.

"Obviously, you know I got married. After college, I started working as an executive assistant in the Cities, and Brad and I were happy, well, at least what I thought was happy. I got pregnant with Presley not long after, and things were still good. As soon as she hit two, we decided to start trying for our second."

Jason is nodding, not saying anything, but also showing

me he's still listening. I continue the story, telling him how I had trouble getting pregnant for years, and things started to get strained, but then as soon as we stopped trying, things were better. When I get to the part about finding out I was pregnant again, I see the slight twist of agony appear on his face. It doesn't take much to know something happened. I don't have two kids running around the zoo today with us.

"I had a miscarriage when I was barely over eight weeks pregnant. Brad was on what I thought was a business trip to Orlando, but I hadn't heard from him outside of a few random texts." I take a deep breath. "In reality, I don't know where he was. Still don't. He left me. Took me and Presley off the insurance plan, which I found out while I was in the hospital having a procedure for the miscarriage. He stopped by the house the day after I was in the hospital, told me he was done, he'd met someone else. It's not something I like to remember, but he said some pretty awful things to me, and about me. He left without saying goodbye to Presley, and I got the divorce papers in the mail a week later."

I don't risk glancing over to Jason, afraid of what I might see. Surely, there will be pity, that's usually what happens when people hear what happened, but I'm afraid there might be something more there. Something I don't know if I'm ready to see from him.

The girls lead us into the aquarium section of the zoo, and I'm thankful for a reprieve from the sun. "Mom, look at this fish!" Presley shouts, pointing at a gruesome looking fish.

After I tell her how cool the fish is, I call both her and Lennie over to drink some water. We reapply sunscreen to the girls before heading back outside. The inside break is short lived, and both girls are ready to see the zebras.

Jason still hasn't said a word about the demise of my

marriage, and I'm not quite sure *what* he could say. I get over myself for a moment and glance up at him. Sweat is beading on his brow, same as my own, but the shade from his baseball hat is preventing me from seeing his eyes.

"Fuck," he murmurs under his breath. His brows furrow and he stares down at the ground. "I don't even know what to say, Fallon. Sorry probably doesn't quite cut it."

I shrug, doing my best to keep my face passive. "Thanks. I'm doing better now. It was rough for a while, but now that I'm settled here, and have my mom close by, things are good."

"I'm glad you're here, even if I want to break Brad's nose for the way he treated you," he says, and I can't help but look at him again. He's looking down at me, those brown eyes so full of emotion because of me.

"I'm glad I am too." My chest almost seems lighter after telling him. Sure, he knew the basics of my story, but being the one to get it all out in the open, to give him that piece of me, it's cathartic.

The girls are both red faced as they point and croon over the zebras, so I offer them more water, making sure they both drink a good amount, and even go as far as putting some on the back of their necks to help cool them down. We definitely won't be here much longer. The heat is getting to me and I'm not running around the way they are.

We take another break inside, and I sit down on one of the benches by the penguin exhibit. Jason stands behind the girls, pointing out one of the smaller penguins up in the corner, lifting each of them so they can see it.

He's such an amazing dad. He even reminds me of my own father when he was alive. He treats his daughter with the utmost care and love. It makes me grieve for my own father, and wish he was around to see my daughter, to give me a hug and tell me I'm doing right by her, that she's going to be okay even though she doesn't have a dad. Once you get past Jason's hard exterior, he's like a soft marshmallow inside. He loves his family so fiercely, and would do anything for them.

I also know that if I let myself, I could fall for Jason Cunningham, even harder than I already have. That realization burrows its claws into my chest. Heavy and unforgiving. Because that's the reality of it all. No matter what I say about the bullshit of being friends, I want more, crave it. Crave the comfort he brings me, the same comfort he did back in college.

The heaviness in my gut spreads through my body, making me lightheaded. The heat is doing wild things to me. That's all this is. *Right?* My heart pounds rapidly, and suddenly, I can't catch my breath.

I look to where Jason stands with the girls, holding each of their hands, and there's that apprehension again. Out of control. Leaning back into the metal bench, I try to get myself together, but it's no luck. Jason turns, catching my eye with a soft smile, and I try to smile back, but I'm sure it looks more like a grimace.

He furrows his brows when he sees me, and tugs the girls away from the penguins, heading over to me.

"Fallon?" His concern is evident in his tone. "Are you okay?"

I lift my hand in a wave. "Oh, yes, fine."

He doesn't buy it.

"Mommy, are you okay?" my daughter asks, and I nod. My mouth has gone so dry I physically can't form the words. Have I been drinking water? My skin is clammy, and I'm totally out of sorts.

"Shit," Jason mutters, dropping the girls' hands, and

rushing to my side at the bench. "Have you been drinking enough water?"

I nod, but I'm not really all that sure. My hands are shaking as I try to reach out for Presley, but I can't move any more.

Jason pulls my water bottle from the pocket of our bag, handing it to me right away. "Drink, slowly," he says, and I hold the heavy bottle in my hands. I sip the cool water, letting it soothe the dryness consuming me.

Jason takes his hat off, and starts waving it in front of me, giving me a semi-cool breeze on my clammy face. It's nice. He then digs into his bag, grabbing an extra shirt of Lennie's. He takes his own water from the bag, and douses a corner of the shirt in water before pushing my ponytail to the side and dabbing the back of my neck. The cool fabric helps immensely. "Keep drinking, but not too fast," Jason keeps saying, asking me over and over if I'm alright, if I think I'm going to pass out or not.

I shake my head every time. I don't think I'll pass out, but I guess you never really know for sure. I glance up to my daughter and nearly cry at the sight. She looks utterly terrified, and Lennie is standing at her side.

Presley is trying not to cry, and Lennie is holding her hand, her face as scared as Presley's. "I'm okay," I repeat, trying to reassure her. "Come here, sweetie." I reach out to her and she rushes to my side, sitting on my left, while Jason is on my right. He's still dabbing at my neck, my forehead, my cheeks, my chest, everywhere with the wet fabric.

We sit on the bench for a long time while Jason makes sure I'm rehydrating and cooling down. In between waving the hat in my face, he's also making sure the girls and himself are drinking water. Thankfully, no one seems to have noticed us in this little corner, or if they have, they've ignored us.

Once I'm doing better, no longer shaking or light-headed, I stop Jason from waving his hat. "I'm better, prom-ise." He raises his brow in question, and I nod. "Really. I'm good. Thank you."

He leans back into the bench, and puts his hat back on, only this time, he puts it on backwards, and shit. It's like he's trying to make me have a flashback to college. That damned hat. He used to wear one nearly every day, and it was almost rare to see him without it. It almost looks better now than it did back then.

"Should we go home?" Jason asks, and I glance down at both the girls. I don't want to cut the day short, but also, I definitely don't want to go back into the heat for a long time.

They're both nodding before I can even say anything, and I'm grateful for it. "You three stay here," Jason says, his eyes darting from me to the exit. "I'll go start the truck and pull it around. I'll text you when to start coming to the entrance."

I agree, grateful for him. The thought of climbing into a burning hot vehicle right now sounds like my worst night-mare. The girls and I stay on the bench, watching the penguins play and splash around their space, and within ten minutes, there's a text from Jason telling us to head to the entrance.

I gather the girls and we walk hand in hand through the zoo. It's still as disgustingly hot, but now that I have some water in me, I'm not quite as sick. Jason's waiting for us in his truck at the entrance as promised, and he opens the passenger door for me, helping me in and closing the door before helping the girls get buckled in. My heart pitter-patters in my chest at the sweetness of it all. He didn't have to help me into the car, I'm perfectly capable, but he did anyway.

Jason gets in the driver's seat, and takes a deep, long, breath. As he exhales, he looks over to me. The girls are in their own world, talking about all the animals, so they aren't paying us any mind.

"You're okay?" he asks me, his tone questioning and unsure.

"Yes." I reach over to rest my hand on top of his. "I promise. I'm really sorry. I should have taken better care of myself. I was so focused on the girls, I forgot about myself."

Jason's eyes are narrowed as he looks over again. "You can't do that, Fallon. I get you were taking care of the girls, but you have to take care of yourself too."

"I know," I reply. "You're right."

"You scared the shit out of me," he says with a lowered voice so the girls don't hear him curse.

My throat thickens and I swallow hard, trying to get rid of the lump that's appeared. "I'm sorry, Jason. I'm better now. I'll relax once you drop us off, and everything will be fine."

He doesn't reply as he looks away and shifts the truck into gear and drives us away from the zoo. His fingers are clenched tight around the steering wheel during the entire drive, and he doesn't say another word to me. He's frustrated with me, I can tell.

We pull into my driveway, and Jason unbuckles, surprising me. "What are you doing?" I ask as I unbuckle myself.

He ignores me, shifting his body backwards to speak to the girls. "Girls, head inside. Lennie, we're going to play here for a while."

The girls squeal in delight and quickly unbuckle and

run to the front door. I glance over at Jason, my eyes wide. "You can't be alone right now," is the only explanation he gives me. "Keys," he says, holding out his palm. I hand him my house keys, and he turns off the truck, climbing out and grabbing the bags from the back seat. Slowly, I follow him, completely at a loss.

I know he's probably stressed I almost passed out, but I'm fine now. There's no reason for him to stick around if he's mad at me. Brad used to stick the knife in and twist it every time he was upset with me, and make the argument drag on for much longer than it needed to. I don't want that now. I want to relax.

I follow him into my house, and the cool air is incredible. I do a quick glance around to make sure it's at least semi-clean, and thankfully, there isn't any dirty laundry in the living room, or unwashed dishes on the counter.

Jason walks through the house with purpose, as if it's not his first time here, and heads straight to the kitchen.

"What are you doing?" I ask as I rush to follow him.

"Getting them a snack. Go take a shower." His voice is clipped, and he still won't look at me as he searches through my fridge. "You still need to cool down, and a shower will help you feel better."

"I'm fine, Jason," I reply. "I can do this, go relax."

He shakes his head, not meeting my eyes yet again. "Fallon, go." When he finally looks at me for the first time since we pulled away from the zoo, there's a mix of stress and emotion all over his face. "I've got the girls for a little bit. Please."

"O-Okay," I stammer, turning and leaving the kitchen. "Call me if you need anything?"

He agrees, and I head down the hall to my bathroom, turning the shower on. He's right, I still am overheated, despite the water and sitting in the cool car. And I probably stink from all the sweat.

I take a quick, cool shower, not bothering to do much besides rinse myself and wash my sweaty hair. When I'm dressed in fresh clothes, my hair towel-dried, I head back to the sound of happy, squealing voices.

I'm shocked when I round the corner into the living room at what I see, though. The girls are dressed up in Presley's princess gowns, with plastic tiaras on their heads, and clip-on earrings and necklaces adorning their skin.

That's not what's jarring, though. No, it's Jason. He's sitting next to them with his own tiara and earrings. I notice the game board in the middle of them, and realize they are playing "Pretty Pretty Princess." It was my favorite game as a kid, and my mom still had my old game from when I was young. We had to replace some of the jewelry and add a few crowns, but the game was still intact, so I took it when Presley was old enough to play. She absolutely loves it, and clearly, Lennie does too.

Before they realize I'm here, I whip my phone out, snapping a few photos. It's an adorable sight, and proves even more how much of an amazing dad Jason is. When he spots me, he immediately stands, telling the girls to keep playing and he'll be right back. He strides toward me, turning me and placing his hand at the base of my spine, leading me into the kitchen.

Once we're in the quiet of the kitchen, he spins me around to face him. "How are you feeling?"

"Better," I reply. "The shower helped. Thank you. You don't have to stick around, I promise I'm good now. It was a fluke."

Jason sighs heavily, and tilts his head back. With the

motion, he realizes he still has the tiara on his head, and quickly removes it, as well as the earrings.

"Why do you seem so frustrated with me? I'm fine," I say, taking a deep breath.

"You're not fine. You should be more careful." His voice is tight, like he's trying to hold back something he's feeling, something I can't quite place.

"Where is this coming from? Jason, what is going on? I told you, I'm fine." I reach out, trying to grasp his arm, but he shakes his head.

"I can't bear the thought of something bad happening to you, Fallon. What if I wasn't there today?"

"Jason, it was an accident." I am trying to understand what is going through his brain right now, but if he won't let me in, how am I supposed to know? "It was ninety-five degrees out today. I could have been doing everything right, staying hydrated and cool, and I still could have passed out. It's not my fault. Why are you reacting like this? You took care of me. I'm fine. The girls are fine. We had a fun day, and the girls are happy."

Jason turns, resting both his hands on the countertop, his head bowing between his shoulders as he takes a deep breath.

25

JASON

The bone deep fear that is seated in my body isn't going away. Fallon is safe. She's standing in front of me now, and is breathing and talking. I shouldn't be reacting like this, but it's like some sort of response in my brain, and I'm reacting on auto-pilot.

I let out a weary sigh. I know I have to tell her, it's the only way I can explain my reaction to her in a way that makes sense. I don't look over, but I know she's still standing there, waiting for an explanation from me.

"Seeing you, sitting on that bench, pale with your eyes glazed over, brought back some really bad memories for me," I state, bile rising in my throat as the memories assault my brain.

Fallon doesn't speak, giving me the time I need to get the words out.

"I'm not sure how much you know about Talia, but she was a drug addict. Off and on throughout the years we were together, she would use. One night, I got home from work, and she was sitting on the couch. Her eyes were completely empty of emotion, her face a shade of white I'd never seen on her before. She was swaying back and forth, her high in full swing. Things were still newer with us, and I'd never seen her high like that before. Sure, we'd smoked weed together before, but something told me this was more. In retrospect, I realize now she'd been using harder drugs for the entirety of our relationship, but until that point, I didn't put it together."

I can hear the sharp intakes of breath coming from Fallon. She takes a few steps toward me, and her small hand rests in the middle of my back, rubbing in soothing circles.

"She could barely string two words together, and then she'd passed out. I thought she'd fallen asleep, and then she started puking. I called 911, not sure what was happening, and Thomas was on duty, of course. I watched as my younger brother gave my girlfriend multiple doses of Narcan, trying to rouse her until paramedics arrived."

My arms shake. Watching my little brother try to save her life is something I'll never forget. "Only after the third dose did she start to wake and finally tell us what she had taken. When she admitted she tried heroin for the first time, I ran into the kitchen, and threw up in the sink. I was in such a state of shock."

"It wasn't your fault, Jason," Fallon says quietly. I shake my head. No, it wasn't my fault, but could I have been the one to stop her? Could I have done more?

"I knew she drank heavily, and smoked a lot of weed, but heroin? That's something I never could have antici-pated. I rode with her in the ambulance, crying along with her as she apologized and promised to turn her life around and get help. She went to rehab the next morning."

I turn and face Fallon, showing her the grief that's

surely covering my face. This isn't how I wanted tonight to go, but I needed to tell her, it had to happen sooner or later. Fallon wraps her arms around my middle, and holds me in a tight hug. My arms reflexively surround her, breathing in her sweet perfume as I prepare to tell her the rest.

"After she came home sixty days later, she broke things off with me. We got back together a few months later, and the cycle continued. I never saw her OD again, but she wasn't clean. She'd end things with me when she would start using again, and after her second round of rehab, she vowed to stay clean. I don't want to say that Lennie was an accident. Maybe surprise is a better word, but we had gotten back together after one of our longest stretches apart. About a year and a half. I know how toxic it was, but I loved her. I thought I could fix her. Make her better. I thought I was enough. When I wasn't, and she found out she was pregnant, I thought maybe..." My voice cracks on the words. "Maybe the baby would be enough."

"She was a good mom, Fallon," I continue, taking a shaky breath. "In the first months we had Lennie, she was so good. Lennie was a good baby, but I think that's because Talia was such a natural. I know I say she was a bad mom, or imply it, but really, it's me being an asshole, mad she's gone. Mad my daughter doesn't have a mom, or that she left because drugs were more important than her. I never want Lennie to experience that. I will do whatever I can so my daughter never feels that way. I want her to have the most fulfilling life. I need her to know how loved she is, even if her mom couldn't stay."

I let out a long breath, thankful that Fallon let me get these words out. "I took out my resentment for her on you today, and I will never be able to say I'm sorry enough for it.

I have no excuse, other than I was scared, and that fear was enough to try to push you away. I can't even explain how sorry I am, Fallon. You didn't deserve my anger." I squeeze Fallon gently. "Please, know how sorry I am," I whisper in her ear.

26

FALLON

My mind whirs with all the information Jason shared. I knew he carried so much in his heart, in his mind, but I never realized the extent of it. I rest my head on his shoulder, holding him close to me. He is in so much pain, and I want to do what I can to ease it. I'm reminded by our time in college. This is that man. He still exists. The man who will fight tooth and nail to do what he can for his family, for those he loves. The man who doesn't shove down his emotions and pain so no one can see who he really is.

He finally looks at me. Our faces are so close I can see the wet streaks still on his cheeks and make out the small gold flecks in his chocolate brown eyes. I cup his jaw with my hand, swiping at his wet cheek again.

"You are an amazing dad. Lennie could not have lucked out anymore if she tried. It's horrible that Talia isn't here to see her daughter grow up, but addiction is a disease. She might want to be here, but she can't."

He nods into my palm.

"Tell me you believe me," I urge. "I need to hear you say those words, Jase."

"I'm a good dad," he responds, and it's so half-hearted.

"Not good enough," I tell him. "You need to believe it."

"I'm a good dad." This time, he says it with more gumption, and I can tell he's starting to believe me, and himself. Only then, he surprises me. "Your turn."

"Huh?" I ask, confused.

"Your turn," he repeats. "You're a good mom. Say it. Believe it."

I shake my head. "This wasn't about me." I lean back, my anxiety churning.

"No, but we're doing it anyway." Jason reaches forward, cupping the back of my neck, bringing my forehead to his. "Say you're a good mom."

I shake my head. The insecurity is burning a hole in my chest. "We're more similar than we think, you and me," I tell him instead.

"Sunshine," Jason uses that name again, his eyes no longer wet with tears, but glistening with a new determination. "Say it. I did. It's your turn."

"I'm a good mom." Like his first try, it's half-hearted. I shake my head right away, knowing it's not good enough. "I'm a good mom," I repeat, this time, slowly believing in myself. Believing him. Believing the words I made him say was one thing, but saying them about myself? It's hard. But I know it's true.

My daughter is happy. She is healthy. I am doing everything in my power to keep it that way. I should be reinforcing the boundary I've worked so hard to build between us, yet here I am, ready to use a sledgehammer to knock it down. I'm sick of fighting whatever this is. I'm so sick of it, so sick of trying to keep myself from him. It's making things harder in the long run. Why can't I be a good mom and also do something for myself? Why can't I be a good mom *and* have a partner?

The fear is still there. Presley had a father figure in her life, and he walked away without a second glance. What if it happens again? Will she be able to cope with it a second time? Can I open myself up to this and let the fear take a backseat? Can I risk both mine and my daughter's hearts for this?

"Fuck yeah, you are," Jason states, and he's shifting, cupping my face in his hands.

"Daddy?" A small voice calls from the living room.

"Coming!" he calls, but doesn't move. He holds me still, eyes locked on mine. Jase presses a long, lingering kiss to my lips, holding me close. Against my lips, he whispers, "I will make this up to you."

I nod against his forehead, wishing I could stay in his arms longer. Jason grabs his tiara and his necklace from the counter and heads into the living room, sitting down next to the squealing girls.

27

JASON

Once the many games of "Princess Pretty", or whatever it's called, is through, I risk a glance at Fallon. She's sitting on the couch behind us, chiming in and laughing at the girls as we play. I noticed her watching me a few times with a small smile on her face every time I earned another piece of jewelry. I wore each piece with pride. My phone says it's nearly six o'clock, and Lennie has started to complain about being hungry.

"Should we get home and make supper?" I ask Lennie, and of course, she frowns.

"No, Daddy," she pleads. "Can we please stay? I want to stay."

I shake my head. "Sweetie, we should go, we don't want to overstay our welcome."

"Actually," Fallon interjects from the couch. "I already ordered pizza. It should be here soon. I figured we could have a movie night."

"Really?" I ask, honestly a little surprised. After I spilled everything about Talia, I figured maybe Fallon would want some time by herself to process. It's a lot. I know that.

"Yeah." Her cheeks pinken. Her hair is dry now, and she's braided it while we played, so it's laying on one side of her neck. The same way it was when I fucked her in the wine cellar. "It should be here in about fifteen minutes."

The girls cheer in excitement. "Alright girls, can you please clean up the game and go wash up for supper?"

They agree, and start pulling off the plastic jewelry. "Presley, make sure you hang up your dresses in your closet nicely," Fallon directs.

I stand from the floor, stretching out my body, ignoring the ache in my back. Fallon heads into the kitchen, and I follow behind her like a lost puppy. She grabs paper plates from one of the cabinets, and a few glasses for her and I, and plastic cups for Lennie and Presley. She sets them on the counter, and I stand behind awkwardly.

"Can I help with anything?" I ask.

Fallon jumps, clutching her hand to her heart. Her chest heaves as she catches her breath, and I do my best not to notice the way her breasts rise and fall with each inhale. I fail.

"Sorry," I state, waving at her. "I should have announced my presence or something."

She chuckles. "It's okay. Um, can you bring these to the kitchen table, and I'll grab the juice and some fruit?"

"Sure," I say, grabbing the plates and cups from her. I set them out on the table, and there's a knock on the door. "I'll get it," I call, and head to the door. I grab the pizza boxes from the teenage kid and give him a cash tip from my wallet, and head back into the house, setting the boxes in the middle of the table.

"Come and eat," I call, and footsteps rush down the hall as the two young girls clamor to get to the table.

We eat, the girls talking non-stop about our day, and what they want to do on their next play date. All the while, I'm stealing glances across the table at Fallon. She's invested in the children's' conversations, offering interjections every so often. I note the hint of sadness in her eyes, and her avoidance of my gaze. Did I ruin this? Did I take something that hadn't even had the chance to start and taint it with my past trauma? I didn't want a relationship, not with her, nor anyone, and yet, here I am, stressed about ruining the possibility of something with her.

We finish eating, and the girls help us to clean and store the leftover pizza. We decide on a movie, and I whip together some "sprinkle popcorn" per the request of Lennie. Awkwardness settles on my skin once the movie ends, and I'm unsure of whether or not I should stick around, or if I should get Lennie packed up and out the door.

"Daddy, can we have a sleepover?" Lennie's voice pulls me out of my internal thoughts.

"I don't think so," I reply with a grimace.

"Pleeaaase," she whines. "Presley already asked me if I could, and we're going to listen really good I promise!"

I sigh, glancing over to Fallon. I'm not going to be the one to make this decision. If Lennie wants to stay over, I don't mind, but I really don't want her to feel like she has to say yes.

Fallon has a soft smile on her face. "If your dad says it's okay, then it's fine with me, Lennie."

"Really?" Lennie shrieks.

"Really," Fallon agrees. She glances over to me. "Jase?"

"It's fine with me if it's okay with you," I respond, leaving it ultimately her choice. "I can pick her up in the morning." Fallon nods. It's nearing eight now, and it's close to bedtime for them anyway. "I'll run home quickly and grab a few things for her?" I offer.

"No need," Fallon says, waving her hand. "We have plenty of extra pajamas she can wear tonight. Presley, why don't you and Lennie go pick out some pajamas from your room."

The girls excitedly stand and run down the hall toward her room, leaving Fallon and I alone. "Are you sure about this?"

Fallon stands from the couch, gathering the popcorn bowls together. "Of course, it's really no big deal. They'll be asleep in thirty minutes anyway."

I stuff my hands into the pockets of my shorts. "Right." I shift back onto my heels. "I should probably get going then?" I jerk my thumb toward her front door.

"Or you could stay?" Fallon glances up to me with her doe-eyed gaze, and I know I'll say yes. Even if I didn't want to, or didn't need to spend hours apologizing to her, I would stay. Much like my daughter, those eyes could get me to do anything. I would fall to my feet and worship the ground she walked on if she asked me to.

"I can stay," I agree.

Fallon nods, glancing down at the bowls in her hands, and I note the pink staining her cheeks.

28

———

FALLON

I can't believe I asked him to stay. I shouldn't have, but something about him is pulling me in. If anything, I can't let him be alone tonight. *I* don't want to be alone tonight.

The girls are in their pajamas and ready for bed now, and we're setting up the trundle bed in Presley's room for Lennie to sleep on. Lennie is about to lay down on the bed, when she looks up at Jason standing in the doorway, leaning against the frame.

"Daddy, you can go now," she states matter of factly. "I don't need you to say goodnight, I like sleepovers."

Jason chokes out a laugh. "Wow, sweetheart. Nice to know you don't need me anymore. I guess I'll go then without saying goodnight." He jerks his thumb over his shoulder, and starts to turn out the door.

"Wait!" Lennie shrieks. "I need a goodnight kiss!"

Jason hadn't even turned his body fully, so he shifts back, a smile reserved for only his daughter on his face. He walks to the bed, leaning down to one knee and pressing a gentle kiss to her forehead. "Goodnight, Len. I love you."

"Love you more, Daddy," Lennie responds, her eyes already blinking harder, voice more slurred.

"Not a chance," Jason responds, brushing her dark hair out of her eyes.

"Goodnight, Jason," my own daughter says, surprising me. "Thank you for letting Lennie stay over."

Jason stands from his knees, leaning over to tug on my daughter's ponytail. "Anytime, kiddo. I know you two are good friends."

My heart clenches at the smile Presley gives him. She deserves a father in her life. She does have one, but he chose to fall off the face of the earth.

Presley looks like she wants to say something else, but she changes her mind at the last minute. "Goodnight, Mom," she says to me instead, glancing at where I stand at the foot of her bed.

"Goodnight, Presley, I love you." I move so I can reach and give her a quick hug and kiss on the cheek.

"Love you," Presley responds through a yawn.

I leave the bedside, turning on the small night light she has on her nightstand, and following Jason as we step quietly out of the room. I flick off the overhead light, and pull the door shut behind us.

Jason is leaning against the far wall, his legs crossed in front of him, hands shoved into his pockets when I turn away from the latched door. The look he gives me is unfamiliar. Sure, I can see that hint of guilt still, but there's something more, an almost heated look.

I walk down the hall toward my living room. I hear the soft footfalls of Jason following me, and I turn off the TV that's stuck on a screen playing previews of varying movies on the streaming service. I grab the knitted blanket off the back of the couch, wrapping it around my body.

I'm not necessarily cold, but I need the comfort of it right now.

Jason sits beside me on the couch, our legs nearly touching. He doesn't speak, but he does reach over and rest his palm on my thigh. "Today was heavy," I finally say after a long moment of silence.

He nods. "Yeah. It really was. I want to apologize again. I shouldn't have reacted the way I did."

I lean over, cupping his palm in my hand. "Thank you for the apology. It means a lot, Jason." Our faces move closer together, and I know where this is headed. "Comfort from another person?" I ask, our lips barely brushing.

Jason shakes his head. "I don't know what this is, what we're doing, or what is going to happen, but this is more than just comfort between us. I can't let you go." Then his lips are on mine.

He drags his lips over mine, his five o'clock shadow rough on my chin as he kisses me roughly, fiercely, like he can't get enough of me. I lean forward, pressing against his chest until he is laying back on the couch, and I'm hovering over his body.

I run my hands down his chest, loving his softness. "Fallon," he breathes my name like it's a prayer. I straddle his hips, rocking my own as he hardens underneath me.

I don't want more tonight, though. Tonight, I want to know he's here with me. I want him, not a frantic fuck in a wine cellar, or a sexually charged moment in a hotel bed under the guise of comfort. No, tonight, I want *him*. I want to be held, to hold him in return. I want the familiarity of his friendship. I want those moments again. They were never about sex, never about frantic sentiments. They were real, true, friendship. I need that from him again.

"Can you just hold me?" I ask him, my voice growing soft.

He nods as I shift off him. I stand and hold a hand to him, pulling him to his feet. I drag him down the hallway to my bedroom, not even caring that it's barely nine pm. I'm emotionally exhausted, and need this.

I rip off my shirt, leaving me in my ratty sports bra and old cotton shorts. Jason tears off his tee, shoving off his shorts so he's wearing only his boxer briefs. I can see the outline of his hard cock, and while my mouth waters, I remain steadfast in the fact that tonight, we don't need more. Tonight, we need each other.

I should be insecure about the fact that I'm not in some cute pajama or underwear set. Maybe I should be insecure about my belly, wide hips, or the back rolls that never went away no matter how many diets I went on, or exercises I did. I'm not though. Jason looks me over with a satisfied hum, making me feel like the sexiest woman alive.

I knew I didn't need to feel insecure with him, even after all these years, after I've changed in more ways than I can count. He's never seen me completely naked, not yet, but maybe someday, someday soon, he will. I want him to. I want to experience the heat of his gaze, feel the confidence he gives me just by existing. He helped me with my confidence all those years ago, and now, he is doing it again.

Pulling back my sheets, I climb into the bed. Jason follows, pulling back the sheets on the other side and climbing in beside me. I shift down, and he lays on his back, opening his arms to me. I shuffle so I'm next to him, and rest my head on his warm chest. The soft tufts of hair on his chest tickle my cheek, but I love it. I run my hand over the soft hair and revel in this closeness.

Jason leans down, kissing my forehead. "Thank you, sunshine."

"I was going to say the same," I respond, tilting my chin to look into those deep brown eyes. "I needed this. Thank you for telling me everything tonight."

I cuddle in close to him, hitching my leg up and around his waist. I need to be as close to him as physically possible right now. I need to be touching him everywhere I can.

"Goodnight, Jase," I say into the dark room, my body warm and fuzzy under his embrace.

"Goodnight, sunshine."

29

JASON

I wake up entangled in Fallon. Her body is still hooked around mine, leg up around my waist, fingers splayed against my chest. It's almost like we didn't move all night. I try to shift, but I'm stiff and achy. Yeah, we didn't move all night long. Jeez. There's a weird, warm, coolness on my chest, and it takes me a moment to realize what it is. Fallon is drooling. On my chest. That's how hard she's sleeping.

I want to be grossed out, but to be honest, it's kinda adorable.

The sound of whispers and giggles pulls me out of my *drool-emma*. I lift my head, opening my dry eyes. To the sight of Presley and Lennie, sitting cross-legged at our feet, whispering wildly back and forth to each other.

Whispering is a word I use lightly, since I can hear them quite clearly, but at least they're trying. Presley is currently leaning over, her hand up to her mouth as she tries to whisper in my daughter's ear.

"Does this mean they're getting married?" she asks, her voice growing louder with each word.

Lennie's brown eyes widen with excitement. "I think my dad loves your mom, Presley," she whispers back.

I do my best not to groan, because we are well and truly fucked now. I don't even know what Fallon and I are right now, and here are our daughters trying to marry us off to each other, and declaring love.

If it wasn't so fucking cute, I might be upset.

Lennie glances back to us, and catches my open eyes. I raise my brow at her, and she shrieks. Her shriek causes Presley to shriek, which causes Fallon to wake up, and also start shrieking. Soon, I'm surrounded by three shrieking women.

"Hey!" I yell. Fallon sits up rapidly, pulling the sheet with her to cover her chest, her eyes darting around as she searches for something to be afraid of. "Stop screaming!"

It's like a light switch. All three girls stop their yelling, and I sit up, rubbing a hand across my forehead. We're in for a long morning.

I WAS RIGHT. We get the girls settled, and then the constant barrage of questions begins. Fallon is quick to come up with responses to each of their questions.

"Are you getting married?"

"No, we're friends, remember?"

"Do friends snuggle like that?"

"Daddy, why weren't you wearing a shirt?"

"Mommy, where were your pajamas?"

So. Many. Questions.

I feel hungover from all the constant questions. My head aches, and so does my body, after laying in one position all night long. We have breakfast together, then it's time to go.

Lennie, of course, doesn't want to leave, and I can't blame her. I'd love to stay and have a lazy day with Fallon and Presley, but I have to get to work, and my mom has a few events planned for Lennie today. There's an almost awkward tension between Fallon and me as we say good-bye. I'm not sure whether to hug her, or kiss her, or what this all means for us. Was last night more? Was it an opening to a relationship? Do I want that? I've been so against a relationship for so long, so what is changing?

My reasons are still reasons. I don't want to introduce someone to my daughter and have her get attached only for things to end badly. But that's already happened, hasn't it? Lennie is attached to Fallon, and Presley too. So do I really have reasons not to let myself fall into this with her?

30

FALLON

September

In the time since Jason and Lennie's impromptu sleepover, things have been interesting. Jason isn't nearly as standoffish as he's been in the past six months, and he's even started texting me every so often, asking how I am, how my day was, and so on.

It would be weird if we didn't have that breakthrough that night. All in all, I'm still not quite sure how I feel about it. But I can't dwell on it for too long, because I have a task at hand. Josie and I are currently having a meeting with Beau, discussing the engagement party he's planning for Marley. Of course, she has no idea of any of it, so it's all very hush-hush.

The event will be at Jason's brewery, and he's agreed to shut it down for the night for us to use. Beau's really laid back about it all, he mainly wants all his family and friends there, and he's leaving the rest to us.

"Okay, I have to ask. Do you know how you're going to do it?" Josie asks, leaning forward to rest her chin on her hand. Her eyes are bright and curious as she looks at her brother-in-law.

Beau shrugs, running a hand through his shoulder length hair. "To be honest, I haven't really planned out what I'm going to say or anything. We're having a little family photoshoot that day, and it's her first day back to work. I figured at the end of it all, I'd get down on one knee, speak from the heart, and go from there."

"Awww, Beau!" Josie says, her voice tight with emotion. "That's perfect. It's absolutely perfect."

"Thanks, Jos. Now, unless you need anything from me, I'm going to head home. I told Mar I had a showing, and I wouldn't be long, so I want to get back to her and the babies." He rises from the small table, and gives us both a quick hug before leaving the small coffee shop.

Josie and I chat about things we need for the party, what kind of flowers she's wanting and more. We've talked and taken notes and planned it all out when I look at the clock and realize we've been here for an hour longer than I anticipated. I told Isaac I wouldn't be long, but I don't think he'll mind.

I shoot him a quick text message to let him know I'll be a little while longer, and he responds with a thumbs up.

While my phone is unlocked, I see another message. This one, from Jason.

JASON

Hey, sunshine. How's your day going? I hear we have a party to plan at the brewery.

ME

We sure do. It's good. Meeting with Josie to go over final touches. Do you want us to come there so we can chat with you too?

JASON

Sure, that might not be a bad idea.

"Who are you talking to?" Josie asks, glancing across the table at me, her brows raised.

I swallow thickly, hoping I can play this cool. "Oh, um, Jason, actually. He wants to meet with us quickly if you have time so we can plan with him too."

"Yeah, we can head over there. What's going on with your face?" she asks nonchalantly. God, why must she be so perceptive?

"Nothing," I squeak, but I know my face must be bright red. I turn my gaze back to my phone, letting Jason know we are on the way. We are within walking distance, so we head toward him. As we walk, I sense her skeptical eyes. "Are you and Jason finally together? Is that what's happening here?"

Oh god, she's cracking me open. My resolve isn't very strong to begin with, but I need to confide in someone. I've told Megan the bare minimum, but Josie is so easy to talk to. And she knows Jason. She's part of his family.

The brewery is in sight now, and I'm about to explode. I need to tell her. I stop in the middle of the sidewalk, pulling her aside so we're not blocking the path. "Fine, but you literally can't tell anyone. Not even Andrew. I don't know what's happening between us, but I need to tell someone."

Josie's blue eyes widen and her mouth drops open. "I was teasing you, I didn't really think you were together. I mean I suspected after the whole wine cellar thing—which you *totally* banged down there, didn't you?—and the hotel thing, but I didn't know for sure. *Oh my god*, this is the *best* news. Tell me everything."

I grab her hand and sit down on a bench nearby. "I'm not really sure what there is to tell. We're in this weird limbo. We both didn't want a relationship, but a few weeks ago, I almost passed out at the zoo, and he confided in me about some stuff, and I did the same to him, and now we're texting sometimes, and calling too, and I don't know what this is." I finish my speech with a huff, and sink back onto the bench.

"Okay well first off, I'm saying this honestly. If you do choose to get together, I think you two will be amazing for each other. And your girls love each other. So that's a perk."

I nod, my brain sort of numb. "I'm scared, Josie. I'm scared to let myself fall. What if he breaks my heart, and in the process, he breaks Presley's too? What if Presley loses Lennie as a friend because of me?"

Josie leans toward me, wrapping me into a hug. "I can't imagine how hard it is. To have to be thinking about someone else, and not only yourself. Trust me when I say this, though. Jason may outwardly put out the vibes that he doesn't care, that he doesn't have emotions, but I'm sure by now, you've experienced how he is with his family. How he is with the people he cares about. With the people he loves. He won't hurt you if he can help it. And that goes for your daughter, and his too."

"You're right," I say with resolve. I have witnessed first-hand how he is, how amazing he is to his family. To me and my daughter.

"Go with the flow. If something happens, which I think it might, don't stress. Take things as they come. We're all on your team, and are here to support both of you no matter what."

I squeeze my friend. "Thank you, Josie. You mean so much to me. I'm so grateful for you."

"Right back at ya," Josie responds. "Now, let's go see your man."

I chuckle, because she's such a goofball. "Technically, he's not my man."

"Yet." She winks.

We finish the short walk to the brewery, and Jason is sitting at a table, leaning forward as he talks to an older man I recognize as his grandfather.

"Gramps!" Josie yells, and he turns in his chair to see Josie.

"Cindy," Gramps greets her. Josie bends down and kisses him sweetly on the cheek. "Jason here was telling me about the party you're planning for Marley and Beau."

"Fallon's the one planning," Josie says, gesturing to me. "I'm doing the flowers and being a helping hand."

I offer a wave to Jason's grandfather. I've met him a few times, and he's always been the sweetest man. "Hi, Earl," I greet.

"Call me Gramps, young lady," he tells me, and I correct myself.

"Gramps. Nice to see you."

"You too. How's that little peanut of yours?"

"She's great. Getting ready for school to start next week, even though she says she's not excited, she is."

"I'll bet."

Jase's eyes are on me the whole time. He's staring so intently at me that I'm almost scared to look at him, scared to give him my full attention. Who knows what will happen if I do. I'll probably melt to be honest.

"Cindy, can you call that husband of yours and tell him to come pick me up. I want to see what he's working on," Gramps asks Josie, and she smiles easily in return. I love that Gramps still uses the nickname he penned for Josie after he met her. Josie and Andrew had a bit of a missed connection, leaving him with only a hair clip to find her by, and Gramps has lovingly called her Cindy, or Cinderella, since then.

She turns her smile to me before grabbing her phone from her back, and walking away to call Andrew, leaving me with Gramps and Jason.

As soon as I lift my eyes to meet Jason's I know I shouldn't have. He's staring at me with such affection, such genuine lust in his eyes. When he sees me standing still, he jumps to his feet. "Here." He pulls a chair up to the table for me. "Sit."

"Oh, thanks," I reply, sitting in the offered chair between him and Gramps. Why is this so awkward? I'm so uncomfortable. I need Josie back as my buffer.

"So, when are the two of you going to tell everyone you're together?" Gramps asks, no filter, no preamble, simply drops the bomb.

"Gramps," Jason nearly scolds him, meanwhile, I'm choking on my tongue. I cough and gasp for air. Jason leans over, patting my back like I'm an infant.

Once I've caught my breath, I lean back in my chair, trying to come up with something to say.

"Am I wrong?" Gramps asks with pure sarcasm in his voice. He knows he's not wrong.

I glance at Jason, and find him already looking at me. I have no idea what to say to his grandfather, so I figure maybe it's best to stay quiet.

"We're... figuring things out," Jason finally says. He reaches over, taking my palm and giving it a gentle squeeze. "I don't really know, Gramps. We haven't talked about it."

"Oops," Gramps responds, though he's chuckling, like maybe he's not really all that sorry. Josie arrives back at that moment, and narrows her eyes at my hand in Jason's. I react, pulling it away and back into my lap.

This is such a mess. We really need to talk.

Gramps and Josie are two peas in a pod. They spend the next ten minutes talking amongst themselves as we wait for Andrew to arrive. Once he does, we spend another few minutes chatting with him, before Andrew helps him out of his chair and out the door.

Jason brings us around the brewery, pointing out places we can hang string lights and decorations. I'm already coming up with so many different kinds of ideas that I cannot wait for this party. Not only for the fact that Marley and Beau will finally be getting engaged, but because I think it's going to be a beautiful event. The brewery is the perfect backdrop. It has such a cozy vibe, while also providing enough space and room so the guests aren't over crowded. Once Jason is through with his mini tour and explanations, we sit back down to discuss the final touches.

Josie not so subtly declares that she has to get back to work a few minutes later, and after she leaves, it's just Jason and I. There's still an hour before the brewery opens for the night, and his employees are starting to file in for their opening procedures.

I stand from my chair. "I should probably get going myself. Isaac probably thinks I got lost or something on the way back."

Jason chuckles, nodding. "You look beautiful today, Fallon." His comment surprises me.

I glance down at what I'm wearing. It's a simple black sundress, and my hair is in a ponytail because I couldn't be bothered to curl it today. "Oh, thank you," I reply. "This is nothing."

"It doesn't mean you don't look beautiful."

I nod, not really sure what more I can say. "I guess I'll get going." *Run.* Leave the awkwardness. Between Gramps totally calling us out, and this, I might die of awkwardness. I run out the front doors of the brewery, and take a deep breath, letting the warm summer air ground me.

I don't know how to act around him when there's other people with us. I'm not used to it. Sure, we've been around our daughters together, but around other people, when there is attention on us? Yeah, no. I don't know what to do with myself.

I'm nearly to my car at the coffee shop when I hear my name being called. I turn toward the voice to see Jason striding down the sidewalk to me. "Wait," he calls. I stop in my tracks. When he reaches me, he's out of breath. "That was weird. Wasn't it?"

I can't stop the laugh that bubbles out from me. "Yeah, it was weird. I didn't know what to say."

"Me either," he chuckles. "Gramps and Josie are always the ones to notice little things, so I shouldn't be surprised he said something."

"It's okay. Josie talked to me about things earlier too."

"We're okay?" he asks, and it's so sweet, like an insecure teenager.

"Of course," I respond. "To be honest, I don't know what we're doing here."

Jason steps into my space, threading his arms around my waist, bending down so he's at my level. "I don't either. I don't know what's going to happen, and I'm trying not to overreact, or think too hard, if I'm being honest."

"Yeah, I get that," I respond. "Everyone is going to ask, and I don't know what we're supposed to say."

"Say it's none of their business," he retorts.

I swat at his chest gently. "Jason, I can't say that and you know it. I love your family, but everyone is very open and tells each other everything."

"Then we tell them that right now we are figuring things out together. It will have to be good enough for them. It's good enough for us, right?"

"Right," I reply. He leans down, resting his forehead against mine.

"All I know is I'm happy when I'm with you. Things are easier."

"Same."

"Then we do what's best for us."

I nod, and he presses a soft, sweet kiss to my lips. I lose myself in the kiss for the shortest of moments. When we break apart, I cringe. "I really should get going. I have a lot of work to do."

"Go. I'll talk to you later, okay, sunshine?"

I nod my response, and get into my car a few moments later, waving to Jason as I drive away.

31

JASON

String lights are hung across the ceiling of my brewery, and flowers are placed on each table in mason jars. Josie and Fallon really did a beautiful job decorating, and my brewery is almost unrecognizable. We've greeted Marley and Beau with a loud cheer of "surprise" as they entered the room, and now they're being passed around from person to person. They each have a baby carrier on their arm, and I can see the subtle glint of the ring on Marley's finger.

I've barely seen Fallon tonight, she's been running around making sure everything has been in order since she arrived hours ago. Presley and Lennie are around here somewhere, coloring with Lennie's stash of crayons and coloring pages she keeps here. I was able to help Fallon get things set up, and hoped I'd be able to talk with her more, but so far, no luck. I want to check in and spend some time with her.

I swing by the bar and have Laila pour me two glasses of Marley's favorite ale before I head over to my brother and his new fiancé. I greet them with hugs and congratulations, and then say hi to my niece and nephew. Their little brown eyes are both wide as they look around the room, taking in all the loud noises and new faces. They seem to be taking it in stride though, and haven't let out a peep of noise.

Now that they have drinks, I make my way through the crowd. I want to find Fallon, and check in with her. I've been stopped a few times by various people, but not for long. Once I reach a corner booth, I spot Lennie and Presley.

"Hey girls," I say, sitting down briefly. I kiss Len's forehead, pulling her in for a quick hug.

"Hi, Daddy," Lennie says. "Do you like my picture?" She holds up her coloring book so I can see the page. On it, is a princess holding a cat, while sitting on a fancy bench. She's wearing a poofy dress, and a crown. Lennie is not the best at staying in the lines quite yet, so there's scribbles all over the page.

"Beautiful, sweetie," I tell her. "We'll have to put that one in my office."

"Look at mine, Jason," Presley pleads. "It's a cat playing with a ball of yarn."

"Wow." I'd never admit it out loud, and especially not in front of my daughter, but Presley's really good at coloring. She stays in the lines, and even has some shading going on, giving the cat more dimension and color. "Yours is beautiful, too, Pres."

"Thank you," she replies. "Can we hang it in your office next to Lennie's?"

"Absolutely. Have you seen your mom?"

She shakes her head. "Nope."

"Okay, thanks. Keep coloring girls, we can hang all your pages in my office if you want." I stand from the booth and head to one of the back rooms, still searching for Fallon.

After a few minutes and no luck, I start to head out into the main room again.

I stop when I see movement in my office. The door is barely cracked, and I can see Fallon's leg as she bounces it up and down. I open the door, finding her sitting in my chair, her head in her hands as she leans over the desk.

"Hey," I say softly, hoping I don't scare her. "What's wrong?"

She jerks her head up, and her face is void of color and emotion. It's something I've never seen on her before, and it's freaking me out. Fallon leans back into the chair, trying to wave me off. "I'm fine. Needed a minute."

I walk over to her, and lean against my desk, crossing my legs in front of me. "Tell me what's going on." Reaching forward, I cup her cheek in my hand. She leans away from my touch, and my heart drops.

"I can't. Because if I do, I'll lose it. I can't lose it, Jason. I need to keep it together," she snaps. I've never seen her like this before. Sure, I've seen her mad, emotional, crabby, but never like this. Never broken.

"Okay," I concede. "Do you want me to go?"

She shakes her head. "No. I just, I needed a minute. I'm fine now." Like she's trying to prove her point, she stands from the chair and adjusts her dress. "Do I look okay?" she asks, quickly swiping under her eyes so fast I didn't even see that there were tears.

"You look beautiful, sunshine," I tell her honestly.

"Great." Her voice is thick around the words. She steps around me and leaves my office without another word. I'll definitely spend the next few hours worried about her, but I'm not about to force her into telling me anything.

I follow her as she walks down the short hallway back into the main room of the brewery. I watch as Lennie and

Presley stand up to greet her, and follow close by. I keep my distance, watching her from afar as Beau stands up in front of the crowd, raising a glass. He surprises me, turning his body toward me, and smiling, saying, "Thank you all for coming, and Jason, thanks for letting us have the brewery for the night."

I nod, realizing I don't have a drink to hold up in response.

Beau shifts his gaze to Fallon in the corner, Presley standing right by her, holding the coloring pages. "And to Fallon, for whipping his ass into shape long enough to help plan the event."

Laughter rings through the crowd, and I glance down at my feet, kicking at the ground. I've never been one for attention, but I turn my gaze to Fallon anyway, knowing there are eyes on us. She's focused on Marley, a soft smile on her face, totally different than the blank look she wore only minutes ago. She offers Marley a small shrug, and then shifts her focus back to Beau as he continues to speak about his future wife.

He finishes his toast, and everyone raises a glass to them. I still don't have one, so I raise my arm in support. From the corner of my eye, I see Thomas trying to sneak in. He has a haggard look on his face, dark-rimmed circles under his eyes. Shit. Work has been so stressful for him recently, and I wish there was something I could do to help.

The party continues for a few more hours, and the whole time, I keep missing Fallon. I truly think she's avoiding me. Something had to have happened, and I'm worried about her.

It's nearing eight-thirty, and Lennie needs to get home. She's been clinging to my side for the last hour. I know she's exhausted. Hell, I'm exhausted. Laila and the crew can handle the rest of the event, but I don't want to leave without talking to Fallon. Her mom, Elaine, came by about an hour ago and picked up Presley for the night. I make my way through the crowd, carrying Lennie on my hip as she rests her head on my shoulder.

Beau and Marley are sitting at a table with pretty much everyone. Josie and Andrew are next to them, and Thomas, Isaac, and Megan are sitting on the other side. The only person missing is Fallon.

Marley's mom and dad took the twins home about an hour ago, giving Marley and Beau some free time on their engagement night.

"Hey, have you guys seen Fallon?" I ask them. They all crane their heads, looking around the thinning crowd to find her.

"No," Josie replies. "She was running around a bit. I told her to sit down like an hour ago, but haven't seen her since."

I furrow my brow. Where could she be? "Can Lennie sit with you guys for a few minutes? I'm going to go find her."

"Absolutely," Thomas responds. "Come here, Lenners." I love how over time Lennie has received an assortment of nicknames from all her family.

Lennie reaches her arms out for Thomas, and I drop her into his lap. Sure, she's five and getting taller each day, but she's still a little snuggle bug. Thomas has taken off all his work gear now, leaving him in a simple cotton tee, so she snuggles right in. In all honesty, I'd be shocked if she was awake in five minutes. I know I need to get her home, but this is important. I can't leave, knowing something was up with Fallon earlier.

"I'll be back," I tell them. Megan stands as I turn away.

"I'm going to use the restroom," she announces, but I have a gut instinct she's going to tell me something.

I stride away from the table, and Megan follows. I head toward the restrooms, hoping I can be subtle. When we're hidden in a hallway, Megan grabs my attention, saying, "She left."

"What do you mean, she left?" I glance around me, like she'll suddenly appear in the hall.

"Today is a hard day for her. I offered to go with her, but she said she needed to be alone." Megan doesn't look at me, only at the floor.

"Why is it hard for her, Megan?" My heart is pounding in my chest, a dull sense of fear creeping in.

"I can't tell you. It's not my story to tell. I was going to go over there as soon as I dropped Isaac off. She may want to be alone, but she shouldn't be."

"Fuck," I curse, running a hand down my face. "You really can't give me any more information?" I need to know what's going on. If she's hurting, I want to be there. I want to help her.

"I can't. She needs to be the one to tell you, Jason."

"Should I..." I trail off, not finishing my sentence. Even if I wanted to go over there tonight, I can't. I have to get Lennie home and in bed. "Shit."

"Should you go over there?" Megan finishes my thought out loud. "Honestly? I think you're the only one she'd want right now."

"I can't, Megan. I have Lennie to worry about."

"I'll take her home. Isaac and I will spend the night at your house."

"I can't ask you to do that, Megan," I breathe, trying to think of my options.

"You're not asking, Jason. I'm telling you. She needs

you, even if she doesn't know it. She's been doing things on her own for so long, even before Brad left her, and she puts on a bright, happy face, but she trusts you. She'll let you see her crumble. And I think she needs to let you see it."

Decision made. I need to get to her. I pull my keys out of my pocket, taking my house key off the ring. "Her pajamas are laying out on her bed. It shouldn't be a problem to get her to sleep. She'll probably fall asleep in the car, and shit, you need her booster seat," I halt my words, thinking of all the things Lennie will need.

"I have a seat for Presley she can use," Megan responds. "I've got her. Go tell Lennie that Isaac and I are taking her home. Then go."

I nod and rush back out to the table where Thomas is still holding Lennie. She's curled into him, her cheek resting on his chest. When I reach the table, I bend down to her level. "Hey sweetie. I have to go check on Fallon. Auntie Megan and Uncle Isaac are going to take you home and put you to bed, okay?"

Lennie nods. "Is Fallon okay?" she asks. She's so laid back, she doesn't even care about Isaac and Megan taking her home, she only cares about Fallon.

"I think so, but she really needs one of Daddy's hugs," I tell her. The eyes and ears of the entire table are on us, and hopefully it doesn't raise too many questions.

"You do give really good hugs, Daddy," Lennie replies, reaching her arms out to me for a hug herself.

I squeeze my daughter tightly, then pass her over to Megan. "Okay, I'll see you in the morning, sweetie."

The table says their goodbyes, everyone's eyes concerned and worried, but I don't have time to address them right now. Hopefully Megan can take care of it. If I was worried about people figuring out something is going on between Fallon and me, they definitely know now.

With a final goodbye, I rush to the bar, updating Laila that I'm leaving, and head out the front door to run to my car. I may be running in blind, but Fallon needs me, so that's where I'll be. I drive across town to her house, focusing on getting to her.

When I pull into her driveway, her house is dark, silent, and almost eerie looking. Her car is parked in the driveway though, so I know she's home. I get out of the car and take a deep breath, heading up to her front door. I knock on the door loudly.

After a minute with no response, I try again. Is she sleeping? I try the door and find that it's locked, so it's not like I can try and sneak in. I'm about to raise my arm to knock one more time when the lock clicks and the door opens a crack.

Fallon peeks through the crack. Her blonde hair is a tangled mess around her head, her face blotchy, green eyes leaking a steady stream of tears. When she sees it's me, she crumples.

FALLON

I sink to my knees at the sight of Jason at my front door. His eyes are full of so much anguish, so much worry, I lose it. He's here. I don't know how he knew I needed him, but he did. He's here, and I finally break. The final piece that I've been trying to hold together for hours finally shatters.

"Shh," Jason croons, opening the door further to let himself in. He kneels in front of me, wrapping his arms around my body and pulling me into him. "I've got you, sunshine. Let it out."

I do. I let all the pain I've kept buried explode as he holds me in the entryway of my house. He closed the door at some point, giving us privacy from the leering eyes of my neighbors.

I let him hold me until some of my tears dry, and all the while, Jase is murmuring words of encouragement in my ears, telling me it's okay to cry, to give him my pain. He doesn't even know what's wrong with me, and yet he's here, taking care of me.

I pull away from him and work to stand. Jason helps me,

holding me up and in his embrace. I was trying so hard to keep my shit together today, but something finally made me snap. I still don't know what it was. I knew today was going to be hard, but I'd hoped the festivities would help keep my mind off things. It did to an extent, but there is only so much I could do to keep myself present.

I lead Jason down the hall toward my bedroom, where I've been wallowing since I got home. He follows, kicking off his shoes and holding my hand. I'm still in my dress from earlier. When I got home, I was unable to even think about changing. Now, I want it off. I need to get rid of the scratchy fabric and out of this fucking bra.

Tears are still silently streaming down my face, but having Jason here is sort of like a Band-Aid on the bullet wound. I'm not naive. I know I'll need to give him some explanation, but for now, all I can do is change.

I dig in my dresser, sliding my dress off my shoulders and letting it fall onto the carpeted floor in a puddle of fabric. I throw on a cotton shirt, and take my bra off underneath it, throwing that to the ground as well. Jason stands close by me the entire time, his hand resting on my hips and moving to let my dress fall, and help me pull the shirt down. His constant contact is helpful, something to ground me.

Once I'm ready, I head over to my bed, climbing in. I reach my hand out for Jason, and love that he doesn't question it. He strips down to his boxers and climbs in behind me. His body molds into mine, and he pulls me against his chest.

"Thank you for coming," I tell him through a shuddering breath.

"I'm sorry I wasn't here sooner," he replies. "I was trying to find you for like an hour. No one knew where you were, until finally Megan told me you weren't okay and left."

A watery laugh leaves my mouth. "Yeah, that's putting it lightly. I kind of yelled at her when she tried to come home with me. I was so intent on being alone, but I know now I really didn't want to be." I gasp as I realize something. "Where's Lennie?" I try to sit up, but Jason holds me down.

"Shh," he calms me. "She's at home, with Megan and Isaac. When I knew I needed to come here, Megan offered to take her home."

"I owe Megan so much," I say with resolve.

"She's the best," Jason responds. "I think everyone knows, or at least suspects, there is something going on between us, though."

I shrug in his arms. "Oh well."

"Oh well," Jason repeats, squeezing me gently. His nonchalance toward everyone knowing gives me goosebumps. "Lennie wanted me to give you a hug from her. I told her I needed to check on you and give you a hug. She said I give good hugs."

"You do give good hugs," I respond. I turn around in his arms so I can look into his eyes. "I didn't know how badly I needed one."

"I've got you." He squeezes me. I rest my cheek against his chest, letting him hold me and breathing in his scent. I let him hold me, building up the confidence to say the words out loud.

"Three years ago today, I lost my baby," I say the words into the silence, letting the heaviness fill me again. "Three years ago, I went to the hospital to find out my husband took me off the health insurance, was filing for divorce, and waived his rights to be Presley's dad."

Jason sucks in a breath, holding me tighter to him as my tears fall again. "I don't miss him, and I don't want him back. That's not why I'm crying," I try to explain, but Jason stops me with a finger to my lips.

"I know, sunshine. You don't have to explain it to me. Let me hold you while you get it out."

His words break down another dam. Brad never held me while I cried. He would give me a hug, and then send me off into our room to cry it out. For a while, I was convinced that was for the best, that that's what I needed. But no, I needed someone to be my strong tower, the one to keep watch while I let myself endure this. Something I have been avoiding for almost three years. It was easy to put on the happy exterior, to shove everything down.

"Thank you," I murmur, embracing the warmth of him around me. I let myself cry and rage and yell about how horrible Brad was for hours, and Jason lets me. He rages with me, he wipes away my tears, he even cries with me.

I was his strong tower the night he broke down about Talia, and now, it's his turn to be mine. We can be this for each other, we can be what the other needs.

When I look at the clock, it's nearing three a.m. I know that tomorrow is going to be a disaster. My mom is dropping Pres off at nine-thirty, but I don't want to close my eyes. I don't want to dream of a little baby I'll never get to hold. I don't want to dream of the little life that will never be.

Jason's barely keeping his eyes open, and I finally whisper, "You can go to sleep, Jase. I'm fine."

He shakes his head hard, like he's trying to shake off the sleep. "No, you're not. I'm going to stay awake as long as you need me."

I lift my head to press a gentle kiss to his lips. "You need to sleep. I need to sleep, but I can't turn off my mind."

"How can I help you?"

"I don't know," I say shakily. "I'm so tired, but every time I close my eyes, I start to dream."

"Do you want me to read to you?" he asks out of the blue. "Sometimes, Lennie has nightmares, and the only thing that helps her is when I read to her. Can we try that?"

I nod into his chest. He rolls over, grabbing his phone from the nightstand. I adjust so I'm laying on his chest, my ear pressed so I can hear the steady thump of his heart. One arm wraps around my shoulder, and his thumb moves in soothing circles on my skin. He opens up his Kindle app, and picks a book. I don't care what it is, as long as I get to hear his voice soothing me.

Without preamble or question, he reads. The words don't mean anything to me. I'm not focused on the story, or what I've missed in the book thus far. I'm focused solely on his low, gravely, sleep deprived voice holding me captive.

He reads until my eyes grow heavy and finally fall shut.

33

JASON

I'm getting used to waking up with Fallon in my arms. It's happened three times now, and each time, it gives me so much happiness, I don't know what to do with it.

I'm laying on my side with Fallon tucked into my chest. Her back is to my front, and we are about as close to each other as we can be. She fell asleep soon after I started reading to her last night, and as far as I'm aware, she stayed asleep the rest of the night. A glance at the clock on the far nightstand tells me it's eight forty-five, so we have a little more time before Fallon's mom drops Presley off.

I inhale deeply, breathing in Fallon. She's snoring lightly, her lips parted as she breathes. Her makeup is all but washed away after her tears last night, leaving only a few flecks of mascara on her cheeks and under eyes. I'm falling for this woman. I fell for her all those years ago, but now, all those feelings are coming back. She's the only person who has truly seen me, truly seen the emotions I've held back in the last five years since Lennie was born, and it's so good to have someone see all of me.

"I can feel you staring at me," Fallon says, her voice

sleepy and raspy. She tries to subtly wipe at her mouth, but I already saw the small pool of drool. It's adorable.

"Yes, and?"

"And nothing," she answers, shimmying her body even closer to mine, if that were possible. "Just making the statement."

Her shifting has awoken other parts of me, and I try to shift my hips away so she doesn't have to feel my growing dick.

Of course, she doesn't let that fly. She shifts herself closer to me, reaching back and pulling my hips back into hers. "Stop moving away," she mutters. "Did you ever think that maybe I want to feel you?"

"Jesus." I chuckle low and gruff, leaning my head back and running my hand through my sleep mussed hair. "I was trying to be respectful, sunshine."

"Well stop. I like it."

Heat creeps through my body at her words. Of course, the blood is rushing south, but the temperature everywhere else has gone up a few degrees. I lean my head forward so my mouth is right at her ear. Pushing her hair away, I press kisses to her neck, traveling up to her ear. "You like it, huh, sunshine?"

A shiver wracks through her body. Sliding my hand so it's wrapped around her throat, she swallows thickly. I trail down further, sliding between her shirt covered breasts. Her nipples pebble under my grazing touches, giving me a burst of pleasure that I can make her like this.

"I love it." Fallon reaches underneath the sheet to caress my hard dick through my boxers. She squeezes gently, making me jerk into her touch.

"Tell me sunshine, do you need this right now?"

"Yes," she breathes. "I need you, please, Jase."

I kiss her neck in response, taking her chin in my fingers to tilt her back to me. I move so I can take her lips, gently tracing my tongue around her lips and gently breaching the entrance. She kisses me back roughly, snaking her hand around the nape of my neck. Her fingers tangle in my hair and she scrapes her nails on my scalp. She needs this, I can tell, and lucky for her, I'm happy to provide her this. I need it too.

We kiss and my hips grind against her ass, needing the friction. My hand slides down her body again, and I shift away from her mouth, bringing my attention back to her neck. I reach the hem of her panties and slide my fingers underneath. Fallon shifts, trying to get my fingers further into her panties.

"You are desperate for my cock, aren't you, pretty girl?" I tease, my fingers finally gliding through the wetness of her pussy. I slide my fingers through her slit, finding her clit soaked and waiting for my touch. Fallon lets out a breathy moan at the first swipe of my fingers across her clit.

She grips my cock tighter in her small fist, stroking me through my boxers. Then, she shoves my boxers down and wraps her hand around my girth, stroking me up and down sensually as I follow the same rhythm on her clit. Her breathing staggers as I bring her to the edge, and then catches as I slowly back off. She does the same to me, though her angle isn't as good as mine, so she's having a hard time.

When I know she's close after a few minutes, I give her clit the tiniest of pinches, and she comes. Fallon groans low and long as she twitches in my arms, her body relaxing as she comes down from the high. I hold her and strum my fingers on her clit as she rides through it. She's stopped her ministrations on my cock, and if anything, I'm thankful. Now I can keep my focus on her.

"That felt so good," Fallon murmurs, still breathing heavily as she tries to compose herself.

"That was the intention." I kiss her cheek. I shift, trying to pull away. This morning was about her. I'll be fine without a release, and I probably should head out before Presley gets dropped off.

"Where are you going?" Fallon whines, reaching around to pull me back to her body.

"I should get going, right? Your mom will be here with Pres soon." I kiss her soft lips, and Fallon surprises me, turning quickly and grabbing onto my cock.

"We still have time," Fallon says. She glances over at the clock to confirm, and god, I hope she's right. Rising to her knees, she pushes me to my back, pushing my boxers down, urging me to lift my hips so she can shimmy them down the rest of the way. She tosses them to the floor, taking in my leaking cock.

She literally licks her lips, biting down on the bottom one as she takes in my naked form. "I've never seen you totally naked before," she mutters, her eyes raking me up and down with a new heat simmering behind them. "So sexy."

Her words make my cock twitch. I've never seen her totally naked either, but I'm not going to bring that up right now. Right now, I'm giving her what she wants. She drags her fingernails up my chest, trailing across my chest hair and nipples. She takes in my body with her hands and fingers, like she's almost memorizing it. She's still in her panties and t-shirt, and I crave to see more, to touch her everywhere the way she's touching me.

As if she heard my internal thoughts, she tears her shirt

off, giving me the perfect view of her breasts. Her dusky dark pink nipples I have the vaguest memories of from our hurried wine cellar time are pointed and hard, begging for my touch. I reach out, cupping her heavy breasts in my palms, swiping my thumbs over her nipples.

"Ah," she moans, then stops herself. "It's my turn to play, baby."

She moves my hands from her tits and above my head to rest on the pillows. Her words are enough to make me ready to come in two seconds flat. The tone of her voice is so low and seductive, so different than anything I've ever heard from her before.

"Please, sunshine." I'm not above begging at this point. My length is so hard it's nearly throbbing, the veins dark and purple against my flesh.

"I like hearing you beg," Fallon announces, then without giving me much time to prepare, she's dipping her head, her tongue flicking my crown, licking up the drop of precum. She flicks her tongue around the round head and slides down, lapping up the few stray drops sliding down my length.

"Fuck, Fallon," I curse, straining my body so my hips don't buck and choke her with my cock.

"Mmm," she moans around my cock, taking me further into her mouth. She hollows her cheeks, sucking and soaking me with each drag of her mouth. Her mouth is fucking magical, but if we're doing this, I don't want to come like this. No, I want to be deep inside her.

Her tits lay heavy across my thigh, and I move my hands from above my head, collecting her hair from her face, giving me the most perfect view of her gorgeous features.

Her green eyes are watering as she gags, trying to take

me deeper and deeper. I groan, not wanting her to stop, but knowing I'm about to come within seconds if I don't.

"Hold on, sunshine," I stop her, pulling her hair so she pops off my cock. A bead of saliva drips out of the corner of her mouth and I swipe it off with my thumb. My cock is dripping with her saliva, which will be perfect for what I have planned. "As incredible as this is, I need to be inside you. Can I?"

Fallon's eyes grow wide, and she nods. "Yes, please, get inside me." She moves, and I drop her hair, letting it fall in waves around her shoulders.

"On your back," I tell her. I need to be close to her, need to see her face when I slide inside. This time, I'm going to savor it. I'm going to feel every clench, listen to every breath, every moan, and I'm going to take my time.

This isn't a hurried fuck. This isn't a release of emotions, this is coming together, becoming one, giving into the other person, letting them take and care for a piece of your soul.

There isn't a person in the world I would rather do this with.

Fallon shifts to her back, and I rise to my knees, and reach to pull her soaked panties down. I can see the large wet spot in the white cotton, and I want to preen, knowing I was the one to do that to her.

Her pussy is revealed to me, and my god, she's perfect. Perfectly pink and soaked with her desire. I slide my fingers through it again, collecting that wetness and bringing it to my mouth for a taste. It's fucking heavenly, better than I could have ever imagined.

When I glance back down at Fallon, her cheeks are flushed, but not out of anticipation, out of... embarrassment.

Did I do something? She covers her stomach with one hand, the other covering her breasts.

"Hey now," I murmur, trying to move her hand. "What's going on?"

"Nothing," she replies, but clearly, it's something.

"You have nothing to be embarrassed about, Fallon. I fucking love your body. Your hips, your stomach, your breasts, *god*, you're incredible. I don't think I'll ever get enough of it," I say with such conviction. I hope she knows how incredibly serious I am.

Fallon sighs, looking away from my eyes. "I... I hate my stretch marks. I hate the way my body looks sometimes. I didn't used to have them."

"They're beautiful," I tell her the truth. "Your body has done incredible things. You know that, right?"

She nods. "I do, but it's hard to reconcile that with the body I have now. Some days, I love my body. I love what it's given me, but some days, it's hard. It didn't help, the way Brad spoke about my body, about me. He said some nasty things that are hard for me to shut out of my brain."

"Can I show you?" I ask.

"Show me?"

"Yes. Can I show you how incredible your body is, and how incredible it can make you feel?"

Fallon nods, giving me the permission I needed. God, I can't wait to show her how beautiful she is. I'll spend every day making sure she knows. That she can see how truly I love her figure, the dips of her hips, the softness of her belly, the heaviness of her breasts.

"Show me," she pleads, shifting her hips and cupping my cheeks in her hands.

"Gladly, sunshine." I move between her open thighs,

running my hands up and down her soft skin. I lean forward, one hand resting on the bed above her right shoulder, while the other grips my cock. I slide my length between her pussy, soaking the tip and settling it at her entrance. "Jesus, you're soaked," I murmur.

I push in my cock enough to make both of us gasp at the pressure. She's so fucking tight. She's going to strangle me.

I slide in a few more inches, giving her more of me, letting her take me. She sighs once I'm seated inside her, my hips flush with her skin. My free hand reaches up, squeezing one of her breasts as I bend down, taking her mouth with mine. "You feel like a dream, Fallon."

She gasps into my mouth and rocks her hips. Her legs rise, wrapping around my waist, pulling me even deeper inside. Her walls clench as I start to rock.

I thrust into my girl, knowing that's what she is now, loving the way she responds to each thrust and movement. Her body is made for me.

"More," she keens, digging her heels into my back, urging me in and out of her body. I pump my hips, giving her what she needs, and kiss my way down her jaw, her neck, all the way to her breasts. I suck on her skin, leaving little marks in my wake. I want her to bear my marks, want to have it known that I'm the one who did this. I need to have her perfect skin covered with the marks my mouth leaves behind.

I take her nipple into my mouth, sucking and pulling, giving it the gentlest of tweaks with my teeth. Then, I reach between us, already knowing I'm not going to last long. The familiar ache in my balls tingles, a surefire warning I'm going to come sooner rather than later.

I flick at her clit, loving her reactions as she squeezes

around me. I'd love to give her one more orgasm, but at this rate, I'm not so sure I'll be able to make it. She's clenching so hard around me, I'm having trouble keeping a steady pace. My hips stutter and shake as I try to maintain some sort of rhythm.

"Come, Jason," Fallon begs. "I want you to come inside me. Fill me up."

Her words set me off like a firework. My sight blurs, and all-consuming pleasure takes over my body as my cock jerks, spurting cum inside her like she wanted. I cum so much that it drips out of her cunt, leaking onto the bed sheets as I thrust a few more times, giving into the last few moments of hazy pleasure.

Completely wrung out, I slowly pull my cock from her weeping pussy, watching our combined releases dripping from her. "Fuck," I groan, watching it slowly drip onto the mattress. Watching her drip with my cum is one of the hottest things I've ever seen, especially when she clenches, giving me even more of a show.

I drop onto the bed beside her, pulling her into me. We're both breathing heavily, but I'm kissing her every-where, touching her, stroking her soft skin and giving her all of my attention. Fallon pulls the blanket up around us, and I know we can't go back to sleep, but god, it sounds so good right now. To fall asleep holding her, after what we did? A dream.

"How do you feel?" I ask her. I need to know that was as good for her as it was for me. "I'm sorry I didn't give you another orgasm."

She chuckles, the sound reverberating through me. I open my eyes to see her own glassy green eyes looking at me with mirth. "I did come again, but you were too lost in your own orgasm," she admits. "But Jason, that was incredible. I feel so good, so... loved."

"That was my goal," I tell her, squeezing her into me. "I know we talked about it briefly at the winery, and you said you had an implant, but I wanted you to know, I haven't been with anyone in five years. I haven't wanted to. Not until you."

Fallon shifts in my arms so she can see my face clearly. "Really?"

"Really." I shrug. "I was focused on being present for my family, and for Lennie, but now, I think I was waiting for you."

"I think I was waiting for you, too."

I kiss the tip of her nose, and glance behind her at the clock on the nightstand. "Shit, it's almost nine-thirty. I need to get going." I reach around, grabbing my discarded boxers and pulling them up my legs. I toss Fallon her shirt, and she throws it on over her naked skin. The sound of the front door opening and heavy footsteps running down the hall makes me look at Fallon with wide eyes.

"What do I do? *Why do we keep getting interrupted?*" I whisper with panic.

"Shit," she murmurs. "I don't care that you're here, but Pres really shouldn't see us in bed together again. I don't need more questions. Not yet."

The footsteps grow closer and louder, and Fallon throws the blanket up over my head. Her hands press on my shoulders and she shoves me off the bed. I roll and land on the floor between the bed and the wall with a loud thud. I groan, but shut up immediately when the door opens.

"Mommy!" Presley yells, and I hear the telltale sounds of her jumping into bed. Fallon is still naked from the waist down, and I really hope she didn't shove all the blankets down with me for her sake.

"Hi, my sweet girl," Fallon croons to her daughter. She asks how her sleepover was with her grandma, and Presley talks a mile a minute about everything they did in the short amount of time and about the breakfast she helped make.

A small spear of guilt hits me as I realize I haven't even bothered to text Megan or Isaac with an update, but I know they'd call with any issues.

There's another set of footsteps approaching, Fallon's mother. Shit. Presley might not notice the man sized lump on the opposite side of the bed, but her mom probably will.

I hold as still as possible as she enters. "Oh, hi, Mom," Fallon says, greeting her mother. "Let me get dressed and I'll meet you in the living room." Fallon shifts, and the blankets make a rustling sound as she covers herself more.

"Come on Presley, let's give your mom a minute," Elaine says. The door shuts behind them, and Presley's excited chattering begins.

"Oh my god," Fallon breathes. I pop my head up the side of the bed, watching as she flops back down onto the pillows. "That was close. My mom *totally* knows you're here, by the way. She kept flicking her eyes to the ground where you were laying."

"Crap," I grumble, standing from the floor. "Sorry."

"Nothing to be sorry about. She knows I'm an adult."

"How the hell am I going to get out of here?"

"Shit," she mutters. "I didn't think of that. Um, you could climb out the window?" I give her a glare that says *absolutely not*, earning me an adorable giggle from her. "Yeah, I figured not. Honestly, I have no idea. I can text you when my mom leaves and you can sneak out?"

"That works. I'll hang in here."

"Great." Fallon finishes throwing on a pair of pajama pants and a sweatshirt, and throwing up her hair in a pony. "I'll see you soon?" she asks, coming back to where I'm standing at the end of her bed, putting my own clothes on. She rests her hands on my chest, looking up at me with round eyes. It's the perfect equivalent to puppy dog eyes, and I know that if I have two, *make that three*, including Presley, girls in my life giving me these eyes, I'm done for.

I lean down, kissing her pouty lips. "I'll see you soon. Do you and Pres want to go to Sunday Brunch tomorrow?" Fallon bites her lower lip, and I kiss her to make her stop. "You don't have to, it was just a suggestion," I offer.

"No, I want to. It's a big deal, that's all."

I shrug. "You already know everyone."

"I know, but... still. Won't they want to know what we're doing? Why I'm there?"

"They will. But I'm at a point where I am comfortable with them knowing about this, us. Think about it, sunshine. No pressure. If you want to come, then you can, but if not, then we will find another time."

"Is that what we are? An us?" Fallon asks, her voice tentative.

I let her words sink in. In the last few weeks, things have changed for me. I want her, and I don't want to hold myself back anymore. It's going to be a transition, but I'm ready for this, ready to at least try, and face the potential consequences. "As scared as I am, for the same reasons you are, I also don't want to fight this anymore."

"So we are giving it a try?" she asks.

"If you're in, I'm all in," I respond, taking her hand and squeezing. "I should really take you on a real date."

She waves me off. "You don't have to do that."

"Yes, I do."

Fallon smiles softly and reaches on her toes to give me another swift kiss. "I'll text you."

I watch her leave, giving her a wave when she turns to look at me one more time before latching the door behind her. I have no idea how I lasted this long without falling for her, but now that I'm allowing myself these emotions, I'm done for.

34

FALLON

After Jason not so sneakily snuck out of my house, I asked Presley if she would want to go over to Lennie's grandparents' house tomorrow. Of course, she said yes, which is why I am now standing in front of my house with a plate of cookies Presley and I spent yesterday baking and decorating.

Jason insisted I didn't need to bring anything, but it felt wrong to show up to a brunch with nothing to offer. If anything, it's something for me to do with my hands, at least for a little bit. It saves me from the panic of whether I should hold Jason's hand when we walk in, or if I should hold Presley's, or shake his mom's hand, even though I know her quite well.

Ugh. You're a mess, Fallon. Get it together.

Jason pulls up right as my spiral goes downhill even further, and he climbs out of his car, greeting me with a panty-melting smile. Dammit. Why must he do these things to me? He kisses me on the cheek before picking Presley up and giving her a hug and spin. "Ready to go?" he asks.

He takes the plate of cookies from me and puts them in

the backseat between the girls, helping Presley get buckled while I shift anxiously in front of the car. I wait until he closes Presley's door, and then I burst with questions.

"How are we doing this?" I ask, my mind whirling. "Are we announcing we're dating? Is that what we're doing? *Are* we officially dating? I don't want to take any of Marley's thunder. Remember that episode of *Friends* when Monica and Chandler get engaged and Rachel kisses Ross and Monica says she stole her thunder? I don't want to do that. They're going to ask questions. What are we telling the girls? They're going to think we're getting married."

"Breathe." Jason cups my face in his large hands. "We can tell them whatever you want, or nothing at all. This is our relationship, so it's none of their business. As for the thunder thing, Marley won't give a shit about that. She won't think you're taking her thunder. She will be happy for us, no matter what. But as far as I'm concerned, yes, we are dating. We're in a relationship, and seeing where that takes us."

"Right," I murmur. "So what about the girls? We can't not tell them anything."

"I'll think of something," he says, kissing my forehead. "Now, are you ready?"

"I think so." I take a deep breath, and Jason opens my door for me. I climb in and buckle up while Jason gets in on his side.

He pulls out of the driveway and shifts his right hand, placing it on my thigh. I wore another sundress today, so he shifts the skirt, resting his hand directly on my skin. He rubs his thumb over it, back and forth in a soothing motion.

The simple touch from him helps soothe my nerves. The girls are in their own world in the backseat, talking about who knows what. When we pull up to Jason's childhood home, that's when the panic really kicks in. Of course, gentleman that he is, Jason takes the plate of cookies, leaving me defenseless and with nothing to do with my hands.

Jason leads us into the house, and Lennie kicks her shoes off, telling Presley to do the same, before taking her hand and running through the house, announcing our arrival.

Jason directs me through the house, and I desperately want to snatch the cookies from his hands so I have the distraction, but when I try, he simply says, "I've got them, sunshine."

In the bustling kitchen, Jane, Marley's mom, and Nikki, Jason's mom, are standing side by side at the stove, preparing the meal. Marley is sitting at the table, with her nursing cover over her front, and one of the babies underneath it. Beau holds the other baby in his arms, giving them a bottle. Josie and Andrew sit beside them, and Josie is crooning over the baby, playing with the soft tufts of dark hair. No one seems to have noticed our arrival quite yet until Thomas comes in the sliding door from the deck.

"Hey guys," he says, a huge grin on his face. He has a little gap in his front two teeth I've never seemed to notice before, and a set of dimples on his cheeks. "Fallon, it's good to see you."

"You too," I say, waving awkwardly. Josie sees me now, and gives me a knowing smile. I shrug, and Jason rests his hand at the small of my back, leading me into the kitchen.

"Ma," he greets, kissing his mother's cheek, and doing the same to Jane's. "I brought Fallon and her daughter with us, hope that's okay."

Nikki turns to greet me with a smile. "Absolutely, we're so happy to have you here." She pulls me into a hug, meanwhile, I'm still a little shocked over the fact that Jason didn't tell anyone we were coming.

"I'm so sorry," I murmur. "I would have thought he told you we were coming. We don't have to eat, but I brought some cookies to share."

"Oh hush," she responds, pulling away from the hug and taking the cookies from Jase. "We have plenty of food, I'm sure you will even be taking leftovers home with you."

I glance up at Jason. He's looking at his mom and I with a softness in his gaze. If I weren't slightly irritated with him for not telling them we were coming, I would find it adorable.

We finish saying hello, and Jason leads me back toward the dining table. "I can't believe you didn't tell anyone we were coming, Jase," I scold, lightly swatting his chest.

"If I would have told them, they would have overreacted, and I know that's not what you wanted. This way, things are chill." He glances at his brothers, "Right?"

Beau is the one to respond. "He's right. We probably would have pressed him a lot harder for information, Andrew especially." He glances at his youngest brother, who shrugs, and nods in agreement. "But we're happy you're here."

"Thanks," I respond. I sit down next to Marley, and she gives me a side hug as best she can with her baby latched onto her breast. A slight pang of heartbreak rears its ugly head in my chest. No, my baby wouldn't be a baby anymore, but I still grieve the moments I lost out on with them. What I would give to hold the baby for a moment, tell them how much I love them, and miss what could have been. It can be hard to be around babies, and I'm ashamed to admit that's part of why I haven't made as much of an effort to see Marley as I should have. "How are you? I'm sorry I haven't seen you much lately. Life is crazy, but that's no excuse."

"I'm good," she responds. "Happy. It's been a rough few months, adjusting to the twins, and finding a good system and meds for my mental health, but I'm good. I'm in a good spot now."

I squeeze her shoulder. "Good. I hope you know if you ever need a break or an hour to yourself, I'm happy to pop over and offer a hand."

"Thank you. I'll keep that in mind. I'm getting better at accepting help lately."

"Is it safe to say things are going well?" Josie changes the subject.

I can't help the smile that comes across my face. I glance up across the table, watching Jason as he converses with his brothers. "Yeah. Things are going well."

"You two are adorable," Marley says.

"Thanks." My cheeks heat under the attention. "It's... new. Very new."

"That's okay, it means you're still in the honeymoon phase. It's going to be amazing, I can already tell." Josie reaches over, clasping my hand in hers and squeezing gently.

"Mom!" Presley's voice calls from somewhere upstairs. If she didn't sound excited I might be worried. I go to stand, but two sets of pounding footsteps stops me. Both she and Lennie bound around the corner, arms full of coloring books, Barbies, and an assortment of crayons. "Look! Lennie's grandma and grandpa have so many fun things here for her to play with! Lennie said I could play with her stuff too."

"Wow, that's amazing, sweetie. And so nice of Lennie to share with you." I push back a piece of hair that's fallen into her face, and smile at Lennie, standing beside her with the sweetest smile on her face.

"Presley's my best friend. Even more my bestest friend than my friend Natalie. I like her a lot, but I like Presley mostest," Lennie says.

"Most," Jason corrects, coming up to stand behind the girls. "Girls, why don't you bring the stuff back upstairs for now. It's almost time to eat. You can play afterwards."

"Okay!" Presley and Lennie agree, running back toward the stairs and up to the playroom.

Marley and Beau stand, announcing they're going to lay the babies down in one of the bedrooms. Andrew comes in with his dad and Gramps from outside, and greets me with a hug and a smile. I've never formally met Richard, so it's nice to meet him. It's fun to see the resemblance Jason shares with his parents.

A few minutes later, we are all settled in at the table, dishing up an amazing smelling egg bake Jane and Nikki have made. The table is packed full of people, full of *family*. It's something I'm not used to. Growing up, it was me, my mom, and my dad. Both sets of my grandparents passed early, and both my parents were only children, like me.

I never wanted that for Presley. I wanted to give her a big family, with so many people to love her in case something ever happened to me. I thought that was something Brad and I could have, but clearly, that didn't work out.

As I sit at this family brunch, surrounded by these people who love each other so much, it hits me how much I want this to work. Not only because of Jason, but for the sake of my daughter and me. To have this family too.

"Fallon, how are you liking working for Isaac?" Nikki asks, bringing me out of my reverie.

"Oh, I love it," I admit. "He's a great boss. I love working at Meadow Grove too. It's such a great environment."

"Fallon's incredible at her job," Jason says, glancing down at me. He reaches under the table to rest a hand on my thigh, and I nearly burst into tears. I try to shrug off the compliment. I've never been good at receiving them, but Josie pipes in.

"She's amazing. Great under pressure, and is so good with her clients. I love watching her in action," she says, smiling at me across the table.

"I mean, you did such great work for our wedding, so I'm not surprised at all," Andrew says.

"Thank you," I say to them, unsure as to why this is hitting me so emotionally.

Jason squeezes my thigh gently, leaning down to kiss my forehead. I look up at him, and I see so much adoration in his eyes that I could simply burst.

What I don't expect, however, is for Lennie to screech. *"YOU'RE GETTING MARRIED!"*

And then for my own daughter to respond, also screeching, *"I KNEW IT!"*

My face turns the brightest shade of red I think it's ever been, and I squeeze my eyes shut in embarrassment. There's a hushed laughter at the table, and I don't know what to do.

I open my eyes, and Jason reaches to clasp my hand in his. "Girls, we talked about this. We're not getting married."

I look over to Marley, cringing internally as I hope she isn't upset that I might be taking over her special moment, but all I see is a giant smile and laughter in her eyes. My worries about upstaging her go away and I let out a deep sigh.

"But you kissed my mom," Presley counters, pointing at me. "And she's all red! You're getting married! You said people who are in love get married, and she's definitely in love."

"Presley, quiet down please," I say, trying to get her to lower her octaves. "We're not getting married."

I look to Jason for guidance, and he's still looking at me with those chocolate brown eyes full of love. "No, we're not getting married. We are together, though. We are dating," he announces, and the table lights up in cheers and congratulations. I can't help but be overwhelmed by the complete outpouring of love.

Jason continues, "It's still new, and we are figuring things out, but I guess the cat's out of the bag." He wraps an arm around me, pulling me into his embrace.

He's so different when he's not fighting his feelings, though I guess I am too. It's much easier to fall for him than fight the connection between us. I can take a full breath and sink into the possibilities the future might hold.

35

———

JASON

Everyone knows. Everyone knows Fallon and I are dating, and I didn't spontaneously combust. Now that we're here, I don't quite understand what I was so worried about all this time, but it seems as though it was all wasted energy.

After brunch, Fallon and I took the girls back to my place, and we explained our relationship. We told them we are dating, and even though we are, we might not get married, because sometimes people break up. The girls seemed to understand, and were happy with that response for now. Time will tell if they really understand and don't tell everyone they see that we are getting married.

Fallon still has to tell her mom that we are together, but she doesn't foresee it being an issue. We'll have dinner with her the next few weeks so she can get to know me. I've really only met her in passing, and I'm looking forward to getting to know her mom better. I'm in my office, working on some back end things, when there's a knock on the door. Thomas and his dog, Arson, are standing in the doorway.

Thomas is still in his full uniform, like he recently got off a shift.

A glance at the clock confirms my thoughts. "Hey, what's up?" I ask my younger brother.

He shrugs, flopping down in one of the extra chairs I have. "Just another day," he responds, his voice gravelly.

Arson bounds over to me, shoving his head in my lap as he tries to get some head scratches. I do, scratching behind his ears, earning me a low moan from him.

"Did something happen?" I ask. We can usually tell when Thomas has an off day at work. He leans on us, usually without even realizing it. You kinda have to pry the information out of him though. He shrugs again, and a knot forms in my gut. When he is reticent to even give you any information, it usually was a very bad day. "Thomas?"

"I don't think I'm ready to talk about it, yet," he admits. "I didn't want to go home."

"That's fine. Do you want to come have dinner with Lennie and I?"

He glances up, and I see how bloodshot his blue eyes really are. "Can I?"

"Of course. I wouldn't have offered it if I didn't mean it. Besides, Lennie will love the one-on-one time with Arson."

"Thanks, man." He comes across the small room to give me a hug. I hold him tight, letting him take his time, listening as his breaths shake in my ear. I'm not going to push him for information, but hopefully he knows he can tell me anything. It makes me wonder if it has anything to do with the drug circles that seem to be popping up locally. He's run more OD codes in the last year and a half than he has in his entire career, and they can't get to the bottom of it.

When he pulls away, I squeeze his shoulder. "Can you distract me?" he asks, and I nod.

"Sure."

"What's going on with you and Fallon?"

I smile, honestly a little surprised it's taken him this long to bring it up, though it has only been a few days since Sunday Brunch. "What would you like to know?"

"How did it start? Last I heard, you were avoiding her like crazy."

I shrug. "We have a history."

I tell him the story about how we were friends in college, and then after she started dating Brad, I was too butthurt to be around her, so I distanced myself. I tell him how we reconnected at Josie and Andrew's wedding, and with the brewery becoming contracted to the winery, we saw each other more often. Then the girls became such fast friends, and we became drawn to each other all over again.

I tell him everything, well, *almost* everything. I'm not about to tell him about our sex life. When I'm done, he looks so much better than he did when he came in here. "And now, we're seeing where it goes. I like her, Tommy. I like her a lot."

"I can tell," he agrees. "She's good for you. And that kid of hers is cute as shit."

"She's adorable, and Lennie and her are so close. It's been fun to watch their friendship grow."

"Who knows, maybe they will be sisters someday," Thomas states, a sly grin coming across his face.

Before I can make some sort of rebuttal to him, he veers away from Lennie and Presley. "Have you heard from Talia's parents lately?"

"Yeah, actually," I reply. "We had a FaceTime call with them a few weeks ago, and they sent Lennie a gift card for some back to school clothes."

"That's sweet of them."

"It is. I wish they could get out here to visit, but it's okay. I think I'm going to take her to California to see them soon. It's been about a year since they saw her in person." Talia's dad had a stroke before Lennie was born, and it's hard for him to get around now.

"That will be fun."

"I think so. It's getting harder as Lennie gets older, trying to explain everything to her, and why her mom isn't around."

"She's a smart kid," Thomas says. "She's more intuitive than you think. I think she knows it's something deeper than her mom not being around."

"I know. But how do you tell a five-year-old about drugs? How can they understand that?"

Thomas shrugs. "It will come, I'm sure."

"I hope so. I'm running out of ideas." With a deep breath, I stand from my chair. "Come on, let's go pick Lennie up, then we can get pizza for supper."

"Sounds like a plan to me."

36

JASON

October

"Hey, sunshine." I sneak behind Fallon as she strides across the reception hall, wrapping her up in my arms.

She spins into my embrace, a cheeky grin on her face. "Hey handsome."

I lean down, pressing a kiss to her soft lips. "I missed you," I tell her.

"It's been like three days, Jase."

I shrug, pulling her closer. My arms band around her waist as I hold her to me. "So? I can't miss you in three days? Admit it, you missed me too."

With another kiss to her pink lips, she sighs. "Alright, fine, I missed you too."

"I knew it," I murmur against her lips. "How's today going?"

"Really well. Everything is on schedule, and the bride is happy."

"Good. I thought I would say hi."

"Do you work tonight?" she asks.

"Nope." I point back to the bar where Laila is training two new employees. "I stopped by to check in with Laila and my new hires."

Fallon nods. "Where's Lennie?"

Lennie pops out from behind the bar, running toward us. "Fallon!" she yells, squeezing between us to wrap her arms around Fallon's waist.

"Hey, sweetie," Fallon says, picking her up and giving her a hug. "How's your day so far?"

"Really good. Daddy and I went out for breakfast, and then he got me a new bookshelf for my room, and then we came here to say hi," she rambles.

"Wow," Fallon says. "Sounds like a fun day to me."

"It is. Laila said that one day she's going to teach me how to make beer."

"I bet you'll be amazing at it." Fallon smiles warmly at her.

"Not for a long time," I tell her. "At least until you're twenty-one."

"How many years is that?" Lennie asks, and I can see the gears turning in her mind as she tries to figure it out. As far as I'm aware, first graders don't learn subtraction, so I don't think she will get it. It's hard to believe I have a first grader, but with the school year starting a few weeks ago, it's official.

"Sixteen years," Fallon supplies.

"That's *so* long," Lennie gripes.

"It will go by fast, I promise," I tell her.

I expect Fallon to say something in response, something witty or cute like she does since she's so good with Lennie, but she doesn't. She's focused on the door to the reception hall, where a man has entered with a woman on his arm.

He's wearing a black suit, and his dirty blonde hair is slicked back with what appears to be an obscene amount of gel. There's a woman clinging to his side, an almost bored look on her face.

"Hey, what's going on?" I ask Fallon, but she doesn't reply. Her face is pale, eyes hollow as she looks at the man. "Sunshine. Talk to me." I take her chin between my fingers, purposefully taking her eyes from the man.

When her eyes focus on me, there's a sense of fear in them. My daughter is still in her arms, and I can tell she's starting to get scared. "Lennie, go back to Laila, please. Tell her I need her to watch you for a few minutes."

"Okay, Daddy," she quickly agrees, sliding down Fallon's body and running back to the bar.

"Eyes on me, sunshine," I tell Fallon. "What's happening?"

Finally, the dead look in her eyes disappears, replaced with anger. "That's Brad."

"Brad?" I ask, confused, looking back at the man. He's walking around with the woman, and he looks lost. Then, it clicks. "Your ex-husband, Brad?"

Fallon nods, and I snap into action. I take her hand in mine, watching Brad as he turns in the opposite direction, then I lead Fallon down the hall to her office. I sit her in her chair, and rub my hands on the tops of her shoulders. "How do you want to do this?" I ask her. "Do you want to talk to him? Do you want *me* to talk to him?"

"Why is he here?" Fallon asks absentmindedly. "He's never reached out to me before, why is he here? Why now?"

"I don't know, sunshine. I really don't, but I can find out for you."

She shakes her head vehemently. "No. Who knows, he's probably here for the wedding or something. It's fine. I need to get back to work and pretend like everything is normal."

"Is that really what you want?" I ask. "Because if it's not, I won't hesitate to go ask him why the fuck he's here, and kick him out."

"No. Please don't, Jase. If he's here as a guest, that will reflect poorly on the company, and we can't have that," she pleads.

While I see her point, I can't help but be irritated. I don't want that man within a seventy mile radius of her or Presley if I can help it. He's done nothing to deserve a spot in their lives. He gave them up.

"Fine," I grumble. "But I'm not leaving. Lennie and I can stick around until you're done."

"Jase, you can't stay that late. It will be midnight or later by the time I'm done. Lennie can't stay up that late."

"I'll figure it out. Maybe I'll call Andrew. He's been wanting to have her over for another sleepover." I use my thumb to swipe across her cheek, pushing away the few stray tears that have fallen.

She shakes her head. "I'll keep my head down, and keep to the edge of the crowds. I want nothing to do with him, but I'm not going to run from my job, or cower from him."

"I don't like this," I admit. I mean really, what are the chances he knows the bride or groom? Fallon told me he grew up in the Cities, though I suppose some people are willing to travel for the perfect wedding venue.

"It's fine," Fallon says, pulling out of the embrace. "I can do this." She stands, adjusting her clothes and smoothing her hair. She takes a few tissues, dabbing gently at her cheeks. Her makeup is still perfect, and despite her eyes being slightly red, she looks flawless.

I watch as she dons a metaphorical mask, and strides out

of her office. She doesn't even look back to me. I'm left jaunting to catch up with her, finally taking her hand in mine when I reach her. I don't say anything, not wanting to crack the facade she has placed, only squeezing her palm in mine.

I don't care what she says, Lennie and I are sticking around for a while. When we reach the entry to the reception hall, I pull her into my chest.

I bend down, kissing her deeply. Cupping her cheeks, I hold her close for an extra moment. Her arms are wrapped around my neck as we hold each other. I rest my forehead against hers as we break apart, catching our breath. "You are the strongest woman I know. I'm *so* proud of you. Watching you be amazing at your job, be an amazing mom, all by yourself, makes me so proud to call you my girl. Sunshine, you are so much stronger than you think. You did this. You built yourself a life without him, and I get to stand by your side and watch you thrive. Don't let him take away your shine."

"Thank you," she murmurs, stretching up to take my lips one more time. She unwraps her arms from my neck, trailing her hands to rest her palms on my cheeks. "I..." She stops herself, but I have a feeling I know what she was going to say. I've been feeling the same. I just don't know if I'm ready to put those emotions into the world yet.

"I'm so thankful I get to have you at my side," she says instead.

I kiss her nose. "Go, be amazing." I turn her toward the reception hall. She heads on her way, and I skim my gaze through the crowd, searching for Brad. I don't see him, but I know I'm going to do everything in my power to keep an eye out for him the rest of the night. I'll stay as long as I can.

37

JASON

It's been nearly a week since the wedding where Fallon saw Brad, and she's heard and seen nothing of him. He didn't see, or interact with us at the wedding, so we figured it was a fluke.

Only now, he's sitting at a table in *my* brewery with the same woman he was with last week.

"Jason," Brad calls from one of my high rise tables across the brewery. *How the fuck does he know my name?* Has he been watching us?

Trying to maintain a neutral expression, I walk over to the table. "Hi, how can I help you?" I ask. I'm not about to act like I know who this fucker is.

Brad offers me his hand, and I reluctantly shake it. I want to punch his face in, not act cordial, but I'm also in my business with other customers around.

"Jason, it's been years," Brad continues. "We went to school together. Well, college. You were a senior when I was a freshman."

"Hmm," I mutter noncommittally. "Sorry, I can't say I remember you."

His smarmy face tightens, his eyes narrowing. Of course this fucker would expect me to remember him from college. Had Fallon not told me all about him, I guarantee I wouldn't know who he was.

Brad grits his teeth, and waves his hand. "The past is the past. Say, I was going to ask, have you seen or heard from Fallon Douglas? Or I suppose you would know her as Fallon Vosk. You two were pretty buddy-buddy if I remember right." He narrows his eyes, and I can tell he's digging. He has to know Fallon and I have been in contact, well, more than that, and he's trying to get me to break, to give him information.

I try to make it seem like I'm pondering the name he's given. I decide to be at least semi-truthful. "I've seen her, yes."

"Great. Can you tell me where she is? I was at an event she worked at last week, and couldn't seem to connect with her. Or better yet, call her for me and let her know that her ex-husband is looking for her? I'd do it myself but I'm not sure she still has my number."

This. Mother. Fucker.

"No can do," I say through gritted teeth, trying to keep my calm.

"Don't play stupid, Jason." He rolls his eyes. "Clearly, you've been in touch with her. It's a small town, and your reaction is quite telling."

"So what if I have? Why should I tell you where she is?"

"Because, we need to speak about private matters."

"Listen here." I move closer to him. The woman he's with blanches, not expecting me to get so close. "I know where she is, but if she wants to see you, you'll have to hear it directly from her."

"I have the right to talk to her," Brad tries to argue. "You know where she is. I have very important things to discuss with her, and you are doing whatever you can to prevent that."

"No." I hold my hand up to stop him. "You lost the right to talk to her the moment you decided to end your marriage without a second thought."

Brad chuckles, an eerie, almost nauseating sound. "Is that what she told you happened? You don't know what you're talking about." He shakes his head.

"Either way, I'm not going to tell her to answer your call. That's up to her." He recoils like I've slapped him, though maybe my denial and lack of bending over backwards to give him what he wants isn't something he's used to.

"Fine. I expect you'll tell her of this... altercation, so you can tell her to anticipate my call. I've been keeping tabs on her through social media, but her privacy settings didn't allow me to message her. You'll tell her it's in her best interest to answer." He turns his face away from me, effectively ending whatever this interaction was. All the better. I need to get out of here before I punch him straight in the nose.

I stride back into my office, shutting the door behind me. I kick my chair, sending it rolling across the floor and into the wall with a thud. Pinching the bridge of my nose, I try to figure out how I'm going to bring this up to Fallon. I don't want to do it in front of the girls, but she needs to know what happened.

I pull out my phone to call her. She's off today, spending the day with Marley and the twins. She answers on the second ring. "Hey, sunshine," I greet. I'm gathering my keys and anything else I need to head to my car.

"Hi," she responds. "I was about to call you, are we still on for tonight?"

"We are," I state. "But I need to talk to you first."

"Jase..." Her voice is tight and anxious, obviously picking up on the tone of my voice.

"Is Presley with you?"

"Yes, I picked her up from school, and then came back so she could see the babies. Your mom and Lennie are here too. That's what I was going to call you about. I was going to offer to bring Lennie straight from here so you don't have to run to your mom's. Then your mom can stay here for a bit. Beau has a later showing this evening."

I sigh. "That works out well, but I need to talk to you. I'll be there in fifteen, okay? Come out to the car when I get there." I head out the back entrance of the brewery, avoiding any more confrontation with Brad.

"Um, yeah, okay," she replies, and I can hear the anxiety in her voice.

"It's going to be fine, sunshine. This isn't something I wanted to tell you over the phone."

"Okay," she says. I climb into my car as we say good-byes, and then I'm heading off to Marley and Beau's house.

I don't know how I'm going to tell her this. How do I tell her that him being at the wedding the other night more than likely wasn't a coincidence like we thought? No matter what, I'll figure it out. She needs to know.

38

FALLON

I sit on the couch at Marley and Beau's house, listening to my daughter and Lennie coo over the babies. I stopped paying attention to the conversation between Nikki and Marley a few minutes ago. I wasn't able to provide any insight or information, and besides, I'm spiraling.

What could Jason need to talk about that is so important he had to come right here? I was going to be at his house in an hour anyway. Something deep in my brain tells me it has to do with seeing Brad at the wedding last weekend, but until I know, I'm going to pretend it's not. Jason pulls up the driveway a few minutes later, and I'm standing from the couch as soon as his car is in view.

"Nikki, can you watch Presley for a few minutes? I need to talk to Jason quickly." I told her he was coming, but didn't tell her anything else.

"Sure," she replies with a smile. I do my best to smile my thanks in response, though it probably comes out as a grimace.

I rush down the stairs and out the front door quickly. Jason is waiting for me in front of his car.

"Hey sunshine." He opens up his arms for me, and I throw myself into his comforting embrace. My anxiety lightens at his touch, but I can sense how tense he is, and it doesn't take long before I'm as anxious as I was before.

"Tell me." I pull back from his embrace.

Jason sighs, running his hand through his hair. When his brown eyes meet mine, I can see the look of anguish there. "Brad came by the brewery. Called me by name."

My heart drops into my stomach. I'd hoped it was a freaky coincidence. "What did he say?"

Jason pulls me tighter against him. "He asked about you. Said he remembered us being friends in college. He asked me where you were, and if I knew anything about you. I didn't tell him anything, but he wanted me to tell you to expect a call from him."

I drop my head to Jason's chest. I thought I was done with him. Done with that chapter of my life. Why is he back now? It's like he sensed I was happy and couldn't accept it. Couldn't let me live my life in peace.

"Why is he doing this?" I mumble. "Why now? It's been three years, Jase. I don't get it."

Jason cups the back of my head, holding me to him as he rubs a hand up and down my back. "I don't know. He was insistent. You have no idea how hard it was not to punch him in the face."

"I might punch him when I see him," I admit, then reel back, shaking my head. "I don't want to see him."

"You don't have to. Just because he's here, it doesn't mean you have to see him."

"He won't leave. He'll find some way to sneak up on me and talk. He's always been like that. He won't give me any space until he gets what he wants."

"What do you think he wants?" Jason questions.

I shake my head into his chest. "I don't know." I'm holding back tears now, because I don't understand. Three years. He's been gone without a word for three years, not caring about me or our daughter. A realization strikes me. "What if he tries to take Presley from me? Can he do that?"

"No," Jason states. He squeezes me tighter. "We won't let him. He doesn't deserve any time with her. He waived his rights to custody, didn't he?"

"Yes, but what if he tries to get custody? He didn't give up his parental rights, so what then? That's a long legal battle that I don't want to deal with." I start to cry into Jason's chest. *He can't take her.*

"I will be by your side every step of the way. If you want me there to talk to him, I will. If you want to avoid him and only talk to him with the lawyers, that's what we will do. You tell me what you need, Fallon."

"I don't know what I need," I sob. "I'm overwhelmed. I don't want any of this. I want it to go away. I was happy. I was living my life. Things are good. Why now?"

Jason holds me, letting me cry into him. I appreciate it. He doesn't offer false hope or a false narrative. He simply lets me get my emotions out. I'm scared. How could I not be? Sure, Brad was never physically abusive to Presley or me, but he hurt me in so many other ways, ways that I'm still trying to work through.

As if he knew Jason told me to expect his call, my phone starts to ring in my pocket. I pull it out, cringing when I see Brad's name on the screen. Stupidly, I never blocked his number. Back then, I had hope that maybe he'd come to his senses and come back and be a father to Pres. Then, I forgot.

"I don't want to do this," I reiterate, shoving the phone into Jase's palm. I step away, threading my fingers through my hair at my scalp, pulling at the strands. I need some sort of pain, something to distract me from this all-consuming anxiety currently eating me.

Jason silences the call. He sets my phone on the hood of his car, coming to my side and pulling me into him. He takes my hands from my hair, resting them on his chest. I curl my fingers in his shirt, squeezing the fabric tightly.

"I don't think I can do this," I say, repeating my earlier sentiments yet again. "How do I do this? What does he want?"

At this point, Jason's letting me get my thoughts out, letting me rage. He doesn't stop me, or tell me it's all going to be okay, because he can't promise me that. He can't promise me anything right now. What he can do, he's doing. He holds me against him, rubbing my back, my head, my shoulders. "I'm here for you," he repeats, over and over.

When my phone rings again, I lean back from Jason, taking his hand in mine. "Don't leave my side," I ask him.

"Never."

I take a fortifying breath and grab my phone from the hood of his car. Brad's name is on the screen, unsurprisingly. I swipe to answer the call, and turn it on speaker.

"Hello?"

"Fallon, so great of you to pick up," Brad says in a condescending tone.

"What do you need, Brad?" I get right to the point. Hearing his voice for the first time in three years is like a shot to my gut. Unwarranted, unwanted, and painful as hell.

"I was hoping we could get dinner."

"No," I state coldly. "Try again. What do you want? You suddenly appear after three years of no contact? What do you want?" I'm surprising myself with the sudden level of confidence I'm bringing to this call, but I'm not mad about it. Jason squeezes my hand, offering his steadfast support.

"Fine. I wanted to talk to you about things. We didn't leave off on good terms, and I'd like to change that. I would like to see Presley. I also have some things I would like to discuss with you."

A shudder rolls through my body. I don't want this. I want to live my life with my daughter, and Jason and his daughter. I don't want this interference from him.

"No. First, you and I can meet, with a third party present. Then, we can discuss things, and the potential of you seeing Presley. I'm not going to bring you back into her life, only for you to decide you don't want her again and leave without another goodbye."

"I never said I didn't want—"

I interrupt him. "Like I said. We can meet with a third party present. Otherwise, we will go through the lawyers. Don't mess with me on this, Brad."

I will do whatever it takes to protect my daughter.

"Let me guess, that third party is Jason Cunningham?" Brad sneers. Before I can respond, he continues. "Fine, but I get to bring my wife if you get to bring your... Jason."

I want to scream. I want to rage. I want to throw the phone across the yard and hit it with a hammer until it shatters.

"Fine."

"Great. I'll see you tomorrow evening at the diner. Does five work?"

"Yes," I say through gritted teeth. He hangs up the phone with my confirmation, and I try to hold in my scream.

JASON

Fallon was quiet most of last night. I easily convinced her to spend the night as Presley has a few sets of clothes at my house anyway. I held her in my arms all night. I didn't make her talk or share what she was going through in her head. I was a comforting presence for her. I dropped the girls off at school this morning and arranged for my mom to pick them up so we could meet with Brad. I'm not looking forward to having to spend any amount of time with the asshole, but I'll do it for Fallon.

The plan is for her to meet me at the brewery after work, and we'll head to the diner together. I don't know why the asshole suddenly wants to meet after three years, but I'd be lying if I said I wasn't nervous. I worry he's going to try and pull some shit to get custody of Presley.

All day I've been extra alert, almost like I've been waiting for Brad to show up here again and confront me. When four-thirty rolls around and he doesn't appear, I let out a breath of relief. Fallon should be arriving any minute, and I know I'll be better when she's in my arms. My mom sent a photo of the girls playing in the backyard a few minutes ago, so I know they're having a fun time.

The front door to the brewery opens, and all three of my brothers walk in. I toss the rag in my hand into the bucket of sanitizer water at my feet and greet them. "What are you guys doing here?"

Beau shrugs. "Had the afternoon off. Andrew was at Josie's shop and she needed to work, so I took him with me. We ran into Thomas and figured we'd all come here."

"I finished a big project and figured I would take the afternoon off. I was going to help Josie with some arrangements, but she said I was doing them wrong," Andrew explains.

"They looked like shit," Beau says. "I don't know much about flowers, but it was not good. Poor Josie was trying so hard not to cringe."

"She was not!" Andrew smacks Beau's shoulder. "She loves my flower arrangements."

"That's what she tells you," Thomas says with a snicker. "I'm off duty. Where's Lenners? Is she back in the office?" He gestures toward the back where my office is.

Usually she would be. After school, we come back here for an hour or so while I finish things up for the day, then we head home. I shake my head. "Nope. Mom picked her and Presley up today. It's a long story, but Fallon's ex is in town."

"The fucker who disappeared on her?" Thomas asks, eyes widening. "Didn't he leave her super unexpectedly?"

I nod. "Yep. We don't know why he's back. Fallon's worried he's going to try and get partial custody of Pres, even though he waived his rights to custody on the divorce papers. He wants to meet tonight, so mom took the girls. We'll pick them up later."

"Damn." Thomas shoves his hands in his pockets. "Want us to go with you? We don't have to sit at the table with you, but we could be stealthily hiding somewhere."

"No." I shake my head. "Fallon probably wouldn't want that. We can ask, but I don't think so. I appreciate the offer, though."

I sit down at one of the tables with my brothers. It's been a while since the four of us have hung out. Life has been changing, and for the first time in a while, I'm not upset about it. I'm happy with the direction my life has taken. I want my future to include Fallon and Presley. I want them to be a part of my family, part of this crazy life we share.

Beau shows us pictures of the twins, who seem to be growing like weeds. I saw them yesterday, but they already look bigger in the pictures that Marley sent him today.

"I really think Josie and I are ready to have a baby," Andrew proclaims. "Sure, we watched Lennie that weekend a few months ago, and maybe we should watch the twins, but I'm so ready to be a dad. Thinking about it makes me want to go knock her up right now. She's going to be the best mom, and *god*, she's going to be *so beautiful* pregnant."

Fallon appears behind him, a smile on her face. "I agree." She smiles as she sits beside me.

"See!" Andrew gestures to Fallon. "She gets it."

I tug her into my side, kissing the top of her head. "Hey, sunshine." She smiles up at me, her eyes dimmer than normal, but still carrying so much of her usual shine.

Fallon squeezes my hand, then directs her attention back to Andrew. "For what it's worth, you're never really ready to have a kid. You learn as you go."

"Ain't that the truth," Beau agrees. He runs his hand through his long hair, putting it up in one of his signature buns. "And every kid is different. I mean heck, Arlo is a champion sleeper and eater, and getting Ariel to sleep is like pulling teeth. The girl has some serious FOMO. You could read all the baby and parenting books—I did—and still not know what's going to happen. What works for other people won't work for you."

Fallon smiles, offering an encouraging nod. "But if you are ready to start that chapter of your life, talk to Josie, and if you're on the same page, then go for it."

Andrew nods furiously. "You're so right. Everyone thinks I'm joking, but I'm totally not."

I look down at Fallon, wondering if she wants more kids. In all honesty, it's not something I ever gave much thought to. I was always so focused on Lennie, and I never thought I would end up with anyone. Would I want more kids? More little Lennie's or Presley's running around the house? I can't say I'd be against it, but only if Fallon wants it.

Perhaps I'm getting way too far ahead of myself. We have other things to be focused on right now, and we've only started dating. But I'm all in. I'm happy to be a father figure for Presley, and I'd love to have Fallon as Lennie's step-mom. Like I said, I'm getting too far ahead of myself. I need to focus on dealing with whatever it is Brad has planned, and we can go from there.

I glance at the time, realizing we should probably get going. "Ready?" I ask Fallon, watching her expression morph from one of joy and relaxation to anxiety and fear.

"Do we have to?" she asks quietly. She leans into me, and I focus only on her. The conversation around us has shifted to other topics, leaving us alone. "My brain is telling me that if we don't go, or avoid it, then it's not real."

"You know that's not what will happen," I tell her regretfully.

She leans her forehead on my chest. "I know." Her voice is muffled against my shirt and I rub her back soothingly. After only a minute, she leans back. "Okay. Let's go."

"Fallon." Thomas stops us, reaching out his hand. "I don't think Jason was going to mention it, but..." He hesitates. "He told us your ex wants to meet. Do you want us to come too? We wouldn't be at the table, just at the restaurant. You wouldn't even see us. We'd be there as silent support. It's up to you, but the offer is there."

She glances around the table, locking eyes with each of my brothers, seeing the sincerity in their eyes.

"You would do that?" she asks, her voice that is usually confident, now small and reserved.

"Of course," Andrew chimes in. "You're part of the family. We don't mess around with family."

"What about Marley and the babies? And Josie? Don't you need to get back to them?"

"I think Josie will be pissed if she's not invited." Andrew stands, rounding the table to squeeze Fallon's shoulder. "But like Thomas said, we won't make our presence known."

"As for Marley and the twins, Mar would probably love a night out, even if it's simply to the diner," Beau states. "But I'll check in with her first."

"I have no life, and no one to report to, so I'll be there if you want me." Thomas shrugs. I can tell it hurts him a little that he doesn't have anyone to call his own, but I don't bring it up now.

"Wow," Fallon breathes. "That means so much. If you're okay with it, then, yeah, I would love your support."

"Then we're there. Anything you and Presley need, we are here for. "

The way my family is rallying around my girl and her daughter is enough to spring a tear to my eye. It means so much to me to know that they care for her as much as I do.

"Thank you," I tell my brothers. I know I told them that she may not want them there, but I'm glad they asked. Having them there will help. "We should get going."

I tell my staff working the bar that I'll be back later, then Fallon and I are heading out the door hand in hand. The diner is a block or two away from the brewery, so we walk there. "Tell me what's going on inside your head," I say after we walk in silence for a minute.

With a sigh, Fallon shakes her head, looking up at me. There are dark circles under her eyes, and her demeanor is defeated. "I don't even know, Jase. I barely slept last night. What if he really does want custody of her, and takes this to court, and takes her away from me? I don't even know where he lives now. He could live halfway across the country. I'd have to move. Then what?"

"We'll figure it out," I try to soothe her. Her breaths are coming in faster pants, her anxiety growing. I try to speak, but she interrupts me.

"And what's this about him being married again? How long ago did that happen? What does she have to do with all of this? There are so many unknowns."

We reach the front of the diner, and I pull her into a tight embrace. "Deep breaths. I'm sorry I made you think about it again. We won't know until we go in."

She inhales and exhales against my chest, and I'm thankful she's listening. Thomas pulls up outside the diner in his patrol car, and I see Beau in the passenger seat, with

Andrew in the backseat behind the Plexiglass. I can't stop the chuckle the sight elicits, and I slowly pull Fallon away from me. "Look." I point to them. She chuckles when she sees Andrew in the backseat.

My brothers are clearly arguing about something, and if I had to guess, it would be about who has to sit in the back next time. Jokes on Andrew, though, he's always going to be in the backseat. Perks of being the youngest of four.

Another vehicle pulls up beside the car, and I spot Josie in the driver's seat. She climbs out and sees Andrew in the backseat behind the bars, and starts laughing. Fallon and I watch as Josie snaps a few pictures from the front of the car with Beau and Thomas in the front seat offering a thumbs up, and Andrew in the backseat frowning.

"We should go in," Fallon whispers, pulling my attention away from them. Josie turns, offering Fallon a gentle wave and sympathetic smile before we head into the diner. Fallon looks around as soon as we enter, and when she doesn't see Brad, she heaves a sigh of relief. I reach down and take her hand in mind, squeezing it tightly and offering my support.

The waiter brings us to a table for four and leaves us on our own to wait for Brad and his new wife. Anxiety practically radiates off her, but I know she can hold her own. She's the strongest woman I know, and it also helps that she was married to the guy, so she knows how he might react.

The door opens with a chime, and my siblings walk in, Josie, Marley, and the babies in tow. Marley waves as they walk by and are seated a few tables away from us. They won't be able to hear the ins and outs of the conversation, but they will still be able to see us.

Fallon sits in silence beside me as we wait for Brad to

arrive. I don't try to fill the void with conversation. There's not really a point. She's too lost in thought right now for anything to stick. The waiter drops off some waters, and extra menus for us, and a moment later, the door opens and Brad walks in. Fallon's head snaps up, and a grimace crosses her face almost instantly.

40

FALLON

Brad saunters through the door with a smug look on his face. It's like he already knows this meeting, or whatever you want to call it, is going to go in his favor. His new wife, the same woman that was with him at the wedding last weekend, follows behind him like a lost puppy. I really didn't want to believe it until now that he was here, that this was happening. I'd hoped that it was all a really bad dream, but no. Here we are.

He greets the waiter, who points over at us. When Brad looks our way, he gives me a killer-watt smile I recognize as his fake one. The one he used when we went to his work events, and he wanted to impress his boss and co-workers. Anger roils in my gut at the sight of it. We were married for a long time. He should know I can see right through his bullshit, even after a few years.

Brad reaches the table and holds his arms out. "Fallon," he greets in a condescending tone. Does he really expect me to give him a hug?

I glare, not giving in to his desire, and hoping he gets the hint. After a long moment, he drops his fake ass smile, along with his arms, and sits across from me. His wife follows suit.

When she sits, I get a waft of her *extremely* strong perfume. The small whiff of it gives me an instant headache. With it, a sense of irritation blooms. So her perfume doesn't bother him, but my much more subtle perfume did? Apparently, his issue wasn't with my perfume. It was with me.

The table is silent for a long moment until I'm fed up. "Well?" I ask. "You show up after three years after you left me with no explanation. What do you want?"

"Can't we just catch up, Fallon? There's no need for the third-degree here." Brad runs his hand through his slicked back hair, leaning back in his chair like he's got all the time in the world.

"No. The time for 'catching up' was before you left me for another woman with no warning the day after I was in the hospital having a miscarriage, leaving me alone to grieve and raise our child on my own, Brad." I didn't expect myself to be quite so forward, so aggressive with him right off the bat, but I'm a little proud of myself. Jason's hand is under the table, and he reaches over, squeezing my thigh. I let out a little breath of air. I'm doing this.

Brad sighs. "I wanted to bring up the concept of what it might look like to spend some time with my daughter. My wife, Trixie," he gestures to the woman sitting awkwardly beside him, "wants to meet Presley. How old is Pres now, seven?"

I cannot believe him. Three years, and not a word, and now suddenly he wants to be in his daughter's life? Or is it that Trixie found out he had a whole other family when they met, and wants to be a good person and help us reconnect?

"You're kidding me, right?" I ask incredulously. "Because either this is some sort of cruel, twisted joke, or you're serious, and I can't decide which is worse."

Brad has the audacity to look shocked. Trixie can't even look at me. She's staring down at the napkin in her palm as she rips it to shreds. My chest is heaving as I suck in lungfuls of air. Jason rubs a soothing thumb over my hand, keeping me grounded.

I hold my gaze on Brad. He swallows roughly, taking a sip of the water in front of him.

"This isn't a joke. I want Presley to know me, and to meet Trixie. I suppose maybe I did some things wrong."

"Just a few." Jason scoffs, earning him a glare from Brad.

"Why now?" I ask. I have to know. "You left me. You told me you met someone new. Is this her? Or is this another woman in a line of women you will love and leave? What changed that you want to try and be father of the year?"

"It sounds harsh, but I didn't love you anymore. I met Trixie at a work conference about six months before I left you. Remember the trip I extended in Boston?"

The memory flares in my brain. I'd been home with a very sick Presley, and he told me he had to stay an extra three days to network with his boss. I begged him to come home. I needed help. Presley was miserable, and so was I. I was exhausted, trying to care for my toddler who was so sick I was scared she would have to be hospitalized. The anger returns with a vengeance.

"You knew your daughter was sick at home and yet you still decided to stay with her?" I point at Trixie, who flinches. Perhaps I'm being too harsh on her, but what the fuck?

"Trixie isn't at fault for any of this," Brad explains. "She didn't know any of it until a few months ago. I kept all of it a secret. I wanted to start over, leave my past completely behind. Maybe it was a mid-life crisis. But I needed a change. For me, the easiest way to do that was to disappear. I quit my job, filed for divorce, and started over with Trixie. I never told her anything until she found an old picture I had saved of us on my phone."

Trixie sniffles. "I thought he was cheating on me. Only to find out I was actually the other woman."

I ignore Trixie, going back to Brad. "Did you even miss your daughter?" I ask. I could give two shits if he missed me. I've moved on, and made my peace with that time of my life. But Presley? She lost her dad, and she's still confused and hurt over it. I don't look at Brad, but the way he doesn't answer right away gives me a bit of his answer.

"I did, but probably not as much as you think I should," he finally replies. Well, at least the asshole is honest about it.

"Why, then?" I ask. "Why are you suddenly appearing in my, in *our*, life again?"

"Trixie and I are starting a family. I thought it was only right that she knew our child had a sibling. That Presley be part of our family, too. We'd like to meet with Presley and have her spend some time with us."

"No," I blurt before I can think twice about it.

"*No?*" Brad cocks an eyebrow at me, and I can already see the cogs in his brain turning, figuring out a way he can win this battle.

"No," I repeat, shaking my head. *Stand your ground, Fallon.* Like Jason said, we can go through the lawyers. "You signed away your custody and visitation rights, Brad. We've been on our own for years now. I'm not going to have you meet with Presley until I know you are serious about being in her life. You have no idea the amount of hurt you have put that little girl through. Her dad *left* her. Do you know how many times I rocked her to sleep as she sobbed in my arms, because she didn't understand why she didn't have a dad who loved her enough to stay? How many times I had to tell her he loved her, even though I wasn't sure that was the truth?"

Brad tries to interrupt me, but Jason stops him with another glare, his brown eyes growing even darker as he stares across the table at my ex-husband.

"I'd think twice before speaking, if I were you." His voice is menacing, something I've never heard from him. I've heard him grumpy, and I've heard him mad, but never have I heard him enraged like this. Jason glances away from Brad, giving me a soft nod to continue.

"Have you ever tried to explain to a child that their dad is alive somewhere out there, but doesn't want to see them? She asks me why my dad died when he loved me so much, but her own father is alive out there, somewhere, and didn't love her enough to stay. So, no. You can't see her. You have to prove to me you're here to stay, to play a part in her life."

"Fallon, you might want to reconsider this," Brad tries to say, his voice low and threatening.

"If you want to meet with her, we will have to have a discussion with the lawyers, Brad. I'm doing what's best for my little girl, and right now, it's not you and Trixie suddenly deciding you want to play *present father*." I turn my attention to Trixie. "I'm sure you're a nice woman, but when you have a child of your own, you'll understand."

Trixie nods, dropping her palm to her stomach. Shit, she's already pregnant, isn't she? I guess that explains the sudden need to reconnect.

Brad scoffs. "Fine. Make this more difficult. Remember this, though, Fallon. You started this. I wanted this to be amicable. I wanted to discuss an arrangement, for this to be done without lawyers and money and hoops to jump through, but no."

"The time for being amicable passed a long time ago, Brad. *You* started this. You filed for divorce and left, waiving your rights to custody of your daughter," I finish with a heavy breath. Anxiety pumps its way through my veins. Maybe I did fuck up and will put us through hell, but I will stand by what I said. I have to do what is best for my daughter.

Brad stands, holding his hand out for Trixie to take. When she stands, I notice the smallest baby bump I didn't notice before. Brad tosses a business card with his lawyer's information down on the table. "Expect to hear from my lawyer, Fallon."

With that parting gift, he and Trixie leave. I take a few deep breaths, trying to keep calm until they're out the door, but as soon as the bell chimes, signaling the door opening and closing behind them, I crumble.

Turning into Jason, I fall into his chest, heaving sobs wracking their way through my body. His arms pull me in tight, and he lets me cry. This is exactly what I didn't want to happen. I didn't want him to ask for partial custody of Presley, and he did. I didn't want a fight or drama. I want to live my life with my daughter, with Jason and his daughter. Things were going so well. Why now? Why did Brad have to storm back into my life after all this time?

41

JASON

She's incredible.

Watching her stand up to him, tell him what she thought of his sleazy ass and stand up for herself and her daughter was the most incredible thing I've ever seen—aside from Lennie being born.

Holding Fallon in my arms as she falls apart is eye opening. I love her. And I love Presley as my own. I've been falling for her, for them, but now, I'm gone. I will do whatever it takes to keep her and Presley safe.

"Shh," I whisper. "You're amazing. You're so strong."

I almost forget we're at the diner, until the scraping of a chair sounds at the small table. I peek out from where I'm holding Fallon in time to watch Marley and Josie pulling their chairs up next to Fallon. They rub her arms and her back while I hold her, whispering words of encouragement. My brothers come up to the table too, scooting around and making room for everyone.

In the thick of everything, I'd forgotten they were all here, but I'm thankful they were.

Fallon pulls away from me for a moment to give Josie

and Marley hugs, then she's leaning back into my side. I wipe the few remaining tears off her cheeks, and wipe the running mascara from under her eyes.

When she looks up at me, I take her chin in my fingers. "We can do this. He doesn't have much of a case. He willingly waived his rights to custody and made no effort to be a dad. Sure, he's back now, but he will have to jump through so many hoops. Who knows, he might decide it's not worth it."

"Is it horrible to say I hope he decides it's not worth it? But then, it sounds like I'm saying my daughter isn't worth fighting for." Her lower lip trembles as she speaks those words, and I run my thumb over it to soothe her.

"Presley is worth any fight. *You* are worth any fight. For him to not try in the first place gives me some idea that maybe this will be all too much for him. He wants it easy."

Fallon nods. "And we aren't going to give him easy."

"No, we're not."

One of the twins chooses that moment to squawk, making their presence very known. Fallon leans back into me, while Beau passes a baby across the table to Marley who hoists her shirt up to feed them.

"Thank you for being here," Fallon says to the five people surrounding the very small table. "Even though you weren't next to me, it was still nice knowing you had my back."

"Always," Thomas says, lamenting his earlier words. "Every step of the way, we'll be here, supporting you and Pres." He pauses for a long moment, a shit-eating grin pulling on his lips. "Hey, not to change the subject, but... Trixie? Sounds like he picked her up at a strip club."

The table bursts into unceremonious laughter. Thomas

is always the one to lighten the mood when things get heavy.

"I wouldn't be surprised," Fallon says through her teary laughter.

I squeeze Fallon's shoulder, kissing her temple. The waiter comes back, taking in the fact that the other two guests have left, but we've gained five adults and two babies. "Uhh, do you guys want to move to a bigger table?" he asks.

"Probably," I say with a laugh.

FALLON AND PRESLEY have spent the last few days at my place, and the girls couldn't be more happy. They are still all aboard the "Mom and Dad are getting married" train, and we've had to shut them down a few times.

I'd be lying if I said I hadn't thought about our future more in the last few days. Having them here with us feels right, though we definitely need more space. The girls deserve to have their own rooms, their own spaces, and neither Fallon, nor I, have enough bedrooms in our respective houses for them to have their own.

I stir the macaroni and cheese on the stove, watching the neon orange powder melt into the noodles and milk. Fallon comes into the kitchen, her blonde hair pulled into a messy bun, wearing one of my old T-shirts. I love seeing her in my clothes. Maybe it's cavemanish of me, but it's sexy. She has a pair of leggings underneath, though I wish she were only in underwear, or perhaps nothing. I'd love to slide my hands underneath the shirt and grasp the bare skin of her supple ass. The dark circles under her eyes stop me from initiating anything, though. She's exhausted, and I don't know how I can help her sleep.

"Where are the girls?" Fallon asks, coming up behind me, and wrapping her arms around me.

I turn so she's wrapped around my front. I lean down, kissing the top of her head. "Last I checked, they were in the living room, coloring."

Fallon nuzzles her head into my chest, tightening her arms around me. "Thank you for picking up my slack these last few days."

"No need to thank me. That's what partners do."

"You're a really good one," Fallon states, tilting her head up. I give her lips a tender kiss. "Presley and I should probably go home tonight. I don't have any more clothes."

"Stay," I murmur, kissing her again. "Please."

"We don't have any clothes, Jase."

"Then get some and come back. Or Lennie and I can spend a few days there."

"Someone is clingy," Fallon teases.

I run my hands over her ass, giving her a gentle squeeze and resting my hands on her hips. "Yes, I am. I don't care, I'll openly admit it, sunshine. I want to be with you all the time. Six months ago, I would have laughed in your face if you told me I was diving headfirst into a committed relationship, but here we are. I'm here. I'm committed, and I want to be with you and this little family we're building."

"Who would have thought Mr. Grumpy Grumps would be begging me to spend the night again."

"I want you to spend all the nights," I tell her. There, I said it. It's out in the open.

Fallon leans back, her eyes narrowing, brows furrowing. "Jase, what are you saying?"

I step away from the stove, and lean against the countertop. "I want you and Presley here all the time. Things are good. Great, and I want to be with you guys all the time."

"Isn't it a little too soon?" Fallon mumbles. Her body tenses in my arms. "I mean, we've been officially together for, what, a month? I'm about to potentially be dealing with my ex-husband and a custody battle for who knows how long. Is that really a good idea? I don't know. I don't want to overwhelm Pres." She rambles on, her voice growing more stressed as the moments pass.

"Hey, slow down." I reach up, cupping her cheeks in my palms. "It was a suggestion. We don't have to do anything now, but I know what I want."

Fallon's chin wobbles, her green eyes growing wet with tears. "I want that too. I do. But it's so fast."

"I understand." I kiss her forehead.I'll do whatever she needs to be comfortable. "At least stay the rest of this weekend. We can run to your house and get more clothes. Okay?"

She nods. "Okay."

I turn my attention back to plating the macaroni and cheese. "Can you tell the girls to wash up and head to the table?" I ask Fallon.

She agrees, heading into the living room. I finish adding some strawberries and carrots to the plates. Fallon appears behind me again, her mouth turned down in thought. "Why do you think we haven't heard anything yet from him?"

I hand her two of the plates, taking the other two in my own hands. "I'm honestly not sure. He could be talking with his lawyers, and making a case, or he could be over it, and forgotten about it by now like we hope."

"I don't think he'll let it go that easy, as much as I may want that."

"I agree."

"I hate this waiting. I called the lawyer I had for the divorce and told her what was happening. She's happy to take us on again, but maybe I should wait? Is he going to have someone pop into my work one day and serve me papers? Ugh, I hate this."

"I know." I wish I could hold her again, but both our hands are full. "Come on, let's feed the girls, and then we can talk."

42

FALLON

At this point, I'm waiting for the papers to come. I know it's inevitable. Brad sees this as a challenge, and it's one he wants to win. I haven't decided whether or not I should tell Presley about her dad. It's gotten to the point where she's not asking about him everyday or crying when she comes home from school because it was "bring your dad to school day."

I click out of the spreadsheet I'm working on when there's a knock at my door. Isaac saunters in, wearing his usual button down and dark jeans. "Hey, how are things?" he asks. I can tell he's trying to be casual, but it's not working.

"I know you know," I state, gesturing for him to sit.

He sighs, sitting down in one of the chairs across from my desk. Megan and I went to lunch on Sunday afternoon and I told her she could tell Isaac everything that happened. If anything, it's one less person for me to tell.

"I do. Is there anything I can do to help?" That's one of the great things about Isaac. He's a great boss, but more than that, he's a great friend, and all too willing to help anyone who needs it.

I shake my head, fiddling with my fingers in my lap. "No, I don't think so. At this point, it's a waiting game to see if I get served with paperwork petitioning for custody."

"I'm sure Megan and I sound like a broken record, but we're here for you, Fallon."

"Thank you." My heart clenches because I know I have so many people in my corner willing to help me through this.

I meet with a bride in about an hour, and then tonight, Jason is taking Lennie, Presley and me out for dinner. He was very insistent that he was not only "wooing" me, but Presley, too. It's adorable. Last week, before all this craziness began, he sent me a bouquet of flowers from Josie's shop, and also made sure to send a smaller one for Pres, too. She was completely over the moon obsessed with the flowers, and made sure to tell everyone she saw that Jason had gotten her flowers.

Quite frankly, it's adorable. I told him he didn't need to do that but he didn't listen. He also made sure to get Lennie flowers, so she was included as well.

A knock on my door pulls me out of my thoughts to an unfamiliar face in the doorway. "Hi, can I help you?" I ask. The man stands still in the doorway, one hand in his pocket, the other, firmly gripping a manilla envelope. My gut churns, as I immediately know what this is.

"Are you Fallon Douglas?"

Swallowing the lump in my throat, I nod.

"You've been served," he says.

I don't bother standing, simply hold out my palm. "Thank you." He serves them to me with a grimace, and I wonder why he does this if he's that uncomfortable to be serving me legal paperwork. You would think he does this often enough that he's used to it by now.

The man exits, pulling my office door shut behind me. For a few long minutes, I sit and stare at the envelope. With trembling hands, I go to open the seal, but I hesitate. Do I want to do this alone? I know of a handful of people who could be by my side within minutes, my mother included. After everything happened last weekend, I made sure to call and update her. To say she's upset would be an under-statement.

Do I want Jason by my side as I open this? I've done things alone for so long, gotten used to it, even, but now, I don't have to. Even if I call him, and he's on the phone with me, I think that will be more than enough.

Decision made, I tap on his contact and call him.

"Hey, sunshine, I was about to call you," he says. The sound of his car door opening and closing sounds in the background.

"You were?"

"Yeah. One of the tap lines is cracked at the winery, so I'm replacing it this afternoon. I just pulled in. Want me to swing by your office and say hi? You have a meeting this afternoon, right?"

"Yeah, in an hour. Can you come here right away please?" I nearly beg.

"Sure, I'll be right there. Is everything okay?" I can hear the concern in his voice, and I know I made the right choice by asking him to be here with me.

"Not really. Brad sent over the paperwork."

"Shit," he curses. "I'll be there in a minute."

Not even thirty seconds later, the door to my office opens again. Jason flies through the door and rushes to my side. "Have you opened it yet?"

I shake my head, looking at the floor. "I couldn't. I didn't want to do it alone."

Jason pulls a chair up right next to mine. "That's okay. I'm here. Do you want me to open it?"

I take a deep breath, and shake my head. "No, I can do it." My fingers are still trembling, but I slide my pointer finger under the seal of the envelope. It slides open easily, and I reach in, pulling the thin packet of paperwork out.

Skimming the first few lines, which mainly contains Brad, Presley, and my full legal names, I take in more of the information. It is an official legal petition for shared custody.

He has it all laid out. He wants to have custody of her the entire summer break, and every school break, including alternating holidays. There is also an addendum that he can request a long weekend or time with her for special events.

Reading it makes me want to be sick. It makes it seem like she's not a person, but a toy they can cart around and show off. That's all I really ever was to Brad, anyway. It makes sense that's what he'd want of our daughter, too.

When I've read through all the legalese a few times, I take in a few shuddering breaths. I can't believe this is really happening. When he signed the form, I thought I would never have to worry about this. It hurt like a bitch knowing he was so willing to give up our family at the drop of the hat, but now it's like he's using us to turn me into the bad guy.

Jason's practically shaking with anger next to me. "In other words, he wants to be the fun parent." He swears under his breath. "He wants to be the one that gets all the 'fun time'. Summer breaks, any time she has off school. He wants that to be associated with him, so he can try to reverse her perspective."

When he puts it like that, it clicks. Initially, I thought it was because of location, and him being in Boston, but this makes sense. He never wanted to do the tough stuff of parenting. I was always the one getting up at night, doing the feeds. The one who took care of her when she was sick, or potty training, or taking her to doctor's appointments. God, it all makes sense now. He never wanted to be a real parent. He wanted the glory of being a "Dad".

"You're right," I murmur. I think I'm numb. I should be raging. I should be coming up with a plan to fight this, but right now, all I can do is be numb. Try to process.

"We'll figure a way around this, Fallon," Jason says, his voice firm and promising.

I nod, my eyes unseeing, only focusing on Presley's name written on the form.

43

JASON

Fallon's lawyer sits in front of us, her hands folded on her desk. A hearing date is officially set, so we are meeting with her to go over everything and file a response to his petition. "I really do think we have a strong case. He legally waived his right to custody and visitation three years ago, and has made no effort until now to be a dad. He also hasn't paid child support in those three years, nor has he ever called to check in on Presley's wellbeing. I think we could win the case and have him walk away with no rights at all, if that's what you want."

Fallon's attention is focused on her hands in her lap. She's been picking at the skin around her nails all week, and they're practically raw. "I don't know what I want," she whispers. "I don't want him to take her from me every holiday or all summer."

Her lawyer, Haley, is a badass. She's been extremely helpful so far, and I know this whole thing is stressful for Fallon, but I really think her lawyer will help ease our minds.

"Brad is going to have to jump through a lot of hoops

before he can even get visitation with Presley. They aren't going to decide one day that he's fit to parent and drop her off at his doorstep. He'll have to move back to Minnesota more than likely, pay back child support, and go through parent education," Haley explains, surely trying to ease some of Fallon's anxiety.

"Okay." Fallon takes a deep breath. Reaching over, I tug her fingers from her hand, hoping to save some of the skin around her fingers from more pain.

"What are his chances even if he does all that?" Fallon needs to hear it out loud to believe it, so I ask the question she's too scared to ask.

"Even if he meets the minimum requirements, the judge will still first and foremost take into account the best interests of the child. Placing her with an almost complete stranger who abandoned her and went zero contact when she was barely five-years-old would most certainly not be in her best interest. The probability of his motion tricking an investigator into thinking Brad actually wants to parent is low." Haley's conviction has Fallon straightening in her chair.

"So, what do we do now?"

"For now, we need to file the response and be ready to argue our position in court. I'll get the response drafted and send it over to you to review. I'll be in touch plenty before the hearing, too. If you have any questions, please contact me anytime."

"Thank you, Haley," I say, dropping Fallon's hand to reach across the desk and shake hers. My mind is whirring with all of the information she gave us today.

We leave the meeting, Fallon still eerily quiet. The girls are hanging out with Fallon's mom today, and we have an hour or so before we go pick them up. "Should we get some lunch before we head to pick the girls up?"

When I glance over to the passenger seat, Fallon nods. "Sure, that's fine."

"Where would you like to go?"

She shrugs. "Doesn't matter."

Reaching across the center console, I take her palm in mine. "Hey," I murmur. "I know this is a lot, but like Haley said, it's going to be a slow-moving process. That will help give you time to process everything. Nothing will happen at the drop of a hat, remember?"

She nods, but I don't fully think she's convinced. "What would you do if Talia came back and asked for shared custody of Lennie?"

I lean into my seat as I do my best to rationally think about what I would do. "I—I don't know. To be honest, it's not something I ever thought about. Realistically, I don't even know if she's alive or dead."

Fallon looks out the window. "I'm sorry. I shouldn't have brought it up. We're in two completely different scenarios."

"It's okay." I lift her hand to my lips, placing a tender kiss on the back of her hand.

44

———

FALLON

I am the definition of a mess. I've kept it together on the outside, working, being a mom, and doing my best to be happy, but on the inside, I'm falling apart. The only thing keeping me sane is Jason. Despite me saying I wasn't ready to move in, Presley and I practically have. We haven't gone home in well over a week, except to grab more clothes and other random things.

The hearing is early next week and I'm spiraling. I don't know what to do. Do I tell Presley about her dad being back in town? What if the judge decides he's fit for custody and we start the transition to him having partial custody? There are too many things ping-ponging in my brain.

I need Jason. I've been craving the comfort only he can provide. He's been handling me with care, and I appreciate it more than he knows, but I need more. I need the intimacy he offers me. I can't help but wonder that maybe this is all too much for him. Is the custody case too much? Is that why he's been distancing himself from me physically? We haven't done anything besides hold each other, or the occasional make out session here and there, though I suppose that's my fault. I've been stuck in my own head. Maybe I should make it up to him.

He's been in the garage for about an hour now. We put the girls to bed together, and then he went back out there. I stand from the couch, leaving my glass of wine and Kindle behind. Music plays softly over the stereo sitting on top of a toolbox, and I find him sitting in a lawn chair, drinking a beer.

"Hey," I greet, running my hand over the back of his neck. "You okay?" I round the front of the chair and straddle his legs, lowering myself onto his lap. My arms go around his neck, fingers threading in his hair. He leans forward, setting his beer bottle on the ground before wrapping his arms around me, pulling me even closer.

Jason rests his head, using my boobs as a pillow. He doesn't answer my earlier question, which makes me think something really is wrong, and he's avoiding it.

"Jase, what's wrong?" Leaning back, I lift his head to look into his eyes. Something is definitely wrong.

He takes a heavy inhale, and my stomach clenches with anxiety. "I don't know how to say this," he finally says.

I try to shift from his lap, and he grips me tighter for a moment before letting me slide off. I step away from him, my heart pounding faster with each step. I rest against the countertop where all his tools are.

"I've been thinking. Depending on how the court hearing goes, I think maybe we should hold off on officially moving in together," he finally states, his eyes cast to the cement ground.

"You're..." I stutter, trying to gather my words. "You're having second thoughts?" I should have known this would happen. He's been distant. He's separating himself from me. Like Brad did. He's trying to push me away. He was the one that brought up moving in together, and now he's regretting it.

Jason abruptly shakes his head. "No. Not in the slightest. I want nothing more than for you two to be here, in my home, in my family. I'm worried about the court case, that's all. They're going to be taking a deep dive into Presley's life. Her living situation, who her mom is dating, *everything*."

He's going back on everything he said. "So what? You're going to give up? Break up with me?" I ask, my voice trembling. I want to be strong right now, but my heart is breaking.

"Sunshine, I never said that. You're taking words out of my mouth," Jason tries to say, but it's like I'm underwater. My ears are whooshing with noise, and I can't think, can't breathe.

"You lied to me." My voice breaks as I spit the words out.

Jason shakes his head. "*No.* I didn't lie to you, sunshine. I'm trying to do what's best for you and Presley."

"He abandoned me, and look where that left me! How is this better for me? Everyone leaves, Jason! That's what I've been so afraid of all this time. He left me, and now I can't trust anyone to stay."

Jason steps forward and tries to pull me in closer to him, but I slide away from him. "Fallon, stop."

"No, Jason."

"I'm not him, Fallon!" Jason yells as I turn my back to him. He stops me in my tracks, turning my legs to stone.

He comes up behind my back, wrapping his arms around me. "I'm. Not. Him," he whispers in my ear. "You need to listen to me when I say *I am not leaving*. I want you in my life, in my home, in my bed. I want Presley to have her own room, her toys and coloring books here. I want her playing with my daughter every night, being the sister she's never had."

Shuddered sobs break through my body. "You said you would fight for us, Jason. You told me you would fight for Presley."

"This is me fighting for you. You think I want to step back? You think I want to be anywhere but at your side as you do this? Of course not. But this is me fighting for you. This is me doing what I can to protect you, to protect *both of you*. If that means holding off on something I want so desperately, in order to make your fight for your daughter easier, then I will do it, no question."

Jason turns me so I'm facing him and rests his hand over my heart. Some of the fight leaves my body as I realize what I've done. I compared him to Brad, someone Jason is nothing like. On his worst day, Jason could never be the type of cruel Brad is.

"You're not him," I affirm, hating that he had to call me out on it in the first place, because he's not. I heard him having what I thought were second thoughts, and I panicked. Because of Brad, my stupid trauma response is to assume the worst in people, to assume they'd leave someone who they once claimed to be a partner to. "I'm sorry. I need you at my side through this, Jason. I'm sorry I reacted that way. I panicked thinking you were leaving too."

"If you think I will willingly walk away unless you tell me to, you're dead wrong." His voice is strong, and I know he's telling me the truth. He wanted me to have all my options, and be aware of all the circumstances.

I rest my head against his chest, his rapidly beating heart is thumping against my ear, knowing mine is matching pace.

"I will stand by your side and fight if you want me, or I

will stand in the background and cheer you on from afar. Whatever you need to make this easier, sunshine. That might mean we have to take a step back from moving you two in for longer than we wanted. I won't do anything to interfere with this battle, Fallon. I want you to have the best shot you can."

"By my side?" I ask, knowing I'll need to lean on him.

"By your side," Jason confirms, his fingers digging into my hips as he pulls me closer to him.

I reach up onto my toes and crush my lips against his. I need to have this connection with him right now. Need to know that I have him, that he's really not going to leave to do what he thinks is protecting me.

Jason's hands skim down to my ass, squeezing my skin through my thin leggings. Heat races through my body at his urgent touch, and I rip at his shirt, desperate for his skin against mine. "Jase, please," I cry, pulling away from his lips. He tugs my leggings down, his fingers rough against my soft flesh.

My underwear is still a barrier between us, and I'm so eager for him, skin on skin. His shirt ends up on the dirty garage floor, giving me access to his chest. I caress the soft hair on his skin. His heart hammers like a metronome underneath my palm. Jason kisses me again as his fingers grip at my hips, trailing around to the front of my mound, slipping underneath the fabric of my panties.

Jason bites my bottom lip, tugging softly as he finds my soaked pussy with his fingers. I groan into his mouth, jerking my hips to get closer to his touch. "Look at you," Jason croons, one digit sliding inside me. "You're soaked."

He pumps his finger lazily in and out of me, giving me a tease of what I need and what's to come. "Jason, please, I need you inside me. It's been too long." And it has. Ever since all this started with Brad, I've been so stressed. I've neglected the intimacy of our relationship, something I love so much and crave even more.

Jason removes his finger from my needy center, lifting it to my lips. "Taste," he mutters. I open for him, closing my lips around his finger, tasting myself on him. I suck, flicking my tongue over the tip, doing exactly what I'd do if it were his cock in my mouth.

Abruptly, he pulls out, reaching down to yank my shirt up and off me. He reaches around my back, unhooking my bra, and I let it fall off my shoulders, my breasts now free. Nipples pebbling in the cool air, I shiver as I stand bare before him in only my soaking wet underwear.

Jason undoes his belt, sliding down his pants and briefs all at once. His dick is freed and he strokes it roughly. A drop of cum slides from the tip, and he takes it between his thumb and forefinger. Reaching down, I grip his wrist, the one stroking his cock, and bring his fingers back to my lips. I flick my tongue over the subtle wetness, enjoying the little taste of him that I get.

With my other hand, I wrap my fingers around his length, caressing and teasing him the way he did to me. Jason drops his head back, letting out a feral groan as I continue to work him, all while sucking his fingers. The sound is so fucking hot that another burst of heat swoops in my belly. "Turn around," Jason commands, and I follow his direction immediately.

In front of me is a countertop that Jason has a few tools on, so I push them to the side, a few clattering to the floor. I rest my elbows on the wood, jutting my ass out and swaying. "Sunshine." Jason steps up behind me, his hands rubbing over the skin of my ass, squeezing harshly. He pulls the fabric of my underwear down, and I kick them off, and I'm completely bare to him. To this incredible man who I fully believe when he says he will fight for me, for my daughter.

"Please," I beg. "I need you, Jase."

Jason's palm rests at the base of my spine, and I turn back to glance at him. He's staring down at my pussy, eyes completely enraptured. His fingers are gripped around his cock. The blunt tip of his cockhead presses against my opening, and I gasp as he slowly pushes in, taking his time. This is what we need. We started off frantic, but now, it's intimate, like we're taking our time, savoring the moments when it's only us.

He fills me, inch by inch until I'm completely full of him, his pelvis flush against my ass. "Fuck, I've missed you," Jason says, his voice rasping as he slowly slides back.

Instantly, I miss the fullness, but luckily he doesn't make me wait long before he's pushing back in, giving and taking as he finds a pace. Jase runs his hand up to the middle of my back before reaching around, cupping my breasts as they move in motion with his hips. I reach down to circle my clit, bringing me to a near immediate climax.

I clench around his shaft, loving how he groans, pinching my nipple. "That's it, sunshine. Come on my cock like the good girl I know you are."

"Oh god," I cry, his words sending me into another spiral. The moment his release hits him, his body shudders against mine, and his warm cum fills me up, spilling out of me down my thighs as he thrusts a few more times.

Jason holds there until he starts to soften, and he pulls out of me, letting our combined release drip between us. I rise from my bent position, leaning against his chest, tilting my head back. He takes my lips in a kiss so soft that I melt. I adore how soft and sweet he can be with me, but also how hard and rough he can take me. Something niggles inside of me, and I know what it is. I know I love this man. I need to find the right moment to say it. I don't want it to be too soon, but yet, I'm still scared. Scared he might not say it back, though his actions prove otherwise every day.

"Stay here," Jason says, giving me one more peck on the lips. He returns a few moments later with a wet cloth, and cleans between my thighs. Once I'm at least semi-clean, Jason wraps a blanket around my body. "Come on, let's get to bed."

He leads me through the house where I clean up a little more in the bathroom, and he heads back to the garage to pick up our discarded clothing. I throw on a pair of underwear and one of his shirts before climbing into bed to wait for him. As much as I would love to sleep naked tonight, I know sleeping naked with two little girls who love to come in bed and wake us up in the mornings is not smart.

A few minutes later, Jason comes in wearing a fresh pair of boxer briefs. He slides into bed next to me and pulls me into his chest. "I'm sorry about reacting earlier. I panicked, thinking it was happening all over again," I admit, realizing how much it sent me over the edge to think he was leaving. I lean my head against his skin, hearing his steady heartbeat.

"I know, sunshine. But I'm here, I'm not leaving. I will show you every day that I won't leave you. I will never leave you the way he did."

I nod into his chest, his warmth and his heartbeat soothing me.

"Thank you," I say.

Jason tilts his head to mine, kissing my forehead. "Goodnight, my sunshine."

JASON

My ringtone plays over the stereo speaker on my car, interrupting the podcast I was listening to. I'm leaving work to pick up Lennie and Presley from my mom's house, then head home for dinner. The hearing is tomorrow, so we are going to have a relaxing night at home.

A look at the caller-ID has my anxiety simmering through my body.

Talia's dad.

I press the button on the screen to answer the call, swallowing the sudden lump in my throat. Usually, they text first before we set up a call, and the only other times they've called unexpectedly is when they have news regarding Talia.

"Hey Lou," I answer, trying to keep calm.

"J-Jason, son, how are you?" he asks, his words stammering. He's had a type of stutter ever since he had his stroke.

"I'm alright Lou. How are you and Ella doing?" I don't ask the question I really want to ask.

"W-we're o-okay." He pauses, more than likely to get his words right in his brain. "She's alive."

A heavy sense of relief seeps its way into my body. "Is she with you?" I ask.

"No. She called from a homeless shelter in O-Oklahoma. We tried to get her to call you, b-but she wouldn't. She talked to us for ab-bout three minutes, and then when we tried to get more information, m-maybe go get her, she hung up. The call was private."

I let out a deep sigh. "Shit." I pull the car over, needing to process, knowing it's not safe for me to be on the road right now.

"S-she asked about Lennie," Lou says, stumbling over his words more with his emotion. "Asked how o-old she was now. Said she was s-sorry, but not to l-look for her anymore."

"We aren't going to stop," I say through gritted teeth. I might not love Talia anymore, but she is my child's mother, and I care for her. I want the best for her, even if she's not in our lives. And sure, we aren't searching for her high and low, but we are still keeping an eye out for her, hoping she's safe and healthy.

Lou sighs heavily. "That's w-what I told her. She hung up shortly after."

"I'm sorry, Lou. Do you need anything?"

"No. J-just calling to let you know. How are y-you two?"

I decide now is as good of a time as any to tell him about Fallon and Presley. Lou and Ella always encouraged me to move on, so hopefully they're happy. "We're good. I met someone."

"G-good for you. Tell me about her."

"Her name is Fallon. We actually met back in college, but lost touch. She moved to Ivy Ridge last summer after living with her mom in the next town over for a few years.

We recently re-connected. Her daughter, Presley, is seven, and she and Lennie are best friends."

He makes a contented sound, and honestly, that's good enough for me. He's not always a man of many words, even more after his stroke, but that little noise is enough for me. "I'm h-happy for you, son. Promise you'll bring them to visit s-sometime."

"Promise. And we will have to do a video chat soon with Lennie. She'd love to chat."

"We would l-love that. Anytime."

"Thanks for the call, Lou."

We say goodbye, and the call ends, leaving me alone in my thoughts. In a way, I wish we could find Talia, so she could see how perfect her daughter is, and how much love she's surrounded by, but it's hard to find someone who doesn't want to be found. I've been thinking a lot about what I would do if she came back ever since that night I spoke to Fallon about it.

It's hard to know for sure, but I think if she came back and was clean, I'd be willing to have Lennie get to know her mom. It would take a long time for me to trust her enough to be on her own with her, but if she fought for it and was clean, I don't think I'd be able to deny her time with her daughter. Her addiction is not something she can control at this point, but maybe someday, she will be able to, and then she can be a part of her daughter's life. Talia isn't a bad person. She's been dealt a shitty hand and hasn't been able to overcome it.

Another call comes through, and this time, it's Fallon.

"Hey, where are you?" she says when I answer the call.

"On my way to get the girls," I respond, taking a deep breath before I get back on the road. "I pulled over for a minute."

"Why? Is everything okay?" Her voice is panicked, so I do what I can to ease it right away.

"It's fine. It was Talia's dad. They heard from her earlier today, so they wanted to give me an update."

"Oh my god, they did?" she breathes. "Is she okay?"

"As far as we can tell. All she told him was that she was at a shelter in Oklahoma, and not to look for her anymore."

"Now what?" Fallon asks.

"Now... nothing," I state. "It's hard to find someone who doesn't want to be found. We keep doing what we're doing, and if one day she ends up coming home, then we go from there."

"How are you doing?"

"Okay," I respond. "I wish she was healthy so Lennie could know her, but at the same time, if she's not healthy, I don't want her near her. Does that make me a bad person? A bad dad?"

"No." Fallon replies firmly. "You aren't a bad dad, Jase. Doing what is best for Lennie is what makes you a great dad. Talia will have a lot of work to do if she ever wants to get clean, but I know you'll do what you can to make that easier for her."

"Thank you," I murmur as I pull into my parents' driveway. "I'm at my mom's. I'll talk to you more when I get home, okay?"

"Okay. I'll see you soon."

The phone call ends with a click, and all I can think about is how hard it was not to say *I love you* at the end of it. I do love Fallon. So much. Both her and Pres have become so intertwined in my life, in my family, that I can't imagine wanting to spend a day without them. It hurts knowing Talia is out there somewhere, but at least for now, we know she's alive, and has a bed to sleep in tonight.

46

FALLON

"Can I ask you something?" I ask Jason, my fingers smoothing over the hair on his naked chest.

"You can ask me anything, sunshine," he responds, twirling a piece of my strewn hair around his finger. We've just laid down after putting the girls to bed, and I'm doing everything in my power to stay calm as I think about tomorrow.

"Tomorrow," I start, taking a deep breath. "I know you said you'd be by my side, but I think I changed my mind." Before he can panic like I did last week, I rush to fill him in on my thoughts. "I think I want you to be by Presley's side."

"What do you mean?" Jason tilts his head back to look me in the eyes.

"The plan was for you to come with and wait outside the courtroom. The girls were going to be with your mom, and my mom would be with me, right?" I ask, though I know the answer, since we've gone over it countless times.

He nods, waiting for me to continue.

"I think I need to do it alone, but... I think I need you to take Presley. It's not that I don't trust your mom, I do. It's really that I need to know she is totally safe while I'm in there debating her future. And you're the only person I can trust with that. She is my entire life, and I trust you more than anyone else that you will keep her happy and safe while I am fighting for her."

Jason swallows thickly, and I can see the emotion rising in his face. "You do?"

I nod, a tear leaking from my eye. "I do. Maybe you could take her out for breakfast or something, the two of you, and then someday I can have some one-on-one time with Lennie."

"If that's where you need me to be tomorrow, then that is where I will be, sunshine."

Weight lifts off my body with his answer, and I can breathe, knowing he will have my girl during that time. If he can't hold me during my time of need, then at least he can hold her.

"Thank you," I breathe, tears freely streaming down my cheeks now.

"Hey now," Jason coaxes. "No more tears. We've got this, remember? Haley is confident it won't be easy for him to get any form of custody right away. If he really wants to see her, he will have to fight hard and prove himself."

Words aren't my strong suit anymore, so I simply nod into his body.

"Come on, you need some rest, sunshine." Jason holds me, caressing my hair until I drift into a fitful sleep of nightmares where Brad takes my daughter from me.

THIS ENTIRE THING seems like something from a movie, not my actual life. Haley leads me and my mom into the courtroom. My mom holds my hand as we stride down the aisle, and she squeezes it one last time before sitting on the bench closest to the table Haley and I will be sitting at.

I take a deep breath and smooth out my black pencil skirt, cursing myself when I see a piece of lint on the hem. Haley gestures for me to sit beside her, and we wait for Brad and his lawyer to arrive.

Not a minute later, Brad and his lawyer stride in. They're both dressed in neatly pressed black suits, with Trixie following behind in a black fitted dress. I can barely see the swell of her stomach as she cradles it. She's pale, her hair in a tight ponytail, but strands are falling loose, and not in a stylish, cute way. She looks frazzled and stressed beyond belief.

For a moment, my heart aches for her. I've been in her position, and if he treats her the way he did me, she may not even realize how wrong it is. She may not know how much better she could be being treated by someone who really cares.

Brad takes his seat next to his lawyer, and the bailiff calls to the courtroom, "All rise."

We all stand as the judge enters wearing her black judicial robes. She takes her seat at the head of the courtroom.

She motions for us to sit and rifles through the paperwork on her desk. My belly swoops with nerves, but I try to stay calm. I wipe my clammy hands down the front of my skirt and pick at the polish on my nails.

"Alright," she says. "My name is Judge Harris, and I'll be presiding over this case. We are here on a petition to revise the initial custody agreement between Fallon

Douglas and Brad Douglas, who is petitioning for joint custody of Presley Douglas. Is that correct?"

Haley waits a moment for Brad's lawyer to answer, but when he doesn't, she stands to answer the judge. "Yes, Your Honor."

Sweat beads on my brow as I try to remain focused and not let my mind wander to the worst case scenario.

"Thank you, Ms. Wilkins," Judge Harris says to Haley.

"Mr. Douglas, it appears you waived your custodial rights when you filed for divorce against Mrs. Douglas, is that correct?" She turns her attention to Brad.

He stands and clears his throat, tugging at the tie around his neck. "Yes, Your Honor."

"And that was three years ago?"

Brad nods.

"Hmm." Judge Harris clucks her tongue, flipping through the papers she's holding. "And you haven't paid any child support in those three years?"

It's like I can see the defeat in his posture as she speaks the words. "No, your honor," Brad states, gritting his teeth.

"Well, I think that in itself is pretty telling."

"Your Honor," Brad's lawyer rises from his chair, attempting to speak.

"Ms. Douglas." Judge Harris turns her attention to me. I rise, and the chair squeaks loudly as I stand. My face heats. "You have been the sole caretaker of Presley for three years now. Is that correct?"

"Yes, ma'am—Your Honor," I correct, my cheeks heating even more.

"In that time, was any child support paid to you, any visits, or any indication that Mr. Douglas was interested in being a parent to his child?" she asks, her eyes holding mine.

"No, Your Honor."

Judge Harris offers me a soft nod, and I take my seat again, wiping my sweating hands down my thighs yet again.

"I think I have everything I need," Judge Harris announces. "Mr. Douglas, I am denying your petition for joint custody. You can re-petition in two years when you have paid the back child support you owe and can show you continued to make an effort that supports your statements that you wish to be in the child's life. Until then, court is adjourned."

My mouth is dry, my mind whirling as I try to process what happened. Is it normally that quick? I know Haley said it would be about a half an hour, but that was all of ten minutes. Is that all Judge Harris needed to decide he wasn't fit?

I sit in the chair, my mouth dropped open in shock as I take in the last few minutes. Oh my god, does this mean it's done? He's not getting custody of her?

When Judge Harris stands to exit the courtroom into her chambers, Haley pulls me to my feet, releasing me once she's out of the room so I can sink back into my chair. Brad and his lawyer immediately leave the room; Brad practically running in what is surely anger. He has always been a sore loser.

From the corner of my eye, I notice Trixie rise to her feet and follow in the direction they went in. Her eyes are downcast, but she looks up in my direction at the last second and offers me a sad smile.

When the room is empty, I stand, and Haley offers me a kind hug, and a quick congratulations. My mom hugs me tightly, whispering words of love and excitement into my ear that this battle is over, for now at least.

He can always try again in two years. And to be honest, if he does what the judge asks, and tries to show some interest in being a father, maybe next time will be different. But we will cross that bridge when we come to it.

I can't stop the whirring of emotions flitting through my body. Excitement, anxiety, happiness that it's over, and fear for the future of having to go through it again.

Now though, I can't wait to get my arms around my baby girl, and show her how loved she is by me, by all of the family we've created here in Ivy Ridge.

47

JASON

"Jason, what's your favorite color?" Presley asks. We're sitting in one of the girls' favorite parks in town, just her and me. We got breakfast to go, and are sitting at one of the picnic tables coloring in her favorite coloring book while we wait for court to finish. Presley still doesn't know what's going on today, only that her mom had a meeting, so I got to take her out for some one-on-one time.

She practically squealed in excitement, and was even more excited when we told her that Lennie will get to spend one-on-one time with Fallon later this week to make it fair for both of them.

"Hmmm," I ponder. "Green. What about you?"

"Purple," she answers instantly. "One day when I get married, I'm going to wear a pretty purple princess dress. That way everyone knows how much I love purple."

"Wow, I bet you will look beautiful, sweetheart," I respond. I can't help but think about a wedding that might happen sooner than hers. I know that someday, I will marry Fallon. It might not be right away, but it will happen. I love her, something I haven't even told her yet, and for that, I'm regretful. I know I need to soon, but I didn't want her to be stressed over the court hearing and say it back to appease me when she doesn't really mean it.

"When you and my mom get married, can I wear purple?" Presley asks, peppering me with questions. I should have known that was where her brain was heading when she brought up weddings, but I'm not mad about it.

"Sure, kiddo. But remember, we aren't getting married yet. Maybe not for a while."

"But someday?" she asks, a shining glint in her eyes, the eyes that match her mothers.

"Yeah, kiddo. Someday."

She squeals, and gets back to coloring the page in front of her. The kid is a true artist. I've seen her freehand a few things, and she's a natural. I can't wait to watch her talent flourish.

I love my daughter, but art is not her forte. She has skills in other parts of her life though, and I can't wait to watch her grow and develop them.

My phone buzzes on the table, and I glance at it, figuring it's work, or my brothers. To my surprise, it's Fallon. Court was only scheduled to start fifteen minutes ago, so there is no way they are already done. Right?

"I gotta answer this call, okay kiddo?" I ask Pres, and she nods, engrossed in her work. I stay seated across from her and swipe to answer the call.

"Hey, sunshine. Are you done already?" I ask, my heart pounding as I stare down at Fallon's little girl in front of me. The little girl whose life might have changed and she doesn't even know it.

"Yeah, I'm done," Fallon answers breathlessly. "The judge denied his petition, Jase. It's done. He can try again in two years if he back pays child support, and continues to pay and shows an effort, but the judge called it within ten minutes. It was over and done before I even had a chance to truly freak out."

"Are you serious?" I ask, my heart beating faster, this time in excitement, rather than anxiety.

"So serious. Haley said it was so cut and dry, she barely had time to blink or start taking notes."

"Now what?" I ask.

"Now, we get to live our lives as normal," she breathes, and I can practically hear the anxiety that's been holding her hostage for the last few weeks melting off her.

"Sunshine, that's amazing news," I say.

"I know. In a way, I feel guilty for being so happy, I mean, Presley should get to see her dad, right? But then again, he never fought before, why now?"

I nod, though she can't see me. "I'm so proud of you. Presley and I are hanging out at the park, but we will see you at home, okay?"

"Okay," Fallon takes a deep breath. "Can I talk to her quick?"

"Of course." I hold the phone out to Presley. "Kiddo, your mom wants to say hi."

Presley holds the large phone to her ear. "Hi, Mom," she says, continuing to color with her right hand, her left holding the phone.

They talk for a few minutes before Pres passes me back the phone. "I'll see you guys in a bit," Fallon says.

"Alright, see you soon. Lo—" I stop myself before I say the words. I do not want the first time I say I love you to her to be over the phone. "Lunch?" I try to play off.

Fallon softly laughs. "Sure. Pick up pizza? I can go get Lennie from your mom's and we can eat outside."

"Sounds like a plan," I state, saying goodbye and

hanging up the phone. I don't know how I'm going to tell her I love her, but I know I need to do it soon.

On the way home, Presley spots a field of sunflowers in full bloom, with a basket of cut flowers beside it. "Jason, look at the flowers!" she yells.

Without question, I pull over my vehicle to the side of the road. There's even a sign that says *free will donation* with a basket below it holding a few dollars and some spare change underneath. Presley climbs out of the car to follow beside me and helps me pick out three separate flowers.

One for each of my girls.

When I was a kid, my grandma used to love sunflowers. Every year she would find a place on the side of the road, much like this one, and grab one for each of her four grandkids. It's one of the things I remember most about her. She was so strong like Fallon is.

Grandma used to find the meaning in everything. Whether it was a single flower, a butterfly flitting about, a sunflower on the side of the road, or a dragonfly, it always represented something. A good omen, one might say. Grandma used to preach to us the meaning of each thing as they happened.

She loved sunflowers because they represented strength, loyalty, and admiration. The sunflowers on the side of the road almost seems like a sign from her. On a day like today, it definitely feels like it. Things can only go up from here.

Presley squeals in delight as I carefully place the three sunflowers on the passenger seat and help to make sure she's buckled in. We pick up a few pizzas and finish the drive home, Presley talking the whole way about how excited she is for the flowers.

When we pull into the driveway, Fallon's vehicle is

already there. I grab the flowers and pizza and we head inside, Presley calling out for her mom and Lennie as soon as we are inside.

I find Fallon in the kitchen, grabbing napkins and paper plates for our outside lunch. "Hey, sunshine," I greet. Setting the pizza and flowers down, I wrap my arms around her waist, nuzzling my face into her neck. I breathe in the sweet smell of her perfume. She's been wearing it more often, and I love it. Something about her perfume drives me insane, in the best way.

"Hey you," Fallon says as she spins in my arms, resting her head on my chest. She takes a deep inhale and closes her eyes. "It's so good to be home in your arms. Where's my girl?"

I press a kiss to her head. "In the living room. She was excited to find Lennie. We got you and her something on the way home."

She raises her brows in surprise. "Oh, did you?"

"Mhmm," I mutter. Presley rushes into the kitchen with Lennie at her side.

"Jason, can we show them?" she asks.

Before I can answer, Fallon pulls away from me. She leans down and opens her arms for Presley, who runs into them. Fallon holds her tight, whispering words into her ear meant only for them. They have a special bond, one I could never replace or emulate, but it's also one I have with my own daughter.

I know Fallon needs privacy with her after their morning, and I'm all too happy to give it to them. Lennie steps up to my side, reaching up to grab my hand. "Daddy, did you get flowers?" Lennie asks in a not so subtle whisper.

I softly chuckle, and offer my daughter a small nod.

"Mom, we need to show you the flowers," Presley says from Fallon's arms, in an excited voice.

"Yes, show me them!" Fallon says, standing and subtly wiping tears from her eyes.

Presley beams as she holds up the three flowers, handing one to her mom, another to Lennie, and holding one in her arms for herself. "We stopped on the side of the road and Jason let me pick one for each of us!"

Fallon looks up at me, her eyes still wet with tears. "Thank you."

"Absolutely, sunshine." I press a kiss to her forehead. "My grandma loved sunflowers on the side of the road. She would always stop and grab them when we were with her, and once I saw them, I knew I had to stop. Maybe it could be a new tradition for us, too."

A smile stretches across Fallon's face. "I would love that."

"It's settled then. How are you, my sunshine?"

"So good," she replies, resting her head on my chest once more. "It's like a weight has been lifted off me. Like I can relax."

"You can." I lean down and kiss her deeply. "And I have every intention of helping you relax in *multiple* different ways." I wink, squeezing her sides as she laughs.

"I can't wait."

48

FALLON

"Can we have a Barbie movie night?" Lennie tugs on my arm as I make dinner. Jason's still at work for another hour, but I picked the girls up from school today.

"I don't see why not," I say, shrugging as I pull her against me for a quick hug.

"Yay!" she squeals, running into the living room. I can barely hear her when she calls out to Presley, "She said yes! We get to have a movie night!"

I laugh, stirring the chicken stir fry on the stove. I pull out my phone to update Jason on our night.

ME

Apparently it's been decided that we are having a Barbie movie night. I know how much you love them.

JASON

Lovely. As long as we watch Barbie Swan Lake, I'll survive. And I'm calling dibs on sitting next to you.

ME

Good luck with that one, I can already hear them discussing seating arrangements. Sounds like I'm in the middle, babe.

JASON

Dangit. I knew I should've left an hour early. I'm missing all the important conversations. Lou texted me to confirm, are we still on for the call tomorrow night?

We're planning on having a FaceTime call with Talia's parents tomorrow night, especially now that things have settled down. I haven't heard from Brad since the court hearing. I have a feeling the only reason he reached out in the first place is due to Trixie's prompting, so him falling off the face of the earth again does not surprise me in the least.

My phone buzzes in my hand again.

JASON

Screw it, I'm leaving early. They've got it handled here anyway.

ME

Yes, I have it on the calendar. I'm excited to meet them. Supper will be ready when you get here. 😊

Twenty minutes later, I'm calling the girls to have them set the table for us to eat. I'm finishing up preparing the meal when the front door opens and closes and Lennie shouts, "Daddy!"

"Hey, peanut," he greets. "What are you doing?"

"Fallon told us to set the table. Supper's almost ready. It smells really yummy."

"My mom said we can watch Barbie movies tonight,

and Lennie and I want sprinkle popcorn. Can you make some pretty please?" Presley asks.

"After we eat, then I can make some," Jason states. "But only if you both eat really well."

"We will!" They chorus, and their thundering footsteps rush toward me. "Mom, is dinner ready?"

"Yes, go wash your hands and we'll sit down and eat."

Jason saunters into the kitchen, wearing a dark dress shirt and jeans. He looks handsome as hell. "What's that look for, sunshine?" Jason's lip curves into a smirk, his eyes heating as he takes me in.

"Nothing specific." I wink. "You're looking particularly handsome today, Mr. Cunningham."

"Is that so?"

"Mhmm," I reply. He saunters over to me, snaking his arms around my waist. I tilt my head up, eager for a kiss. He appeases me, pressing his lips to mine in sensual touches. His tongue slides into my mouth, gently prodding and swiping. His hands cup my ass, squeezing and kneading through my jeans.

"Ewww!" the girls cry, their voices shrill. "That's so gross Daddy!" Lennie says.

"It's not gross," Jason says, his voice irritated as he pulls away from me. "You're gross."

"I'm not gross," she says with a hint of sass. She sets her hands on her waist, popping out her hip.

"Whatever you say, Lenners."

"Daddy, I'm not gross."

"You're not gross," Jason concedes with a smile.

"Go sit down," I tell the girls, turning to grab the skillet with the stir fry in it. The girls rush to sit at the table, leaving Jason and me alone again.

"Why do we always get interrupted?" he asks. I turn to look at him. His forehead is wrinkled, lost in thought.

"Well, we have two kids, Jase, we're bound to get interrupted."

"No, I mean really think about it, sunshine. Even back in college. The night of the Christmas party, I was going to kiss you, and that dude walked in. The night I was going to ask you out, Brad appeared. Then, in the wine cellar, Josie interrupted us. Throw in the morning your mom almost caught us, and now this?" He shakes his head with a laugh. "It seems like we're always getting interrupted."

"Hold up," I say, holding my hand out to him. "You were going to ask me out that night in the library?"

"You didn't know?"

I shake my head. "No. I mean, I had an inkling, but I didn't really know for sure. I had the biggest crush on you, but I never thought you reciprocated my feelings. I didn't truly think you actually liked me, Jase."

"I did. *I do.* A lot," he says with a wink.

I smack him in the chest with a pot holder. "I like you too," I tell him. "Now, let's go eat."

"MOM, do you like the sprinkle popcorn?" Presley asks me after we've finished the first movie.

"I love it," I tell her. We're all bundled up in a blanket fort we made before we started the movie. There are pillows lining the floor, with chairs holding up blankets around us. Jason even moved the TV onto the floor so we could all lay under the blankets and watch the movie. The girls are determined to have a sleepover in the fort rather than their beds, and I don't see why we can't. Though, Jason and I might end up in bed, rather than sleeping on the floor, for the sake of our backs.

"It's my dad's specialty," Lennie announces. "One time, he even got glitter to put on there. That was the best."

"Mom?" Presley leans up on her elbow. I'm squeezed in the middle between her and Lennie, with Jason on Lennie's other side. He looks like he's about ready to fall asleep, but he's holding on.

"Yeah, honey?"

"Can we stay here?"

"Tonight? Of course, we're going to stay tonight." I wrinkle my brow in confusion.

"No." She shakes her head. "I mean like, always. Can we stay here forever?"

My eyes meet Jason's over Lennie, and she's nodding furiously. "Please? Can you stay?"

"I... I don't know," I say honestly. "It's something Jason and I need to talk about."

Jason raises his brow. We haven't brought it up again now that things with the custody petition have settled, but I would be open to it.

"But if you stay, then you can be my mom, and my dad can be Presley's dad." Lennie folds her hands. "Pleaaase?"

My heart absolutely melts. I glance over at Jason again, and his gaze has softened. I don't even have words.

"Girls, we will talk about it, but it's up to Fallon and me, okay?" He looks at them intensely. "And if we decide it's not the time yet, that doesn't mean it won't happen some-day, or that you get to be too upset, right?"

They both nod frantically. I offer Jason a mouthed, *thank you*. We choose the next movie, and press play. Lennie is tucked into my left side. Her finger is wrapped around a lock of my hair, and she's gently twisting it. Presley is on my right side, also tucked into me, playing with my hand.

Jason subtly reaches over, entwining my free hand in his. He squeezes it gently, and I look over, giving him a grateful smile. I'm surrounded by what I hope will someday be my new little family, and through all the stress of the last few weeks, I'm so happy, and so relaxed.

49

JASON

Both girls have fallen asleep in Fallon's arms, and I can tell she's fighting sleep too. The movie is almost done, and the only light left in the room is that of the tv screen.

"Psst," I whisper. Fallon stirs, her eyes fluttering back open. I smile at the sight of her. She's so gorgeous. I can't believe I ever fought this. Fought my feelings or the concept of finding someone again.

"What?" she responds, tipping her chin to gesture at our sleeping daughters in her arms.

"You know my answer," I state. The confusion in her eyes is instant, and my smile grows.

"What answer?"

"To staying forever. You know my answer. I want you, *both of you,* to stay forever."

Her eyes soften, and in the glow from the movie, I can see the misty glistening in her eyes. "Yeah. I know."

"So, what do you say? Will you stay?" I'm hopeful. So damn hopeful, because I know things have been stressful for her, but now that the court hearing is over and done with, it seems things are falling into place.

"We'll stay," she nods. A smile unlike one I've ever seen on her takes over her face, and god, I wish I could pull her into my arms right now. I can't wait for us to start this part of our lives together. As partners. I rise to my knees, leaning over my daughter to gently kiss her lips.

"We're going to need a bigger house, though," she murmurs against my lips. "I don't think there's enough room for all of us here, or at my place."

"Not at all," I tell her. "Good thing I know a really good realtor. Who knows, maybe we could even build a house out by Beau and Marley's, or my parents."

"That would be amazing," she replies. Glancing down at the girls in her arms, she whispers, "Can we leave them out here?"

"Totally," I respond, and slowly work on rolling Lennie off of Fallon. Once she's disentangled from the girls, and have them covered in their blankets, we crawl our way out of the quite impressive blanket fort. I turn off the TV, and make sure all the doors are locked before meeting Fallon in my, *our*, bedroom. The overhead light is off, only the lamp on my side of the bed is one, leaving the room warm and cozy.

"I don't think I'm going to be able to fall asleep," I admit. Fallon turns to face me as she changes out of her shirt, taking off her bra. Her breasts fall from the cups of her bra as she slides it to the floor, and her nipples immediately harden.

"I didn't intend on sleeping," Fallon states, shimmying her sleep shorts off her full hips.

I withhold a groan, biting my tongue as my cock stiffens in my shorts. "Fuck, sunshine. You're so goddamn sexy, I don't think I'll ever get enough of you."

"Your turn," she says, her cheeks flushing deep pink under the glow of the lamp. She takes two steps toward me, her hips swaying with each step. When she reaches me, she lifts the hem of my shirt up. I hold my arms up, helping guide my shirt off. I'm left in only my cotton shorts, and Fallon trails her fingers down my chest. Her fingernails scrape through the soft curls of my chest hair, sending a shiver trembling through my body.

With each passing second, my dick grows harder, and my heart thumps louder. In all honesty, I'd be surprised if she couldn't hear it. "Fallon," I breathe her name as she slides her fingers under my waistband, pushing my shorts and boxer briefs from my hips. My length springs free, and Fallon immediately wraps her fingers around it.

"Wait," I say, though my body is totally disagreeing with my brain. Fallon lets me go, and I slide my hands around her waist, leading her backwards toward the bed. We're both completely naked, and god, I love having her skin on mine. Fallon giggles as she flops onto the bed on her back, her golden hair fanning around her head. I follow, climbing onto the bed so I hover over her. "I need to tell you something."

"What is it?" Fallon says. Her arms wrap around my neck. She plays with the hair on the nape of my neck as she gazes into my eyes. I can plainly see the love in them. It's so raw, so deep, that I know I'm making the right choice.

"I'm going to sound like a sap, but when you walked back into my life all those months ago, I think deep inside, I knew I was going to fall for you. I tried so hard to stop it. I was so convinced that all I needed in life was my little girl, and that feeling something for someone was a weakness. That I'd lose a part of me, and risk hurting my daughter if I did. I realize now I was waiting for you to come back into my life. I fell for you the first time I saw you in our Econ class, and even though we had to wait to find each other again, I wouldn't change a thing. Because now, we get to have our own little family."

Fallon nods, the tears brimming her eyes again. "Yeah, we do."

"Fallon, I love you. I love your daughter, and the way you care for my daughter. I love that our girls are best friends, and who knows, maybe someday they will be sisters. I love the way you care for me, and make me get out of my head without even trying. I love you so much that I don't know how to live without you anymore. You are my sunshine, and you bring so much light to our family."

She's smiling, her eyes beaming with so much joy that I don't know how she contains it. "I love you, too, Jase. I love you so much that I can't imagine doing life without you. I love that you've taken me and my daughter as a part of your family."

Her hands cup my cheeks, and I lean down, kissing her. Our kiss quickly turns into something stronger, our bodies reacting to each other again.

I hold her to me, taking my time to savor each moment with her. When I finally sink inside her, I'm home. She is my home, the person I will choose over and over, through every fight and hard time.

I rock my body against hers, thrusting together as I reach down and thrum her clit in a cadence I know will have her falling off the edge in moments. "I love you," I croon over and over, kissing every part of her body I can touch. She repeats my words, her lips finding mine as we make our way to a deep climax that spans all the way to my toes.

We hold each other as we catch our breath, and finally pull apart, only to rejoin moments later after putting some clothes on and falling into the bed to sleep. I cradle her in my arms all night, and in the morning, we snuggle in bed as a family, our daughters waking us with their laughter and making their way between us.

50

JASON

I can't help but be nervous as the phone rings in my palm. The four of us are seated together on the couch in the living room to talk to Talia's parents on the phone. I shouldn't be, but I am. Lou and Ella have been nothing but supportive of me throughout the years, and I'm thankful for them, thankful my daughter has them and the connection to her mother.

I swipe my finger across the screen, smiling when their wrinkled faces appear. "Hi, Lou, Ella," I greet.

"Grandma Ella, Grandpa Lou!" Lennie wastes no time calling their names, swiping the phone from my hand.

"Hi pumpkin," Ella chimes, her voice cheery. "How are you doing?"

"Grandma, this is Presley," Lennie states, turning the phone to Presley as she sits next to her mother.

"Well hello, Presley." Ella smiles sweetly. "I've heard so much about you."

"Hi," Presley says, a moment of shyness appearing.

I take the phone from Lennie, setting it on the coffee

table in front of us so they can see all of us. "There," I state. "That way they can see all of us, Lenners."

"This is Fallon," Lennie says, leaning over to hug her. My heart warms at the sight. Lennie has been so excited to introduce Fallon and Presley to her other set of grandparents. It makes me happy. I'm glad we've been able to keep the connection there so she knows and loves them, even though they are across the country, and Lennie doesn't really know her mom.

Recently, she's been asking more questions about her, and I've answered them as honestly as I can. It hurts bringing her up, and trying to explain it to a five-year-old, but I'm doing the best I can.

"It's nice to meet you," Fallon says with a wave.

"Y-you too," Lou says.

They chat, and it's mostly Lennie and Presley talking about how excited they are for school to start next week. In a way, it's weird to see these two parts of my life collide into something new, something I never anticipated.

I never would have guessed I'd be introducing the woman I love and her daughter to Lou and Ella, but I wouldn't change a thing. I love the way my life has turned out, and if someday, Talia is able to get clean, and stay clean, then maybe she can be a part of it too.

I hope she can. Then she can see how beautiful life is, how beautiful the daughter we made is, and how incredible she is.

We talk for a while longer, and Ella makes sure to get Fallon and Presley's birthdays written down so she can get cards and send them in the mail when the time comes. We even make a tentative plan to fly out and visit them over Thanksgiving this year. It's been over a year since we've seen them last, so it's time. It's hard for them to travel, and I know I need to be better about making an effort to get out to California and visit more. Lennie deserves to have a strong relationship with them, not only over the phone.

When we hang up, Lennie and Presley talk about how much they love Lou and Ella.

I wrap my arm around Fallon's shoulder, pulling her in for a kiss. "How was that?" I ask.

She nods. "It was good, I think. They're so sweet. I was so worried they would think I was replacing Talia, but I don't think they thought that."

"Not at all." I shake my head. "They've been encouraging me to find someone else to share my life with since day one. They've never wanted me to be alone. I was too stubborn to do it. Though I suppose maybe I was waiting for you, sunshine."

"I must have been waiting too," Fallon says. "I love you, Jase."

"I love you more, sunshine."

51

FALLON

"Mom, when do we get to move into our new house?" Presley asks. She and Lennie are in the back seats of my car as we head over to Jason's parents house for Sunday Brunch. The plan was to ride over together, but apparently there was a leak at the brewery last night that Jason wanted to take a look at before they opened for the day.

I laugh under my breath. "Not for a while, honey. We have a lot to do before we can move. It will be a few months, probably more. You need to be patient."

"I don't want to be patient, Fallon," Lennie states. She crosses her arms over her chest, and looks out the window. "I want you guys to live with us now."

"We are living with you now, sweetie, but it's going to be a while before we find a new house. That's all."

"I guess that's okay then. As long as you don't leave."

"We aren't leaving, I promise."

I pull into the driveway, and shift into park as my phone starts to ring. I glance down, expecting for it to be Jason, but an unknown number rings on the screen. I let it play to voicemail, figuring maybe it's spam.

Spam doesn't usually leave a voicemail though. My phone dings when the completed voicemail pops on the screen. My phone works to start transcribing it, a new feature that can sometimes come in handy.

I'm surprised to see that the message reads, *Hi Fallon, this is Trixie. I'm sure you won't—* I don't read any more before I'm climbing out of my car to bring the girls inside so I can actually listen to this unexpected voicemail.

I grab the first person I see when we get inside, which so happens to be Gramps. He's sitting on the couch in the living room watching TV.

"Gramps, can you watch the girls for a minute? I need to go listen to a voicemail quickly."

He looks up at me, that familiar humorous glint in his eye that's always there. "Sure, honey, but if they go upstairs, there's no way I'll be following them."

"That's fine. Thank you, Gramps!"

I rush back outside, ignoring Josie when she calls my name from the dining room. I'll tell her what's going on in a minute. First, I need to listen to this voicemail.

I climb back into the driver's seat, and unlock my phone, pulling up the voicemail. It starts to play Trixie's voice immediately.

"Hi Fallon, this is Trixie. I'm sure you won't listen to this, or call me back, but I had a few things I needed to say to you." I pause the message, taking a deep breath before pressing play again.

"I'm sorry. I can't even begin to express how sorry I am. I'm the reason Brad put you through all the stress of a petition for joint custody. When I found out about you and your daughter, I was absolutely gutted. I wanted my child to know their sibling, for your child to know their father. I was wrong. I put you through hell, and all for my own selfish reasons. To be honest, I don't think Brad wanted anything to do with custody."

I suck in a shuddering breath at her words.

"As you know, I'm pregnant. I've been having my doubts about him for a while now, but he was so excited to start a family. I thought maybe things would change."

Deja vu rings through my veins. I thought the same thing. At least she's realizing it now, instead of ten years into a relationship and marriage.

"I've decided to leave Brad. I'm giving him the option for shared custody, but I'm not sure if he will take it. I guess I don't know what I'm doing leaving this voicemail, I guess I wanted to apologize for what I helped put you through. I realized in that diner how skewed my judgement was, and for that, I'm sorry. If your daughter ever wants to meet her little brother, please reach out. I'll be happy to meet. Good-bye, Fallon."

The voicemail ends with a click, and I'm left sitting in the front seat, taking deep breaths. Holy shit. I take a few minutes to process what played, and try to come up with any sort of response. I'm not going to call her back, not now. But maybe someday I will.

Instead of making the choice, I can leave it up to Presley in the future, when she's a bit older. She can choose to meet her sibling, and who knows, maybe she will want to reach out to Brad when she's older. If that is what she wants, then I won't stop her. For right now, though, I will do what I can to protect her, and that is keeping her away from him.

Presley has a family. Even if things don't work out between Jason and me, she has a family in the Cunning-ham's. She has a family in me and my mother. In Megan and Isaac. She is surrounded by so much love and so much joy everyday.

A soft tapping on my window pulls me out of my mixed feelings. Jason is standing outside my car door. I fling the door open, hitting him in the process.

"What's wrong? Is everyone okay?" Jason cups my cheeks, scanning my face and my body for harm before scanning his parent's front yard.

"Everyone's fine," I say, shaking my head and swiping at the tears I didn't realize had fallen. "Trixie left me a voicemail."

"She did?" Jason asks in surprise.

"Yeah." I play the message for him, and watch as his eyes widen as the seconds pass by.

"Woah," Jason finally says when it's done playing. "Are you going to call her back?"

I shake my head. "Not now. I'm not in a good place right now, and I don't want to talk to her. I think someday, I'll give Presley the choice to meet her sibling, maybe we can do it sooner rather than later so she doesn't miss out on him growing up, and go from there. And maybe someday, she will want to reach out to her dad and try to have a relationship. But that's up to her. I won't stop her."

Jason breathes out a heavy sigh. "Wow, sunshine. That's a lot."

I nod, resting my head against his chest as tears fall down my cheeks. "You're telling me," I say with an unamused chuckle.

His lips press a kiss to the top of my head, and he squeezes me tightly. The air is chilly now that fall is starting to make an appearance, and I didn't wear a jacket.

"Do you want to go inside, or go for a quick drive to warm up and try to relax a little?" Jase asks.

"We should probably check on the girls. I didn't even say hi to anyone. I dropped them in the entryway and asked Gramps to watch them," I say with a small laugh.

Jason chuckles. "Yeah, he probably is feeding them candy by the handful."

"Probably. Is my makeup a mess?" I ask, stepping back to look in the side mirror of my car and swiping at my tear stained cheeks.

Jason grimaces, and I watch as he stammers, trying to come up with something to say. "It's... not great," he finally says. "You're still beautiful, but your mascara is a little racoony."

"Racoony?" I laugh. I open my vehicle and dig in my purse for an extra makeup wipe I keep on hand for my brides. I swipe the cloth under my eyes, and Jason offers me a thumbs up. I still check in the mirror, pleased that my eyes didn't get too puffy. "Ready to go in?"

Jason nods, and takes my hand, leading me into his childhood home where I'll be surrounded by a family that supports and cares for each other, no matter what.

52

JASON

This weekend we are officially moving Fallon and Presley into my place. Lennie and Presley could not be more excited to be sharing a room, even if it's temporary. I'm sure once they get older they won't want to share a room, but for a few months, it will be fine. It worked out pretty well, actually. Fallon's lease ends in a month anyway.

Fallon and Presley are spending one last week by themselves at their house, mainly so they can pack. Luckily, I have quite a bit of space in my basement and garage, otherwise we would probably have to rent a storage unit for a few months.

Beau, Fallon, and I have a meeting in a few days to discuss what our price range is, and what we're looking for. Beau's already sent me a few options, but nothing has quite matched what I have in mind.

It's crazy to think that this time last year, I was lost, still in a zone of never wanting to find someone else. So determined to live my life alone, thinking that is what was best for my daughter and me.

Then the bright sunshine that is Fallon and Presley fell

into my lap and even though I tried to fight it, she wormed her way into my heart and my life and I wouldn't have it any other way.

There's a knock on my office door, and Gramps and Thomas are standing in the doorway. "Hey, son," Gramps greets, walking in and sitting down in the extra chair.

I greet them, and don't bother asking why they're here. Honestly, it's par for the course at this point for any of my family to show up at any time, anywhere. "Big week coming up," Gramps says, his voice full of his familiar mirth.

I lean back in my chair, rubbing my hands together. "You could say that."

"Ready?" he asks.

"More than ready."

"Good," he murmurs. "I knew she was the one for you the day I met her at Cindy and Andrew's wedding. She and that little girl are perfect additions to the family."

"You knew even then?" I ask, a little shocked. "How?"

"An old man knows these things. I knew Cindy was perfect for Andrew, and Marley and Beau were a no brainer. Thomas hasn't found his perfect match quite yet, but if I had to guess, it'll happen soon."

Thomas lets out a disbelieving chuckle. "Yeah, right. I'm not holding out too much hope."

"You'll find her," I state. Thomas has never really been one to date, even back in high school.

He shrugs. "We'll see."

"Don't question an old man," Gramps says, shoving Thomas's shoulder.

"I'm not," Thomas defends, crossing his arms. "I'm only saying I don't have much hope. I'd love to find someone. We all know how much I want a family of my own."

I stand, striding over and pulling him into a tight hug. "Don't give up."

"Oh, hey," a familiar voice says from the doorway. "I can come back."

I pull away from my brother to see Fallon and Presley in the doorway. Lennie bounds through, rushing into Gramps' lap. "Gramps!" she yells. "Did you hear that Fallon and Presley are moving in? They're totally going to get married, even though they keep telling us '*not yet*' and '*we have to be patient*'." Her voice lowers to a whisper that everyone can still hear. "Gramps. I am not patient."

Gramps laughs boisterously. "I'm not patient either, Lennie." Presley strides over to stand next to him, resting her hand on his arm.

"Gramps, can you be *my* Gramps too now that I'm moving into Jason and Lennie's house?" she asks so tentatively I can practically see the nerves radiating off her. "I don't have a Gramps. I love my grandma a lot, and she can be Lennie's grandma too, but I want to have a Gramps."

"I would love to be your Gramps, Presley," Gramps voice is choked up, and I swear I can see a hint of a tear in his eye. "Lennie's Grandma Nikki and Grandpa Richard, as well as Jane and Gabriel will be your grandparents too. Soon, you'll have so many grandparents, aunts and uncles, and cousins that you won't know what to do with it."

Fallon covers her mouth, covering the wide smile settled on her lips. I pull her across my small office and into my arms. Her back is to my front, and I lean down, my mouth brushing the shell of her ear. "They're your family too, you know."

She nods, leaning her head back onto my chest. "Thank you for making me a part of it."

"Thank you for being a part of it," I reply, kissing her cheek. "I love you."

"I love you more," she responds.

I shake my head, whispering in her ear, "Not possible."

The girls continue to talk with Gramps and Thomas all about the upcoming move. Thomas even offers to take the girls in his patrol car for a ride with Arson someday.

Everything is falling into place, and I'm more settled than I ever have been.

FALLON
EPILOGUE

9 Months Later

I look around our new house. We've been here for over a week now, and I'm finally starting to get settled. It took a lot longer than we would have liked to find a place we all loved and felt like could be our home, and ironically, it's only a mile away from Jase's parent's house. It will be nice to be so close to them, as well as Marley's parents, Jane and Gabriel. My mom is only fifteen minutes away, and is already planning nights she can come have sleepovers and spend time with the girls.

Jason's arms wrap around me from behind as I take in our bedroom. He let me have creative freedom over the bedroom. Of course I included him in the process, but he really let me do whatever I want.

The house is old, and still has the beautiful hardwood flooring. I got a gorgeous rug to go in the room, and painted the walls a soft cream, giving the room some warmth, while also making it easy to match things if I ever want to switch it up. Our bed is covered in a fluffy cream duvet and all the accent and throw pillows I could ever want, a few of them in different colors to give the room a bit of a pop.

"Presley has declared that her room is officially done," Jason murmurs. "And my back hurts."

"I'm sorry," I whisper, turning in his arms to kiss him. "If it makes you feel any better, so does mine."

"It does." He bends down, groaning softly and kissing me. "I could flop down on the bed right now and fall asleep."

I hide my grimace. "I'm all on board for you taking a nap, but... can you shower first? You're kinda sweaty. And you still have paint all over your arms. You'll probably leave a man-shaped stain on the bed if you climb in now."

Jason groans. "I know I have to, but the thought of showering is exhausting."

"You're being a little dramatic."

"Can you blame me? Our daughters are entering their teen stage, I swear. They kept making me rearrange things in their rooms until it was perfect, and then it wasn't after five minutes."

"You're such a sucker for them. I would have made them leave it."

"Can you blame me?" he questions with a raise of his brow. "I love them so much it hurts. I'd do anything to make them happy."

"And that's why you're the best dad." I lean onto my tip-toes to give him another kiss. I reach around and swat his ass. "Now, go take a shower. You stink."

Jason nuzzles his sweaty forehead into my neck. I squeal and squirm, trying to get him off me. "Jason!" I cry. "You're gross!"

"Yeah, Dad is gross!" Lennie yells from her room down

the hall. It reminds me of a memory of a similar conversation so many months ago.

Presley also chimes in. "Dad, you're gross!"

Jason freezes, and I do too. Presley has never called Jason *Dad* before. Is he okay with it? Am *I* okay with it? It doesn't take me more than a second to realize that yeah, I'm more than okay with it. Jason is Presley's dad in all the ways that matter. Sure, we're not married or even engaged. We haven't really talked about it other than knowing it will happen someday. But knowing my daughter considers Jason a dad, *her* dad, is something I will always cherish.

"A-are you okay with that?" Jason tentatively asks as he pulls away from my neck. His forehead is wrinkled in concern, eyes full of worry.

"Yeah, I am," I tell him honestly. Pulling him in for a kiss, I murmur, "If you're okay with her calling you dad, then I am."

He nods. "Yeah. I am. It's right. If Lennie wants to call you mom, I would be okay with that too."

Jason and I have talked extensively about Talia, and how there's a chance that someday she'll return. We've talked about how much we would love it if she were healthy, and could be a part of Lennie's life.

I nod. "If she wants to, she can, but I don't think she's there yet."

"I agree. Something else I wanted to mention, and the timing seems right, but we've talked about marriage, and what our family would look like. If you're okay with it, I'd also like to look into adopting Presley. Formally."

"You would do that?" I ask, my eyes welling with tears. "Really?"

"Brad would have to officially terminate his rights, which at this point, I could see him doing since he still hasn't paid a dime of child support, back pay or otherwise, but absolutely. I would love to be her dad, officially. I know you technically can't adopt Lennie because of the circumstances, but I would do it. I would adopt Presley."

"How did I get so lucky with you?" I ask.

"I think I'm the lucky one. I have the love of my life in my arms, and two beautiful little girls that I can't wait to see grow up into incredible women."

"I love you."

"I love you, too. I can't wait for this incredible life with you."

I hug him, resting my face against his chest, not even caring about the sweat and grossness anymore. The best is yet to come, and I cannot wait to see how our life unfolds.

WANT MORE JASON & Fallon? Read the Christmas party flashback scene for free now!

Want to see if Josie & Andrew decide to have a baby? Read a bonus scene for them here!

ACKNOWLEDGMENTS

Honestly, this is just insane at this point. How am I already writing the acknowledgements for my sixth book?

This book took me on a journey. What was supposed to be an early winter release turned into late winter, and then a spring one. It just didn't feel right for the longest time. Throw in a death in the family, moving (again) and seasonal —and regular— depression, and it made for a hard to finish the book.

Aria & Tiff- Thank you thank you thank you. This book would literally not be finished had we not had that three hour long FaceTime call and many texts and questions about whether or not something worked. I love you two and am so insanely grateful for your friendship. Expect a long hug when we meet in person finally.

Indie Queens- My emotional support group. I love you all!

My Beta Readers, Emily, Brittany, Abbey, and Jessica- your kindness and suggestions are so incredible. I appreciate you taking the time out of your busy lives to read and make this book better!

My ARC and Street Team- The fact that you are all so willing to take time out of your lives and days to read my books and hype me up will always be amazing. Each and every one of you mean more to me than you know!

My family and friends- for listening to me gush about my characters and stories, and being my biggest supporters.

Victoria- For being my person, and standing by my side through this journey.

HBC- Cause I accidentally forgot to include you in the last book... sorry!!! Just know how much I love you and don't know what I'd do without you.

And lastly, to my readers. Thank you for making this dream of mine a reality.

ALSO BY ALICE DANIELS

Cinder Valley Series

Tip Of My Tongue- Lainey & Colin

How Do I Tell You?- Mallory & Tyler

Give Me A Minute- Theo & Peyton

Ivy Ridge

Flowers in Your Hair- Andrew & Josie

Never Really Mine- Beau & Marley

Can't Let You Go- Jason & Fallon

In Plain Sight- Thomas & TBA

Minnesota Blue Herons Hockey Series

TBA-Grace & Adam

ABOUT THE AUTHOR

Alice Daniels is a born and raised Minnesotan who loves to write books based on the small town she grew up in. Her books are sweet, heartfelt, and sexy, with relatable characters.

As a child, she was an avid fiction reader, which evolved into a deep love for romance novels and the community surrounding them. She recently discovered a passion for putting her ideas into writing and decided to pursue her childhood dream of becoming an author.

She spends time with her family and friends when she's not writing, especially on the lakes or outdoors in the summer.

Follow Alice on Facebook, Instagram, and Goodreads for book updates, teasers, and future releases!

Join her Facebook Group, Alice Daniels Reader Group to get all the insider info, sneak peeks, and more!

https://alicedaniels.com/

amazon.com/author/alicedaniels

facebook.com/authoralicedaniels

instagram.com/authoralicedaniels

goodreads.com/authoralicedaniels

bookbub.com/authors/saylor-ann